MW01128122

# The
# Mistress's
# Black Veil

# Other books by M. K. Baxley

The Cumberland Plateau: A Pride and Prejudice Modern Sequel
Book 1
In
*The Modern Pemberley Series*

Dana Darcy
Book 2
In
*The Modern Pemberley Series*

*"From the very beginning -- from the first moment, I may almost say -- of my acquaintance with you, your manners, impressing me with the fullest belief of your arrogance, your conceit, and your selfish disdain of the feelings of others, were such as to form that groundwork of disapprobation on which succeeding events have built so immoveable a dislike; and I had not known you a month before I felt that you were the last man in the world whom I could ever be prevailed on to marry."*

*"You have said quite enough, madam. I perfectly comprehend your feelings, and have now only to be ashamed of what my own have been. Forgive me for having taken up so much of your time, and accept my best wishes for your health and happiness."*

*And with these words he hastily left the room, and Elizabeth heard him the next moment open the front door and quit the house ...*

—Jane Austen

The House of Pleasure

# The Mistress's Black Veil

A Pride and Prejudice Vagary
Book 1
In
The Regency Adaptations

*M. K. Baxley*

RAVEN BOOKS

*The Mistress's Black Veil* is a work of fiction. All other characters are either from the author's imagination, or from Jane Austen's novel, *Pride and Prejudice*.

No part of this book may be reproduced without prior permission. mkbaxley@bellsouth.net

ISBN-10: 1449974767
EAN-13: 9781449974763

© Copyright March 05, 2011 by M. K. Baxley

All rights are reserved.

First Edition: July 2011

Front cover photograph purchased from Istocks.
Back Cover photograph purchased from Isctock 02-04-07 © Kateryna Govorushchenko

http://www.istockphoto.com

Graphics are from Dover Publications

Photograph of Fox Theatre San Francisco, Ca is from Dover Publications used by permission

Cover and internal design © M. K. Baxley 2011

# Let us begin.....

# Chapter 1

It is a truth universally acknowledged that a fine-looking woman in possession of a good figure, a beautiful face, and all the trappings of youth, regardless of her circumstances, must be in want of a gentleman. And that, my dear gentle reader, is exactly where we find our heroine, Miss Elizabeth Bennet and her three remaining sisters, of this story I am about to tell. It begins five years after the death of their dearly beloved father.

Mr. Bennet, it seems, caught his death of a cold upon searching for his youngest daughter, Miss Lydia, after her elopement with that notorious rake, Mr. George Wickham, in the year of our Lord eighteen hundred and thirteen, whilst her sister, Miss Elizabeth Bennet, was away visiting their cousin in Kent.

Mr. Collins, said cousin whom Miss Elizabeth Bennet was visiting at the time, happened to be the parson of Hunsford Church in Kent under the patronage of the Grand Dame and formidable Mistress of Rosings Park, Lady Catherine de Bourgh, who, upon hearing of the death of Mr. Bennet, instructed her parson to remove the Bennets at once from Longbourn, the estate of which he was to inherit due to entailment. Mr. Collins, dutiful to his beloved mistress's ever dictum, did as he was instructed, much to the severe consternation of his wife, Charlotte Lucas Collins, the former best friend of Miss Elizabeth Bennet.

And Mrs. Bennet, unable to reconcile herself with being cast into the hedgerows, went quite insane. She now passes her time in a rocking chair by the fire, living in a time long since passed, whiling away the hours, conferring with the mice scampering about and consulting no one. Comfort of the heart was a fleeting state for poor Mrs. Bennet, for now there was none to be had. Mrs. Bennet was lost completely to senility, crying for her dear Lydia, unable to accept the dire circumstances in which she now found herself. For Miss Lydia Bennet was not to be found until she was discovered in London's Lower East End near the banks of the River Thames, quite alone and quite heavy with child.

Lydia Bennet was taken in by her Uncle Gardiner to his house in Cheapside on Gracechurch Street where she gave birth to a healthy robust child with a full set of lungs, but, alas, Miss Lydia was not to survive. Succumbing to childbirth fever, she lived only long enough to surrender her babe, a strapping boy, into the hands of her two beloved elder sisters, Miss Jane Bennet and Miss Elizabeth Bennet; for upon

1

William Bennet's birth, his mother did die and was laid to rest in St. Mary's Churchyard in Whitecastle.

The following year, an outbreak of grippe swept through England, claiming the lives of Miss Mary Bennet, Uncle Edward Gardiner, Aunt Madeline Gardiner, the two eldest Gardiner children, and Mr. and Mrs. Phillips as well many of the residents of the Southern counties, Hertfordshire in particular, and London's East End, leaving the three remaining Bennet sisters: Miss Catherine, Miss Jane, and Miss Elizabeth, along with Flora and Edward Gardiner and little William, now known to his doting aunts as little Wills, all alone in the world with Mrs. Bennet for company. And, to complicate matters even more, Mr. Gardiner's partner in business exercised his right by law, and took possession of Gardiner & Bateman, giving the poor family only a smattering of their rightful due, reducing them to poverty.

With all that has passed, we find our dear courageous sisters holding together, facing their dire circumstances as best they can. Miss Kitty works as a seamstress in Madam Hamilton's modiste shop, and our dear Lizzy has attempted to fill the position of governess for three prominent families, all ending in disaster as the master of each house desired more than an instructor for his children. Thus our poor Lizzy has just lost her third position, fleeing from the house through an alleyway and into the street where she stumbled into the path of an old acquaintance from Hertfordshire, Harriette Goulding, now Ophelia Dior, widow to the late Mr. John Dior of Devonshire. Ophelia is now employed at the fine establishment of Madame Papillia's *House of Pleasure*—a gentlemen's club—also known as a brothel.

And so my good reader, we are now joined in on the scene in the meager living room of said family as they discuss their happenstance of fate and what they will do about it.

Elizabeth walked into their tiny sitting room where Jane was sitting by the fire, mending the gown Elizabeth had worn earlier today. Jane looked up from her work. "Is William finally asleep?" she asked, never missing a stitch.

"Yes," Elizabeth replied. "The poor little dear wanted to hear the story of how the Prince comes to rescue the fair Princess. I fear he never tires of it even though he must have heard it at least a thousand times."

Jane smiled as her needle went in and out, repairing the tear in Elizabeth's bodice resulting from Lord Weatherly's amorous and unwanted advances.

Kitty entered the room. "Mamma is finally resting peacefully. Poor Mamma. Every night she asks for Lydia, and every night I shake my head and tell her the same. Then she tells me that Lydia will be home soon with Mr. Bennet. I have told her countless times that Papa and Lydia are gone, but she does not hear me."

Kitty took a seat beside Jane and picked up her workbasket. Pulling out her sewing, she began putting the final touches on a pair of kid gloves.

"The Lady Hanover will be in the shop before noon expecting her gloves to be finished and stitched to perfection," Kitty said. "I will have to work late tonight. I am afraid Mamma took more of my time than I had to spare."

"Poor Mamma." Elizabeth sighed. "It is best she does not know the truth of our circumstances. Let her continue in her happy thoughts. However," Elizabeth paused, pursing her lips, "there is something of great import of which we must speak." She stopped and took a deep breath. "Going over the ledger, I have calculated that we

2

have enough money to last until the end of the month. After that, I have no idea how we will eat."

"Lizzy," Jane softly spoke, "somehow we will make it. We always have."

"Yes, but the material point, Jane, is this," Elizabeth said as she paced in front of her sisters, looking from one to the other. "I have lost three posts in five years. I will not be able to find another position. Word gets around. I never imagined the other responsibilities I would be expected to assume when I began soliciting work."

"Lizzy, it cannot be as dire as you think. Surely there are good and decent men who will not take advantage of you or expect…" Jane's voice trailed off.

"You think that, if it gives you ease." Elizabeth arched one eyebrow.

"No, Lizzy, tell me you will not take Ophelia's offer. 'Tis too much. We can manage."

"No, we cannot, Jane. I have been over the books all evening. With the lost capital in Uncle Gardiner's final venture before he passed and what we spent to bury Papa, Lydia, and Mary—not to mention the debts we had to pay from Mamma's extravagance before Papa died, there was not much left but a small stipend; now that that little bit is gone, there is nothing at all. It has been five years, and we have had to use what little we had for housing, food, clothing, and the essentials of life for six people—and let us not forget what Mamma had spent before I took control. At long last, we have finally exhausted what there was of our inheritance. Things are desperate, and desperate times call for desperate measures. There will be no knight dressed in white satin breeches, riding a white steed coming to our rescue. It is up to me to save us in whatever way I can. It is this…or the parish workhouse, and I prefer this."

Taking the seat across from her sisters, Elizabeth folded her hands in her lap. "Now, let us discuss the Courtesans' Ball. I will spend most of the week at Madame Papillia's learning the skills and manner in which I am to deport myself. I want you," she said, looking at Jane, "to fashion me a black gown from the silk mourning dress I wore after Papa's death, and I want you, Kitty, to design a black veil. I have discussed it with Madame Papillia, and the only way I can go through with this, is that my true identity is to never become public knowledge. I am to be Sofia Molina. I will speak only Spanish." Her lips curled softly. "I will let them wonder about my identity and my background."

"But, Lizzy, we must remember who we are," Jane said softly, glancing up through thick lashes. "We are the daughters of a gentleman."

"No, Jane, Lizzy is right," Kitty interjected. "The Bennets of Longbourn are no more. With no living relations to help us, we must help ourselves in whatever way we can. It is not only ourselves with whom we must be concerned. We must think of the children. They are innocent. If we do not provide for them, they will become street urchins. I cannot bear that. Can you?"

Jane shook her head.

Elizabeth placed her hand on her sister's knee. "Jane, this is not forever. I have thought it through. None of us will ever marry. You know that."

Jane nodded and paused to wipe a tear.

"Jane, this is only for a short time. I plan to make as much money as I can, and then we will disappear. I want us to go far away to a place where we can live in peace and quiet solitude and raise the children—a place where they will have a chance to grow up away from scandal and perhaps marry well. We shall go to the

Ulster Mountains of Ireland or perhaps to the West Indies where it is warm and sunny. That would do Mamma a world of good. Ophelia says I can make two thousand pounds, perhaps more, and then I can shed the charade, and we will be free, free to live as we should. I am doing this for all of us. It is our only hope."

"I know, Lizzy. It is just that I had hoped that somehow…maybe…Mr. Bingley might hear of our plight and return, but I suppose that it quite impossible, given our circumstances."

"Jane, I do not know why you still hold to that foolish notion. I, for one, would not have such a weak and simple minded sapling!" Kitty declared. "Lizzy," she said, turning to her sister, "I am behind you, and I will work extra hard to see that you succeed."

Jane glanced up with a timid smile. "As will I."

"Then it is settled." Lizzy drew back and raised her chin. "I will attend the Courtesans' Ball as Sofia Molina, the woman behind the black veil. Now," Lizzy said as they huddled together, pulling their shawls a little tighter, "the Courtesans' Ball is to be on the 12th of December and is to be a masquerade ball, therefore my veil needs to have a black mask underneath which I want to be black silk-satin trimmed in lace and clear glass beads. The dress is to be plain but low cut and fashioned with red silk twist rosettes intermingled with the same clear glass beads used on the mask. Do you think you can do that, Kitty?"

"Yes, I can, and I can make it from the scraps of twist and cloth at the modiste. Mrs. Hamilton will not mind. She often tells me to take this or that for the children, so she will not suspect anything. Oh, this is going to be such fun. I will fashion you the most beautiful mask and veil that ever was seen. When we are through, you shall be the most striking courtesan at the ball, but Lizzy, do pick a handsome man, an officer, perhaps a general, if you can. Do not let it be some stuffy old man who is fat!"

They both laughed. "Never!" Lizzy said as she and Kitty clasped hands.

Jane only smiled while her needle slipped in and out of her sister's torn dress. The three women talked late into the night, discussing the ball and their future lives.

# Chapter 2

It is also a truth universally known that all work and no play makes Jack a dreadfully dull boy, or in this case, Mr. Darcy an extremely overwrought man in need of a diversion in the way of a night out on the town. And that, dear reader, is exactly where we find our dear hero, studiously slaving over his ledgers and calculating his wealth. Gold coins stacked upon his desk with little else in his life but money, business, and a memory of a country miss whom he had severely underestimated. Let us recollect our hero's mishaps.

After delivering his infamous letter to our heroine, our hero, Mr. Fitzwilliam Darcy, left Kent five years previously with his pride humbly in his hand sufficiently served back to him as a cold dish by our heroine.

At first, Mr. Darcy, like any man so eloquently set down by someone so decidedly beneath himself, was furious. He flew as fast as his barouche box could carry him to his London townhouse to ceremoniously lick said wounds inflicted upon his person by our heroine. But, upon further inspection of her accusations, he had deemed she was perfectly right and justified in her assessments of his character. Well, at least some of them, that is. And so he went about attending to her judgments.

Believing that he had allowed his one chance for happiness in the married state to slip through his fingers, our knight in shining armor went about trying to put out the flame Miss Elizabeth Bennet had ignited in his heart, but it was to no avail. The following year on his annual visit to Kent, he had hoped to hear some news of her, perhaps that she might still be single and in want of a husband and that he might be given a second chance to make amends for his so disastrous proposal of the previous year. Instead, what he discovered alarmed him.

Lydia, her youngest sister, had eloped with his boyhood friend and arch nemesis George Wickham, and Mr. Bennet, in an attempt to rescue his youngest daughter, had succumbed to a cold and died. Mr. Collins, under the direct influence of the Right Honourable Lady Catherine de Bourgh, had flung the Bennet family into the hedgerows to starve and had taken possession of his rightful inheritance under the rules of entailment. What had become of the Bennets was unknown. Once again Mr. Darcy was furious and let it be known in no uncertain terms what he thought of his relation's infusions into matters that were clearly none of her business. Once he had said his piece, Mr. Fitzwilliam Darcy quit the room as soon as could be, leaving Rosings Park forever.

He had immediately set out for Longbourn only to discover that no one knew what had become of the Bennets, but it had been widely believed they resided in

Cheapside on Gracechurch Street, or so Sir William Lucas had said. However, upon arrival at said address, our hero discovered another family residing in the residence. The Bennets had disappeared with no forwarding address. Mr. Darcy had searched far and wide, high and low, without success. Some in the warehouse district said they, and their relations, had succumbed to the grippe epidemic that had raged through London that year, but had no idea where they might be buried. And so, with a heavy heart, our hero had given up, surrendering to grief and guilt once more.

With nothing left but a fantasy, he poured himself into his work, buying up businesses and investing in capital ventures until he had amassed a vast fortune which some rated as the highest in the kingdom, rivaled only by the royal family itself. He invested in real estate, banking, shipping, importing goods from the Americas and the Far East. Everything Darcy touched turned to gold.

And whatever time he was not working, he had buried himself in charity endeavors, always making way for progress, giving money for hospitals and caring for the less fortunate, especially the sick and needy. It was his way of repaying his dearest Elizabeth for the lessons she had taught him.

Yes, my dear reader, Mr. Darcy had all the trappings of wealth and the prestige of philanthropy, but he did not have love. So each night when he lay down to sleep, he entered into his imaginary dream world in which his love, Miss Elizabeth Bennet, would come to him as a mystical temptress. He would love her all night and in the morning there would often be evidence of his dreams.

Mr. Darcy's work habits were so extreme that his family worried excessively about him. His beloved sister who doted on him, attempted to introduce him to fine young ladies of the *ton*, but it was of no use. None could replace his country miss, the most accomplished lady of his acquaintance. Alas, Miss Darcy married and moved to Scotland, leaving her brother to the care of his cousins, General Fitzwilliam and the Viscount Wexford, heir to the Earldom of Matlock.

In the fifth year of Mr. Darcy's self imposed exile, the general and his brother had decided that enough was enough. It was time their cousin pulled himself up by the bootstraps and left his cocoon, time for Mr. Darcy to join the realm of the living once more, and they had just the thing for him. Determined not to be put asunder, they lifted the doorknocker and rapped firmly upon his door at No. 2 Grosvenor Street.

And now, dear reader, we are joined in their conservation.

"Come, Darcy, I must have you join us. It pains me to see you wasting your life away, piling up more money than you can ever spend, working with the disadvantaged, sponsoring orphanages. Darcy, all work and no play makes for a very dull life. I must have you attend Madame Papillia's soirée with us. I must!" Viscount Wexford exclaimed.

"Go to the Courtesans' Ball? Are you mad, man? You remember what happened last year. A score of Tahitian virgins and a sex orgy. I think not!"

"Darcy, that was the *Cyprian Ball*. Madame Papillia runs a respectable business. She is *not* Mrs. O'Kelly!"

Darcy gave a disgruntled "Humph!"

"Besides," General Fitzwilliam interjected, "if you remain insistent that you will not marry, then you must at least take a mistress. Madame Papillia has the most beautiful girls in all of London. There is even a new one that is all the rage. Everyone is vying for her attentions, and she is not even formally out. His grace the Duke of Ancaster has already fought a bloodless duel with the Duke of Castlebaum over her."

"Fitzwilliam, I have told you countless times I am not interested in a paramour."

"But, Darcy, you are the most eligible man of the *ton*. You can have your pick of females, even more so than I," the viscount pleaded. "You must come with us to this year's Courtesans' Ball. It promises to be the most splendid event London has ever seen in that venue. Come, cousin, you must accompany us."

"Henry, you know how I detest such things. Women fawning all over me, desiring my affections, not to mention my money. I despise it all. For the few seconds of pleasure a Cyprian can give, you find your coffers reduced by an unequal amount. It is not worth it. The expense is damnable, the position ridiculous, and the pleasure fleeting."

"Darce, I would not be as fastidious as you are for a kingdom. Upon my honor, man, you might as well enjoy it, for you cannot take it with you. Without an heir, which you say you no longer desire, what good is it to amass untold wealth if there is no woman to warm you bed?" The general walked over to the side table and lifted a decanter of port. "As I see it, you are wasting away. This is not like you. I know Elizabeth Bennet meant a great deal to you, but you have to face it. She is gone, and her death is not your fault. Here," he said, handing his cousin a glass of wine.

Darcy took the proffered drink and slumped down in a chair by the mantelpiece. "Fitzwilliam, I loved her, and I lost her. I have no desire to replace her even for a night. There is no woman who can take her place in my heart."

"But cousin," the viscount interjected, "you are looking at this all wrong. A courtesan is not a replacement for a lost love; she is a diversion, something to take your mind off things and relax your body. Darce, you are in dire need of a woman's comforts, and you do not have to take her on as your paramour. Simply enjoy her for the night."

Darcy passed his hand over his face and looked up at his cousins standing over him. "You say this new Cyprian is very beautiful, and Ancaster and Castlebaum are in competition for her charms?"

A wide smile spread across the viscount's face. "That is right. No one knows what she looks like, but that is part of her sensual allure. She wears a black veil, and every man thinks he will be the one to remove it. But she will remove it only for the man she chooses...and I have heard only when *she* chooses and not a moment before. If, however, gauging her figure counts for anything, well, I must tell you she has a body that will light any man's lust to flame—even yours, cousin.

"You don't say."

"I do say."

"Henry, it will take quite a woman to set me to blaze, but you have sufficiently enticed me. I must see this woman for myself. Though I must warn you, I have no intentions of taking a mistress or spending a farthing more than I have to on a common whore."

"I can assure you, Cousin, common she is *not*."

# Chapter 3

*Sofia Molina
the Cyprian
with the
Black Veil*

nd now, dear reader, we join Miss Elizabeth Bennet who has left her dear family in their meager and not quite so modest house on Beggar Street in Whitecastle for the Grand Dame Madame Papillia's *House of Pleasure* in the fashionable district of Covent Garden. Upon entering the grand house, her veil securely in place, our heroine is whisked away to the Grand Dame herself, whereupon she is given a contract to sign with an advance in funds, *The Cyprian's Handbook* to study, and the lovely Oriental lady's maid Ling-Ling to prepare her for her coming out as the newest addition to Madame Papillia's *House of Pleasure*.

Under the skilled hands of Ling-Ling, master herbalist with secrets from the Orient, our heroine is transformed. Her hair is dyed with henna and indigo from Persia and India, her skin softened with shea butter from the Karité tree in East Africa and perfumed with exotic scents from the Far East. Her announcement is placed in the *Ladies of Pleasure*—a listing of London's top courtesans and their specialties. She is presented in the throne room of the Grand Dame to gentlemen of the highest breeding. For three weeks, our brave heroine, the new siren of Madame Papillia's *House of Pleasure*, has been the talk of the town. Finally it is time for her début.

Bathed in buttermilk and perfumed in the sweet scents of sandalwood and myrrh, blended with spikenard patchouli, her skin softened to the perfection of silk with the exotic butters prepared by her maid, and instructed under the careful eye of Madame Papillia and *The Cyprian's Handbook*, our lovely temptress is ready.

The higher his pulse rate, the less a man cares what a snatched moment of delight might cost[*] in the arms of a beautiful woman.

Let us see what our beautiful Cyprian has learned.

The Courtesans' Ball was a magnificent event, the most elaborate in the old city for the month of December. Elizabeth, who normally enjoyed a ball, took little pleasure in this one. She shifted about nervously, her mind on her sisters and all that this night meant for their security and future happiness.

To her, this was but a dream or some novel she might have read. As long as no one discovered her true identity, all would go well, she hoped, and soon they would be on a ship bound for the new life of promise she aspired to give them. She gave a gentle sigh. Her thoughts drifted to the events of the last few days...

Madame Papillia had given her an advance of ten pounds when she had signed the Cyprian contract, thus sealing her fate. The money, however, was desperately needed. It had allowed her to purchase not only the needed food for the house and pay for their lodgings, but also two new muslin gowns and a new cloak for each of her sisters. There was even enough for each of the children to have a much needed set of new clothes and a new coat with a trifle to spare for some sweetmeats along with gumdrops and penny-candy, something they had not had in a very long time.

After all that had to be paid was paid, Elizabeth took the remaining money and went by coach to Hertfordshire. She had not seen her father's grave since that fateful day over five years ago when they had laid him to rest. This would be her only chance to see his resting place before leaving her past behind her for good.

With her cloak pulled tightly about her, Elizabeth had slipped into Longbourn Churchyard. It was near dusk and not a soul was around, nor could a sound be heard as she stepped softly and made her way back to the lonely stone in the far corner of the garden where her father lay under the shade of tall oaks. Elizabeth recalled how she had bent low and spread herself across the cold marble slab, resting her head upon her arm as she had prayed a simple prayer and spoken with her father, asking for his forgiveness. She was his favorite daughter, and before he died he had called her to his bedside where he pressed one last request, his words still crystal clear in her mind...

*"Lizzy...As a father I have failed you...and your sisters. Lydia is lost, and now all of you must partake of her shame...and when I am gone...I know not what will become of you."* Her father released a ragged breath. *"Mr. Collins...Given his thoughts and feelings on our recent disgrace, I fear there will be little mercy from our dear parson."* Mr. Bennet shook in a sputtering of coughs as he continued. *"I should have done more...I should have put back a nice sum, but you see my dear Lizzy, I intended to father a son, and he would thereby care for my widow and daughters."*

*"Please, Papa, please do not speak of it."*

---

[*] Lucas Cranach The Elder (1472-1553)

*"Ah, but I must, and you must hear me out," he said. "When I came to the realization that would not be the case, it seemed a little useless to begin saving, and then there was your mother's and sisters' spending habits. They kept me but one step away from debtor's prison on a number of occasions... but somehow I managed." He gave a small laugh between hacking coughs.*

Lizzy closed her eyes and shook her head as she recalled his last words.

*...Her father took her hand in his. "Find a way, Lizzy...find a way to provide for your mother and sisters...you are the strongest one. It is up to you, Lizzy, to protect them...to provide for them as best you can. Forgive me...*

With that, Mr. Bennet breathed his last and faded away.

*"I promise...Papa..."*

Elizabeth shook her head to dispel the painful memory. So much had changed...so much more would change. All she wanted was enough money to move her family far away. She had told her father at his graveside about Ireland and a cottage she had dreamt of where she and Jane and Kitty could raise the children and have a small garden, flowers for her and vegetables and herbs for Jane and Kitty.

Elizabeth closed her eyes and breathed deeply. This would be the only time she would ever know a man's touch. After this she would take a vow of celibacy.

She could do this. Tonight she wore black...black for mourning...black for mystery...black for the loss of her identity as Elizabeth Bennet...and black for her rebirth as Sofia Molina, the Spanish temptress. She smiled ruefully. Yes, she could do this because she was not Elizabeth Bennet—she was *Sofia Molina*.

Her musings were interrupted by a sharp jab in the ribs. "Pay attention to what you are about, Sofie. They will soon be coming our way. And remember to smile in a coquettish manner...*flirt*," Ophelia said, flicking her ivory feathered fan open as she shifted her gaze across the crowded ballroom to the three men who had just entered.

Ophelia, known for her allurement, had come as the mystical Freya from the garden of Odin in Valhalla.

"He looks marvelous tonight," she said.

"Which one?" Athena, the girl dressed as Aphrodite asked.

"The tall one, the one with the dark hair," answered Ophelia. "He has not been here in years."

Pandora, a beautiful blonde, scantily clad as a mythical mermaid, fanned herself as they waited. "They say he is a wonderful lover you know—a tall, handsome, fine specimen of a man with a noble mien—the epitome of a wealthy gentleman."

"Who?" Dorothea, the Irish courtesan clothed in sheer fabric, dressed as a sultan's harem beauty asked.

"Why Fitzwilliam Darcy, of course," Ophelia answered. "He has not been seen in society in over five years."

"Why ever not?" Athena asked.

"I do not know exactly, but from the report in general circulation they say a woman is to blame."

Elizabeth stiffened and fanned herself as she listened closely.

"It appears that the enigmatic Mr. Darcy lost his heart some years back to a mere country lass. Rumor has it that he proposed marriage and she turned him down. Can you believe that? Mr. Darcy finally falls in love, and the simpleton turns him down." Ophelia declared with the musical laughter that set her apart and secured her status as the most desired and sought-after courtesan in all of England. "What do you think of such a thing, Sofie?"

"I am sure I wouldn't know anything about it." ...*Oh, God, it could not have been me!*

"Um...no, I do not suppose you would at that. However, he is handsome, don't you think"? Ophelia asked as she fanned herself.

"Yes, he certainly is..." Elizabeth muttered more to herself than to her friend. Yes, he certainly was a fine looking gentleman indeed. Mr. Darcy cut a fine figure as he mingled in and out of the crowd as if searching for someone. Elizabeth had heard of the enigmatic Mr. Darcy through the years and had wondered about him many times, especially after she would reread the letter she had kept since that fateful day in Kent. He was known for not only his wealth, but for his benevolence to the poor and less privileged as well. She took a deep breath and shook her head. What had she done all those years ago?

As much as she wanted to linger in her musings, she was unable to, for her quiet reflections were disrupted by her friend. "Since then, he has been out of circulation. I have been told that he has poured himself into his estate and business. He has amassed a great fortune they say, making him one of the richest men in the Kingdom." Ophelia's lip curled slightly. "It looks like the magnificent Mr. Darcy has returned."

"Yes, I would say he has," Pandora responded. "What do you think, Sofie? Is he not the handsomest man you have ever beheld? And he is quite a good lover, too."

Elizabeth's senses suffered a jolt as she lifted her gaze to the man in the archway. "You have been with him?"

"No," her laughter tinkled merrily, "But I have heard. The General is *my* man. He is quite a lover, too, and that I *do* know for certain."

Elizabeth felt an uncomfortable surge in the pit of her stomach as she watched Mr. Darcy through the black lace of her veil. He was dressed in a black formal suit with a flowing cloak, but wore no mask and was indeed every bit as handsome as she remembered. No, he was more handsome with a touch of silver framing his temples, giving him the appearance of being distinguished.

His attendance was obviously welcome to every woman in the room, for all noticed him and soon were vying for his attention—all except her. Pandora, Dorothea, and Athena had even stepped in his direction. Only she and Ophelia remained where they stood.

"What makes him so desirable?" Elizabeth asked, her veil dancing in the current of her warm breath.

"Why his money, of course...that and the fact that he has been known to bring a woman to the pinnacle of raptures. He was known for his tender touch and his slow hand, coupled with a commanding prowess. Mr. Darcy is one of the few gentlemen who actually cares whether or not a woman is satisfied. I have been told by the women lucky enough to be chosen by him that he always saw to their pleasure before taking his own, a definite plus in this business."

Elizabeth glanced in his direction and their eyes locked. She could feel the heat of his penetrating gaze.

"Smile, Sofie. He is looking directly at you," Pandora said, returning with the others. "From what I heard just a moment ago, they are interested in us. The taller one especially expressed an interest in *you*, Sofie."

"Umm…it would appear he prefers the more innocent ones then," Dorothea remarked, turning to Elizabeth. "But that is hardly surprising. I can tell he is a very refined gentleman and your costume is more elegant than the rest of us. From what I know of him, you are just the sort of girl he would prefer—dressed in black satin with just enough décolletage to be interesting…mysterious even, but not enough to give away your secrets."

Elizabeth blushed. It was true. She had remained firm. She would not dress like a common prostitute. Her gown had been fashioned by her sisters to be sensual and alluring, very promising, but not revealing. The neckline was cut low enough to entice with a single red rosebud fashioned in the middle of her bodice just above her whalebone in the daintiest of little hollows. It was enough to make any man lower his eyes.

In addition to that, Elizabeth wore an elegant black and white cameo strung on a velvet cord, resting just below her throat. Kitty had fashioned tiny red rosebuds in silk twists interspersed with glass beads along the edge of her satin mask that lay beneath her black lace veil, and Jane had created a sash of black velvet tied just below her bosom, helping to lift them in a pleasing and provocative manner. Her dress was just revealing enough to be inviting, but not enough to give everything away before the ink was dry on the courtesan's contract. If Elizabeth was to be a rich man's paramour, she would do so in style, *and* she would command her price—a price high enough to give her family the country cottage and new life they desired.

"Look…he is moving toward us. I hope he picks me," Athena giggled in delight.

"No, me," Dorothea interjected.

"Hush," Ophelia said, fanning herself. "He will hear you."

As Fitzwilliam Darcy and his cousins made their way across the room, Darcy remarked to himself. …*Except for the woman in black, it is as I remember…much pomp and circumstance with very little substance.*

When they reached their destination, Ophelia lowered her fan. Turning to Viscount Wexford she said, "Viscount, it has been a while."

"Ophelia," he smiled, "you are still the same sultry siren I remember, alluring as ever, and if you are not otherwise engaged, I would like to claim the first dance."

"I am not engaged, sir." Her lips curled pleasantly.

"Splendid! Now, allow me to introduce my companions. My brother you know, but my cousin I do not believe has had the pleasure of your acquaintance."

"Madam." Mr. Darcy gave a curt bow.

"I am honored to make your acquaintance, Mr. Darcy," she replied. "Now," looking directly at Viscount Wexford, she continued, "if you will allow me gentlemen, I will introduce my friends." Ophelia turned to her companions. "To my right is Miss Sofia Molina. She is new and seeking a protector. And this is Pandora, Athena, and Dorothea with whom you, Viscount, and your brother, are well acquainted, but I do not believe Mr. Darcy has had the pleasure." Ophelia said with a smile. "All are looking for a gentleman tonight and are at your service." Ophelia lips curled upward as she glanced between the enigmatic Mr. Darcy and her three friends, all of whom were especially eager to please him.

The gentlemen bowed, the General's eyes never leaving Pandora whom he had apparently chosen already.

Mr. Darcy, however, lifted Elizabeth's hand and placed a gentle kiss on the back of her black fingerless lace-gloved hand, his eyes dropping from her face, focusing on her bosom before returning to her intense stare beneath the black veil. "If you are not engaged, Miss Molina, may I have the honor of the next waltz with you?"

Elizabeth smiled and accepted in her most elegant Spanish.

To say he was surprised would have been an understatement. He was shocked. The melodious sound of her fluent Spanish was pleasant, but unexpected. "Señorita, ¿habla usted inglés?"

"No, Señor, no hablo inglés. Hablo español."

Seeing the dilemma, Ophelia interjected. "Mr. Darcy, Sofia is English, but she prefers to speak Spanish. It is part of her mystique."

"I see," he answered with a smile. "Then let us speak Spanish. It will be an exercise I am in sore need of."

Darcy had spied the enchantress when he had first entered the room and was intent on seeking her out. He was indeed attracted to the alluring princess, but it was more out of curiosity than anything else. However, this aspect of the dark beauty entranced him even more. The Cyprian had class and sophistication. He gave her an intense smile as he led her to the center of the ballroom.

Floating over the dance floor, the woman felt familiar. For some reason, the lilt of her step, the lightness of her figure, and the ring of her laughter and melody of her voice reminded him of a woman he had known long ago.

"¿Señorita, que libros le gusta leer?" he asked.

"¡Libros!" She merrily laughed. "Oh, no Señor, no se debe hablar de esos temas en un baile."

Darcy raised an eyebrow. *She doesn't discuss books in a ballroom...* Again his mind drifted back to another lady he had known and a ball five years ago at Netherfield Park. Perhaps the Cyprian would be a reasonable facsimile of the woman he had once loved. He smiled to himself.

He had not come tonight to find a paramour, but folding her into his arms, the corporeal scent of her perfume filled his senses, creating a carnal desire he had long since forgotten he possessed. It was not a fragrance he was familiar with. It was exotic, sensual, and intoxicating. Pulling her against his chest, he felt his body tighten in response to the lush Spanish siren in his arms. If only for the night, he would pay her price and have her. His body demanded it. He wanted her for one night, and one night only, for had he come seeking a mistress, it would not be a sultry temptress who played with his senses and threatened to overwhelm his emotions with her allurements.

"Señorita, you are acquainted with the rules of engagement, I presume."

"Sí, Señor."

"Then would you care to accompany me to your room above stairs?"

"No, Señor. *I* set the rules of engagement, and there are no samples of my wares, even for a fee. It is a contract or nothing. ...And, Señor Darcy, you must be made aware, I am not *cheap*," she said in perfect fluent Spanish.

Gazing down at the siren in his arms, he could make out just enough from beneath the veil to see that her eyes twinkled and her lips turned up in an impetuous smile that had alarming repercussions on his senses. Already fully aroused, he could think of nothing more than losing himself in her arms, sinking deep into her mossy grotto, and the thought of not finding his release caused him to inwardly groan in pain. How much would she cost? Would he be willing to pay it? In all of his memory, only one woman had been brave enough to challenge him, and he had let her slip away. Would he let her only rival, a Spanish siren, also slip away?

"And what is your fee, my Spanish Cyprian?"

"For that, Señor, you must speak with Madame Papillia. She knows my limit. But I assure you, the higher the price, the better your reward."

He laughed. "You are quite the business woman. I admire that quality in the female species. It is rarely seen, sadly," he said. "I shall indeed speak with the brothel keeper, and, within reason, pay your price, but I am not sure I want to keep you for a full year."

"We can negotiate monthly, but the price rises sharply, as I desire a secure future."

The folds of her black veil danced with every word she spoke, captivating him even more as their bodies swayed to the sound of the orchestra. He smiled. The Cyprian was indeed his match. Perhaps it was time he took a mistress after all since he knew he would never take a wife, or at least if he did, it would not be the love match he had desired when he had met Elizabeth Bennet all those years ago.

After releasing her hand, the Duke of Ancaster claimed her for the next two sets, and then the Duke of Castlebaum, each enjoying her laughs and smiles as they floated across the dance floor. While she danced, Darcy stalked the perimeter of the room, watching the gentlemen vying for Elizabeth's affections, a contemptuous look of disapproval shadowing his features. Darcy stared, but never asked for her hand again.

Dukes, earls, marquises, members of the beau monde and gentlemen of the highest caliber courted her interest. They enjoyed her smiles while she enjoyed their rapt attention, but she could not help stealing glances every now and then in a certain gentleman's direction, catching his stern expressions and disgruntled look. Had she not known better, she would have thought he gave her looks of disapprobation as she laughed and flirted with first one and then another of her many admirers. As the hour grew late, it seemed that two of her admirers claimed her time more than any other. Between the Duke of Ancaster and his grace the Duke of Castlebaum, her time was limited, but every time she glanced in Darcy's direction his eyes were riveted on her, burning her with the intensity of his stare.

Darcy glowered. However, this time she did not misread his reserved stares, for Elizabeth did not miss that she was the only courtesan he danced with that night. She knew that he was attracted to her and that his attraction was strong. Of all the gentlemen applying for her favors, she knew which one she would choose. And thus she enjoyed her evening with Madame Papillia's words fresh in her mind.

*...With a figure like yours, my dear, you can open doors with a mere smile. Treat the gentlemen well, Sofia, and **they** will be good to you...*

And so dear reader, before the evening closed, Mr. Darcy had negotiated a contract for the alluring Spanish Cyprian. He hadn't even flinched at her price of three thousand pounds per annum. Instead, he smiled wryly. Knowing the Dukes of Ancestor and Castlebaum had already offered up to six thousand pounds, he upped it to ten thousand pounds—an amount he dared his competitors to top. He had even agreed to purchase the contract of her maid, Ling-Ling, whom she refused to leave behind, and he gave her an additional twelve hundred in pin money to be paid monthly as well as the promise of an entirely new wardrobe with the specification that he would select at least half the gowns and accessories, for he intended to dress her in style with the latest fashions from Paris and enjoy his fantasy for as long as it lasted. In addition, he further agreed that, for a full year, she would have use of his second home, a country townhouse located in Richmond on the outskirts of London. If she pleased him and he renewed her contract, he would deed it to her.

However, Miss Molina had insisted that a trial duration clause be inserted into the contract. If either she or he wished to break the contract for any reason after a trail living arrangement of three months, they were free to do so with the stipulation that half the money was to be hers. So sure was he of his ability to hold the young Spanish siren that Mr. Darcy had agreed to all of her demands and then some. He had stipulated that at the end of the trial, she must remove her mask and reveal her identity to which *she* agreed provided that he did not seek her identity before the said time of three months. If he broke the agreement and looked upon her face, the contract was terminated and she would receive the full amount of ten thousand pounds.

# Chapter 4

**T**is yet another universal truth known that, though delightful and beautiful, menacing and alluring, passive and predatory, women will always hold the men they encounter in the palms of their hands. Or so they say.

In the fine sentiments of our dearest friend, Mr. Shakespeare…

> *O, she doth teach the torches to burn bright!*
> *It seems she hangs upon the cheek of night*
> *As a rich jewel in an Ethiop's ear—*

Now, my dear reader, let us see how it goes.

### Christmas Eve

Darcy took his watch fob from his waistcoat and flipped the gold casing open.
A quarter to six.
He snapped it shut and returned it to his vest pocket. Where was she? He passed his hand over his face and lifted his brandy glass to his lips. He had sent his best coach to Madame Papillia's over two hours ago. Sofia should have arrived by now. Settling back into the soft, comfortable divan, he glanced over at the black velvet case on the side cabinet. He had bought her a gift, something he had seen while shopping for his sister. Tomorrow, if all went well, he would present it to her for Christmas.
Darcy glanced around the room as he settled back and crossed his long legs. Although it needed a little work, Richmond House was a fine piece of property. He had acquired it as part of an estate sale the previous spring, intending to refurbish it

and sell it for a profit, but, if things progressed as he thought they might, he would redecorate it to Sofia's specification and deed it to her.

He dragged his hand over his face once more in agitation. It was so unlike him to let lust cloud his thoughts. His logical mind still reeled at how his emotions had got the better of him. What was it about this woman that lured him to her like a moth drawn to the flame? He smiled sadly. It was because of Elizabeth Bennet. All these years he had carried her memory in his heart—a torch that burned with a consuming desire that would never be satisfied. At least not by Elizabeth Bennet. He had loved her, but now that memory was fading. He could scarcely recall what she looked like.

Darcy sighed as he sat his glass aside and twisted his signet ring. Had he been willing to lay aside his pride and expose Wickham, Elizabeth would still be alive, and maybe he would have been given a second chance when his former best friend Charles Bingley would have returned to Netherfield. But no, he had held his pride and his tongue until it was too late.

He winced as he recalled Bingley's reaction to the news that Miss Bennet had been in love with him all along. He and his best friend had come to blows. Darcy had let Charles knock him to the ground. After all, Bingley was justified. His pride had been his own downfall. Elizabeth was gone. She was dead. And in part, it had been his fault.

However, he smiled, in some small way, Sofia reminded him of Elizabeth. She was about her build, possessed Elizabeth's same sharp wit, and she was admired wherever she went, albeit for her sexual allure. Elizabeth had been a fantasy—one he had taken to bed every night since their time together at Netherfield and then again later at Kent. It had consumed him.

Elizabeth was but a dream. Sofia was flesh and blood. He could have Sofia even if he had to buy her. He could never have Elizabeth.

Darcy rose from his seat and moved to the large picture window, parting the heavy brocade curtains. It had begun to snow heavily. Where in God's name was she?! He ran his fingers through his hair. Perhaps he had made a mistake in letting his lust get the better of him. No, it was too late for regrets. Darcy tossed the curtains back. He had paid her well enough. By God, she had better come!

Just then he heard the coach pull through the gate and into the drive, making its way to the house. A wide smile crossed his features. She had come.

He parted the curtains once more, staring out the window as the coach was unloaded. There she stood with her maid Ling-Ling and an odd looking cat as the snow steadily came down on her brown cloak and black veil. Releasing the curtain once again, he stood and waited for her to be announced.

Hobbs entered the drawing room, and Darcy smiled as he turned and left for the entryway.

When Darcy entered the vestibule, he immediately froze. *...she doth cause the torch to burn.* And his torch was certainly on fire.

The scent of her perfume filled the room with traces of honey flower, tactile wood, and amber, matching the woman perfectly. Sofia was more captivating than the night he had danced with her at the ball. That night she had been a temptress, but today she was simply beautiful.

Conservatively dressed in cream colored brocade with brown embroidered silk trimmings and a dark brown woolen cape stitched in peach colored twist, she was the epitome of elegance befitting any gently born lady. Her brown woolen-felt bonnet with its black veil was very attractive. His manhood stiffened as his eyes caressed her body.

"¡Brr! Hace frío afuera," she said merrily as she brushed the snow from her cloak.

"Señorita Molina." He bowed formally. ...*still speaking Spanish, I see. Well, Señorita, it's anything but cold in here.*

Darcy smiled to himself. *...If my growing erection is any indicator of your charms, the night holds a promise of exotic pleasure untold... my pretty Señorita.*

"Señor." She curtseyed.

He turned to his butler. "Hobbs, see to it that Miss Molina's things are taken to the mistress's quarters. Her maid is to have the room in the family servants' wing. The one closest to our quarters. Once it is taken care of, you may be dismissed."

"Muy bien, Señor."

The butler directed a few servants to take the trunks above stairs and then left the vestibule.

"Señor Darcy, allow me to introduce my maid and cat," she said, turning to the small Oriental woman by her side. "This is Ling Hua. Her name means delicate flower, and that she is. She is invaluable to me. However, she is called Ling-Ling."

"Ling-Ling at your service, Sir." The maid dropped a deep curtsy.

"I am indeed pleased to meet you, Miss Ling-Ling."

"And this is my cat, Cocoa." Sofia smiled, noting the frown on Mr. Darcy's face. "Sí, I know Cocoa is unusual. There is not another cat like her in all of England. She is Siamese* and comes from Siam. Ling-Ling gave her to me."

"Indeed she is unusual. I have never seen a cat with blue eyes or markings like that," he said, reaching out to stroke the cat's fur.

Cocoa purred and licked Darcy's fingers, rubbing her head against his hand.

"Sí," she said, handing the cat off to a servant. "Her chocolate color is very unique, and she appears to like you."

As Sofia went to loosen her wrap, Darcy stepped forward. "Allow me to help you with your cloak and gloves, Señorita?"

Taking her gloves from her delicate hands, Darcy noticed their roughness. He frowned. These were not the hands of a lady. Who was she, and where did she come from?

Darcy slipped the cloak from her delicate shoulders and hung it on the rack, and then placed her gloves in the silver salver. "Señorita, I will show you to your quarters. Dinner is at eight. I expect you to eat with me. Then we will retire for the

---

* There were no Siamese cats in England in 1817. The first recorded pair came when Edward Blencowe Gould, the British Consul-General to Siam, brought a pair back from Bangkok in 1884 for his sister Lillian Jane Veley who went on to be co-founder of the Siamese Cat Club in 1901. The cats were shown at The Crystal Palace in 1885.

—Courtesy Wikipedia

evening. Over dinner I shall tell you what is expected of you as my mistress," he said, leading her to the expansive staircase that wound around as it climbed upward and split into two sections.

Sofia glanced up at him and swallowed back a faint smile as they took the stairs together. She followed a few steps behind him, allowing herself to take in the lean, strong build of the man to whom she had committed her future.

Once in the confines of her room, Sofia fell on her bed. "Oh, Ling-Ling, what have I done? Did you see the way he looked at me? I do not know if I can go through with this."

"Oh Miss, you must. He good man. Ling-Ling know. He like Cocoa. And Cocoa like him. Ling-Ling help you. Miss Sofie must relax. First time always hard. Hurt, yes, but once it over, Miss will like gentleman's attention. Ling-Ling make you very pretty. Make Mr. Darcy fall in love with you. You marry protector. My last mistress now Lady Berwick. She marry protector."

Sofia softly laughed. "No, no, Ling-Ling. I do not want to marry. I want to earn enough money to take care of my sisters and mother. We have two young cousins and a nephew to care for. It is for them that I do this. When the time comes, we will go to Ireland or maybe to the Islands in the Caribbean. There is no room in my life for such a foolish thing as love."

Ling-Ling shook her head. "Sad about family. Ling-Ling have no family. Ling-Ling's life hard. Me come to England on sailors' boat. Me disguise as cabin boy escape uncle. Uncle beat Ling-Ling after father die."

"Oh!" Sofia went to her maid and hugged her like she would one of her cousins. "I am so sorry. I forget myself. I know you have suffered, too. Forgive me, Ling-Ling."

"No...no be sorry. Ling-Ling very happy now. Ling-Ling help people. Father taught Ling-Ling ancient Chinese medicine. Ling-Ling help girls be beautiful. Make hair beautiful and potions for silky skin. Make perfumes from ancient recipes for ladies. Make men fall in love. Make gentleman fall in love with Miss Sofie so he pay well." The girl giggled. "Ling-Ling make Miss Sofie most beautiful of all courtesans. Mr. Darcy marry Miss Sofie."

"No, Ling-Ling. I do not want Mr. Darcy to fall in love with me. We can never marry. Too much stands between us. It can never be."

Ling-Ling sighed and shook her head. Within the short time she had come to know Sofia Molina, Ling-Ling had come to love her, even giving her prized Siamese cat to her. It pained Ling-Ling to see her mistress unhappy. Ling-Ling was an excellent judge of character. She had not missed the way Mr. Darcy looked at her mistress. If she knew anything, she knew he was half way to being in love, and when he discovered his mistress was a virgin, Ling-Ling knew his heart would soften.

Ling-Ling clapped her hands. "Chop-chop. We must prepare you for dinner...and tonight. You wear green dress with cream lace. It make mistress very pretty. Show figure yum-yum. With figure like yours, it go long way to making Mr. Darcy fall in love."

Sofia rolled her eyes and laughed. "Ling-Ling, you are impossible, but I do adore you."

Ling-Ling sent below stairs for a cup of buttermilk and steaming water. She collected her essential oils from her case and prepared Sofia's aphrodisiac bath: one cup of buttermilk, four drops of jasmine, four of ginger, four of neroli and six of clary sage with one drop of black pepper, and her mistress's bath was ready.

Sofia's hair was scented, her skin smoothed, her dress fitted to entice. Sofia was ready. She turned and kissed Ling-Ling's cheek. "Thank you, Ling-Ling, for all you do."

"You very welcome, Miss Sofie. You go and enjoy yourself. Ling-Ling and Cocoa wait."

Dinner was a formal affair. The meal was excellent and the wine was of the very best vintage. Mr. Darcy sat at the head of the formidable cherry wood table and Sofia sat to his right. The clatter of their silverware clanking against the fine china was the only sound in the room.

"Señor Darcy, we must have some conversation."

"¿Sí, Señorita, of what would you like to speak?"

"Oh, I do not know. I might compliment the meal, and you might say, 'Yes, Cook is an excellent servant.'"

Darcy placed his silverware aside and looked her straight in the eye. "Sofia, let us dispense with the small talk and come to the point. You are my mistress for the next three months. I do not expect frivolous conversation; nor do I expect to sit around and exchange polite little pleasantries with a woman of your profession. I expect you to pleasure me in whatever way I wish." Darcy picked up his knife and fork and began to cut his meat as he continued.

"If you please me, Miss Molina, your contract specifies the reward. If not, you are paid fifty percent of the agreement and sent on your way. Now, listen carefully to me. I expect you to be available to me whenever I wish it. If you happen to be on your courses, you are to pleasure me at my discretion in whatever way I specify. I will provide for you, and you will please me. You are to have no expectations of me other than those specified in your Cyprian's contract. Is that understood?"

She stiffened and looked away. "¡Perfectamente!"

"Muy bien."

He picked up his goblet and took a sip of wine. He had not wanted to be so blunt, but truth be told, she was driving him to distraction with her sweet-scented perfume and low-cut dress. Her veil allowed no indication of her beauty, but if her face was half as handsome as her body, he knew he would never be able to have enough of her. And that was the material point. She was a whore. He did not want to share anything with her apart from satisfying his physical lust. Loving her was out of the question. She might remind him of Elizabeth Bennet; however, she was *not* Elizabeth. Miss Elizabeth had been a lady—a gentleman's daughter. Sofia was a Cyprian. He would not have her engaging him in conversation as Miss Elizabeth had.

He slowly sipped his wine as he watched her from the corner of his eye. With dinner concluded, he instructed her to be ready for him within the half-hour.

Sofia stormed into her room, stamping her foot as she slammed the door shut. She was furious.

"What matter, Miss Sofie? Dinner not go well?"

"Insufferable man! He has not changed one bit—not in the least. He is just as I remember. He as much as called me a trollop!" She stopped with a look of shock. "I guess that is just what I am, is it not," she muttered more than asked. "Oh, never mind."

Ling-Ling tilted her head. "Ling-Ling no understand. Does mistress *know* Mr. Darcy?"

"It does not matter. Help me prepare. Bring me the most provocative dressing gown I own. If he wants sex for the evening, then he shall have it. I have been paid well. I will not disappoint." Sofia took a deep breath, recalling Madame Papillia's words. *...Open your legs wide, my dear. That's what men want.*

Elizabeth Bennet was more determined than ever to become Sofia Molina, the Spanish Cyprian Mr. Darcy expected. He would get her virtue, and she would get his money.

# Chapter 5

From Mother Eve down through the ages, man has justified his need to dominate woman by claiming superiority. However, in the bedchamber, it is the man who willingly surrenders his hypothetical dominance to the supposedly weaker sex.

Darcy gave two firm raps on the door joining their rooms.

"¡Entre, Señor!" she called out.

He entered and paused, standing just inside the room, his eyes drinking in the sight of her. His senses were instantly heightened by the fragrance in the room. He glanced about. The bed was turned down, dressed in red satin. She had lit scented candles now scattered in jars throughout the room. A fire crackled in the fireplace. The mood…the atmosphere—all of it was stimulating and inviting, a playground for one's fantasies to run wild. His eyes became riveted on her form.

Clothed in red and black, a scarlet mask beneath the black veil, she stood by the hearth with a red fan trimmed in black lace provocatively positioned, covering her breasts. Were they bare? His jaw twitched. She was more beautiful than he had imagined. Her gown was of the finest silk; her negligee, the sheerest black lace. The folds of the translucent material fell elegantly about her figure, revealing just enough to cause his blood to boil, but not enough to completely reveal her secrets. Those he would explore in time. The siren…*his* siren…had excellent taste and knew how to arouse a man's sexual appetite and indulge his fantasies.

Finally he strolled over to the dressing table and opened a decanter of port, pouring two glasses.

"¿Care to drink with me?" he asked in flawless Spanish.

"No, Señor Darcy."

"Señorita, in the confines of this house, and especially in our bedchamber, I am Fitzwilliam or Señor, if you prefer, and you are Sofia. When we are out in the public square, then you are Señorita Sofia Molina, and I am Señor Darcy," he said with a commanding tone, his eyes intense and focused on her. "Take the wine. You may need it." *…we both may.*

Sofia took the proffered drink and raised the goblet to her lips.

"¿Señor…Fitzwilliam, would you have a seat?" She motioned to the settee near the mantelpiece.

He walked over and settled himself among the silk pillows she had placed there. "Come, join me," he said, his eyes never leaving her form as he sat and beckoned her to come.

She did as he asked and strolled in his direction.

A small smile curled his lips. She looked alluring with the fan hiding her secrets, her scarlet mask concealing her face, and her black veil dancing about her lips when she spoke—all of it stimulating to him. He looked forward to the day when he would remove it, revealing the mystery behind the black veil. Perhaps tonight would be the night.

Darcy took a small sip of wine. "Drop the fan."

As the fan slowly lowered and dropped to the floor, his eyes flashed. Taking in a deep breath, he slowly drank in the sight of her, the whiteness of her neck and shoulders, the smoothness of her skin, and the swell of her lush breasts, rounded with firm, dark nipples—his for the tasting—were barely visible through the sheer fabric of her gown. All of it transformed this woman of flesh and blood into a mythical creature—his Spanish Cyprian issuing the siren's call to his baser emotions.

He cleared his throat. "Now, drop your robe." He set his wine down as he watched the black lace fall to the floor, his eyes tracing over the curve of her figure through the thin cloth. The only thing separating him from her was her scarlet gown.

"Step closer."

With a sharp intake of breath, she did as he said.

He rose to his feet and took the wine glass from her hand, setting it beside his. Turning back to his Spanish Cyprian, he reached to caress her face and remove the veil, but she stayed his hand.

"No, Señor," she said, her lashes beneath the black veil sweeping downward.

"When?"

"In four score and ten days." She turned and looked at him. "Then you may remove the veil. If you still want me after that, I will remain, but if not, I will go. Never is my veil to be removed in public, nor are *you* to reveal who I am. No one is to know. It is part of the contract."

He smirked. "Señorita, I am well aware of the contents of our contractual agreement."

Taking her hand, he sat down and pulled her into his lap, burying his nose in the curve of her neck, inhaling her exotic scent. Then he reached up and pulled the pins from her hair one by one, being careful of her veil and mask, letting her raven tresses cascade down over her shoulders, covering her body like her veil covered her face.

"Usted tiene un hermoso cabello, Sofia. It is truly your crowning glory. Wear it down for me, loose and free, especially in our bed." His Spanish was flawless.

She nodded and closed her eyes as his soft warm lips found their way to her throat, gently moving and suckling over her delicate skin. She had never been kissed by a man before. The sensation of his lips on her flesh was exquisite, but also puzzling.

After their exchange at dinner, this softer, gentler side of Mr. Darcy was not expected. She had assumed he would take her, as so many others had aspired to do, with little desire other than to satisfy his primal need. Gentleness, she had not anticipated. She swallowed and breathed deeply, her hands instinctively going to his face, her fingers sinking into his thick dark curls.

His lips finally captured hers, kissing her deeply, his tongue moving in and out while her fingers played in his hair. He moaned and broke the kiss. Burying his face in her bosom, his tongue ran down the cleft of her breasts, suckling and kissing as he cupped one lush mound of flesh, gently fondling it, running his thumb over the erect nipple.

She ran her hand over the expanse of his chest to his arousal, massaging it through the thin layer of his nightshirt, feeling it pulsate as she stroked the tip. Dampness spread in the cloth.

He groaned and took her face in his hands, whispering her name as he kissed her aggressively. Deepening the kiss, his body tightened as she turned in his lap and straddled him, rocking back and forth over his swollen member. The Cyprian knew her art as she drove him to the point of no return.

He wanted her in every possible way. He'd almost forgotten how good it felt to hold a woman in his arms, to kiss her, to caress her, to make love to her. Only in his dreams with Elizabeth had he imagined how good this would feel. In many ways Sofia reminded him of his Elizabeth, and now his longing…his need for his Elizabeth would be satisfied tonight with her Spanish complement, a sultry and sexy vixen as he imagined Elizabeth would have been under his skillful tutelage.

His hunger reaching its peak, Darcy repositioned her in his lap. "Are you lonely for a man, Sofia? Well, I'm lonely for a woman. Together we will find our way," he whispered against her lips as he ran his hand to the hem of her gown and lifted the silken fabric, his fingers tracing her leg to her thigh, stroking and exploring. Her legs were exquisite, firm and athletic, the finest pair of legs he'd ever caressed.

His hand traveled upward to the center of her womanhood. She parted her thighs, allowing him full access. Feeling her hot dampness as his fingers slid inside of her, he paused and quickly withdrew. Scooping her up into his arms, he carried her to their bed where he gently set her on her feet and ripped back the coverlet.

"Querida," he said softly as he untied the strings that held her bosom secure and then unfastened the loops of her gown.

Reaching up, he touched her collarbone and slipped the strap from her shoulder. The red silk fell in a pool at her feet. "This is the way I want you, Sofia. You are to be naked when you are in our bedchamber." His voice was hoarse.

He then picked her up and placed her in their bed.

Removing his clothing, he walked over to the small desk and pulled a lambskin sheathe from the drawer. He removed it from the casting and secured it in place.

Sofia's eyes widened. She had never seen a naked male before. Her eyes fixed on his bare chest. A tuft of dark hair streaked with a touch of silver spread across his breast and downward to his loins. His buttocks and limbs were lean and fit. Mr. Darcy was magnificent, strong and graceful, formed like the statue of David she'd seen when she had toured Florence with her aunt and uncle. And then there was his arousal. Her eyes widened even more. How would she take *that* inside of her?

Her breath caught as he climbed in beside her and pulled her into his arms, touching her, tasting her, savoring her, tenderly kissing her all over, caressing her every curve. Nothing she had read prepared her for how it would feel to be loved by a man skilled in lovemaking, and Señor Darcy *was* skilled in the art of lovemaking.

His lips traced the line from her collarbone to her breast. Taking her breasts into his hands, he suckled them, going from one to the other, slowly licking and caressing with his lips and tongue, swirling around her nipples and gently grazing his teeth over her soft skin, sending shivers coursing through her body as her heart raced.

"Eres muy bonita, Señorita...Eres tan hermosa...you are so beautiful," he whispered, inhaling her exotic scent as his hand descended, gently stroking her silken mound.

Sofia writhed at his touch as he found his way to her center once again, touching and caressing her. A rush of heat spread throughout her entire being. She softly moaned his name.

His mouth covered hers, suppressing a cry as his hand continued stroking her. She shook violently when his fingers slid inside.

Darcy recognized a fully aroused woman when he saw one, and Sofia Molina was fully aroused and more than ready for him. Rolling on top of her, he gathered her into his arms and parted her legs with his knee, settling between her thighs and adjusting himself.

When Darcy pushed into her, he felt instant resistance and froze. Pulling back in shock, he cried, "Good God, woman. You're a virgin, and you didn't tell me. What is the meaning of this? Who are you? Do you not realize how badly I could have hurt you?"

"I...I...did not think it would matter. After tonight I would no longer be. ¿What does it matter to you if I am still intact? You are getting what you paid for."

"It matters a great deal, Señorita. I had every right to know. You could have been badly hurt had I been more aggressive, and believe me, querida, I considered plunging into you with unrestrained passion. Had I done that, you would be writhing in agony, and I would be mortified."

Withdrawing from her, he fell back on his pillow. "I thought you were an experienced Cyprian. I paid for and *expected* an experienced woman. Instead, it is I who will have to teach *you*...not at all what I bargained for. I am of a mind to return you to Madame Papillia, or better yet, to your father, except that he would expect me to marry you."

Sofia flinched. "I have no father or brother. There is only me to provide for myself, and Señor, I do not expect matrimony nor do I wish it. I can take care of myself, thank you very much."

He drew a deep breath and glanced in her direction. "¡Señorita, you are indeed a strange woman! Innocent as the day you were born."

"Señor, do not underestimate me. I may be a maid, but I assure you I have been well instructed. I have studied The Cyprian's Handbook to a fault. I am only in want of a partner to perfect what I have learned."

Darcy threw back his head and gave a hearty laugh. "Señorita, you are incredibly naive. The art of lovemaking is not learned in a book." He looked at her with a soft smile. "I am not opposed to becoming your teacher. At least this way, neither of us need be concerned about disease. In that knowledge, I am well pleased. I will not need to take the usual precautions. Pregnancy, however, is another matter, but you can be assured that I will honor and provide for any children we produce." He tapped her nose with a kiss.

"I take no particular comfort in that, Señor," she said, clearly flushed, "for I have no intentions of begetting your child or anyone else's. My handmaid prepares a tea that is supposed to prevent pregnancy. I shall take comfort in *that*."

"No, mi belleza," he said, pulling her into his embrace. "Many a courtesan has lost her life following that course. I would rather you conceive and give birth ten times than to have you die from blood letting."

"¿How old are you, mi bonita?" he asked.

"Old enough."

"¿One and twenty?"

"Older."

Realizing no answer would be forthcoming, he smiled and ripped the covering from his swollen manhood, now more aroused than ever, demanding satisfaction.

Once again he pulled her into his arms. This time he would go slowly, making love to her as a young maid was worthy of.

For some reason, knowing she was a virgin thrilled him and changed his opinion of her. The only regret he had was that he would cause her pain and would not be able to bring her to pleasure as he otherwise would have done.

She reached and brushed a lock from his brow, looking intently into his deep brown eyes. Glancing between his dark, passion-filled gaze and his lips, she closed her eyes and leaned in, taking him in a soft kiss, stroking his face as she pressed the kiss, her tongue doing as his had done earlier.

He responded in like fashion and soon they were writhing against one another, kissing, touching and stroking, each bringing the other to the point of seventh heaven.

However, this time when Darcy rolled her over and parted her legs, he was very careful to enter her slowly. When he met her resistance, he raised up and said, "Querida, relajate, relax and follow my lead. It will sting, but I am told that if you are fully aroused the pain is fleeting. Relax and let me love you, my beautiful Spanish siren." With that he took her mouth in a deep kiss, trying to distract her from what was happening. He pushed gently and steadily, feeling her body give way as she opened up, and then with one swift thrust, he broke through her maiden shield and settled inside of her, buried to the hilt.

She flinched and cried out in pain.

"Relajate, Señorita. Let your body become accustomed to mine. When you can, raise your legs and follow my lead."

He breathed deeply as he inhaled her scent and began to kiss her anew, spreading tiny endearing kisses over her face and throat. He took her earlobe in his mouth and suckled, his warm breath in her ear, sending ripples of pleasure throughout her body.

Finally, Sofia raised her legs and encircled his waist.

Darcy began to move, and she followed his lead, slowly at first, but then as the pain gave way to pleasure, she moved against him with equal fervor and equal passion.

Darcy abandoned his reserve and buried his head into her neck, picking up speed.

Utterly spent, he collapsed on top of her and rolled over, pulling her against his chest, awash with emotions, both panting for breath.

"¿Did I hurt you too badly, querida?"

She relaxed against his shoulder and kissed his neck. "No. You were perfect. The pain was fleeting. It was more pleasurable than I ever could have imagined."

A broad smile etched his features. "Next time it will be better, my lovely Señorita, and you shall truly enjoy our coupling as I have enjoyed it now."

It was the truth. If she would have asked him at this moment, he would have given her half his fortune. For an hour spent in her arms was… priceless.

# Chapter 6

The next morning Sofia awoke peaceful and more contented than she had been in many years. She felt young again and alive—alive for the first time since Lydia's elopement. She stretched out lazily and felt for her lover. She frowned and turned to where he had lain the night before. He was gone. Sofia rose up in alarm.

She was just about to arise from her bed when the door to her room opened. A tray was brought up.

Darcy entered from the door that connected the master's suite to the mistress's suite.

"¡Feliz Navidad, Señorita!"

"¡Fitzwilliam! ¡Es una mañana magnífica!" She purred like a lazy cat awakening from its nap.

"Sí, 'tis a wonderful morning," he agreed. "We shall have breakfast in bed, and then we shall bathe. We're to spend the whole day together and enjoy the winter gardens."

They huddled together on the bed eating their eggs and toast. He hadn't felt this relaxed in years—not since that brief time he had spent at Netherfield. Unfortunately, back then he'd been too stubborn and proud to admit that he could actually enjoy a country society that was less varied than that to which he was accustomed. He had lost once. He did not intend to lose again.

Once the tray was cleared away, he removed a velvet box from his dressing gown pocket.

"¡Feliz Navidad, querida!" He beamed.

"¿Qué es esto?"

"Your Christmas present."

"Today we celebrate the Lord's birth. Tomorrow we will celebrate Boxing Day. And by the end of the week, we will go shopping. I want you to have an exclusive wardrobe from the best shops in London. We shall attend the theatre for Shakespeare's performance of Twelfth Night and then a party for a Twelfth Night celebration the following evening. My cousin, Viscount Wexford, always gives a party. I have avoided attending for many years. However, this year we will make an appearance. I intend to show you the world, and for that, you need a fashionable wardrobe."

"But Fitzwilliam, I have no present for you."

"No, Señorita, last night you gave me the best present a woman can give a man; you gave me yourself."

Sofia took the sapphire and diamond necklace from its case and held it up to the light, "Fitzwilliam, it is beautiful. I have never had anything like this. It will be a treasured possession for the rest of my life."

He smiled and took the necklace from her hand. Sofia turned so that he could fasten the clasp. Unable to resist, he bent low and placed a kiss on her slender neck.

Circling his arms around her waist, he pulled her back into his chest and ran endearing kisses along her pulse edging towards that tender spot behind her ear and down her throat in a manner that he knew drove women wild with desire.

Sofia shuddered and turned in his arms, curling her arms around his neck and pulling him into a deep, lingering kiss. Soon they were naked and making love in front of the crackling fire. Slowly, easily, and with deliberate strokes, he took her where she had never been before. It was heaven as Elizabeth Bennet, nay, Sofia Molina, surrendered to his touch and allowed Darcy to love her body once again.

After they had distributed the Boxing Day gifts Darcy had arranged for the servants of Richmond House, Darcy took Sofia to the winter gardens which were unusually pretty this time of year. The former owner had constructed an array of fountains in the garden which were now frozen solid, and the berry-laden trees with their bright red fruit looked spectacular against the backdrop of a winter wonderland covered in white, glistening snow. Off in the distance, the bells of St. Mark's could be heard ringing in the cold, crisp air.

"Come, Señorita, I must have you enjoy the gardens whilst we can," Darcy said, taking her by the hand as he led her into the cold. "The birds have come to celebrate with us. I had Cook prepare a Christmas feast of suet and millet for them, and the finches can have the berries. They are plentiful this time of year. My only concern is that your cat may not allow them to exist in peace."

She gave a small laugh. "Cocoa is a fierce hunter to be sure, but I believe she prefers mice to birds. We shall see."

"And so we shall." He laughed in return.

Strolling in the winter gardens arm in arm, talking and laughing, Elizabeth spied a frozen pond. "Come, Señor. There appears to be a small lake. I have not skated in years."

He laughed. "Señorita, we have no skates."

"We don't need them. When I was a child, my sisters and I skated on ice in our boots. I will admit it is better with a fine pair of ice skates, but one does not need them to enjoy the sport. Now, come," she said, tugging at his hand.

They stepped out onto the ice and began to mock skate, slipping and sliding as they went. "Señorita, how will I keep up with you? You are so vibrant."

"I am sure a man of your means…a man of the world will find a way. You tease and tantalize so well, and I have heard that practice makes perfect." She smiled from beneath the veil.

He tilted his head and gazed at her. "So I have been told." He had heard that before. Who was this woman?

"You had better hurry Señor, or I shall get the better of you. And you would not want a mere woman to best you, now would you?" Her laughter rang out in the clear morning air.

Darcy followed in hot pursuit. He had not had this much enjoyment since his youth back at Pemberley. Catching up to her and spinning her around, laughing and frolicking like two young lovers, he finally caught her in his arms like a small animal.

When she looked up at him, Darcy froze. She was so helpless and lovely at the same time. He wondered at her. How had she come to be a courtesan when she had the breeding of a fine gentleman's daughter…perhaps the daughter of an earl or some other rank in the peerage? Sofia was no common woman. She had no father, no brother…only him, her protector, to care for her welfare. The thought was worrisome.

Sofia reached up and touched the silver at his temples. "Señor, the night we met I thought you rather distinguished by the grey, but when you smile, years drop from your appearance. You are a very handsome man."

"Distinguished…" He smiled and shook his head as he took her gloved hand and kissed her fingers. "Perhaps…but it is *you*, Señorita, who is the beauty."

She shuddered—but not from the cold.

Gazing into her eyes through the black veil, he lifted his hand and gently caressing the side of her face, his fingertips tracing over her black mask. "I look forward to the day when I unmask your beauty, querida, and discover who you are, my lovely Señorita."

"Señor," she murmured as she glanced away and shook her head.

"No, Señorita, look at me." His fingers curled under her chin and tipped her face upward. "Sofia, even if I cannot see your face, I know that you are beautiful, for you have a beautiful mind and a beautiful heart, the mind and heart of a gently bred woman. That much I know, Señorita." He bent low and placed a kiss on her sweet lips.

She pulled back.

"You should not say things that you do not mean, Señor. I am not a woman you wish to conquer. I am your paramour."

She breathed against his lips before engaging them again.

He paused and muttered, "But I do mean it, and I have no wish to conquer you, only to make love to you until you weep from the pleasure of it."

Once again he covered her mouth with his as he felt her tremble in his arms.

Breaking their kiss, Sofia's lips curled in mirth. "Señor, you must catch me first," she teased, slipping out of his arms and scooting away.

Darcy gave chase and just as he caught her, they fell to the ground, tumbling and rolling and laughing. "Be careful of the family jewels, querida, or you may injure me for life."

"¡Never!" She laughed. "I must have you at my service."

"Oh, at *your* service. We shall see about that." He began to tickle her.

"¡Me basta, Señor, enough¡ I surrender," she cried.

He laughed and tickled her again, but then the expression of her countenance changed and caused him to falter. Passion…pure passion burned in what he could see of her eyes.

His breath caught in his throat. "Señorita..." he bent low, and his lips caught hers. Taking her in a deep kiss, a groan escaped from deep within his chest as his body burst into flames, and once more he wanted her. He could not get enough of her. She was alive, and for the first time in many years, he was alive again, too.

Breaking the kiss, he rose and took her by the hand, breathing deeply to cool his passion. "Señorita, we must go inside. It is cold, and you are flushed."

"Sí, Señor," she said as she dusted the snow from her dress and cloak.

"When we're in town, I shall purchase two pairs of skates, and we will do this properly."

The snow had begun to fall once again and the wind rustled the evergreens. Darcy gave a contented sigh as he gazed down at the little woman so full of life by his side. Her black veil danced in the wind. The flush of her cheeks and the glow in her face, brightened by the exercise, were tantalizing. Sofia Molina was indeed a desirable woman. Darcy reached and pulled her to his side as they walked toward the house. They had frolicked and played for what seemed like minutes, though it had been hours. Luncheon had come and gone.

Darcy looked up and tasted the falling snow on his tongue. Glancing at the woman walking beside him, he mused. *...she reminds me of Elizabeth. With very little effort, I could fall in love with her. You have to be mindful of yourself, Darcy. It would not do to fall in love with your mistress. Better to take her inside and ravish her...taste her fruits and nothing more, than to spend a lifetime pining for her... as you have for her complement.*

Once they had eaten and refreshed themselves, Darcy approached her. "Sofia, come upstairs. I want to make love to you by the fire. Undress. I want you naked when I come in to you...and I want your hair down as your only covering. Your second lesson in the art of lovemaking begins this afternoon. I have arranged for us to eat in our quarters. I fear the lesson will require our total attention and a great deal of time."

Her lips curled into an impetuous smile. "Señor, I would not miss it for the world. You are an excellent instructor, and I am an eager student."

"Every professor's dream, Señorita."

They did exactly as they pleased, making love all afternoon and into the night until both were utterly spent from the sheer pleasure that could be had in the arms of an eager and enthusiastic lover.

And that, dear reader, is how our couple spent the first days of their time together. Mr. Darcy hasn't a clue as to whom he has in his arms, not to mention in his bed. All of the evidence is there, but when a man's lower passions are engaged, his mind seldom is.

# Chapter 7

ow good and gentle reader we join our young lovers in the boudoir after an amorous encounter where old secrets and new revelations are disclosed. It seems our hero still carries a torch for a lost love with no realization that his desire is only a breath away. So close…and yet so far.

Let us see what our young lovers are about.

Lying in the arms of her lover, basking in the aftermath of their lovemaking, Sofia felt more relaxed than she ever before. She reached up and tenderly kissed his neck allowing herself the pleasure of savoring his skin beneath her lips. If she were of a mind to fall in love, it would be with the man who held her in his arms at this moment. He was a good man, kind and thoughtful, nothing like she had perceived him to be all those years ago in Hertfordshire. Had she not misjudged him, she would be lying here as Elizabeth Darcy, his wife—not Sofia Molina, his mistress. But the young Elizabeth Bennet was no more. She had matured into a woman, and she no longer teased and laughed at human folly; now she lived it.

When she looked around her and perceived the man he was, she could not help her thoughts *…and to think of all of this I could have been mistress with full legal rights as his wife.*

She released her breath and smiled at the irony.

Darcy glanced down and tipped her chin. "¿My lovely Señorita, what is in your pretty little head? A pence for your thoughts."

She chuckled. "Nada, nothing much. It is of no consequence."

"No, mi querida, if it can bring about a pretty smile, it is of consequence. Tell me what you are thinking."

"Well, if you *must* know, I am thinking of the past and what might have been had another road been taken."

He sighed and pulled her into his embrace, resting her head on his shoulder. "Señorita, tell me about yourself. I very much would like to know and have often wondered. ¿Where do you come from, and why did you choose the path of a courtesan?"

She laughed, her hand playing in the damp curls over his heart. "That is not so easy to explain, Señor," she said. "As I am a woman of no importance, it would not interest you."

"That is where you are wrong, querida. You are important to me, and I want to know. I am certain you could have married well. You have all the elements of a gently bred young lady with wit and charm, and you are better educated than most of your sex—nay more then most of my own. ¿So tell me, Señorita, what brought you to this?"

She snuggled closer and placed her arm around his waist. "As you say, Señor, I was a gentleman's daughter and raised to be a gentleman's wife, but my father was little better than a country squire with not much more to offer. My sisters and I, with no dowry, had little else to recommend us but our charms; therefore, when he died, we were lost to the world to make a life as best we could with no husbands."

"¿Did you have no family to care for you? ¿No uncles?"

"No, Señor. It was but me and two sisters left to survive in a world hostile to us. My sisters are alive and well. One keeps hearth and home, caring for our aging mother, a nephew, and two orphaned cousins. The other works as a seamstress in a small modiste, trimming gowns and bonnets. I worked for three noble families as a governess, but each master tried to seduce me, the last one striking me and ripping my gown when I refused his advances. Needless to say I found myself once again turned out into the cold. That is when I met an old friend, one whom you know." She heaved a sigh. "I felt I had no choices left to me. Ophelia introduced me to Madame Papillia, and you know the rest."

"¿Had you no offers of marriage before this calamity came upon you?"

"Yes, Señor, two. I turned them both down." She softly spoke. "I desired to marry only for affection, a foolish thing, I have been told."

"And you did not love either of your suitors…"

"No," she whispered. *...At least not the first one.*

"That is indeed an unfortunate turn of events, but in some small way, a blessing, because you found me, and I will take care of you. I am your protector. No one will ever beat you or ravish you against your will."

"Sí, Señor, you are indeed a good man." She nodded.

Darcy shook his head and pulled her close.

"I once thought as you did, wanting to marry for love," he murmured. "I agree; 'tis foolish."

Tilting her head, she twirled her finger around in the tuft of hair on his chest in quiet reflection. "¿Señor, were you ever in love?" Sofia knew the answer, but she wanted to hear the words from his lips, to know his inner thoughts.

Releasing a deep breath, he pulled his arm out from under her, flexing it to relieve the stiffness.

"Once." He nodded. "'Twas a long time ago."

Sofia could see the sadness in his eyes, the longing, and it touched her heart. "¿Will you not tell me about her? ¿What was she like?"

He looked at Sofia and smiled. "No, I do not mind. It was years ago. Her name was Miss Elizabeth Bennet. She was the jewel of the county, a country miss from Hertfordshire. A friend of mine had leased an estate in the neighborhood, and I had come from London to help him with estate management. I was not pleased to be in the society of Meryton, and I am afraid that my displeasure showed. You see, I found the society lacking in manners and good breeding, and somewhat wanting in variety."

"¿How did you meet this young lady?" He had her total attention. Her mind was in a whirl as she carefully listened to his every word.

Darcy gave a small laugh. "It was at an assembly on a cold autumn night. I remember it very well," he said with fondness. "I had not wanted to attend and was put off that my friend had insisted on it. I am afraid I was very disagreeable that evening, even to the point of insulting her, her family, and many others in the community. I have to admit, I was not attracted to her at first."

"¿Were you not?"

"No. I hardly noticed her."

"¿What changed your mind?"

"Well," he said in a somber tone, "what caught my attention and held it was her cheeky impertinence. After I had insulted her with a comment—something to the effect of her not being handsome enough to tempt *me*, she walked past me and smiled. It was that moment which caused me to take a deeper look at the woman with whom I had refused to dance. I remember saying I was in no humor at present to give consequence to young ladies who were slighted by other men. Those words were regretted soon after."

"Hmm, a very regrettable choice of words, I am sure."

"Yes, it was." Darcy glanced at his companion and smiled. "In many ways, Señorita, you remind me of her. She was about your height, perhaps a little taller. Her figure was light and pleasing, similar to yours. However, what I found most striking about her were her eyes, green with flecks of gold that sparkled with uncommon intelligence. I once remarked on the very great pleasure a pair of fine eyes in the face of a pretty woman can bestow. Although I can scarcely recall her face now, it has been so long, I shall never forget those luminous eyes."

"¿Señor, when did you discover that you were in love with her?"

"That is difficult to tell, for it came on so gradually. I cannot fix on the hour, or the spot, or the look, or the words, which laid the foundation. It is too long ago. I was in the middle before I knew that I had begun. I was attracted soon after the assembly, especially at a dinner party given by a neighboring gentleman. I listened to her every word. That is also when I noticed her eyes."

Sofia listened intently, her mind reliving the scene he described, remembering it only too well. Her musings were soon interrupted by his affectionate recollections of herself as she once was.

"The attraction deepened when she came to Netherfield, my friend's estate, to care for her sister who had become ill whilst visiting with his sisters. I found I could not concentrate when she was in the room. I would often stare and admire her beauty, but apparently, she misunderstood my admiration. When we would spar in verbal combat she apparently thought I meant to ridicule when I merely meant to challenge her quick wit. I fell in love with her for the liveliness of her mind, I did."

Sofia glanced away and shook her head. "You must have loved her then..." *...when we were at Netherfield,* she muttered more to herself than to Darcy.

"I left the country to escape her, but her memory followed me until my passion became too great to deny. I proposed marriage whilst we were in Kent, she visiting her cousin and friend, and I my aunt, Lady Catherine de Bourgh. It did not go well,

I'm afraid. I insulted her in every imaginable way with my proposal and did not even realize it.

"You see she had discovered that I was responsible for separating her sister from my friend because I did not believe her sister to have affection for him. I am afraid I viewed her family very badly and thought that Miss Bennet was only interested in my friend for his money." Darcy smirked and shook his head. "That was when I learnt her true opinion of me. Miss Elizabeth's accusations were ill-founded, formed on mistaken premises, but my behaviour to her at the time had merited the severest reproof. It was unpardonable. I cannot think of it without abhorrence. Except for one misconception, her words were true and justified."

Darcy folded his hands behind his head and stared up at the ceiling.

"It never occurred to me that she would reject my offer of marriage. After all, I am a wealthy gentleman from amongst the ranks of nobility. My grandfather is an earl. Therefore, I assumed she would be honored to become my wife, and at that point, though I still found her family objectionable, so smitten was I that I was willing to overlook everything and care for them as if they were my own. ¡But she would have none of it! I am unsure how I could have been so blind, for I had erroneously believed she was expecting my addresses, even wishing for them, but I was wrong. I had mistaken her friendly manner for admiration. I can assure you that night was one of the most painful times in my life. It pains me even now to know that I will never have the opportunity to show her how her rebuke has been properly attended to."

"I am truly sorry to hear this account. It grieves me to know it. Pray, continue, Señor."

"As am I…grieved and saddened," he said with a far-away look in his eyes.

"Miss Bennet's father died that spring, and her cousin, set to inherit her father's estate under entailment, apparently turned them out. When I became aware of their desperate situation the following spring, I searched for her, but to no avail. I would never see her again. I learnt from her uncle's business partner that the entire family perished that winter from grippe. It grieves me to think she died without ever knowing how much I loved her… how much she meant to me. I could have saved them…I would have."

"I fear Miss Bennet misjudged you severely, Señor Darcy. I am sure 'tis long forgot."

"No, Sofia, I cannot be so easily reconciled to myself. The recollection of what I then said—of my conduct, my manners, my expressions during the whole of it—is now, and has been these many years, inexpressibly painful to me. Her reproof, so well applied, I shall never forget: 'Had you behaved in a more gentlemanlike manner.' Those were her words. You know not, you can scarcely conceive, how they have tortured me; though it was some time, I must confess, before I was reasonable enough to allow their justice."

Sofia gave a small sob, choked with emotion. "Please do not speak of it. She sketched your character very ill…very ill indeed."

"No, Señorita, she was quite correct in her assessment. I have been a selfish being all my life, in practice, though not in principle. As a child, I was taught what was *right*, but I was not taught to correct my temper. I was given good principles, but left to follow them in pride and conceit. Unfortunately, an only son, for many years an only *child*, I was spoilt by my parents, who, though good themselves—my father

35

particularly was all that was benevolent and amiable—allowed, encouraged, almost taught me to be selfish and overbearing—to care for none beyond my own family circle, to think meanly of all the rest of the world, to *wish* at least to think meanly of their sense and worth compared with my own. ¡Such I was, from eight to eight-and-twenty and such I might still have been but for her, my dearest, loveliest Elizabeth! ¡What do I not owe her! She taught me a lesson, hard indeed at first, but most advantageous. By her I was properly humbled. I came to her without a doubt of my reception. She showed me how insufficient were all my pretensions to please a woman worthy of being pleased."

"So…you had then persuaded yourself that she should accept you…" Sofia said on a soft whisper.

"Indeed, I had. ¿What will you think of my vanity? As I spoke before, I truly believed her to be wishing, even expecting my addresses."

"Her manners must have been at fault, but not intentionally. I am sure she never meant to deceive you, but a woman's spirits might often lead her wrongly. ¡How you must have hated her after *that* evening!"

"¡Hate her! I was angry, perhaps, at first, and even for many months after, but my anger with time began to take a proper direction."

Sofia answered in quiet, thoughtful reflection, "Señor, wherever she is, I am sure she would be pleased to know that you are not thinking ill of her."

"¿Why would she ever think I would think ill of her? It is I who fears she thought ill of me."

"Oh, she does not—I mean did not; I am sure of it." Sofia smiled and nodded. "It is the way of our sex."

Darcy softly laughed. "You are very much like her, you know. Like yours, her wit sparkled. She was the most accomplished woman of my acquaintance. She had the sharpest mind of anyone with whom I had ever had the privilege of sparring. I loved her very much."

"Señor Darcy, I have heard of your good works, always showing compassion to the poor and needy, especially—"

"Señorita, please, do not speak of my charity. It is a debt I owe to mankind…for her…for Elizabeth."

"No, Señor, 'tis not. Wherever she is, I am telling you, as a woman, I believe she understands."

"You are too kind, Señorita. I fear it is not so." He turned and gazed at her. "¿How can you possibly know that?"

"Call it a woman's intuition. If, as you say, she is very much like me, then I feel a kindred spirit, and that spirit says she forgave you long ago. And since she is in heaven, as you say, then she knows all, and she knows you love her. 'Tis as simple as that."

He threw back his head and laughed. "If I live to be one hundred, I will never understand the logic of women."

Darcy grew silent and stared off into the distance. Almost in a whisper he said, "I have loved her with an everlasting love these five years past. She was my one true love. I will never forget her." He glanced at the woman lying on his shoulder "Señorita, I want you to know I can never love another after Elizabeth." His eyes were intense and sorrowful. "I *like* and admire you a great deal, and I desire you, but I am afraid I could never give you my whole heart."

She tensed and looked up at him. Nodding, she responded, "'Tis all right, Señor. I perfectly understand… and…I accept what you can offer me. Your admiration, your esteem, and your respect are enough. I am content."

She smiled and released a gentle sigh.

He pulled her close and placed a tender kiss in her dark tresses.

"Señorita, the hour is late and we must rise early for our trip. Once we arrive in London, I have a meeting with my manager, and then we will depart for our outing."

"Um…yes, I am tired," she said, snuggling into his embrace.

Once they were situated with his hand gently cupping her naked breast, Darcy fell asleep quickly, but Sofia's thoughts were too engaged for sleep. She closed her eyes and shook her head. *…I never knew myself…What a wretched fool I have been…My family could have been saved had I only known…I have so badly misjudged him.*

Now, more than ever, Mr. Darcy must never discover that Sofia Molina and Elizabeth Bennet were one and the same. It would destroy his opinion of them both. Let him give his heart to one and satisfy himself with the other. She, as Elizabeth Bennet, would be content in the knowledge that he had once loved her with his heart. And she, as Sofia Molina, would be content that he had once loved her with his body. Sofia Molina smiled peacefully and closed her eyes in sleep.

# Chapter 8

nd now, my dear good and gentle reader, we are about to begin our adventure as our lovely couple head for the Old City. So far, things are progressing rather nicely, do you not think? Let us see how they fare on their trip to London, shall we?

Sofia came through the door of her apartments with a song in her heart and a smile upon her face, very much looking forward to their trip to London. If she could spare a moment, she planned to slip away and visit her dear sisters and the children whom she longed to see. Now that she had a hundred pounds at her disposal, she planned to move them from Whitecastle to a little house on Newgate Street in Cheapside. And when she collected her pin money, there would be accounts set up for Kitty and Jane to manage the household until she could be reunited with them.

Spinning around and hugging herself, she called for her maid.

"Ling-Ling, are the trunks packed? We are to be in London for a sennight."

"Yes, Mistress. Trunks now being loaded. Ling-Ling take care of Cocoa, too. Cook care for her."

"Thank you, Ling-Ling." Sofia bent down and hugged the small woman tightly. "I don't know what I would do without you. You are truly my friend as well as my maid."

Ling-Ling blushed a bright pink. "Oh, Miss, Ling-Ling love you, too. But we must snap-snap. Ling-Ling now help you get dressed for trip to town. You wear this," the maid said pointing to a burgundy and black traveling suit with a daytime mask made of silk-satin. Sofia could not help but stare at the set of clothing arranged on the bed. The mask was the most delicate and striking accessory she had ever beheld. It was trimmed in black lace with tiny glass beads fashioned in the form of cats along the edge with an elegant sheer-lace netting which was perfectly suited to the matching burgundy felt bonnet her maid had selected to complete the ensemble.

"Oh, Ling-Ling," she breathed out in a near whisper as she moved to the bed and lifted the bonnet. "This is so beautiful and so befitting an outing. Wherever did you obtain it?"

"Ling-Ling make for Mistress. Ling-Ling want Mistress to go in style. It in keeping with your mystique." The young girl giggled.

"And so it is!" Sofia said, clutching the item to her breast. "How will I ever repay you, my affectionate little keeper?"

"You marry Mr. Darcy. That make Ling-Ling very happy!"

Sofia gave her a sideways glance, and they both burst into giggles. "You are impossible! My ever devoted custodian."

Once she was dressed, Sofia turned slowly, staring at her reflection in the mirror. Her lace veil was fastened to her bonnet in a very alluring manner, falling down to the curve of her lips and giving her an aura of confidence. The fitted coat hugged her slim waist and flared at her hips creating a captivating look of style and elegance. And the long skirt, cut on the bias, draped her figure well, enhancing her curves in an hourglass fashion, falling just to the top of her walking boots. Sofia breathed deeply and whispered to herself, "...I am very beautiful as Sofia Molina..."

"Miss Sofie look very lovely. Mr. Darcy will notice. But Mistress need one more thing."

"And what is that?" Sofia turned and asked, one eyebrow arched as she addressed the faithful maid.

"This!" Ling-Ling came close and dabbed a bit of perfume on her mistress's pulses. "Orange blossom with sandalwood and rose. Make Miss Sofie smell so good. Mr. Darcy like."

"Ling-Ling, you *are* impossible, but I do love you as dearly as if you were a sister." Sofia gave the small woman a warm hug, and then pulled back and squeezed her hands. "Now, come, let us go down. Mr. Darcy will be waiting."

"Oh, good. Not want to keep Mr. Darcy waiting. He be angry if we keep him waiting."

Sofia gave a small laugh. "Some how I doubt that. He has been very agreeable of late."

"Oh, yes, Ling-Ling see that. He falling in love with mistress."

"Ling-Ling! Do not repeat that. I am Mr. Darcy's paramour. Nothing more."

"You think that, if it please you. Ling-Ling see man's eyes. Mr. Darcy love Sofia Molina."

Sofia rolled her eyes. "Come," she motioned to her maid.

Hearing the footsteps, Darcy looked up and snapped his watch fob closed, his eyes immediately drawn to the woman coming down the stairs. He examined her closely from head to toe. He had never seen her looking more breathtakingly lovely than she did at this moment, descending the stairway with such style and grace that one would think her to be a fine gentlewoman, raised in the household of an earl or a duke. Darcy smiled to himself. *...I knew she was a gentleman's daughter, but whose daughter was she...and where did she come from?* She was certainly not of the common variety found amongst the demimonde. He took a deep breath, taking in the exotic scent of her heady perfume as she approached him. *...I could lose myself in the arms of this woman...Every time I see her she is more beautiful than before, and this mask and veil is more captivating than the last.* He shook his head to dispel the emotions.

Grinning, he bowed as he motioned with his hand toward the door.

"Well, ladies, shall we?"

After seeing Ling-Ling to the servants' coach where she was to ride with his valet, he helped Sofia into the master coach in which he took a seat beside her and tapped the roof with his cane signaling the driver to pull out.

London was but six miles away, giving Darcy just the time needed to contemplate his situation with his paramour, Miss Sofia Molina, the Spanish siren who drove him to distraction more than he cared to admit. Because of her, he had fallen terribly behind in his work. A stack of papers from both Pemberley and his London businesses awaited him when they arrived in town, some of it needing immediate attention. Sofia had certainly kept his mind away from his work. He chuckled softly and glanced down at the temptress by his side. Having been up most of the night engaged in amorous activities, Sofia was tired and had been promptly lulled to sleep by the rocking of the carriage.

He cast another fleeting glance at the woman whose head rested on his shoulder. She had taken him completely by surprise. He had wanted nothing more than a physical relationship without the constraints of emotional ties, but somehow, just the opposite had occurred. He was beginning to care for her in a deeper sense. It was not wholly the sexual attraction that held his attention, although that was certainly there as evidenced by her lack of sleep and his satisfied smile. Nor was it necessarily her pleasing manner. Perhaps it was her resemblance in temperament to his lost love, Elizabeth Bennet.

He sighed as he closely observed his new mistress. Like Elizabeth, Sofia loved books, and he often caught her in the sparse library here at Richmond, perusing its meager selections. Noting her interest, he had promised to take her to Hatchards in Piccadilly where he planned to open an account in her name so that she could shop to her heart's content and fill the shelves of Richmond with whatever pleased her.

Then, also like Elizabeth, there was her love of nature and long walks. Almost every day he would go in search of her only to discover that if she was not to be found in the library then she was certainly in the garden, strolling through its avenues, feeding the birds and scolding her cat, who more often than not, chased the birds, hoping for a meal. But since Sofia had fastened a bell to her neck, Cocoa had not been able to kill a single one, or a mouse, for that matter. Yes, Sofia Molina and Elizabeth Bennet were very similar.

Reflecting on the matter more closely, he concluded that the two women differed most in the matter of wit. Elizabeth's had been sharp with a humorous bite, especially when she engaged him in a game of social intercourse. Sofia's, though quick, lacked the edge of the former, and there was a color of sadness about Sofia Molina that had not been present in Elizabeth Bennet.

Darcy felt Sofia shudder as a small whimper escaped her throat. He sighed again, pulled her a little closer, and kissed her bonnet. Suddenly Darcy felt an urge to protect her from the evils of the world. He knew that her life had not been without pain and disappointment, but she now had him, and to the best of his ability he would provide for her for as long as she needed him, regardless of whether they lived together or not—especially if she bore his heir. Although he had no intention of taking her as his wife—or any other woman for that matter, he could sire an heir with her. Since he was not titled and his properties were not entailed, he could arrange for the child to inherit his estate and all that he owned.

He looked at her again and frowned. Given the opportunity, she could become well educated with ease. The other evening, he had caught her reading Cicero while she waited for him to come to her, not an easy task for a scholar, let alone a woman. Someone had taught her well.

Darcy clasped her gloved hand. If he *were* of a mind to take a wife, knowing full well that he could not have Elizabeth Bennet, Sofia would be his choice. She was beautiful, charming, and very loving. In fact, she was a great lover. He had to smile as he recalled their many passionate explorations. Her sensual skills were among the best he had ever experienced. Sofia knew how to arouse his passions, what to kiss, and where. In a carnal sense, Sofia was everything he had ever wanted in a woman—nubile, eager to learn, and always there at his leisure.

He sighed once more and shook his head as he lay back to rest his weary eyes and drift off to sleep. Congenial copulation was wearing on him, too.

Sofia snuggled into her lover's embrace and gave a soft sigh as she smiled to herself. The last few days had been wonderful; getting to know the enigmatic Mr. Darcy had been a pleasure in every sense of the word. He was not at all as she had imagined him to be all those years ago. In fact, her ability to sketch a man's character had failed her so completely that she felt quite ashamed of her previous false assumptions. Mr. Darcy was not proud or disagreeable at all. Quite the contrary, in fact. Unlike her other great misconception, Mr. Wickham, who had deceived them all, Mr. Darcy was good and kind, though certainly reserved. She whimpered and sighed. Mr. Darcy had a gentleness about him that she was sure he seldom revealed, except perhaps to those in his closest circle. And she could well imagine, as all she had heard and gave evidence to, that he had indeed been a very good brother to his sister—the kind of brother that she and her sisters would have liked to have had if only their father had sired a son.

She took a deep breath. Mr. Darcy's masculine scent was comforting, filling her with desires she had never felt before. Truth be told, he made her feel things she had never realized a woman could feel, creating in her a thirst for more of what he had to give, a desire to be filled with him until her heart burst from the pleasure and raptures of his very essence. He created in her a desire so strong that it almost overrode everything she had been brought up to believe. As Elizabeth Bennet, she was embarrassed to think about it. As Sofia Molina, he made her lower regions weep at the thought of it. She smiled and clutched his coat a little tighter. Sofia knew with very little effort she could fall hopelessly in love with him, but she did not dare to even consider it. The risk was too great and the stakes too high.

If only she could go back in time to those few short weeks they had spent together in Kent. How different their situation would be if she could then, with the knowledge she now possessed, make a clear and rational decision. She had completely misunderstood him and judged him wrongly. He had loved her. He had *truly* loved her. She swallowed back a sob and softly moaned. They could have been happy and her family saved, but there was no chance of that now. Her scandal, should it ever become public knowledge, would dwarf Lydia's. No, they could never marry, and he must never know who she really was. After all, she had more to consider than her own concerns, and on that, she would remain resolute. She must leave England and begin a new life for herself... and for Jane and Kitty and the children. No matter how much the allure of being loved by the man at her side tempted her, theirs was a bargain—a contract, and she must not forget it. It was his money she wanted, nay needed, not his heart. The world was cold and unforgiving, and she had best remember it.

The carriage gently rocked back and forth lulling her to sleep, and as she drifted off, she thought of Jane, Kitty, and the children—especially little Wills, and even her mother. While in London, she would see them at least once and move them to Cheapside where her mother's welfare could be more easily provided for and the burden lifted from Jane and Kitty. With those thoughts playing in her head, Elizabeth Bennet slipped into a deep sleep.

As the carriage rolled into London, the traffic increased. Darcy was awakened by the unevenness of the cobblestones and by the sound of a company of men on horseback as they passed the carriage, alerting him that they had almost arrived at their destination. For a moment, he was startled and unsure of where he was and of whom he was with, but then the angelic form nestled next to him stirred, and his memory came into clear focus.

He glanced down at the sleeping beauty by his side and closely studied her while she slept. Darcy was shocked to see, even with a mask and veil, just how young she really was—almost a girl nearly as young as his sister. Sofia could not be much more than five and twenty and was probably younger. A twinge of guilt pierced his heart as he studied her dainty features—her small mouth, her delicate upturned nose. She was so much like Elizabeth that he knew with very little effort Sofia could replace that memory with flesh and blood, and he deeply regretted that he had met her in a brothel house. He moaned to himself and closed his eyes as he shook his head. *...But if not you, then who, Darcy? At least with you, she will be protected and her needs provided for.... She will never want for anything whilst she is with you...*

Sofia smiled, and Darcy narrowed his eyes. There it was again...that familiar expression. He touched his finger to the dimple in her cheek. The last time he had seen that smile, Elizabeth was wearing it at Kent. Darcy released a hard breath and passed his hand over his face. *...You have got to get hold of yourself, man. She is not Elizabeth Bennet...*

Sofia stretched out like a cat waking up from a nap. "¿Umm...Señor, dónde estamos?"

He smiled softly and stroked her face beneath the veil, brushing his fingers over the lace of the delicate silk mask. "We are coming into London, mi querida Señorita."

"Muy bien, Señor," she breathed out lazily.

"In fact," he pulled her up and pointed, "over there is Hyde Park. Once we have settled ourselves, we shall take a turn in the park if you like. Soon we will be coming up on Grosvenor Street. That is where I live."

Sofia sat up straight, taking in all that she saw. This was the exclusive Mayfair District—a place she had only dreamt of seeing, never imagining that she would live there. The carriage took one turn and then another and soon they arrived in front of one of the most beautiful houses Sofia had even seen. *...So this is his home...* She smiled and turned back to him as the carriage rolled to a stop.

"¿This is your home?"

"Sí, Señorita, and for now, it is your home, too. I will have Wilson take your trunks to your quarters. Then I want you to meet me in the upstairs landing. I will give you a brief tour of the house before we have luncheon. After that, I have a meeting with my manager, and then I am taking you out."

"¿Out?"

"Sí. We are going to Madam Cantrell's to have you fitted for new gowns, and then I want to take you to Hatchards in Piccadilly as I promised. We are going to open an account so that you can shop to your heart's content. Fill the library at Richmond with whatever you like for your enjoyment. You may also shop for other things to make the house your home. Whatever you want, you shall have," he said with a smile.

"¡Señor, libros! 'Tis the best present you could give me. ¡The gowns are appreciated, but books…they are a treasure, Señor son un tesoro!"

"And you shall have all you want of them. Now, let us go inside and freshen up. I will meet you within three quarters of an hour. We have a great deal to accomplish. Tonight we are going to Drury Lane for the premier of *Twelfth Night*. My cousins Viscount Wexford and General Fitzwilliam will be there as well."

"You are too good to me, Señor. I do not deserve it."

"Yes, you do. You deserve that and more."

She softly sighed as they climbed the stairs together. If he only knew what she would really like to fill Richmond House with; it would not be things. The house on the outskirts of London was the perfect place for her mother, sisters and the children. It had the advantages of a small town, and yet the atmosphere of the country all wrapped into one. She looked up at him with a smile as they turned the corner into the family wing and he led her to her quarters.

*…Mr. Darcy, you are truly a good sort of man…the best of men…*

# Chapter 9

usiness, progress, and the complications of life have begun to close in on our dauntless hero as the reality of existence in this world once again raises its ugly head; a shadow begins to fall as things now take on a more serious nature. However, my dear, good, and faithful reader, fear not, for after the rain there always comes sunshine with a rainbow close to follow. Let us hope that the pot of gold at the end of it is *not* the privy convenience, or shall we say...*le pot de chambre*. Let us take a look and see, my good reader, shall we?

Once Darcy settled Sofia in their apartments, he went directly to his study and looked over the numerous pieces of correspondence piled in neat little stacks across his mahogany desk. One by one, he shuffled through them. There were matters of pressing business, missives from his solicitor, and letters from his London manager. There was even a stack from his steward at Pemberley. A small moan escaped his throat as he laid them aside and fell back in his chair. Once the holiday season was concluded, he would have to bury himself in his work once again. Glancing back at the mounded piles, he dragged his hand over his face with a sigh. He would have to spend their week in London working during the day. Sofia and he could spend their evenings doing whatever they pleased, but having fallen so far behind in his responsibilities, his work had to be attended to before all else.

Darcy released a frustrated breath as he rose to his feet. He would think about business later.

Closing the door on his work, he made his way to the upstairs balcony area to wait for Sofia. But before she made her appearance, he was greeted by a footman.

"This has just arrived, sir," he said, bowing slightly before handing him a dispatch. "It is from your steward at Pemberley. Also, your manager is here. I have left Mr. Steadman waiting for you in the drawing room, sir."

Darcy quickly broke the seal and read the letter.

"Damn," he whispered under his breath. "If it is not one thing, then it is another. Well," he said, "there is nothing to be done for it except to face it."

He turned to the waiting footman and instructed, "Tell Mr. Steadman that I shall meet with him shortly. Take him to my study and see to it that he helps himself to my finest port."

"As you wish, sir," the man said with a bow. "Also, sir, your solicitor, Mr. Mann, wishes to have a word with you. He, too, is waiting. Shall I have him wait in your study as well, sir?"

"What?" Darcy looked up from the letter he was reading.

"I said, sir, Mr. Mann wishes to have a word with you as well as Mr. Steadman; they are both here, sir."

"Ah, yes, have him keep Mr. Steadman company whilst I have luncheon. And bring them some bread with cold meat and cheese as well. I will get to them as soon as I can—no more than three quarters of an hour."

"Very good, sir."

No sooner had the footman left than Darcy heard the door to Sofia's chamber softly open and shut. He glanced up with a smile as he folded the missive and placed it in his coat pocket.

"Señorita, you look lovelier each time I see you."

"¡Gracias, Señor! May I please have a tray sent up for Ling-Ling? She is absolutely famished."

Darcy chuckled. "Very well, then. I shall order a bread platter with fruit, cheese, and some cold meats with a flask of wine."

"Muy agradecida, gracias," Sofia said with a smile.

"Shall we?" Darcy offered his arm.

As they descended the stairs, Darcy said, "Sofia, I have a bit of bad news."

She furrowed her brow beneath her veil and glanced up at him. "What is it, sir?"

"I am afraid I have neglected my duties these past weeks, and I must make amends. We will still go for our outing today as planned, but, before we do, I have a small matter of business that I must attend to after we dine. Also, I will not be able to give you the tour of the house as I had promised. However, my housekeeper, Mrs. Brookmyers, will be glad to assist you. And we can always tour it ourselves a little later."

"I prefer later," she said with a sigh. "I shall rest after we eat luncheon, and then, when you have concluded your business, I will be ready for our outing."

"Very well, then. But there is more."

"More?"

"Yes. While we are in London, I will have to work during the day; therefore, I cannot spend the time with you that I would like, but you will have my full and undivided attention in the evenings."

She smiled. "That will have to do, Señor. For in times such as these, we must make the best of things," she said cheerfully. "Therefore, you need not worry on my behalf. I shall find plenty to occupy my time. Perhaps I shall go for walks in the park or visit with friends. I am sure Ophelia would like to see me."

"Perhaps, mi Señorita, but always take your maid. London is not like Richmond. I do not want you to be out unaccompanied. It is not safe for you."

"Sí, Señor." She nodded. "Ling-Ling will always be by my side."

"Muy bien."

When they had finished their luncheon and Sofia had retired to her quarters, Darcy left for his study and the mountain of work awaiting him there. Entering his office, he greeted his guests.

"Gentlemen, I am sorry to have kept you waiting. I have just arrived back in London from Richmond," he said. "I hope you have been keeping one another company, and that the repast was to your satisfaction."

"Entirely to our satisfaction, Mr. Darcy, thank you."

"Quite right," agreed the second man, who was a little taller than the first. "Darcy, you always have the best port of anyone I know, but," he continued, "this is not a social call. There are many items of urgency that must have your unfettered attention."

The taller one reached into his satchel and pulled out a file, while the shorter one took a seat to await his turn.

"Mr. Steadman," Darcy said, taking the seat behind his desk. "I have read over your correspondence in my absence, and—"

"Then you understand the urgency."

"Yes," Darcy sighed.

"Very good then," his manager said, pushing the documents in front of his employer. "You realize you cannot put it off any longer. You must liquidate these assets before you lose anymore money."

Darcy took the proffered papers and read them carefully. He then took his pen and dipped it in the ink well.

"Sell all shares in Cotter's Bank and use the money to open the orphanage down by the river we last spoke about. Then, what is left from the sale of the bank shares is to be used for the housing development project in London's East End," he said, signing each paper and blotting it. "My assets from the sale of the shares in MacGregor's mining operations are to be set aside. Put them in the Darcy Trust Foundation to be used at a later date. What else do you have for me?"

"This," Mr. Steadman said, handing him another file. "Look it over and tell me what you think. If you are interested, we'll discuss it in more detail on the morrow when we set to work."

Darcy looked over his man's recommendations. It was the invention of a steam locomotive and railway system connecting London to the northern counties and to Liverpool. His manager had researched it well and had concluded that if the idea should catch on, the rewards promised to be thousands of pounds, if not more.

Darcy nodded. "It looks like something I might want to investigate further. If this is as good as you seem to think it is, we stand to make a tremendous profit."

Returning his eyes to the papers, he turned a leaf and continued to read. There were recommendations for the improvement of his shipping line which brought needed goods from the Orient. Many of the vessels needed to be replaced. The last item of business pertained to Darcy's cotton mills in Lancashire. Unrest existed between the new Irish workers whom they had imported and the regular workforce, posing a potential problem which threatened to explode if he did not address the issues at hand.

Darcy glanced up with an exasperated look. "Anything else?"

"One more thing. The problem at Pemberley."

"Yes." Darcy sat back in his seat. "I received an express when I first arrived. I am aware of the situation there."

"Mr. Darcy, you will have to go to Pemberley soon. There is nothing to be done for it. Mr. Meade can no longer contain the problem. Your direct intervention is needed, or you may have more than you wish to contend with should you continue to ignore this trouble."

"Yes, I am aware of it." Darcy released a harsh breath. "Mr. McLarty and Mr. Rathbone are now shooting at one another, and this time someone was injured. Damn!" He pounded his fist. "Can the Scots and the Irish never learn to exist amicably together?"

"Mr. Darcy, it is not Mr. Meade's responsibility to—"

"Yes, yes, I know." Darcy raised his hand in irritation and waved his manager off. "Mr. Meade has enough to contend with in the everyday management of Pemberley, let alone being shackled with this sordid affair. I cannot leave now, but in a fortnight, I will travel to Pemberley and see to the matter personally. Mr. Meade has been taxed enough. Send him an express telling him to expect me by the end of January. I have business here in town that must first be attended to, and then I will need to escort my guest back to Richmond. I will leave from there."

"I will see to it directly," Mr. Steadman said, rising to take his leave. "And I will call round on the morrow to work with you through these projects I am leaving with you now, as well as those on your desk." He placed his beaver on his head and continued. "I bid you a good afternoon, and I will see you at our usual time, eight o'clock sharp?"

"Eight o'clock sharp. I will be waiting," Darcy said, seeing his manager to his study door.

When he returned, he closed the door and took a deep breath. "Well, Mr. Mann, you have been privy to all of my affairs now, and you see how pressed I am to catch up on my duties."

"Yes…and that is exactly why I am here—to see to your affairs and inquire about your duties." Mr. Mann hesitated, and then spoke with conviction. "Darcy, are you mad?" His solicitor threw a document onto the desk. "Tell me this is a mistake, and that the signature on this dotted line is not yours."

Darcy released another hard breath and picked up the Cyprian's contract giving it a cursory once over. "There is no mistake. It is my signature."

"Good God man! Have you lost your senses, and over a woman! What has she done? Bewitched you?"

Darcy collapsed into his chair and buried his face in his hands as his solicitor lectured him like a small school boy on his moral conduct and fiscal responsibility, stressing that he needed a wife and an heir, not something in between.

"Mr. Darcy, I have been your solicitor for many years, as well as your father's before you. It is my job to look out for your best interests, and this, my friend, is not one of them. Did you not read the trial duration clause? Five thousand pounds is to be kept in escrow until the twenty-fourth of March at which time *she* may withdraw it, and there is nothing you can do about it!" He paused and pulled himself up to his full height. "My good sir, if she chooses to leave you after three short months, *you* will find yourself five thousand pounds the poorer—not to mention the twelve hundred pounds you are giving her per month. It is an exorbitant amount. Only fools have been known to lavish such extravagance on a mistress. She is robbing you blind—picking your pockets like a common thief!" he exclaimed in exasperation. "I cannot imagine that the adventure would outweigh the obvious loss of funds, or that a man in his sound mind would surrender to such folly."

Finally, Darcy looked up. "You do not understand, Horace," he said at last. "I have been alone for far too long. I need Miss Molina as much as she needs me. She is not what you think—she is not what I thought. Miss Molina was once a gentleman's daughter who was brought down by unfortunate circumstances—things that, except for the grace of God, might have befallen *my* sister or *your* daughter. England is a flourishing nation, but not all share in her prosperity. We have spoken of it many times, how women are forced into lives of poverty and yes, *prostitution*, because they have no other way to survive."

The older man looked upon him with sympathy. "Like your father before you, you are a good man—just as affable to the poor as he was, always caring about those less fortunate than yourself, but in this matter, you are blind," he said. "Mr. Darcy, those of the demimonde are there of their own choosing. Many *are* women of means. They have fathers and brothers, but choose not to marry because they do not wish to submit to a man's rule!"

"And that is another thing that is wrong with our society." Darcy's eyes flashed. "Why must a woman lose her money, her land, her very freedom, and all of her possessions simply because she marries? Many of them are like lambs led to the slaughter by flattering tongues with polished manners designed to pick their pockets and leave them to a life of misery after they have squandered their inheritance. Women should not be so vulnerable to unscrupulous men like the George Wickhams of the world who lure young girls away from their families only to leave them in disgrace."

Mr. Mann raised a brow, for he was well acquainted with George Wickham, a man who had seduced many a young girl, including his own daughter and an attempt on Mr. Darcy's sister. He sighed and shook his head. "I hear all that you say, but it still does not excuse your utter lack of judgment in this particular matter. It is so unlike you—the careful man with whom I have worked for many years. You are not thinking with your head."

Darcy reflected on his solicitor's words. Finally he nodded in recognition of a truth. "Perhaps I am thinking with my heart," Darcy said as he rose from his seat. "Come, Mr. Mann, let us have a drink, and then I must go. I have an engagement for this afternoon. I will stop by your office a little later this week. I want an account set up for Miss Molina today so that she may manage her household as she sees fit."

"As you wish," Mr. Mann said. "However, I still believe it to be a foolish thing to do."

"It is what I wish—foolish or not." His face flushed with anger.

Mr. Mann sighed as he retrieved his papers. "Do not be angry with me, Fitzwilliam. It is my job to look after your best interests. And this, my good man, is not one of them."

In a somber tone, Darcy replied, "I might have thought as you do once, but I have since changed my mind."

Sofia entered her chamber and closed the door as she folded her arms and leaned back against the thick slab. She puffed out her cheeks and blew out a frustrated breath. "What am I to do?" she asked to herself as she threw up her hands.

Ling-Ling immediately rose to her feet and greeted her mistress. "Miss Sofie, something wrong?"

Sofia turned and quickly recovered, not realizing she had been observed.

"No. Quite the contrary," Sofia said with a smile. "Things could not be better! Mr. Darcy must spend his days attending to business, and that my dear Ling-Ling, is all the better for us. I shall have every day to spend with my family. Once I have my pin money, I can take care of them properly. Jane shall not have to work herself to exhaustion caring for my mother. Mamma will have a doctor and a maid, and Jane shall have a cook and a servant. And the children…they shall have books for a proper education. I must send Ophelia a missive. We shall visit her on the morrow, and then go to Whitecastle to visit Jane and the children. Kitty, though, will be at work, so we shall not see her."

Ling-Ling clasp her hands together. "I shall meet family. This make Ling-Ling very happy. Ling-Ling very good with medicine. Ling-Ling help mother. She get well."

"Ling-Ling, my family will love you. To me, you are already a part of my family. They will love you as much as I do, and when we go to Ireland, you shall go with us if you wish it."

"Ling-Ling like that very much. Ling-Ling want family. Ling-Ling need family."

The maid then turned and moved toward the dressing room. "Now, Miss Sofie must make ready to go out with Mr. Darcy. Miss Sofie must look very pretty for people to see. She must go in style."

Sofia gave a small moan and crumpled herself into a nearby chair. "Must I? …Yes…I suppose I must."

"What wrong, Miss Sofie?"

Sofia glanced up and shook her head. "I might as well tell you since you are my confidante. Ling-Ling, I am nervous about going out. All will be staring at me. Ling-Ling, I am not at all comfortable with the prospect. What if someone should see me and realize who I am?"

Ling-Ling sighed. "No one recognize you, Miss Sofie. You not worry. No one can see face. Veil cover it well." Ling-Ling stopped short as if perceiving a deeper meaning to Sofia's concerns. "You not worry, Miss Sofie! Remember family and children. You go for them. Hold head up high. Miss Molina is lady. She good lady…love family. No be shamed. Women do what women must do."

Sofia smiled. "You know me too well. In so short a time you have sketched my character to perfection. And you are right. It is not *I* who is to be out today—it is Sofia Molina from the South of Spain—at least in disguise that is who I am." She lifted her chin in confidence. "She is the one on display for the public eye." *…not Elizabeth Bennet of Hertfordshire…Besides, if Mr. Darcy does not recognize me, who on earth would?*

"Miss Molina will look her best. She go in style. Let us dress. Must not keep Mr. Darcy waiting. Gentlemen not like to wait."

Sofia smiled once more and rose to her feet. "My confidence has never failed me. It shall not today. Let us dress. I want to be more handsome than even *he* can imagine."

Ling-Ling dropped a curtsey and led Sofia to the dressing room.

When they had arrived at their destination, Darcy gave instructions to the driver to meet them in Vauxhall Gardens at three o'clock. He then turned and helped Sofia from the coach. She unfurled her parasol, and he then offered his arm. With his cane in hand and Sofia on his arm, together they strolled down Bond Street and then entered the *Western Exchange* shopping bazaar. Talking quietly between themselves, they stopped occasionally to sample the wares of a street vender selling food and drink. Sofia laughed and he smiled. Though he could not see her eyes, he imagined how they must be dancing with merriment. Soon they approached a man selling toy soldiers in tin boxes, bags of marbles, and rag dolls, and Sofia wanted them all. He thought it rather odd, but bought them just the same, for her smile was worth the cost of a few toys.

As they walked along, it was not long before people began to look intently upon Sofia as they passed them by. Darcy glanced at the woman by his side. He knew it was more than their mere appearance together as a couple that had captured the attention of the London crowd. It was her black veil dancing about her lips as she spoke. Though he thought it was sensual, he knew others did not understand why she wore it. Finally, after several curious passersby had stopped to gawk, Darcy inquired, "¿Mi querida, why will you not allow me to remove your veil and mask? Are you not concerned that people might stare?"

She tilted her head and looked up at him with an air of confidence and replied, "No, not in the least, Señor. You must come to understand that there is a certain stubbornness about me that can never bear to be frightened or subdued by the will of others. My courage always rises with every attempt to intimidate me. Therefore, I feel no such shame for what others do not understand. If they wish to stare, let them!"

Darcy's eyes flashed. *...Elizabeth...? This woman will drive me to distraction if she utters one more word after the fashion of Miss Bennet!*

"Sí, Señorita. I have always admired a strong woman—one who thinks for herself and does as she pleases. You are indeed a rare breed." *...rare indeed, Darcy...the kind you would marry if you could...Sofia is the Spanish counterpart of my Elizabeth... Yet, no one can ever be Elizabeth; no one could ever compare... and yet...*

Moving on, Sofia noticed a strange man leaning against a lamp post. His beaver covered his eyes; therefore, she could not make him out, but he appeared to stare in a way that seemed different from the rest. She frowned and shrugged it off, thinking he must be an admirer.

Stopping in front of a little shop, Darcy clasped her hand on his arm and spoke, "Señorita, we have arrived. This is Madame Cantrell's *Bits of Lace*. It is the best shop in London for women's apparel. Madame Cantrell caters to the affluent who have discriminating tastes in clothing, and I have arranged an appointment with her for you. Let us go in," he said, pushing the door open and stepping aside to allow Sofia to enter.

"You are to choose five ball gowns, a dozen day gowns for morning dress, several coats, a selection of gloves, and all the accessories to complement them. I will give my approval as I want you to dress for me. However, there is one exception."

"¿Pray, Señor, what is that?"

"*I* alone must be allowed to choose your dressing gowns and undergarments—your chemise, corsets, pantalets, and petticoats."

Sofia blushed beet red and almost fainted from lack of breath. She stopped short. "¡Señor! ¡Surely you jest!"

"No, Señorita, you must recall our bargain. I am to buy your clothes, but with the option to choose what you wear. I am taking my prerogative. I shall choose."

"Señor, 'tis too much. I cannot allow it."

"Ah, but you must. A bargain is a bargain; therefore, I will not be gainsaid."

"Very well. If you must." She raised her chin in obstinacy. "Do as you wish. I am yours, bought and paid for. But I must ask for another one hundred pounds to cover the embarrassment of such a vulgar display."

He laughed. "You are truly a vixen, but today I happen to like vixens. Another hundred it is. Now let us go to the back. Madame Cantrell awaits us."

As they slipped through the curtains into the private fitting room, a lady rose to greet them.

"Mr. Darcy, it is a pleasure to see you once more in my shop. I thought I would never have this pleasure again."

"Madame Cantrell." He bowed. "This is Miss Sofia Molina. I am afraid she only speaks Spanish. Therefore, I must translate."

Madame Cantrell glanced at Sofia with a soft smile. "It will be a pleasure to serve you, Miss Molina. Mr. Darcy has exquisite taste in fine ladies as well as in the clothes they wear. Let us have a seat and begin."

Together they pored over magazines and books, looking at all the high fashions from Paris. Sofia chose the designs she liked, Darcy gave his approval, and then they looked through the samples of cloth and intricate trimmings. Cream colored lace with peach colored silks and tiny rosettes; a pallet of pastels in pinks, lilacs, and periwinkle blue; another of jewel tones, such as purple, crimson, poppy red, deep blue, and jonquil yellow; muslins, linens, woolens, velvets, and silks were among the colors and fabrics they chose. They were to be fashioned in delicate needlework with velvet ribbons and lace netting, silk ribbon tapestry, and shadow embroidery with Italian cutwork. She was to have the finest French evening gowns available, extravagantly trimmed and decorated with lace.

Next they chose cloth for her morning dresses to be worn inside the house. They were to be high-necked and long-sleeved, covering her throat and wrists, plain and devoid of decoration. However, the evening dresses were designed to be quite the opposite. Those extravagant creations were to be cut low with necklines which accentuated her bosom, and sleeves hemmed short to display bared arms which were to be covered by long white gloves. Sofia hesitated, but Darcy insisted that her bosom and shoulders were to be exposed with only the bare minimum covered.

For outings and warmth on winter evenings, they chose fur-lined capes for the very cold weather and cashmere woolens for everything else. There were shawls made of soft angora and silk in paisley patterns, and spencers, along with long-hooded cloaks, Turkish wraps, and mantles. He insisted on one of each, but the spencers were to match her morning dresses; therefore, six were ordered. By the time they were through, Sofia had more clothes than she had ever dreamed a woman could own, and yet the smile on his face warmed her heart. Mr. Darcy truly enjoyed shopping for her.

When it came to her intimate attire, Darcy insisted on Sea Island cotton trimmed in white lace and silk ribbons for her small clothes. She blushed scarlet at the designs he chose; more so because of the fact that *he* had selected them, and that Darcy would know what she was wearing in her more personal areas.

Darcy laughed when she leaned in and whispered in his ear that some of the selections were indecent, and she was embarrassed that the seamstresses would know she would be wearing such things. Darcy reassured her they would think nothing of it. Most would be grateful for the work. She had to acquiesce, knowing how much Kitty appreciated the same and how valuable her earnings had been to the survival of their family, often making the difference in whether or not they ate that day.

When the selections were finalized and the measurements complete, they left for the next shop. Stepping out onto the footpath, Sofia turned to Mr. Darcy with a smile.

"¿Señor, do you often shop for women's attire?"

He gave a small laugh. "Not often."

"¿Then I must ask more specifically, have you ever done so before and, if so, when? For I have the distinct impression that Madame Cantrell knows you quite well. And I would also say from her smiles that she is well acquainted with your particular tastes in women's … hmmm … delicacies."

This time he laughed out loud. "Señorita, I have many gifts and unspoken talents. They are for me to know and for you to discover. But in this instant, you are the first woman, other than my sister when she was much younger, for whom I have ever had the pleasure of being actively involved in choosing her wardrobe—especially those items of a more intimate nature. However, that does not mean that I am ignorant on the subject of the more *delicate* things, as you say, that a woman requires, and in your case, my pretty Señorita, I want you to have the finest things in life."

Sofia paused and looked up at him. "Señor Darcy, while we are on this subject, there *is* one other thing I wish to know, if I may."

"¿Sí, Señorita, and what might that be?"

"I wish to know…that is I would *like* to know," she said, turning her gaze away from him and resuming their walk, "How many other women have you…have you been with…before me. I presume I am not the first since Ophelia mentioned you were known for your prowess and amorous attentions to the female gender, so—"

He laughed again at her impertinence. "You want to know how many women I have taken to my bed before you. Well, we have spoken of much since our relationship began; therefore, I will tell you what you wish to know, though it is of a very personal nature," he replied looking at her pointedly.

He looked off into the distance as if in deep reflection. "There are not as many as you might think, nor are there as many as I am reputed to have had, but there have been quite a few." He hesitated and glanced at her. "I am not the man I once was, Sofia—nor will I ever be such a man again. I will share one more bit of privy information, and then we must desist from this line of conversation, as it *is* rather personal." He took a deep breath and moved forward, clicking his cane along the walkway as they went.

"Before Miss Elizabeth Bennet, I was more inclined towards the wilder side of life, but after her…well, it seemed rather shallow and empty. I was always looking…always desiring—though I had yet to realize it at the time—something else—something deeper in a relationship. I was looking but could not find anything more than mechanical, insipid conversation with empty headed females, vying for my attention. You see, the women of the *ton* are polished—a little too polished in their address, and I despised them all. Their simpering and fawning—I loathed it. Disguise of every sort is my abhorrence. I knew it was not me they wanted. No, it was my money and my position in society which they desired. And I hated every minute I spent at their soirées, their balls, their teas, and their dinners. Marriage is nothing more than a lifelong contract, shackling a man to some cold-fish harpy for the rest of his life, if he is not careful. That is why many men in my class take mistresses. They marry for convenience—to acquire wealth, land, and an heir, and then they take a mistress for the more amorous side of life."

"¿But is it not also true that many women are shackled in such marriages by unscrupulous men desiring *their* money and land, otherwise known as a dowry?"

"Yes, that is also true, but a man can spot a manipulative woman conditioned to sell herself on the marriage mart far better than a good woman can spot a rogue. However, that is not the subject of the moment."

"No Señor, pray, please continue." …*I suppose women have always sold themselves in one form or another*… Sofia mused to herself. …*if not in marriage, then in another way… it is all about money, is it not?*

He looked at her and smiled. "Yes…well, when I first met Miss Bennet, as I have already told you, I presumed her to be one of them—those women to whom I was accustomed. And how could I not make that assumption? Her mother gave all indications that she desired a good match for her daughters based entirely on wealth. Love and affection be damned. Consequently, I struggled until I realized Miss Bennet was not like the others. She was the woman I wanted…the one with whom I could have spent the rest of my life in a loving relationship—the institution we call marriage, but it did not come to be, and that is that." He glanced down at Sofia. "Sofia, if what you want to know is have I ever had a paramour, the answer is no. Miss Bennet was my first and only love, and you are my first in the other regard."

"Oh," was all she said as she raised her parasol and continued to walk. Sofia said not another word on the subject as she was much too stunned and embarrassed to press for more information.

When they came to the next intended stop, he pulled her into the *Boot & Shoe Shop* and there they remained until she was fitted with an assortment of fashionable shoes and boots suitable for the dresses Mr. Darcy had purchased earlier.

Next, they went to the milliner's shop for fashionable hats, bonnets, and parasols. Then to the chocolate shop for hot cocoa and biscuits, and after that to a soap and toiletry shop which Darcy declined to enter, allowing her to make the purchases that pleased her and which would be a delightful surprise for him.

Moving on from shop to shop, they collected many packages to be delivered to Grosvenor Street, and as they shopped, Sofia had the distinct impression she was being watched. She turned to her right and noticed a man standing idly by reading a newspaper, but his face was concealed. She furrowed her brow. It was the same man whom she had seen when they first entered the modiste. Was he following them? And more importantly *why* would he follow them? Cold fear slithered up her spine and clenched its long finger around her heart. Did he know who she was? Sofia glanced up at Mr. Darcy and was relieved that he had noticed neither the man nor her reaction to him. She breathed a little more deeply and gave a small sigh of relief as they moved on.

Their last place to shop was at *Hatchards* in Piccadilly where Darcy opened an account for her so that she might fill the library at Richmond with her heart's desire. As they perused the many books available, it pleased Darcy to see how Sofia went about making her selections, for they were many of his own personal favorites. Yes, he thought to himself, someone has taught her well. It was obvious to anyone who observed her that she was intelligent and well-read. Darcy stood to the side and took it all in as he studied her closely.

*...Darcy, she is so very much like you...she is your complement, so full of life, inquisitive and eager to learn...If you would allow her, she could own your heart, and you could have what you have wanted all these years. ...No, she is not Elizabeth, but she is a reasonable facsimile of what you loved about Miss Bennet...*

He smiled to himself and continued to watch until she signaled for him to come. She showed him all she had selected, and he gave his approval. There was only one thing he found that puzzled him—a collection of children's books: fairytale readers, a geography tome, an atlas, arithmetic books, and primers. He furrowed his brow.

"¿Señorita, why do you need children's school books?"

"They are for a friend whose children are in need. ¿Do you object to my generosity?"

"Not in the least. It merely appeared odd." He shrugged his shoulders and signed the purchase agreement.

Except for the school books, he had the packages wrapped and sent to Richmond. After the book shop, he took her to a nearby café where they had tea, and then they left for a leisurely walk in Vauxhall Gardens which was particularly beautiful at that time of year, with the skaters on the frozen lake sliding over the ice. Perhaps someday soon they would join them.

Casually strolling through the avenues, he told her all about the history of the gardens and that of Hyde Park as well. She seemed keenly interested in all that he relayed, but she kept watching over her shoulder as if looking for someone. Finally, after several such instances, he paused and asked, "Sofia, you seem fearful. ¿Is something the matter, mi linda Señorita?"

"No, Señor. I am well. However, the hour has grown late, and I am tired. I wish to go home."

"Sí, Señorita. We shall leave at once. You must rest before we leave for Drury Lane, and I must reserve my energy for afterwards. All of our exercise has whetted my appetite and made me in need of sustenance of an entirely different sort." He smiled and placed his hand upon hers as they walked towards the carriage.

# Chapter 10

A h, our dear good and gentle reader we have now come to a crossroad for our beloved hero and heroine. What will he do as the shadow of indecision falls over him? 'Tis times like these when I must call upon the help of a friend. "Cupid," I say, "draw back your bow and let your arrow go," for like Beatrice and Benedict in *Much Ado About Nothing*, our gallant hero is in dire need of a bit of a push.

And now we are off to the theatre. Let us see how it goes.

Darcy knocked twice and entered Sofia's room. He smiled as he leaned his shoulder against the door, admiring her beauty, as he often found himself doing of late. As he stared, the thought occurred to him that Sofia could be Elizabeth's double, for she possessed the same grace and elegance of the latter and was very much like her in so many other ways as well. All that she needed was the benevolence of a good man to guide her with a little more instruction in the ways of his class, and she could rise above her situation. His smile deepened as he observed her in front of the looking glass turning from side to back. His attraction was growing stronger, for she was quickly becoming more than a mistress. She was becoming a friend—someone with whom he imagined he could spend the rest of his life. After all, Elizabeth was gone, life must go on, and he knew he also had his legacy and his family heritage to think about. He needed an heir, preferably a son…a *legitimate* son who would not have to suffer the labels that people bestowed, but could he give Sofia what he knew was right?

"¿Señor?" she tilted her head. "¿Le pasa algo?"

"No, not at all. I am simply admiring your lovely figure," he said with a smile. "Señorita, every time I see you, you are more beautiful than the last."

"Señor, you flatter me," she said, teasingly. "I suppose you say that to all the ladies."

"No, mi Señorita. Only to you do I pay such a compliment, and I mean every word I say. I am not the sort of man to give frivolous praises for the sake of flattery. *But* there is one thing that will improve your beauty."

"Sí, Señor, and what might that be?"

He pushed away from the door and moved to stand behind her in front of the large mirror. He circled his arms around her waist and gazed into their reflection. "Tú eres hermosa...so very beautiful," he said leaning into her neck to place soft kisses on her pulses while his hand slowly moved up her body and caressed her breast.

As his lips moved down her velvet skin, he noticed something on her lower neck he had never seen before. He glanced up and furrowed his brow. "¿Señorita, where did you get this strange mark?" he asked, grazing his fingertips over a soft raised swelling on her skin.

"¿This?" She touched her fingers to his as she gazed at their reflection in the mirror.

"Yes."

With a smile, she turned and touched her lips to his jawline. "It is a blemish I inherited from my mother. Usually it is barely noticeable, but about once a month, it becomes irritated and red. It will fade in time and be no more than a slightly raised berry that blends in with my skin. I have always hated it and tried to keep it covered. I find it ugly."

"Well I think it is lovely...a beauty mark," he said, kissing her neck and running his tongue over the rough textured mark while his hand traveled to her lower regions, teasing and stroking. "I almost wish we were staying in tonight. I would like a repeat performance of the afternoon."

"Umm...Señor, it would be lovely—lovely indeed, but I should think that you receive enough of my affections that surely we can spare one evening of entertainment other than another of our many amorous activities," she said with a smile. "I have been looking forward to the play ever since you told me we were attending. I understand that Mrs. Davis does an outstanding performance as Olivia. I should not want to miss it."

He smiled once more as his fingers languidly slid into the opening of her pantalets and began to tenderly caress her. "I do not care for any performances except the ones I share with you, mi querida."

With a soft moan, she regretfully pulled away. "Señor, we certainly shall have time for that and more when the last curtain falls and we are safely home in our bed."

He laughed. "I see there is no persuading you. So, in cases such as these when I must take you out, you should have a gift to set the mood."

He slipped a black velvet box from his coat pocket and handed it to her.

"¿What is this?" she asked.

"Open it."

Sofia slowly opened the box and gasped. "¡Oh, Señor, you should not have!"

"Yes...I should have. You are very lovely inside and out, and when I saw this, I knew it was for you."

Darcy took the diamond bracelet from its case and fastened it around her wrist.

"¿Do you like it?"

"Oh, indeed I do, Señor," she said caressing the diamonds strung together in gold mounts.

She looked up at him in awe. "¿Cuándo…dónde…?"

He smiled. "Whilst you were shopping for soaps and toiletries, I went to the jeweler next door. I wanted to buy you a special present for tonight, and when I saw the diamonds, I knew they were meant to adorn your lovely wrist. It is but one of many I wish to bestow upon you, my pretty little Spanish Señorita. It goes well with this." He pulled out another velvet box.

Her breath caught in her throat as she opened the box. Inside was a beautiful diamond necklace. Sofia removed it from its case and held it up to the candle light, sending sparkling shimmers of light dancing in the dim room. "¡Señor! 'Tis too much. Sapphires and now diamonds." She shook her head. "I do not deserve such generosity."

Darcy was touched and pleased with her modesty. Truly, she was a class above her station in life, and he was beginning to want to take her away to a place where she would never know anything but love and happiness. However, just as that thought passed through his head, he glanced away and winced. *…You cannot fall in love, Darcy…not with a courtesan…You can never marry her… no matter how much you should wish to…*

"¿Señor, are you unwell?"

"Sí, Señorita, all is well. Here allow me to assist you," he said, taking the necklace from her hand. As he fastened it around her slender neck, he thought about their first time together as man and woman. She had been an innocent maid. Could he really release her to a life he knew would destroy the beautiful woman she was? He closed his eyes and groaned. *…Darcy you want to keep her for a lifetime, but you are not the kind of man who can live in between. If you keep her, you must be willing to marry her…but what will Lord Matlock and Lady Catharine say…Do you even care for their opinions…?*

He pulled her into his arms and held her to his chest. *…Darcy…with very little trouble, you could love her…but can you marry her?…And your progeny …What about them? You know there will be offspring if you continue as things are now…*

Releasing her, he said, "Come, Señorita, it is time to depart."

The carriages pulled up at Drury Lane one by one, letting the patrons out in a long procession for the night's presentation of *Twelfth Night*. Darcy had seen it many times, but Sofia confessed she had never before seen a Shakespearean performance, though she had read all of the plays in her father's library. He smiled as he guided her into the lobby and up the stairs to their box. This would be another of the first events that he could share with her, and that pleased him very much. In fact, to see her happy and smiling always brought a smile to his face. His only regret in knowing her was that he had met her at the *House of Pleasure* where her portrait still hung in the great hall for all to see. Someday he would buy it, for he could not bear the thought of other men looking upon with lust what he considered to be his treasure.

Entering their private box, Darcy helped Sofia to her seat and took the one beside her. He looked around the theatre. All eyes were upon them. The ladies sneered behind their fans, but the gentlemen looked on with envious smiles.

Darcy leaned in and whispered in her ear, "*Twelfth Night*, sometimes called *What You Will*, is believed to have been written for the close of the Christmas season in

1601-02. As you know, it expands on the musical interludes and riotous disorder expected of such an occasion, which, from what I have read, were numerous."

She turned and smiled. "Yes, I know. My father told me certain plot elements were drawn from the short story *Of Apollonius and Silla* by Barnabe Rich who based his story on one written by Matteo Bandello. Papa said it was first performed on the second of February, 1602, at Candlemas."

He smiled. "That is correct. One of my ancestors was there for the opening night. It was quite a performance." He paused. "You have been taught well. Did you have a governess for your formal education?"

"No Señor. There was no governess."

"No governess?" He furrowed his brow.

*...How was that possible? Daughters brought up at home without a governess! I never heard of such a thing...If her father did not see to a governess, then perhaps someone else ...*

"Then your mother must have been quite a slave to your education."

She shook her head. "No, indeed. My poor mother was more concerned with other pressing matters which better suited her. She divided her time so entirely between my younger sisters' frivolous amusements and her domestic cares that she had very little time to see to my, or anyone else's, instruction. I am afraid our education was the furthest thing from her mind."

"Then, who taught you? Surely you were not neglected?"

"Umm...compared with some families, I believe we were, but such of us who wished to learn never wanted the means. Mi padre always encouraged us to read and had all the masters that were necessary," she said with a smile. "He had an ample library stocked with all the great classics and volumes of history, philosophy, economics, and geography. Those of us who chose to avail ourselves, certainly did."

"¿And he taught you Spanish?"

"Sí, Señor. He took me to the peninsula when I was but a child. There we stayed for the summer. I learnt from the residents in the village where we stayed, but my father always insisted I speak it properly. I was never allowed to speak the less formal dialect. Oh, I believe we must be still. It is about to begin" she said, her excitement obvious in her voice. She pointed to the stage and leaned back in her chair. The curtains were rising.

Having seen the play numerous times, Darcy sat in quiet reflection and contemplated all that he knew about Miss Molina, and what she had just shared. It was rather disconcerting to discover that her father had not provided her with a proper education, and yet she had apparently learnt all on her own with, perhaps, some small guidance from her father.

He eyed her carefully: the way her lips curled upward when she smiled, and how her small and delicate fingers twisted the program as she fretted in eager anticipation of the next scene. When they first had met, her hands were rough and coarse, but now they were smooth and soft. What sort of life had she come from and to where would she return should they part? The more Darcy thought about it, the more he wanted her for more than a mistress.

Suddenly the curtain fell, and he knew it was time for intermission when people generally mixed and mingled for pleasant conversation. Many a gentleman used this opportunity to parade his mistress for public inspection; however, that was not Darcy's intention—not on this night or any other. Therefore, instead of leaving for the lobby as was customarily done, Darcy and Sofia chose to remain in their box and discuss the play.

While they were discussing the particulars, Darcy looked up and smiled as he rose to his feet.

"Wex, Fitzwilliam, come. Have a seat and join us," Darcy said. "Where is Lady Margaret?"

"Maggie had a prior engagement, but will be present for tomorrow night's festivities, and she is eagerly waiting to see you again."

Darcy laughed. "Tell her I look forward to seeing her again, too. It has been to long." He turned to Sofia and softly said, "Lady Margaret is Lord Wexford's betrothed. They have only recently announced it at a ball given in their honor before Christmas and are to be married next autumn when we celebrate the Harvest Festival."

Sofia nodded.

Darcy then gestured between her and his cousins. "Wex, Fitzwilliam, you remember Miss Molina."

"Indeed." The viscount bowed. "It is a pleasure to see you once more, Miss Molina."

"Indeed it is," the general added with a bow. "We are most pleased to see our cousin has come out of his den and decided to live again." Fitzwilliam winked at Darcy then returned his attention to Sofia. "It is a compliment to you, Miss Molina."

"Señor, you make me blush. I am sure Señor Darcy has not been such a recluse as you say."

Viscount Wexford smiled. "You have not the slightest inclination of the improvement your presence in his life has brought about, but that is a subject for another time. What is your opinion of this night's performance and of Mrs. Davis? My brother and I are most eager to hear your opinion on the subject."

"¡Señor, it is stupendous! Señora Davis es magnifica."

As she began to tell them her interpretation of the first act, Darcy had to smile. Her enthusiasm was enchanting. She enjoyed the play with such eagerness, that he decided they would have to repeat this activity before they left London for Richmond.

Sofia continued to discuss the play and her enjoyment of it until it was time for the final act. The viscount and the general paid their respects and returned to the Lord Matlock's box, both laughing and shaking their heads. Darcy chuckled to himself. He could see Sofia had made quite a favorable impression on his cousins, but what would they think if they knew how he was beginning to feel about the pretty little señorita sitting by his side? He sighed and shook his head as he reached for her hand. ...*Darcy, if you decide to make this arrangement permanent, they will have an opinion, and you know it is not going to be to your liking*...

By the time the final act was over, Darcy was eager to take her home and to bed where he intended to love her slowly, savoring every tender moment they were together. The nights they had shared were amongst the best he had ever spent with anyone. In fact, he could not remember a more pleasurable or comforting time spent in domestic felicity.

Shifting through the crowd of people, greeting those whom he must, he guided her to the upstairs lobby. Just as they came down the stairs to call for their carriage, Their Graces, the Dukes of Castlebaum and Ancaster, approached. Darcy stiffened and gave a formal bow. Of all the personages to be here, they were not among the patrons he wished to see.

"Darcy! Good God. You are out in society again. Good to see you, man," said His Grace, the Duke of Ancaster. Where have you been keeping yourself?" Casting a fleeting look at Sofia, he winked. "Ah, but I can see what, or rather whom, has occupied his time," he said to Castlebaum who smiled in return.

Darcy watched carefully as the Duke eyed Sofia from head to toe as if he wanted to undress her. His Grace finally turned full-face, bowed, and lifting her hand he said, "Miss Molina, what a pleasure to behold such a lovely sight. As The Bard himself would say, you do indeed cause the torches to burn bright. You look radiant tonight, my dear. Blue becomes you, and your diamonds do your beauty justice," he said and then placed a chaste kiss upon her gloved fingers.

Tearing his gaze away, he asked, "Darcy will you be attending Wexford's Twelfth Night ball tomorrow evening?"

Darcy glanced at Sofia. "It is probable."

The Duke of Castlebaum spoke next as he turned his eager eyes to Sofia. "My lovely lady, you will be the crowning jewel of tomorrow evening's festivities. I hope to see you there and perhaps share a waltz if your protector can spare you for a fleeting moment."

"Aye, and I, as well." Ancaster's eyes shifted from Sofia's face to her stimulating décolletage, which nearly pushed her breasts completely up and out of her gown.

Darcy was incensed at the forwardness of the nobles, but Sofia appeared to enjoy the attention. She laughed and spoke in broken English, something she had never done for him—not even once. Darcy was consumed with jealousy, but he would be damned to a hangman's noose before he would show it.

As the Duke of Castlebaum's licentious gaze caressed Sofia's body, resting on her full bosom for far too long, he finally tore himself away and turned to Darcy.

"Darcy, may I have the honor of a dance with your lovely paramour tomorrow evening? You shan't keep her all to yourself. 'Tis not proper. You must allow her to have a few dances with others."

Darcy spat out, "Sofia may do as she pleases. She may dance with you if it gives her pleasure…and if she agrees."

Sofia laughed. "Your Graces." She gave a deep curtsey. "Ask me on the morrow, and we shall see." The merry sound of her broken English mingled with light laughter wafted through the air.

Paying his respects to the Dukes of Castlebaum and Ancaster, Darcy bowed with a cool demeanor and took his leave with Sofia close behind.

During the entire ride back to Grosvenor Street, not a word was exchanged. Sofia quietly mused to herself ...*He is jealous!* With a soft laugh, she took a deep breath and peered out the opposite window into the darkness. From the corner of her eye, she caught sight of a silhouette—a man in the shadows. He tipped his hat, but she could not see his face. A small gasp escaped her throat.

Darcy's eyes riveted to her. "I am not amused!"

"¿Amused by what?" she snapped back.

"¡You know perfectly well *what*!"

"Señor, I am afraid I do not understand your meaning. Tell me what you mean."

"You speak broken ingles to Their Graces, the Dukes of Castlebaum and Ancaster, but not to me. Never once have you spoken en ingles to *me*. I am not amused by your flirting with other men. ¡I will not have it!"

"I was not flirting. I was merely being friendly. Their Graces are amiable men— men of quality with good breeding. If you do not care whether or not I dance with them, then why should I not?"

Darcy turned away and looked out into the night. ...*Because you belong to me...That is why.*

When they entered the house, his temper was engaged more than a little.

"Sofia, go above stairs and wait for me. Undress. I will be in to see you when I am ready."

"¿Where are you going?"

"To have a whiskey."

He turned to leave, but stopped in mid-step at the sound of her voice.

"I think not, Señor. I am tired from our outing. I think it best if you rest in *your* room and I in mine."

Darcy heard the bite in her voice. He slowly turned to face her. "Señorita, I will have none of that. I will not be denied that which is rightfully mine."

"¿Why...why must you have your rights this night when I am tired?" she asked with a definite upturn of her head.

"I think that should be abundantly clear." He paused and released a hard breath as he looked away momentarily. "I want my seed wet between your legs. I want you to remember to whom it is that you belong and who it is that escorts you this night and every other night." He hesitated and took a deep breath, an air of finality in his voice. "Tomorrow evening I will dance three dances with you. You may do as you please for the remainder of the evening, but remember in *whose* bed it is that you belong *then* and *now*."

"Am I to presume you are marking your territory as one of your hounds marks a tree?"

"Presume what you like."

"¡It is *you* that offered my hand to them, not I! If it is not to your satisfaction, then you should not have done so. I do not perform to a standard, Señor Darcy," Sofia said with a smug smile as she turned and started for the stairs.

Darcy jolted. He grabbed her arm and spun her around. "Neither of us performs to a standard, Señorita."

He crushed her against his chest and took her mouth with his in a bruising kiss— kissing her senseless as she trembled in his arms, not wanting to love him, but unable to resist.

"Te quiero este noche...I want you tonight, my little Spanish siren!" he murmured against her hot lips.

"I - I—" before she could answer, he scooped her up into his arms and carried her to their bed. His male scent assaulted her senses as she whimpered in his arms. She did not want to fall in love with him, and yet as he bruised her lips with his kisses, she could not help herself. Sofia Molina wanted him, but Elizabeth Bennet was falling in love.

# Chapter 11

nd now my dear reader, we come upon our hero on the morning after the theatre. He is feeling quite ashamed of himself, I do believe, as he partakes of his morning repast and coffee. Instead of the tender lovemaking he had planned to enjoy all through the night, he savagely took our young heroine until the wee hours of the morning, repeatedly ravishing her body, taking, conquering, and plundering, much like a ram in rut. It appears that my good friend, Cupid, shot his arrow just a little off the mark. 'Tis very naughty of him, do you not think?

Our dear heroine, on the other hand, gave as good as she got, following his lead on every foray into the land of erotic bliss. Her opinion was quite the opposite, I do think. Let us take a peek and see how she fares, shall we?

Sofia stretched out in bed like a lazy cat with a smile on her face, yawning. She reached over for her lover, hoping for one more amorous encounter, only to find him missing from his pillow. She creased her brow.

"¿Señor? ¡Señor! ¿Where have you gone?"

She rose up on her elbows and glanced around the room. "¿Señor Darcy, have you left me?"

"Miss Sofie, you well this morning?" Ling-Ling said, entering the room. "Sleep late. Mr. Darcy gone. He say he work today. You need bath. We go out. Remember?"

"Oh…yes, I do remember now." She smiled and stretched once more. "Ling-Ling send to the kitchen for our morning meal and have them fetch hot water for my bath. Today is a glorious day—the best day of my life. We are going to see Mamma, dear Jane, and the children. And to answer your question, I am well—very well indeed."

*…in fact, I do not know when I have been better…*

She smiled remembering the night and their lovemaking. Mr. Darcy was indeed a magnificent lover, just as Ophelia had told her—a stallion very much like those she had seen on her father's estate. Sofia knew she would remember the previous night with fondness even when she grew old.

As Sofia and her maid were about to depart, Mr. Darcy approached them in the vestibule.

"Señorita," he said as he came closer, "I must have a word with you, por favor."

"Sí, Señor." Sofia turned and signaled for Ling-Ling to wait for her in the coach.

When she was through the door, Mr. Darcy took Sofia by the hand. "Señorita, you must allow me to apologize for my behavior last night. It was abominable and shall not be repeated."

"¿My forgiveness? ¿Señor, whatever for?"

Darcy sighed and shook his head. "Señorita," he said with a contrite spirit, "I am afraid I did not represent myself in a gentlemanlike manner last night when we…when we retired for the evening. I should have respected your wishes and kept to my room. My behavior was unpardonable. I cannot think of it without abhorrence. I can hardly bring myself to talk about it at all. ¿Will you forgive me?" he asked quietly, his eyes cast down.

"¡Forgive you! Señor, I can hardly bring myself to *forget* it. If this is your un-gentlemanlike behavior, please *do* repeat it, for I quite enjoyed it," she said with an upturned smile.

Darcy laughed and pulled her into his arms. "¿Señorita, what shall I ever do with you, mi querida? You taunt and tease and have me in the palm of your hand."

"Love me like you did last night, and I shall be well pleased…most content indeed."

He smiled down at her with merriment sparkling in his deep, intense eyes. "That I do, Señorita. More than you know. ¿When will you return, mi querida? I seem to find myself in need of your affections whenever I am in your presence."

"I shall not be long. I am going to visit an old friend and run a few errands. I shall return in time for tea."

"Good," he said. "I wish I could accompany you, but I must work. Return to me soon, mi querida. I will miss you while you are away."

He dusted her lips with a gentle kiss and walked her to her carriage. After she had handed the driver the directions to her intended destination, Darcy solicitously helped her into the coach. Only when the carriage was to the gate did Darcy turn and enter the house to attend to the mountain of work that awaited him and his manager.

As he walked the long corridor to his study, he paused to reflect on the woman in his life. The saucy impertinence on Sofia's upturned face—the way her lips curled into a smile and her response to their night of passionate lovemaking—caused him to smile. She was indeed every bit the woman he had imagined Elizabeth to be—especially in bed.

*…Darcy, she is your complement in every way imaginable. Her intelligence…wit…passion for life…and especially her passion in bed! You could not ask for more in a woman…That is why Sofia Molina is a danger to you…She is a courtesan… and could never be more than…*

He sighed and shook his head, not wanting to complete the thought. Turning the corner, he left for his study where his manager awaited him.

Sofia's first stop was to the Barings Bank where Mr. Darcy's solicitor had established her household account. Withdrawing half the money he had set aside, she and her maid then set out for Ophelia's house.

The carriage ride to Covent Garden gave Sofia pause to think. She could not remember a time since her father's death when she had felt more secure and content, perhaps even loved. Mr. Darcy was ever present in her thoughts, and, against her will, he had claimed a place in her heart. As she mused about their congenial cohabitation, for a moment—a brief moment—she contemplated removing her veil and revealing her true identity. But no sooner than the thought had occurred, another replaced it.

*...Lizzy, he will despise you! You cannot! You must not! ...What will he think of you if he should discover the truth...? That you have sold yourself for money...his money at that! He once thought of your family as mercenary. He would now believe it to be true.*

She shook her head to dispel the image of his face when he had last looked at her. No, she would not think upon it. Today was to be a good day—her first day home with her family since she had left to become Mr. Darcy's mistress. Pondering her situation with Mr. Darcy was better left to another day.

Sofia smiled as the carriage rolled to a stop. Retrieving her packages, she gave the coachman his leave with instructions to return for her at a quarter 'til four.

Ophelia was there to greet them the moment they entered her small, but fashionably decorated, lodgings.

"Sofia! I am so very glad you have come," she said, embracing her friend. "Let us call for tea and talk. You must tell me all about the enigmatic Mr. Darcy," Ophelia said with a bemused smile.

She then turned to Sofia's maid. "Ling-Ling, if you wish, you may visit Sally. She has been eagerly anticipating your arrival with raptures all morning."

Ling-Ling curtsied and replied that she was indeed agreeable to the notion.

Ophelia gave Ling-Ling directions as to where she might find Sally, and the maid was soon out of sight, leaving Sofia and Ophelia to themselves.

As the ladies entered the drawing room, Sofia lifted her veil and removed her mask. Unpinning her hair, she shook her head to loosen her curls. With a few small touches in front of the looking glass, she fashioned her hair to a different style, and she was once again *Elizabeth Bennet*.

When they had taken their seats across from one another, Ophelia enthusiastically leaned forward. "Lizzy, you must tell me. Is it true? Is he as good a lover as I have heard? I must know it all!"

"Ophelia!" Elizabeth said with a laugh. "Surely you do not expect me to reveal the particulars? I shall not do it. I will only say that he is gentle and knows what a woman desires, but I shan't say another word! I will say, however, that he is as kind and good a man as ever there was. He is amiable and generous with the poor and has been very good to me. Mr. Darcy is as passionate about life as he is about love. I am truly fortunate to have come to know him as I do now."

"Then why must you leave him? I am certain he will wish to keep you forever. Lizzy, why do you not reconsider and stay with Mr. Darcy? From what you have told me, I understand he is quite taken with you. You may even be one of the lucky ones. He may marry you; he certainly seems to hold you in great esteem."

Elizabeth glanced away. "That's the problem. He does seem to regard me with admiration."

"Problem? I do not understand."

"No, you would not," Elizabeth said with a sigh. "On the twenty-fourth of March, I must remove my veil and reveal my true identity or leave. I will choose the latter, of course. Mr. Darcy can never know who Sofia Molina really is."

"And why ever not?"

"Because," she glanced away once more, "Elizabeth Bennet *is* the Country Miss...the one he fell in love with all those years ago."

Ophelia gasped. "Oh no, Lizzy! You?"

Elizabeth turned back and nodded. "I cannot let him know...I cannot bear to shatter the image he has of *his* Elizabeth. He has confided in me things I never knew, and now that I know the truth of the feelings he held for me all those years ago, I... Oh, Ophelia! What would he think of me...of her, especially after all we have done?" *...especially after last night!*

"Oh, Lizzy," her friend said as she moved across the distance and took a seat beside her. "It was *you* who fostered the change in so proud a man. He is what he is today because of *you*, Lizzy. If he loved you then, he still loves you now. I am sure he would understand. Will you not at least try to tell him the truth?"

"No. I would die of mortification should he know the truth of my situation. He would think me a whore in every sense of the word, and that I cannot bear, for I am not a whore," she said with conviction.

She glanced at Ophelia, wringing her hands. "What must you think of me?"

"Think of you! Lizzy, I am a gentleman's lady of the evening. What do you think I think?"

Elizabeth gave a faint smile.

"I think you are a courageous young woman who will do what she must in order to survive in a world that holds no mercy for those of us without the means to protect ourselves. Putting it bluntly, your life—my life, both of our lives are tales of survival if anything. That is what I think. Now, you must not fret. It is not the Elizabeth Bennet with whom I am acquainted with. And, if it is certain that you must leave, then we have important things to discuss. Are you absolutely sure this is what you want?"

"It is."

"Well, then," Ophelia said, moving back to her seat across from Elizabeth. "I have done as you asked and inquired about accommodations in Ireland from my protector. He owns a fine estate in the Ulster Mountains. It is in the village of Livingston in County Down. There are also several small cottages there that are large enough to accommodate you—some as large as Longbourn and just as fine. He is willing to sell one of them. This is it." She produced a sketch of a very handsome cottage.

Elizabeth looked it over carefully. There were many gardens for pleasure as well as practical use, and groves of trees numerous enough to tempt her to take long and peaceful walks to her heart's content. The drive to the front of the house was flanked on either side by a huge hedgerow and was spacious enough that a coach could manage it quite easily. The portico was small, but adequate for their needs. Yes, she thought to herself, it was just the sort of establishment she had in mind for Jane and Kitty.

She nodded her satisfaction and glanced up. "It looks as I imagined when we first discussed the prospect. What is his price?"

"It does not have much land, but it has enough for an income of one thousand pounds per annum. But, because he is in love with me and will do anything I ask, the price is…" she whispered into Elizabeth's ear.

"That much? Well," she puffed out her cheeks, "with what Mr. Darcy is to pay me, I can afford it. Furthermore, with the income the estate will provide, we will get by. My father taught me the particulars of estate management. I can administer a manor as well as any man and better than most," she said cheerfully. "I will take it!"

"In that case I will contact Mrs. O'Brady and make the arrangements for you to take possession by the first of April."

"Then it is done!" Elizabeth exclaimed as she placed the sketch in her reticule. "I have one less thing to worry about."

"Good!" Ophelia smiled. "But there is more news to reveal. I have also made inquiries about the house in Cheapside you requested. Here is the address," she said handing a sealed document to Elizabeth. "I think it is a quaint little house perfectly suited for Jane and Kitty. There is also a small garden for the children to take exercise and play. I think you will like it, and the price is very affordable."

Elizabeth looked over the papers and nodded. "'Tis perfect! And you are right; it is very reasonable—even more so in that it comes with servants, saving me the trouble of selecting them. I shall see the solicitor straight away and lease the property for three months."

"Very well," Ophelia said as she turned in the direction of the parlor door. "I see Phoebe is here. Let us have our tea. Shall we?"

Ophelia poured a cup of tea for herself and another for Elizabeth. The two ladies then settled in to talk while they had their tea and crumpets. They talked about former times and the things they had done as young girls—the trees they had climbed, their mud-splattered frocks from chasing lost kittens found in the woods, their disheveled hair, and the insect collection they once arranged as a joke to set their mothers' nerves on edge. After several laughs and a few cups of tea, Ophelia grew somber and spoke as if in deep reflection.

"Lizzy, all this talk of insects and lost kittens has caused me to recall something I had forgotten."

"And what would that be?" Elizabeth asked as she set her cup aside.

"I was just thinking about something from long ago. Lizzy, do you remember the childhood parable of *The Ant and the Grasshopper*? It was one of Aesop's fables. The one Mrs. Bertram, the elderly woman who lived in the cottage by the woods near the village, used to tell us when we were children. We would go there in summertime and play in her garden. You collected grasshoppers, and I found caterpillars for our collection. Do you remember, Lizzy?"

"Yes, I remember. She would treat us to tea and biscuits, and we gathered her vegetables for her." Elizabeth furrowed her brow. "I also remember when she died. You were particularly sad."

"I was. I shall never forget her or her parables from nature. That particular day after we had collected several very large grasshoppers, she looked at them and then showed us the ants carrying away crumbs which we had dropped from our biscuits. That was when she began her tale. She said the grasshopper plays through the summer months while the ant busies herself saving for the long winter to come.

Lizzy, have you not realized how people are like grasshoppers and ants? If we do not save for the time when our beauty has faded, then we will be left to the fate of the grasshopper in the winter of our lives."

Elizabeth tilted her head and gazed at her friend. "What are you telling me, Ophelia? For I know there is a meaning. A parable always has a meaning for the instruction of the hearer."

"Yes, Lizzy, there is a meaning." Ophelia set her cup aside and leaned back. "I have thought about it for some time now. I know I have encouraged you to remain with Mr. Darcy, but if he will not marry you, then it is best to go while you still have your youth. The life of a courtesan is a difficult one. Soon your beauty will pass, and you will be alone. It is the way of things."

"Ophelia…I hardly know what to say."

"Promise me you will go to Ulster and begin anew as a respectable woman while you still have the bloom of youth clinging to you. Do not re-enter the demimonde. It may be pleasurable for a season, but all things must come to an end, and the end for a courtesan is not pleasant if she has not made preparations. Many of us are left to die in poverty from sickness and starvation. If it were possible, I would find a cottage for myself and become a respectable woman while I still have my beauty. But I have not saved enough money, nor does it look like I shall, for I am not as fortunate as you to win a contract for ten thousand pounds."

"Ophelia I—"

Her friend held up her hand. "Say nothing, Lizzy, for there is nothing to be said," she replied as she moved to pour another cup of tea, but Elizabeth stayed her hand.

"No," Elizabeth said, "I cannot. As much as I would like to stay and continue our conversation, I must go, or I shall not accomplish all that I must for the day. We will talk of this another day. Now, if you will excuse me, I shall change into my Miss Elizabeth Bennet clothes and hire a hackney. Expect me to return at three o'clock in order that I may change back. Mr. Darcy is expecting me for tea, and I shan't be late. We are attending Lord Wexford's ball tonight."

"And you shall be the most admired woman there," Ophelia said with a soft smile as Sofia Molina left to change her identity into Elizabeth Bennet.

While Elizabeth made herself ready, she pondered her friend's words. Ophelia had never given any indication that she was unhappy with her situation, and yet it would appear as if she was. This new revelation was indeed a surprise.

After settling the lease for the house on Newgate Street, Elizabeth took the next few minutes to have a talk with her maid explaining that while she is with her family, her name is Elizabeth or Lizzy, but that Ling-Ling was never to address her by that name when she was dressed as Sofia Molina. Ling-Ling shook her head in understanding. Then they left for Whitecastle.

Once they were as far as she dared go by coach, she paid the driver, and she and her maid made their way on foot through the alleyways and avenues of London's lower East End. With their bundles of packages in hand, they headed for a small cottage on Beggars Street.

Elizabeth's maid looked around in trepidation.

"Oh, Miss, Ling-Ling not like this. Family live in bad town. Ling-Ling may have to *wushu* if we attacked."

Elizabeth glanced down and furrowed her brow. "What do you mean, Ling-Ling? I must travel this way lest we be seen."

"Ling-Ling mean *wushu*. Ancient Chinese method. Wisdom given to Ling-Ling by father. Ling-Ling protect Mistress."

Elizabeth looked at her little keeper in wonder. She was barely bigger than a small boy, but much more of a giant than most men. She smiled to herself. When her family left England, Ling-Ling would most certainly be among the party to depart.

Turning the last corner, they were on the street to home. A few more steps and they were there. Jane greeted them at the door with a warm smile and a hug.

"Mamma!" Little Wills came running and threw his tiny arms around Elizabeth's legs the instant she was through the door. "I have missed you so much."

He reached up his little arms for her to take him.

She set her packages on the table, and then bent down and lifted the child into her arms, squeezing him tightly and giving him a warm kiss as his arms flew around her neck. "Wills, Wills, Mamma has missed you, too! But I am here today, and we are to have the whole day together."

"Weee!" he squealed in delight.

"Lizzy, 'tis so very good to see you," Jane said, giving her sister another hug.

Flora and Edward came forth and greeted their aunt as well, letting her know how delighted they were to see her. Kitty came through the door and hugged her sister with tears of joy springing to her eyes.

"Lizzy, we have missed you so. How have you been?"

"Very well, but Kitty, why are you not at Mrs. Hamilton's today?"

Kitty sighed. "There will be time enough to discuss that when we are alone. 'Tis better to speak in private."

"I see," Elizabeth said, setting William down. "Well, in that case, let me introduce to you someone who is dear to me." She gestured to the small woman next to her.

"Jane, Kitty, this is Ling Hua, my personal maid and close friend. Her name means 'delicate flower,' but she is known to me as Ling-Ling."

Ling-Ling curtsied. "Ling-Ling very glad to meet family of Mistress."

Jane smiled gently. "Miss Ling-Ling, we are most pleased to make your acquaintance. Any friend of our sister's is always welcome in our humble home. Will you not make yourself at home?"

Ling-Ling bowed. "Ling-Ling make herself at home. She care for family and help family."

Kitty reached and embraced their new friend. "You are most welcomed to be a part of our family."

After their salutations were exchanged, Elizabeth exclaimed, "I will be here every day! Mr. Darcy is confined to his work, and I am free to do as I please, *so*, we are going to spend the entire week together as a family. I have enough money for us to have a grand time. We shall go to the park and the marketplace. We will buy each of you a new set of clothes and then some, but the first order of business is to move. I have acquired a house on Newgate Street complete with staff. There will be one maid, a manservant, and a cook. No more domestic duties for *you*, Jane."

Jane smiled. "Lizzy, you very well know I do not mind."

"That is not the material point," Elizabeth said. "We are the daughters of a gentleman, and we will live according to the station to which we were born. I do not want you chopping wood, tending fires, or bringing in buckets of coal. Furthermore, I want the children to have all the things associated with that status. They will have a proper upbringing. Which reminds me; I have purchased a set of books—a set of children's stories for Flora and Edward and a set of fairytales for Wills. There are books for learning mathematics, history, and geography as well."

"Mamma! Mamma! Books!" William exclaimed. "When can I have them? Do they have pictures?"

"Yes," Elizabeth said with a smile. "They are illustrated, but you cannot have them until we move."

William brought his little hands to his chest in a fist of joy. "Mamma, will you be coming home to live with us? I miss you."

Elizabeth looked upon the young child with tenderness as she stroked his curly top. "Soon Wills, we will all be together as a family, and Mamma will never leave you again. But for now, Mamma has to be away. However," she said in quiet reflection, "I promise you it will not be much longer, and then I will be home for good. For the present, however, you must mind your aunts, and be a good boy!"

"I will. I'm always good." He looked up with expectation. "Mamma, what is that?" he asked pointing to the bundles on the tea table.

"That?" she asked, raising her brow.

"Yes, Mamma! What is that?"

"Well, gather around, and I shall tell you."

As they all gathered around Elizabeth began to unwrap her parcels. The rag doll she purchased at the bazaar was for Flora and the leather bag of marbles for her brother Edward. To William she gave the box of painted tin soldiers. Lastly, she gave them each a bag of penny candy.

The children jumped for joy, each clutching their special gift and bag of candy. Flora cradled her doll in her arms and swayed from side to side, singing a lullaby while Edward opened his bag and pulled out the shooter marble. "Look! Now I can play by the fire," he said.

William took his box of tin soldiers and bowed. "Thank you, Mamma."

Elizabeth dismissed the children to go with Ling-Ling to the back room where they slept so that they could play with their new toys, allowing her to have the time she needed with her sisters.

Making themselves comfortable, they all settled in around the table for conversation, Kitty with her workbasket and Jane with her knitting.

"Jane, I want you and Kitty to prepare to move on the morrow. I will be here as soon as I can with helpers to move our family to Newgate. Once you are settled in, life will become much easier. Jane, you can begin to teach the children and give them a proper education. Mamma will be made more comfortable in a room where proper light can enter. That and a bit of fresh air should set her to rights. Nonetheless, in my absence, do make arrangements for the apothecary to visit, and perhaps she might recover."

"Lizzy," Kitty said, shaking her head "Mamma will not recover. That is why I am here today and not at work. Mrs. Hamilton was kind enough to allow me to work from home. Mamma is very ill, and that is what we must discuss at present. The best we can do is make her last days more peaceful. With the money you gave us before leaving for Richmond, we sent for a doctor, and he said she has chronic lung disease and heart failure. Mamma is dying, Lizzy. We must make arrangements to have her laid to rest with Papa; then perhaps she will be happy."

Tears gathered in Elizabeth's eyes. "All the more reason to move quickly. Her last days must be spent in ease. I only wish I could be with her, but I cannot, and neither can I leave my maid. Ling-Ling knows much about ancient Chinese medicine. I will see if perhaps she can recommend teas to help Mamma rest in her final hours. However, when the time grows near, you are to send round a missive. Send it through Ophelia addressed to Sofia Molina." Elizabeth paused. "Do you suppose I might see her?"

"Mamma is resting now," Jane said, "but you might step in for a few moments before you leave. However, I must warn you she still calls for Papa and Lydia. She is quite insensible of her own state and does not recognize Kitty or I. Therefore it is not likely she will recognize you either."

"If only…"

"If only what, Lizzy?" Kitty asked, furrowing her brow.

"Nothing," Elizabeth said, recovered her emotions. Taking a deep breath, she continued with a smile. "Let us speak of it no more. I have happier things to discuss."

She reached into her reticule and pulled out the sketch Ophelia had given her earlier.

"This is to be our new home when we leave England. It is situated in Ulster, Ireland—in the heart of the high mountains in a little village known as Livingston in County Down. Look at this sketch," she said spreading it out on the table for all to see.

"You, Jane, shall have the cottage in the mountains you have talked about, and Kitty will have her little shop to make all the ladies' finery she wishes, and I?" Elizabeth laughed. "I shall have my gardens with flowers, lavender and roses, and vegetables and herbs, of course. We shall have it all, and we will do it on our own without a man to account to for anything."

"Lizzy, 'tis too much. It must cost you a fortune to—"

"That is no concern for you, Kitty. Mr. Darcy has given me my pin money, and I have two hundred pounds to spare. Here," she said reaching into her reticule and taking out her coin purse, "you and Jane are to have one hundred pounds to buy whatever is needed for Mamma and the household. Tomorrow, I will take half the money—six hundred pounds and place it in an account at another bank in your name. That should see you through until this is over, and we can be on our way to freedom."

"Lizzy! It is more than I imagined," Kitty said. "You have done very well. Will you have all the money Mr. Darcy has paid for you?"

Elizabeth drew in a sharp breath. "No, Kitty, and to tell the truth, I am having difficulty taking any of it. If it were not for our very survival, I would not take a penny. However, beggars cannot afford…well never mind," she said, wiping a tear.

Jane sat knitting a pair of socks, listening as her sisters talked. At Elizabeth's last remark she glanced up from her work.

"Lizzy," Jane said, "why do you hesitate, and why are you crying? I saw you wipe your tears. You cannot fool me, for I know you too well. Have you fallen in love with Mr. Darcy? I know you did like him, even cared for him I do believe. Do you now love him after...? Well, I shall not speak of it."

Elizabeth glanced away and shook her head as she chewed on her lower lip. She then turned and caught Jane's piercing blue eyes. "I know what you think and while it is true, I did care for him before...before our living arrangement, love is not an option for me, Jane," she said with a tinge of sorrow in her voice. "Besides, it was always you who held to such foolishness, not I. For me, this is a business venture. Do not fear, my dear Jane. For soon I shall be with you—and all of us will be together again forever. We will have the life a cruel fate has denied us. Soon, Jane, I promise, this will be over."

"But Lizzy, this is not you, and I do believe you are in love with Mr. Darcy. I can see it in your eyes and hear it in your voice. You love him."

Elizabeth shook her head. "Jane, no matter what I feel, I must do what I must do. Should Mr. Darcy discover the truth, it would be the death of me. The image he holds of me would be so wholly shattered that I could not bear his censure...not after what we have shared. Whatever affection he has for me would be utterly and completely destroyed. I cannot allow that. I care enough not to hurt him in that way. Therefore, let him remember Elizabeth Bennet as she was," Elizabeth said in a faraway voice.

She glanced at her sisters and smiled. "Both of you know very well that I have always held the philosophy that we must think of the past only as its remembrance gives us pleasure, and thus dear sisters, that is what we shall do."

Jane smiled sweetly as her needles moved in and out.

They continued to talk for the greater part of the afternoon with the children coming in every now and again to talk as well. When it was time for Elizabeth to leave, she gathered her things and stepped in to see her mother who was in a restless sleep. Mrs. Bennet cried out several times about her poor nerves, and then she would ask about Mrs. Phillips. Elizabeth stepped closer and took her mother's hand.

"Mamma, it is I, Elizabeth. Do you know me, Mamma?"

Mrs. Bennet slowly opened her eyes. "Lizzy, where have you been, child? Mr. Bennet has been searching for you. Such a naughty girl you are, not nearly as graceful as my dear Jane. Just look at you. Your dress is dirty, and your shoes are covered in mud. You are not fit to be seen. What shall I ever do with the likes of you? Leave you to Mr. Bennet that is what I shall do. Go now. Be off with you. Your father is in the library. He has just come from town, and he has a new book. Well, what are you standing there for? Go along, child. I must see to Lydia. She needs a new bonnet."

"Oh, Mamma!" Tears flooded Elizabeth's eyes and spilled down her cheeks. "I shall take care of you. I shall. Soon you will be with Papa and Lydia and poor, poor Mary. Rest," Elizabeth said as she pulled the coverlet up comfortably about her mother's shoulders. "I must go now, Mamma. I shall return again and take you to a more comfortable house. I love you, Mamma."

Elizabeth bent down and placed a kiss upon her mother's worn and withered brow; then she turned and took her leave with a heavy heart.

When she stepped into the sitting room, she glanced from Kitty to Jane. "Mamma has grown grievously ill since last I saw her. It is imperative we move to Newgate without delay. I wish I could leave my maid to sit with her, but *that* I would never be able to explain. Therefore, we shall do the next best thing. Jane, take the money I have left and hire a companion to sit with her. When the time grows near, send word 'round. Somehow I will steal away. I do not want you to weather this alone."

"No, Lizzy. We do not need a companion. The money would be better spent for Mamma's funeral. Kitty and I will manage. Do not trouble yourself."

Elizabeth sighed. "As you wish, but just the same. I want her made as comfortable as possible."

Giving her sisters and each of the children a hug and a kiss, she left for Ophelia's, vowing to return on the morrow no matter what might come of it.

The instant Sofia came through the door, Mr. Darcy was there to greet her.

"¿Señorita, where have you been? It is a quarter past the hour. I was beginning to worry. You are late for tea, and we must prepare for Lord Wexford's ball."

"Señor, the time merely slipped away from me. Surely you know it is the prerogative of a woman to be fashionably late." She smiled sweetly as a servant took her cloak and gloves.

Darcy furrowed his brow and grumbled something about a timely manner and tea.

With merry laughter ringing out, Sofia moved to where he stood. She reached up on tiptoes and tapped his quarrelsome lips with hers. "Let us have tea. I am famished."

When they had finished tea, Darcy escorted Sofia to their rooms to make ready for the ball. She was to go as a snow owl while he would attend as a pirate. After their baths, but before they dressed, Darcy came to her.

"Señorita, I have missed you. ¿Where did you go to spend the entire day? I came searching for you in hopes you had returned, but you were nowhere to be found," he said, slipping his arms around her waist and playing with the lace on her pantalets as he held her close.

"I went to visit an old friend and took the gifts I bought at the bazaar," she said, glancing away with sorrow in her voice. "I am afraid we were making merry and all thoughts of anything slipped from my mind. It shan't happen again."

"¿Is that all, Señorita? ¿Are you certain? Your heart seems troubled."

"Quite certain. ¿Why do you ask?"

"I ask because I care for you. All through tea you seemed sad. ¿Is there not something I can do to relieve whatever troubles you? ¿Is your friend in need?"

"No Señor, all will be well soon. La madre de mi amiga està muy enferma. She is ill, and I wished to sit with her. I shall not be late again, but I must go every day to attend her."

He smiled and pulled her closer. "I think it very admirable of you to think of a friend. If there is anything I can do, you need not hesitate to ask," he whispered as his soft lips caressed her neck, his warm breath sending shivers straight through the center of her.

Sofia pulled back and gazed into his intense eyes filled with compassion, and something inside of her broke. She reached up and took his face in her hands, kissing him in wanton abandonment. Sofia Molina—nay, Elizabeth Bennet, needed him tonight to make the world and all its troubles go away.

His hand found its way to her breast. Pushing her chemise aside, he caressed it before taking a handful and gently massaging it. His lips were soon to follow, and passion once again burned between them as both let go, lost in one another once again.

"Marking your territory again, Señor," she murmured against his lips gently moving over hers.

"Perhaps…more like property."

"Very sure of yourself…umm…Señor Darcy, has anyone ever told you that you are a good kisser?"

"You talk too much."

"¿Do I?"

"Be silent and kiss me." He covered her mouth with his and took her in a deep, passionate kiss.

Darcy, consumed with need, swept her up into his arms and carried her to their bed, making love to her as he had intended the night before. Every kiss, every gentle ministration was meant for her pleasure until they were both utterly spent from the sheer bliss of it.

Basking in the aftermath of their lovemaking, Sofia felt sated and loved. Darcy had been as gentle with her as he had been their first night, making sure her pleasure was complete before he took his own. And it was at that moment that she came within a hair's breadth of telling him what weighed upon her heart. She was so close and yet so far away. With a contented sigh, she smiled and resolved to merely enjoy herself. Tomorrow was soon enough to think about Mamma and all the trials at home.

And so, dear good and loyal reader, it is on a bittersweet note which I must leave you. Our young heroine feels the weight of the world pressing upon her slender shoulders. However, if she would but open her eyes and look about, she might find that there was one who held her in such high regard as to lighten her every load and help her along life's many rocky roads. But our dear heroine is as blind as she is beautiful.

# Chapter 12

Now, my good and gentle reader, we are off to the Twelfth Night Ball at No. 6 Cavendish Square, where several events shall occur, and some secrets will be revealed. As for our hero, well, my dear friend Cupid has assured me this time his arrow will be true to its mark as he will apply a different spell to the tip. But, as for our dear heroine, my friend tells me that her future is a matter better left to a being with superior skills. Our heroine is quite the contrary one, is she not? Tsk-tsk.

Let us come along to the ball and see how matters progress, shall we?

Night had fallen over the Old City, covering it in a cloak of darkness. But that was the least of it, for along with the black shroud of night, a thick veil of dense fog had rolled in from the River Thames, making travel difficult as the Darcy coach rolled through the brick and cobblestone streets. Oil lamps lit the way along the avenue like tiny dots in the dark, but their light was swallowed up by the night. One would not wish to venture out in such weather, but this night had been planned for many months and was not to be missed by the elite of London. Nor would it be missed by the residents of No. 2 Grosvenor Street, no matter how perilous the journey seemed.

As the carriage rolled along with the steady clip-clop of the horses' hooves pounding the cobblestone, Sofia had a strange feeling of foreboding about this particular night—as if it were to be different from any other she had experienced, but the source of her discomfiture was yet to be discovered. She glanced around, feeling as if eyes from the night were peering out from the shadows, watching her, studying her. Deciding it was simply her nerves giving her a fit of anxiety, she took a deep breath. This was to be her first real outing with Darcy since coming to London in which she would be in his inner circle, meeting people of rank and mingling with them, and she had greatly anticipated it. Therefore, she would take her mother's sage advice given to all her daughters whenever they were to be out; she would take every opportunity presented and enjoy herself to the fullest. Settling back against the soft cushions of the elegant Darcy coach, she anticipated the evening.

Sofia had selected a snowy owl for her costume while Darcy had chosen a Caribbean pirate. Together they would appear as the *Lady of the North* and the *Man of the Seas*. Sofia was rather intrigued by the idea when he had first approached her with the theme, and she had to admit, together as a couple, they looked stunning: he in his black woolen cape lined in red with a foil hanging by his side, and she in her white silk gown with a silk organza overlay peppered with velvet flecks of black. It suited her mask and veil perfectly.

Mr. Darcy had requested that she wear her hair down, and so she had. It hung in long ringlets well past her hips and swung gracefully whenever she walked. She smiled to herself. Outside it might be somewhat daunting, but inside it was anything but.

She knew tonight they would be mixing with some of the highest ranking people of London Society. Dukes, earls, and possibly the Prince Regent and his brother Prince William would be among the exclusive guests for the evening's festivities.

As the carriage moved steadily towards Cavendish Square, Darcy must have sensed her apprehension and assumed her to be fearful of the aristocratic gathering. He pressed his hand over hers in a reassuring gesture. "Señorita, do not distress yourself. The nobility are no different from anyone else. They can be a little proud, maybe even snobbish, but they are people like you and me. You must not feel apprehensive. Let me assure you that because of me, no one will dare be anything but cordial. Smile and be yourself. Your elegance and grace will carry the night," he said, then added as if an afterthought, "You may expect many a woman to be jealous of your beauty, and many a man to envy my good fortune."

She turned and looked at him with a smile. "Señor, it is not the mere presence of the nobility that worries me. It is something else entirely. I cannot explain it. 'Tis an odd sort of feeling—one I have only when something is about to happen, but I know not what. It is the feel of the night, cold and wet, as if clammy fingers will reach out from the darkness and snatch me away."

Darcy chuckled softly. "You need not fear, Señorita. You are with me, and this is my cousin's house. Lord Wexford lives in the most fashionable part of London. No such crimes will occur here."

Turning away, Sofia privately added, "A dense fog often spells death where I reside." She took a deep breath and puffed out her cheeks.

"¿Señorita, did you say something?"

"No, indeed," she said, "nothing at all. Nada." She reached for his hand with a smile and snuggled a little closer. As long as he was with her, she would fear nothing—not even the night.

Soon they arrived in Cavendish Square. The carriages pulled into a long procession, and one by one the guests entered the viscount's house. Shedding her wrap, Sofia glanced around, taking in all she saw. To be sure, she had seen fine houses before, but this one was even more elegant than the others. Pausing to gaze upon the chimneypiece, she chuckled to herself and wondered what Mr. Collins would think of *this* one.

Finally they reached Viscount Wexford and his escort for the evening, Lady Margaret Dellafont from Yorkshire. Mr. Darcy had informed her at the theatre that Lady Margaret had recently accepted Lord Wexford and was now his betrothed.

"Miss Molina," the viscount bowed and lifted her hand, placing a chaste kiss on her gloved fingers, "welcome to my home. It is my desire that you will enjoy yourself as much as I shall enjoy your presence."

Lady Margaret spoke next. "Welcome to Lord Wexford's Twelfth Night Ball. I simply love your costume, my dear. Where on earth did you find such a dress?"

Darcy glanced between the women and spoke. "Lady Margaret, I am afraid Miss Molina speaks only Spanish."

"I see," said the regal lady. "Then I shall have to speak Spanish as well. ¿Dónde encontara su vestido?"

Sofia smiled and curtsied. "My maid designed and stitched it especially for tonight," she replied in perfect Spanish.

"It is very beautiful. Give my compliments to your maid," the lady returned with a smile.

They moved into the center of the great hall to mix and mingle with the other guests. Sofia knew not a soul except for Mr. Darcy. He introduced her to the lords and ladies, and dukes and duchesses. Just as Darcy had said, the dukes admired her beauty. And the ladies? They were cordial enough with their upturned brows. Some even complimented her gown, but none were rude as she had expected—at least not to her face.

As they moved along, Darcy tuned to her and spoke. "Señorita, wait here. I shall fetch some wassail."

"Sí," she said with a smile.

As Darcy ambled through the crowd to the refreshments table, Sofia looked around. General Fitzwilliam stood in the corner with a rather handsome fair haired lady, whom Sofia assumed was his escort for the evening. Her eyes moved on. The Dukes of Castlebaum and Ancaster were present, but appeared to be alone and unaccompanied. The Prince Regent was indeed present with his mistress, as was Lord Blackburn with his, and there were several others whom she assumed were of the nobility, but as yet, she had not been introduced.

Finally her eyes rested on a tall, gaunt-looking male figure standing alone in the corner by the chimneypiece. He was staring at her from over the rim of his glass, sending a cold chill up her spine. The man was void of all light, the epitome of death. He wore black—black as the dark of night, black as a *funeral* procession. He had a long flowing cape and wore a mask that fitted snugly over his face down to his mouth. It was silvery grey and reminded her of the pallor of a cold corpse. Another chill swept over her, but she soon chuckled softly. *...Mr. Death is what I shall know him as...*

"Miss Molina," a soft feminine voice called.

Sofia turned. "Lady Margaret?"

The woman smiled. "Yes, that is what they call me, but you may call me Maggie. I have been eagerly awaiting your appearance ever since James told me you would be attending. It is truly a pleasure to meet a woman who could turn Fitzwilliam Darcy's head. And believe me, my dear, it has been tried. Even I had to give it up and settle for his cousin, but then a Lord is better than a country gentleman I suppose, even if the latter is richer than the former."

76

"I see," Sofia replied with amusement.

"But you are not to fear me. I am quite happy with my situation. I only wish you as much felicity in love as I have found. The Fitzwilliam men are truly good lovers in more ways than one. They are good men who esteem the women they love, and that, my dear, is definitely a plus in this life."

"Your Ladyship…*Maggie*, in as much as we have just become acquainted, I have to wonder at your purpose in sharing such intelligence with me. Quite frankly, we hardly know one another, and what you have shared is quite personal."

"My dear Sofia, you are so very young and still very innocent. There is no malcontent in my speaking with you. The truth is that I care very much for Mr. Darcy and his happiness. Therefore, I do not want to see him hurt, and my dear lady, you possess the ability to wound him deeply. It is out of character for Fitzwilliam Darcy to take a lover. He must, indeed, care for you, or you would not be here tonight. See to it that you guard his good opinion. Guard it like a jealous lover."

"Lady Margaret, I have to wonder, since you appear to take such prodigious interest in Mr. Darcy's welfare and you seem to know him in such intimate terms, have you shared his bed?"

Sofia had expected the regal lady of distinction to flinch at such an audacious question, but to her complete surprise, she only smiled and fanned herself.

"Miss Molina, a lady never tells." She paused and then added, "Excuse my interference; it was kindly meant. Enjoy your evening," she said as she moved on.

"Maggie!" Sofia called after her.

"Yes?" The lady faced her.

"I would not hurt him, not intentionally that is, but he may well break my heart."

Lady Margaret softly smiled. "That he might, as he surely broke mine."

The lady once more turned and walked away.

Sofia watched Lady Margaret with fascination as she greeted each and every guest, exchanging pleasantries. The lady would most certainly have fitted Caroline Bingley's definition of an accomplished woman. She had a certain air about her that clearly defined her as a lady of good breeding; so had she shared Fitzwilliam's bed? And why was she sharing the Viscount's now? Of course, she was a widow, and widows were allowed more sexual freedom in this sphere of society. However, Sofia was puzzled by her for she seemed quite free in her discussion of her most private matters. Could it be that all Elizabeth Bennet had been taught applied only to her station in life but not to the one above hers; or was it that a gentleman wanted a maiden for his wife and a more experienced woman as his lover? What type of society was this…this circle called the *ton*? They openly spoke one way while secretly living another.

"Señorita?"

"Sí." She turned to catch Mr. Darcy's smile.

"Here is your wassail." He paused, studying her carefully. "Are you unwell? You seem to be lost in the fog as if you are far away."

"I am well, Señor. I am simply sketching the character of those I see around me."

*…sketching the character of those around her…where have I heard that before…? Netherfield many years ago! If I did not know that Elizabeth was dead, I would think the woman before me was she. Can there be two Elizabeth's in this world, and if there are, could I ever let this one go as I did the former…?*

A sobering chill moved over him. Even though he could not have Elizabeth, he could have Sofia, but how was he to do it without the stain of her past casting a shadow over their lives? It was true. With his money and status, no one would dare show her anything but the utmost respect as his wife while in his presence, but would they accept her in their inner circles and extend invitations to their teas and garden parties without the coldness he knew women were well capable of demonstrating? That, he was unsure of.

"¿Señor…Señor, are *you* unwell? It is now you who looks to be in another world."

"I was lost in thought, swept away by an old memory." Darcy smiled. "Finish your wassail. When the music begins, I shall have the first two dances with you; then you are free to dance with whomever you wish, but I shall have the supper dance and the last. Enjoy yourself, but not too much. Remember, it is I who escorts you."

"Señor, jealousy does not become you, and there is no need for it. Whether you choose to believe it or not, I am an honest woman. No matter what my station in life may be, the quality of my character is *not* to be determined by my circumstances. Nor is it based on my station in life. I am a lady, Señor Darcy, and you would be wise to remember it."

She drained the contents of her glass and handed it back to him, leaving him speechless. No woman except Elizabeth Bennet had ever talked to him in such a manner. Sofia Molina was Elizabeth's equal, and both, as gentlemen's daughters, were his.

The music began and Darcy and Sofia danced. Her long hair swayed to her every move, making her the most beautiful woman in the room. Each of them was captivated by the other as if they were the only ones floating across the floor. Sofia could see the piercing eyes of those assembled watching them, but she cared not. She had her Mr. Darcy, and when he held her in his arms, all her many troubles seemed so far way.

When the second dance ended, he escorted her to the refreshments table, and then excused himself to join his cousins and the other gentlemen in a heated discussion over the recent debate in the House of Commons. Lord Matlock and Lord Heatherton were outraged by what they felt was an attack on the long-held prestige and traditions of the nobility by the Commons, and thus were in a heated argument with Lord Weatherstone, a man who supported what they opposed.

It seemed that certain members of the House of Commons were demanding free trade and an end to protective tariffs, passed to protect the interest of the lords and the gentry. It was this particular petition, which had all the lords and much of the gentry up in arms as they argued over the consequences of such an act.

Darcy was also concerned about the impact such legislation would have on Pemberley and his many tenants who depended on him for their living. But, no matter how heated the discussion became; Darcy's mind and thoughts were elsewhere.

His eyes were constantly watching as Sofia danced and laughed with those around her. It particularly irritated him that Ancaster and Castlebaum still vied for her attention, for he knew full well what their intentions were. If either one of them touched her, Darcy would call him out.

While watching Sofia, Darcy caught a glimpse of another man standing in the corner. The mysterious man in the black cape had kept to himself all evening, but now Darcy realized the man's stare was following every move Sofia made. Who was this mystery man, and what did he want?

"Darcy! Darcy! I say man, what is your opinion on the matter? You have yet to give it. Are you paying attention, or are you so love struck that you cannot divide your concentration between two subjects?"

"I am sorry, Your Lordship; what were you saying?"

The Earl of Matlock gave his nephew a disapproving glare. "I simply asked your opinion on this debacle in Parliament, this new initiative they wish to ram down our throats."

"Lord Matlock, I am afraid my opinion will not sit well with you. Although I am concerned for the impact it will have on our incomes should the Corn Laws be repealed—especially for the tenant farmers at Pemberley—you must also think of the poor. They barely make enough to feed their children. The abolition of the import tariffs would allow them to afford bread for their families. 'Tis true that we would suffer for it, but what are a few pence in our pockets when it will make such a difference to the poor who are starving? Gentlemen", he looked around at those staring at him, "it is our business to take care of those less fortunate than ourselves. If the price of foreign corn is cheap, then we must adjust our pricing to meet it or suffer the consequences. Free trade is a good thing. It stimulates the economy and allows for affordable prices to be had by all. There is money enough to be made elsewhere without placing all of our eggs in one basket. We must diversify."

"Poppycock! What has come over you these last few years? Where is the nephew I once knew so well?"

Darcy sighed and glanced away for a fleeting moment before answering, "He finally looked outside his circle and grew a heart. I do believe the Americans have it right: 'all men are created equal in the eyes of God', but unfortunately all men are not equal in the reality of life. Now, if you will excuse me, I've had enough talk of corn, business, and money for the evening. I must go and see to my partner."

Darcy turned to leave, but Lord Matlock blocked his way. "I have not missed how that *woman* has you eating out of the palm of her hand. *You*, nephew, are cunt whipped! It is disgraceful!"

Darcy straightened his shoulders and looked Lord Matlock dead in the eye. "Because you are my uncle, and out of respect for your station and my mother, I will ignore that remark, but do not ever let me hear those words spoken in my presence again, or—"

"Or what!"

"Or I will forget I ever knew you." Darcy turned and walked away, leaving those behind him astonished at his exchange with the illustrious Lord Matlock.

"Brilliant, Cousin! Bloody brilliant," Viscount Wexford whispered to himself. "Very well done!"

General Fitzwilliam smiled and shook his head. "Sometimes I rather envy you, Darce."

Lord Matlock turned to his sons with a scowl. "You had best remember what side your bread is buttered on!"

While Mr. Darcy spoke with several gentlemen, Sofia danced with nearly every other eligible man in the room. She hardly had time to catch her breath; so much in demand was she. The ballroom was rather warm and the air stifling. Fanning herself, she glanced towards the open door to the winter gardens. She thought a respite on the terrace might be the very thing she needed to renew her energy. Leaving her last partner, she moved towards the veranda in anticipation of the coolness of the evening. She was about to step outside for a breath of fresh air when His Grace, the Duke of Ancaster approached.

"Madam, I believe you have danced with every man here but me," he said with a smile that did not reach his eyes.

Sofia glanced up at him with trepidation. She knew what he had on his mind, and it made the pit of her stomach quiver in a most unpleasant way. She had been avoiding him all evening and, at this point, had thought she might escape such a cruel fate as to be his partner in a dance. However, he took her so much by surprise in his application for her hand, that, without realizing what she had done, she accepted him.

The dance was a waltz which left her even more distressed. The Duke danced a little too close for comfort's sake, and his eyes, caressing her form, made Sofia even more uncomfortable. All of this, and yet he said nothing as they glided over the dance floor. She began to imagine that their silence was to last throughout the entire dance. And then, to her horror, he spoke.

"Miss Molina, you know that I hold a strong attraction for you. I have since that night at the Courtesans' Ball. I tried in vain to buy your contract, but Mr. Darcy outbid me on the last draw. However, that does not dissuade me."

"What do you mean, Señor? I am sure I do not catch your meaning."

"No, I am sure you do not. Your innocence is one of your many charms, my lovely Señorita," he said. "Simply put, if you are ever in need of affections from a man of considerably more rank and distinction than Mr. Darcy, I am here for you. Also, when your trial duration is up, I will gladly take you under my protection for the sum of ten thousand pounds. You will be as successful as a highwayman with fifteen thousand pounds instead of ten. Think about it. Unlike Mr. Darcy, I will not keep you all to myself. You may work for others whilst with me, thus making even more money, and, besides giving you jewels and clothes, I shall take you to the theatre and dancing every night if you wish. And why not? You dance so well. You should not be kept tucked *away* as Darcy's sole treasure. A jewel as rare as you should be shared by many."

Sofia bristled at his insinuation, but kept her composure. "Your Grace, I hardly know what to say, except that I must decline your generous offer. It would be unfair to Mr. Darcy, and though you may think otherwise, I have *not* a faithless heart."

"Señorita, it is *you* who is mistaken about a great many things. You are young, and this is your first season. Therefore, let me educate you to the particulars of how things truly are in the demimonde. You see, you must understand, Miss Molina, women of your kind are never worthy of anything more than satisfying our baser needs—*fellatio* and all matters of exotic pleasures are what we expect. Mr. Darcy, especially, will not marry you. If that thought is in your pretty little head, you had best discard it now."

"And I think *you*, Your Grace, had best discard any thoughts of congenial...*exotic* encounters with *me*, for I have no intention of gratifying them," she said as she turned and walked from the dance floor leaving him standing there with a foolish smirk on his face.

Visibly shaken she crossed the room for a glass of wine. Suddenly she felt the sting of her situation, and she thought back to Ophelia's words. *...The life of a courtesan is a difficult one... the end is not pleasant if she has not made preparations. Many are left to die in poverty and sickness...*

"You need not worry, Ophelia," she murmured to herself. "I will never enter the demimonde again and would not have done so now except for want of survival."

"His Grace can be a bit of a brute," came the sound of a woman's voice.

Sofia turned and nearly spilled her wine. "Your Ladyship!"

"Maggie—my friends call me Maggie. I saw what he did and can only imagine what he said. My dear young Sofia, their Graces, the Dukes of Ancaster and Castlebaum, are notorious rakes. I would not have invited them had not James insisted. They move in Prinny's inner circle. Be glad neither of them is your protector. Have nothing to do with either, for it would not be in your best interest." Her ladyship paused and smiled.

"You may not realize it, Sofia, but you have the best situation of any courtesan in service. As I told you previously, Mr. Darcy has never taken a mistress, and he would not have taken one now if the attraction were not strong." She laughed softly. "If I am any judge of character, I would say he is half in love with you already. Take care, Sofia; do not be a simpleton."

"I thank you for your intelligence, but you need not worry for me. I have no intentions of ever speaking to either of them again. As for Mr. Darcy, that is a private matter. Now, if you will excuse me, Maggie, I must have some fresh air. I find it very difficult to breathe in this stifling room filled with such pretentiousness."

"As you wish," she lifted her wassail to her lips and watched Sofia leave for the terrace.

As she left, another individual, likewise, followed her every move. Lady Margaret scrutinized the mysterious man in black as he followed Sofia to the terrace.

"I wonder what he is about. He has been watching her all evening. I had better fetch James," she said to herself, twisting a strand of golden hair about her finger.

Darcy had seen Sofia dancing with the Duke of Ancaster and sensed her distress. He moved through the crowd of people, trying to reach her, but before he could make much progress, he was stopped by first one and then another congratulating him on his choice of mistress. He bowed and addressed them one by one, exchanging pleasantries for as long as societal rules demanded and then moved on in search of Sofia.

He glanced around the room in frustration. She was gone.

Suddenly he was accosted by another familiar voice.

"Are you looking for Miss Molina, Mr. Darcy?"

He turned and bowed. "Lady Margaret," he said. "Have you happened to have seen her? I seem to have lost her in the crowd."

Lady Margaret curtsied with a smile. "It has been a long time, Fitzwilliam. I see you are well and just as handsome as ever, if not a little more so than the last time we…well never mind."

"I am *quite* well, I thank you." He paused in frustration. "Lady Margaret, I must beg you to answer my question. Have you seen Miss Molina?"

"Oh, very well. I see you have quite gotten over me. She left for the terrace for a breath of fresh air. You might want to rescue her. That strange gentleman dressed in black followed her out. If you should ask me, I would say he does not look like a pleasant sort gentleman with that deathly mask that fits him like a second skin. I was about to fetch James when you came along."

"Lady Margaret, if you will excuse me," he said with a quick bow. "I shall go."

The man in black seemed familiar to Darcy and not in a good sort of way. He quickly moved through the crowd, pushing his way past the sea of people, his eye on the entrance to the terrace. As he approached, his blood ran cold. He drew his blade.

"Madam," a voice called out.

Sofia turned to see *Mr. Death* standing over her with a look of cold steel in his pale grey eyes, the look of a predator. She calmed herself and raised her chin.

"You have been watching me all evening. What is it you want?"

"I think you should know, madam."

"¿Señor? I have not the slightest idea."

"Do you not! Come now, Señorita. Surely you know me. But, if by chance you have forgotten, then let me remind you." He paused with an evil grin, his teeth gleaming in the dark. "I once knew a pretty little wench from Hertfordshire. She lived in the village of Longbourn with her parents and four sisters. She was a country beauty. She and her sisters were known as the jewels of the county. She liked to flirt and tease, a young girl with no proper training, but I found her to be a delight." He stopped short; his gaze bore into her with a frightening look. "Drop the pretense. I do not know where you learnt the Spanish, but I am not taken in by it—not in the least." He paused and moved closer, brushing his finger over the birthmark on her shoulder.

"Did you think I would not know you? I saw your portrait in the *House of Pleasure*. There is only *one* woman with a mark on her shoulder." He paused and gave a deep throated moan, "Yes...red and swollen as it is tonight. I remember another time when it looked as it does now. You were particularly good that night."

Sofia reached up and slapped his face. "Take your hands off of me!" Fire flashed from beneath the mask as she felt her blood boil. "If I could, I would kill you! You destroyed us and took everything we had. I hate you!"

The man grabbed her by the arm and twisted it behind her back leaning in dangerously close. "You little trollop!" he said through gritted teeth. "I always knew you would survive. You have spunk and spirit, but I never expected how it would be—a courtesan to the very rich." His gaze raked over her body. He licked his lips as his eyes rested on her full bosom, heaving in desperation. He slowly raised them to her face. "Yes, I can see you have prospered quite well in my absence, but you are *mine*. You have a gold mine between your legs, and I will not let you go. I want half of whatever Darcy is paying you, or I will tell him and all of London who the pretty little Señorita really is."

He pulled her to him in a painful grip, leering over her and was about to kiss her when suddenly he felt the tip of cold steel pressed uncomfortably to his throat.

"Let her go."

He turned with a sneer.

Darcy pressed. "You worthless excuse for a man. Nothing would please me more than to run you through. Now let her go, or I shall kill you right here and now."

Blood began to ooze and trickle down his neck, staining his cravat.

The man glared but did not release his grip on Sofia.

"I said let her go, or I will slit your throat like the filthy pig that you are."

The man stepped back and dropped his hands to his side.

Darcy slowly raised the tip of his blade to the edge of the man's mask and flicked the flimsy silk fabric. "Now, remove your mask."

The man glanced at the stone railing and then turned back and snarled through clenched teeth.

With a flick of his wrist, Darcy sliced a large X on the man's face, cutting deep into his skin and grazing his left eye.

Crying out in pain, the man fled over the railing out into the garden below, disappearing into the night.

Sofia collapsed into Darcy's arms, sobbing and trembling.

Dropping the bloody rapier, Darcy circled his arms around her in a protective embrace as she cried. Suddenly he was overcome with feelings he had not expected. If he lost her as he had Elizabeth, he would not survive it, especially if it was his fault. "Do not worry, mi amor…do not worry. I will protect you."

"Take me home," she cried between sobs, "Take me home." She clung to him, whimpering and crying, like a lost kitten rescued from a rainstorm.

"Shh…Mi linda Señorita," he said, cradling her in his arms. "We will leave shortly. I cannot take you to Richmond tonight, but I will send you there in the morning. I will join you when I can."

She glanced up. "No, not to Richmond. I want to go home to Ja—I mean, to our home—to Darcy House. I must stay in town. Please, Señor, I do not want to be parted from you. I could not bear to be alone." She cried against his chest, clutching the lapels of his coat in tight fists.

"Hush, my pretty Señorita, I will take you home…to *our* home. No one is going to hurt you. You have my word on it," he said, soothing her with gentle strokes to her back, running his fingers through her long hair. The thought of someone hurting Sofia tore at his heart. He would give his life to save hers. Whoever this man was, Darcy intended to hunt him down and kill him.

General Fitzwilliam and Viscount Wexford rushed out onto the terrace followed by Lady Margaret.

"What has happened out here, Darcy?" the viscount asked. "There is blood on the stone."

"The man in black attacked Miss Molina." He glanced between Lord Wexford and Lady Margaret. "The blood is his. I slashed him with my foil. Which of you invited him? I want to know who he is. I will kill him with my bare hands."

"It was not I," said Lady Margaret. She looked at the viscount. "Wex?"

"Neither did I. I assumed it was Maggie. "Who do you suppose he was? He was a rather hideous looking fellow, dressed as a specter of the night."

"I do not know," Darcy replied, "but I intend to find out. Have your servants search the grounds. Tell them what we are looking for but advise them to be discreet. I slashed his face through to the bone. He will be covered in blood. If we do not find him tonight, we will most assuredly will find him soon after. He is marked for life, and I will know him when next I see him." He glanced at the viscount. "Do the others know what has happened out here?"

"No, we were quite careful. Maggie immediately came for me after you left to follow Miss Molina. Whoever this man is, he had been stalking several ladies—Maggie among them, but most particularly Miss Molina," Viscount Wexford said.

Lady Margaret went to Sofia and put her arm around her shoulder. "I am so very sorry this has happened to you, Sofia. Is there something I could offer you for your present relief? A glass of wine perhaps—shall I get you one? You look very ill, my dear. Let me call the doctor."

Sofia nodded. "A glass of wine will do, but I do not need a doctor. If I could but sit for a moment, I shall be fine." She looked up at Darcy. "Do not take me home. We came to enjoy the ball, and so we shall. I will not let someone like that beast destroy my happiness, but I will dance only with you. For once, I have had quite enough of the activity."

"If you are certain that is your wish, then we will stay. I shall not leave your sight. But you must also tell me what Ancaster said to you. I saw him dancing with you. You looked distressed. It is what caused me to search for you."

"It was not important. Nothing really."

"It is important to *me*. I want to know, Señorita."

"Well, if you must know, then I will tell you. He offered to buy you out when our trial period comes to a close. I told him he had best discard that thought as I would not consider such a proposition. I have not a faithless heart. I belong to you, Señor. And with you I shall remain."

Darcy laughed and pulled her into an embrace. "Mi linda Señorita. How I do cherish you. Come, let us return to the ball."

She nodded and gave a faint smile. Once she had composed herself, Darcy escorted her back into the ballroom where they danced until the supper hour as if nothing untoward had occurred. Her spirits improved greatly, and she once again laughed and teased, her long hair swaying as she moved. Sofia had found the bean in the King Cake and was crowned queen for the evening. When the best costumes were announced, Darcy and Sofia had won those, as well. Sofia laughed and Darcy was sure her spirits were restored, but he could not remove the image from his mind of the trembling damsel in his arms.

Shortly after the last dance, they paid their respects to Lord Wexford and Lady Margaret, and then left for home. For the duration of the ride to Grovesnor Street, Sofia took comfort in Darcy's strong arms. The mysterious man had escaped leaving only a trail of blood in the garden, but not enough to track him down. For fear of what he might say had he been found, Sofia was relieved that he had not. The shock of seeing him again after all these years had been monstrous, but she drew comfort from one small thing: he did not know who she really was. However, fear of what he might do was now an ever increasing threat to her security. She would have to be more careful than ever. Perhaps the slash to his cheek would be enough to keep him away. Nevertheless, tomorrow she would speak with Ophelia. She would know what to do.

She glanced up at Mr. Darcy. In the heat of the moment, he had called her mi amor—his love. He had never spoken those words before. Could it be…was it possible?

Then she recalled the Duke's words with painful recollection. *"…Women of your kind are never worthy of anything more than satisfying our baser needs… Mr. Darcy, especially, will not marry you. If that thought is in your pretty little head, you had best discard it now."*

His Grace's words had taken her by surprise and had stung. Could he see what she wanted to hide, and did she even want Mr. Darcy to love her…marry her? No, she knew that could never be a possibility. This was not one of little William's fairytales. There was no fairy godmother who granted wishes. Therefore, why wish for things that could never come true? She knew when she put pen to paper and signed the contract that it could never be more than it was. Even if he did love Sofia Molina, would it be enough to forgive Elizabeth Bennet? She shook her head and swallowed back a sob.

However, her courage rose to meet her need, and she smiled and snuggled a little closer, determined to live and love for the time she had and to be content in what was hers for the moment, storing memories that would have to last a lifetime.

When they reached Darcy House, Darcy led her to her apartment and gave her a chaste kiss. "If you wish, I will sleep in my chamber tonight so that you might rest."

"No, it is not what I wish. I wish for you to hold me. I cannot bear to be alone. Te necesito. Please, Señor, I need you."

"If that is what you wish, then I shall stay," he said, pulling her into his arms.

Cradling her to his chest as he kissed her head, he stroked her long strands. "I cannot bear to see you unhappy. I will simply hold you throughout the night."

She nodded.

Secure in her warm bed, Sofia snuggled into her lover's arms and engaged his neck with her lips while her small hand roamed over his body. "Señor, I want you to make love to me. You are my knight in shining armor, and I need you tonight."

He turned and gazed at her with real affection. "And you are my lady. You need not fear, Señorita. I am here to slay your dragons. I will protect you," he said. "All will be well, mi amor…all *is* well," his voice trailed off as his hand slowly began to caress her body, his fingertips brushing over her skin with a feathery touch while his lips took hers in a deep kiss. By now, he knew her body well, what to stroke and where, and just how much pressure to apply.

Surrendering to his touch, her body writhed in raptures at the feel of his fingers on her skin. She cried out, calling his name, and he knew she was ready for him.

Parting her legs, he slowly slid between them, and they came together as one. He made love to her until she violently contracted around him. Knowing her pleasure was complete, he let go and felt his body tremble and shake, and then he released his seed, passing his life force into her where it would take root and flourish.

Collapsing on top of her, he gathered her into his arms and held her close. His emotions were overwhelmed, and the feeling in his heart was intense.

Sofia softly whispered against his lips, "Te quiero." *…I love you…* "Te deseo."

He responded in turn, "Te amo." *… I love you…*

She released a small sob, and murmured against his neck, "No matter what happens, Señor Darcy, always know that I love you. Remember me, and do not forget this night...*our* night."

*...I will always love you, Fitzwilliam...for the rest of my life I shall love you. But will you love me once you know the truth...?*

He turned and whispered in Spanish as he took her lips with a kiss, "Tú eres mi mundo...mi amor, mi vida," *...you are my world, my love, my life.* "I shall never forget you, my pretty little Señorita."

Darcy pulled her closer and rolled them over. Gathering her once more into his arms, he held her to his chest. *...forever is not long enough, mi querida...* he thought to himself as he began to make love to her all over again, repeating it until they were both utterly spent.

As Darcy held Sofia to his heart, his mind was in turmoil. He could no longer deny that he loved her, but was it for the right reasons? Was he in love with a memory, or did he love the woman in his arms? One thing he knew for certain. The thought of someone stalking her sent cold fear through his heart.

Ever steady and true to his purpose with his eye on the prize, Cupid let his arrow fly straight to our hero's heart where it found its mark, just as he had promised. But, what of our heroine? Hmm...we shall have to be patient, to wait and see, for she, our good and gentle reader, might prove to be a little more difficult of a nut to crack. Perhaps it is time to call upon Cupid's mother, the goddess of fertility...*Aphrodite* to the Greek and to the Roman—*Venus*.

# Chapter 13

$T$ is with a pleasant repartee that I come before you today, my good and gentle reader, for it seems my friend Cupid has done his duty to perfection. Therefore, dear reader, let us see how goes the game of love with our good hero as we find him deep in thought and quiet reflection.

Come, shall we?

Darcy stood at the window, gazing out across the gardens, watching the carriages and horses come and go up and down Grosvenor Street. Over a month had passed since the incident at Lord Wexford's ball with no further happenings from the masked man in black who had attacked Sofia. Darcy had had the streets and alleyways searched for a man with a large gash on his left cheek, but, as of yet, nothing had been discovered as to his identity or his whereabouts. It was as if the man had vanished into thin air. Nonetheless, he had insisted Sofia remove herself to Richmond, but she had refused, insisting the danger had passed when the man failed to materialize. And perhaps Sofia had been correct. After all, the event in and of itself was enough to scare away any man with good sense, although Darcy had a nagging feeling they would see him again. The question was where and when. Darcy sighed and shook his head.

January had given way to February and February was quickly moving into March with more urgent matters acutely in need of his utmost attention. He had put off his business in the North until it could no longer be ignored. He had received another express this morning, demanding his presence in Lancashire without further delay. The discontent in the mill village was rising and would soon be out of control if he did not intervene. Tomorrow he must leave. However, there was one poignant thing weighing heavily on his mind: Sofia.

The last few weeks had been like a dream: their walks in the park after a long day of work, ice skating in Vauxhall Gardens under the moonlight, evenings at the opera and another at the theatre. It had been a long time since he had known such contentment as she had given him. He breathed deeply. Just as it had been with Elizabeth, he was in the middle of it before he had even become conscious that it had begun. As he thought more about it, he realized that as it had been coming along since he had first seen her in December. He could not fix on the hour, or the spot, or the look, or the words, which laid the foundation. It had simply happened without him wanting or planning for it.

Moreover, as with Elizabeth, he had struggled in vain with what he knew was expected of him, and he knew that he could no longer deny what was so clearly before him. He loved her. He honestly loved her—loved her against his wishes, against his better judgment, and most certainly against his very will. And, although she had not spoken those words of love that he longed to hear fall from her lips since the night of the ball, he knew by their many nights of passionate lovemaking that he held her heart as she held his.

But then, as Darcy thought about it, neither had he spoken words of love since that night, and yet he knew he was deeply and passionately in love with her—very deeply, in fact. Yes, he nodded, a man who felt less might have confessed his feelings and showered her with declarations of undying love, but that was not Fitzwilliam Darcy's way. He was a man of deep convictions who kept a close check on his emotions. He was not one to allow them to cloud his judgment, and yet, in spite of all the battles in his mind—his heart—his very soul, establishing why he could not marry her, just as it was with Elizabeth Bennet, Sofia Molina had conquered them all in her own simple ways. He smiled and chuckled to himself as he breathed deeply and recalled their nights.

The touch of her small and delicate hand when she ran her fingers over his body, bringing him to the point of ecstasy and the way her body felt beneath his, were enough to cause him to push all doubts of her class status aside. It no longer mattered. She meant everything to him, and the thought of losing her was more than he could bear. Therefore, his mind was made up. He knew what he must do.

Just as he was about to quit the room and return to his office, a carriage pulled through the gate and came to a stop in front of the portico. A few moments later, two gentlemen exited. He heard his butler greet them at the door. Darcy turned slightly as his cousins, Viscount Wexford and General Fitzwilliam, entered the room and strolled over to where he stood.

The viscount took a post near him, his shoulder pressed against the window jamb while the general took his station by his side, staring out the window with his hands linked behind his back.

"This is an unexpected but pleasant visit. May I offer you something to drink: a glass of wine or perhaps a brandy?"

"That will not be necessary, Cousin," Viscount Wexford said. "We are here on business—family business."

"And what might that be?" Darcy asked.

"Your mistress," Viscount Wexford responded.

"And what of her?"

"That is what we are here to find out, Cousin. The talk at White's is that she has bewitched you."

"And what if she has? What is it to you?"

"So you think you are in love, do you? Lady Catherine and Father will not approve, and you know it," Richard Fitzwilliam answered.

"I care not one whit what they think." He turned and looked from one to the other. "Not since Elizabeth have I wanted a woman in the way I want Sofia. I love her…and I want her for my wife, to honor her as the Mistress of Pemberley—not merely my kept woman. I want her to bear my sons."

The viscount's jaw dropped. "Darcy! You cannot mean it!"

"I can and I do!"

"But you do not even know her. Exactly who is she?" General Fitzwilliam interjected. "You don't even know what she looks like. She may be beautiful from the neck down. There is no denying that. But what of her face? You have never even seen her face…her eyes. What if she has a wart on her nose, or a lazy eye? Darcy you cannot do this!"

Darcy laughed. "She has no wart, and even if she had, I wouldn't care." Darcy paused and pressed his point. "I love her, Fitzwilliam. I honestly love her."

"Yes…" the viscount said, "I believe you do. But you cannot marry her. You may keep her as a mistress, but not as a wife. Think about what you are doing! What about your children? You must think of them and your heritage. They must be born from a woman of good breeding—one who can bring wealth and status into the union."

Darcy glared in righteous indignation then turned his gaze to the window as if in deep thought. The stillness in the room was stifling.

Finally, in a soft contrite tone, he broke the silence. "You disappoint me, Wex. I thought we were in agreement on the subject of progressive ideology. It appears that we are not."

"Darcy!" the viscount replied in astonishment, "Championing the cause of the poor and underprivileged is one thing, but to marry from the ranks of the demimonde—that is quite another."

"Yes," Darcy nodded as he gave his cousin a look of disbelief. "Quite interesting that you would say such a thing, Wex, considering your own actions. Therefore, let me present it to you in a somewhat different light."

He paused and then addressed his cousin in a clipped tone. "Why is it that *you* can marry Lady Margaret, and I cannot marry Sofia? Have you not kept *her* as your mistress for years? Clandestine meetings in Scotland, cottages by the sea in Brighton where you lay *naked* in the sun, openly copulating by the seashore? How many times, Wex, have you bragged about your many conquests with her and others? And yet you intend to marry Maggie."

"That is not the same. Lady Margaret is Lord Blankenship's daughter and Baron Warmouth's widow. She is a member of the nobility."

"And yet all three of us have slept with her."

"It is different."

"How is it different?"

"Lady Margaret is *not* a courtesan. That is how it is different. She is a lady of distinction and part of our sphere. Can you not see that?"

"No, I do not see it at all. Lady Margaret, congenial as she is, is a young widow with whom you have been having an affair for years, and Richard and I before you while Sofia has only had one lover, *me,* the man who wishes to marry her. Therefore, I fail to see the difference in what you do and what I do. Quite the contrary, in fact."

"Darce, you cannot be serious. Lady Margaret is a respectable woman. She—"

"Wex is correct, Cousin," the general interjected. "It simply isn't done. A member of our station must think about—"

"Think about *what*, Fitzwilliam? The state of affairs as they currently exist? Damn the status quo!" He narrowed his eyes. "I know where the lines of respectability are and what they entail, and I am quite sick of it—sick of it all. We of the noble class, with our rigid rules and elegant manners that apply to some but not to all. The strict regulation of propriety that must be obeyed in the public eye while one does as he pleases behind closed doors. Yes, I know about it all! I have understood it from the time I was a young boy in loose fitted shirts buttoned to high-waisted ankle-length trousers."

He stopped short and glanced between his cousins. "The absurdity of it all. We live in a society where rules apply to one but not the other, a society *rich* in contradictions, *rich* in irony, *rich* in contrasts, and particularly *rich* in its hypocrisy[1]. Should all these *things* we do in secret suddenly become center stage in the public forum, the scandal would rock this kingdom to its very foundations. Everyone knows the behavior of the Royal family and yet nothing is said. The Duke of Devonshire paraded his mistress alongside his wife in front of all of London for years, and yet no one said a word. Lord Berwick marries one of the *Four Graces*, and still no one cares. Why do you think they will care about *me*?!"

"Because *she* is not one of *them*. That is why. One must come from prime stock with good breeding, the right station in life—"

"And Sofia will have it as my wife. I have enough money and enough of the right connections and social status for us both. No one would *dare* not to accept her as my wife."

"But, Darcy," the general interrupted once more, "you do not even know where she goes during the day whilst you work with Mr. Steadman and Mr. Mann. You have told me so yourself that every day whilst you are dealing with matters of business, she leaves for either errands she insists she must attend to, or to visit an old friend. Who does she *really* see while she is out, Darcy? Do you even know?"

Darcy sighed and drug his hand over his face. He knew his cousin was right. No matter how he tried to suppress it, the question was ever present in the back of his mind. He wanted to trust her, but doubts lingered. Who was she seeing?

And then there was the nagging question of the money he set aside for her use each month. He gave her a very generous allotment, and every month she had spent it all with nothing to show for the expense. Where was she going and, more specifically, where was the money going? Finally, there was Richmond. Why had she resisted returning there when he insisted upon it? He did not know the answers to any of these questions. However, he was unwilling to believe what he knew his cousins were insinuating. He glanced between them.

"I know what you are implying, but you are wrong. She would not see another man, Fitzwilliam, and I am insulted that you would even suggest it. *I* am in love with her, and on the twenty-fourth of March, I intend to ask her to become my wife. It is the day when our contractual duration comes to an end. Then I will know all there is to know. Until that day, I will trust her."

---

[1] **A Good Man is Hard to Find**. By Flannery O'Connor. New Jersey: Rutgers UP, 1993. 3-24.

General Fitzwilliam rolled his eyes and shook his head. "Darcy does it not bother you that many men have been with her before you—that she is... a *whore*."

Fire flashed in Darcy's eyes. "You had best mind your tongue, Fitzwilliam, or I shall have to rip it out! But, since you have brought it up, there is one thing I want to make perfectly clear right here and now to the both of you. Sofia is no *whore*. She came to me untouched by any man."

"What are you saying, Darce?" General Fitzwilliam asked.

"I would think that is obvious," he said. "Sofia came to me as an innocent maiden with her maidenhead intact. I am the one who took it."

General Fitzwilliam's eyes widened.

"A virgin?" the viscount asked in astonishment. "Are you quite sure?"

"Oh, yes," Darcy laughed in amazement, "I am quite sure. I would think that something of *that* significance, I would know," he said. "Sofia was a virgin, untouched by any man. I was the first man to ever kiss her, let alone lie with her. She is the daughter of a gentleman. In that sense, we are equal."

"But where did she come from? Who was her mother?" the viscount asked with a raised brow. "You may be of the same sphere, but on opposite ends—especially as things stand now."

Darcy shook his head. "That does not trouble to me. She is my equal in every way that matters. I am in love with her, Wex, and I will not be dissuaded from it. I want to protect her from the harsh life that would crush her for want of a husband," he said. "Sofia is different from the rest, brought up in the ways of a well-accomplished young lady, a gentleman's daughter who was forced into this life by the need to survive. She did as many do in our society whose fathers die and leave them penniless. Our brothels are filled with the likes of such women where men such as ourselves take advantage of their situations."

"That is indeed a misfortune, an unlucky happenstance, but...well," Viscount Wexford threw up his hands in recognition of a battle lost. "I had best be silent as I can see your mind is made up."

"It is."

"Then there is nothing more to say," General Fitzwilliam added. "When will you be leaving for the North?"

"My plan is to leave on the morrow. Why do you ask?"

"No particular reason," the general responded. "We will see ourselves out."

The viscount dropped back as his brother quit the room. He clapped his cousin on the shoulder. "If you follow your heart, you risk censure from society. Father will not be pleased and Lady Catherine will be even more opposed, as you well know. Darcy, I love you like a brother. Therefore, I would be disingenuous if I didn't warn you of the consequences. You had better be damned sure this is what you want before you commit to this course of action. But, if you do as you presently intend, I will abide by your decision, and you may be assured, as the Viscount of Wexford and heir to the Earldom of Matlock, I will stand by you. No one will show you less than the respect due to you as my cousin, or they will answer to me."

"Your warning is duly noted and your acceptance appreciated."

Viscount Wexford nodded his solidarity and then left to follow his brother.

Darcy stayed back and nervously twisted his signet ring as he replayed the conversation with his cousins in his head. He was sure of what he wanted, but, although he knew she held a strong attraction for him, he was not entirely sure of Sofia's wishes.

As they were leaving, the general turned to his brother. "I do not trust her, Wex. For Darcy's sake, I am going to have her followed whilst Darcy tends his daily business. We will discover her true identity, with whom she spends her time and her activities during the time she is gone. She may have been a virgin when she came to him, but I do not believe she is innocent. I will have proof of her unfaithfulness in my hands before his return from the North. Darcy is being betrayed by a woman of dubious character, and he is too love-struck to see it. Marry his mistress indeed!"

"Her pleasing figure and alluring looks have become his bane, but if it be the case that she is *not* faithless and he indeed marries her, I have given him my solemn assurance that I will stand by them, and you had best do the same, Brother."

"I insist upon discovering the truth one way or the other, and if she is not unfaithful, then Darcy will have my support as well. Change is upon us, I suppose, and you are correct, it is best not to resist. But as for Father and Lady Catherine, they will not be so amendable."

"Agreed."

As they stepped out onto the portico, a carriage bearing the Darcy seal pulled into the drive. A frantic Oriental woman exited the coach. The driver, slumping in his seat and bleeding from a wound to his chest, was obviously hurt. The two men rushed to his aid.

# Chapter 14

y dear good and faithful reader, it is with an unsettled and disquieted heart that I bring you this next installment in the love affair of one Mr. Fitzwilliam Darcy and his dear lady, Miss Sofia Molina, also known as Miss Elizabeth Bennet. Our scene opens with our heroine returning from an exhausting day of nurturing those who are dear to her, and for whom she has sacrificed everything to provide for their necessities and comfort. However, dear reader, if she thinks her day has been disconcerting, what will she think of her evening?

Let us find out, shall we?

Elizabeth and Ling-Ling carefully moved through the passageways of the Old City until they reached the alley behind a row of townhouses that led to Ophelia's house. There had been no further incidents since Lord Wexford's ball, and the fear she had felt immediately after had all but disappeared.

Slipping into the kitchen through the back door, they were greeted by the cook. "Aye, Miss, bless my soul! You and the little missy are back again. Miss Ophelia is waiting in the drawing room. Let Sally get your wraps, and I'll fix a spot of tea to warm your bones."

"That would be lovely, Mrs. Gilmore," Elizabeth said, loosening her bonnet and then slipping her gloves from her hands. "I think tea with maybe some biscuits would be wonderful. Ling-Ling will take my cloak and gloves. We need not trouble Sally."

"Aye, Miss, I forget how independent you are. We'll have tea 'fore long, Miss." The older woman turned to the young scullery maid and raised her hackles. "Pollyanna, listen up girl! What are you standing there like a wooden stick stuck in the mud with no mind? Did you not hear th' missis? Set the kettle to boil!"

Elizabeth chuckled to herself as she left through the kitchen door in search of her friend. Moving towards the drawing room, she removed her bonnet and cape, handing them to Ling-Ling. Mrs. Gilmore was a jolly old woman who gave the appearance of being much more arduous than she really was, and poor Pollyanna; she always jumped at the older woman's command. But truth be told, Mrs. Gilmore was quite fond of the young lass.

"Ling-Ling, take my things and wait for me in the servants' quarters with Sally. When I am ready to return to Darcy House, I will call for you. But first I wish to spend time with Miss Ophelia."

"Ling-Ling do as Miss Sofie say. She wait with Sally. Have tea, talk. Sally need lotion for Miss Ophelia. Ling-Ling teach her make cream."

Elizabeth glanced at her maid with a smile as they parted ways.

"Ophelia," Elizabeth said as she entered her friend's sitting room and fell into a chair. "I am exhausted. Mamma is very ill, and it is becoming more difficult for me to make excuses to come out each day. Although we have seen nothing of Mr. Wickham since Lord Wexford's Twelfth Night Ball, Mr. Darcy still contends that I must leave for Richmond where he thinks I will be safer than I am here. He believes the man, as he refers to him, will make himself known once more and insists it is best that I leave London and wait for him until he can join me, but I cannot leave with Mamma like this. What shall I do?"

"Lizzy, you know very well what I think; tell him the truth about everything. Tell him that the man who singled you out at the ball was Mr. Wickham, and tell him about your mother. Mr. Darcy is an understanding gentleman. He may surprise you. I dare say you might find him very sympathetic. Do not be a simpleton. Confide in him, Lizzy."

Elizabeth glanced away. "No, Ophelia, I cannot. I cannot tell him about Mamma or Mr. Wickham. And, furthermore, it has been over a month. If Mr. Wickham was going to approach me again, he would have done so by now, do you not think? I believe his encounter with Mr. Darcy has been his undoing. Surely he will not dare to approach me again."

"No, Lizzy I do not think so at all. He believes you to be Lydia, and he desires to manage you as a common whore similar to the way Robert Baddeley did with his wife, Sophia, one of the most infamous and sought after courtesans of her time, prostituting her out and keeping her money until she had finally had enough of it. If you do not inform Mr. Darcy of Mr. Wickham and his attempted blackmail, then it is my opinion that you are making a mistake. Mr. Wickham is still a threat. It is only a matter of time until he appears again. And Lizzy, I can never say it too much. Mr. Darcy is a good man. You can trust him."

"Perhaps...but, you must understand. I have no choice but to keep such intelligence to myself, for I must save some shred of what is left of my self-respect. Should Mr. Darcy know with whom he has been—no I cannot! I would be mortified to face him with such a revelation." She paused and shook her head. "It makes no difference anyway," she said in a near whisper. "It will be over soon, and I will be gone to Ireland. Everything is tentatively arranged. The tickets are purchased, and I am to meet Mrs. O'Brady around the first of April."

"What do you mean?"

"Simply this," she said. "I fear the end is near for Mamma. She now requires day and night assistance, and poor Jane and Kitty are beside themselves with concern for her comfort. And, as my good fortune would have it, an express came early this morning. Mr. Darcy will be in the North for an extended period. Therefore, I shall come to Newgate and remain there until it is over. Then I will abide by his wishes and remove myself to Richmond until he returns. That is what I must do and nothing less. I know how fond you have become of Mr. Darcy with all my accolades of praise for his generosity, but please, let us not speak any longer of Mr. Darcy or

Mr. Darcy or my relationship with either of them. It is Mamma with whom I must concern myself first and foremost. I am putting Mr. Wickham and his threats out of my mind!"

Ophelia sighed. "As you wish, Lizzy. You are well aware of my feelings on the subject. I shall not reiterate them. However, I am half sorry I arranged for you to go to Ireland in the first place. It is my feeling that you belong here with Mr. Darcy, but no matter." She then reached for her friend's hand. "We will not speak of Ireland, Mr. Darcy, or Mr. Wickham again, but on one thing I must make myself clear. I shall not allow you, Jane, and Kitty to go through this alone. I am coming with you to Newgate. We shall see this through together."

"Ophelia, I do appreciate your generosity, but I cannot allow you to burden yourself with my troubles. It is bad enough that you worry about my safety, and now this, too. 'Tis too much."

"Nonsense! I will not hear of it. Tomorrow when you leave for Cheapside, I am going with you and that is that. Not another word from you! Now," she said, "let us have our tea and you can tell me the particulars whilst you rest."

Ophelia called for Phoebe, the tea was poured, and the two friends settled in for a long talk. When they neared the end of their discussion, Ophelia raised her hand to her mouth.

"Oh Lizzy, it nearly slipped my mind. There is one thing of great importance which I must tell you before you go."

"What?" Elizabeth wrinkled her brow as she set her teacup down.

"Pandora called round today. She had something of an alarming nature to disclose. It seems that Mr. Collins comes once a week to the *House of Pleasure*, and each time he is there, he stands and stares at your portrait."

"Mr. Collins at the *House of Pleasure*? Are you quite certain? He is a clergyman!"

"Regardless of his calling, he has been in Madame Papillia's establishment. Pandora is quite sure it was he. She described him perfectly. Furthermore, she overheard him speaking with one of the other girls. He was asking peculiar questions."

"What sort of question?"

"He said that the woman in the painting garners his attention, that he feels a connection to her and was wondering how much she would cost if he should desire an afternoon with her."

Elizabeth's eyes widened. "No, never! Even if I were not taken, I would rather starve in the hedgerows than spend an evening with him. What else did Pandora have to say?"

"Only that he was disappointed to learn you had a protector."

Elizabeth reached for the teapot and poured herself another cup of tea. "All the more reason that Sofia Molina's identity must never be known. Should that odious little man gain such knowledge, it would be my undoing."

"He will not discover such intelligence, Lizzy. Only I, Madame Papillia, and you know the truth. I will never tell, and neither will Madame Papillia. However, you must be extremely careful when you go to Longbourn to lay your mother to rest. I shall not go with you there, lest he become wise to your situation."

"Yes, he will most certainly be there, and I agree. I must be circumspect. I have come too far to allow such a man as Mr. Collins to destroy everything I have sacrificed to obtain. But I shan't think of such things now. I have more important matters to attend to," she said lifting her cup to her lips.

Glancing at the mantle clock, Elizabeth drank the last of her tea and replaced the cup in its saucer. "The hour approaches a quarter of four. I must excuse myself and once again become Sofia Molina."

She rose and left for the dressing room with disturbing thoughts of the good parson resounding in her head.

While the carriage rolled along the uneven streets of London heading for Mayfair, Sofia leaned back against the soft cushions to rest from her wearying day. She glanced at her maid. The poor girl had worked feverishly to relieve the suffering of Mrs. Bennet, giving her teas and applying warm compresses to her chest. Sofia knew if she lived to be a hundred, she would never know another like Ling-Ling. The little maid was now resting, her eyes closed in sleep. Sofia took a deep breath and smiled.

Closing her eyes, she let her mind wander until it finally drifted to the last thing she and Ophelia had discussed. Mr. Collins. That disgraceful man! How could he! How could he find pleasure in the arms of another woman, particularly one from the *House of Pleasure*, and he a man of the Church? It was one thing if a man was single; quite another if he was married—especially if that man was a parson. Poor Charlotte! How her life must be melancholy to be left to such affliction—to be leg-shackled to such a loathsome man! The stupidest man in all of England! But, as Sofia contemplated it further she had to acknowledge that Charlotte had chosen it with her eyes wide open, and even though she did not seem to ask for compassion, Sofia knew how her life must be.

Reflecting back on their many conversations whilst at Kent, she recalled how Charlotte had expressed the means in which a whole day would pass where she and Mr. Collins would spend less than a few minutes in one another's company. Back then she bore her solitude cheerfully—quite content in her situation. Charlotte was never romantic, only asking for a comfortable home. But was she truly happy? No, Sofia surmised. She could not possibly be. Surely by now, her home and her housekeeping, her children and her poultry, and all their dependent concerns, must have indubitably lost their charms for things to have become as they appeared to be.

Sofia sighed and nodded in gentle recognition of another truth. The unfortunate choices made when one was young and naive of the ways of the world had a way of haunting a person for the rest of their lives. As she considered that thought, her mind shifted to Mr. Darcy. She could no longer deny that she loved him dearly and would give anything if she could go back in time to when they had first become acquainted. Oh, how had she been such a wretched fool as to have let her pride and prejudices cloud her judgment! That she could have been so blind to believe lies and reject the truth, thus allowing a delusion to control her thoughts and actions! If she could but go back...back to Netherfield, back to Kent, she would observe more clearly and choose more wisely. True, his declaration of love had been executed in the worst possible manner, but it had been sincere, and his portrayal of her family accurate. She softly moaned and tossed in her restlessness. Soon she would return to Longbourn for the last time. And that presented another thought.

Although she would miss him exceedingly, she was grateful that Mr. Darcy would be leaving on the morrow for the North. He was to be gone three weeks, maybe more. That would give her the time needed to bury her mother and return to Richmond without his being the wiser. Then she would concentrate more fully on him and what she must do come the twenty-fourth of March. Could she really leave him? Her plans were set, but what she had once dreamed of having had now become her heartache.

Suddenly Sofia was jarred out of her sleep. The coach was weaving and the horses spooked. She glanced at Ling-Ling who was now fully awake.

"What wrong, Miss Sofie? I hear man fight."

Before Sofia could answer, a man forced the coach door open and jerked her out. She wanted to scream, but she was frozen in fear and her voice would not obey her command.

"Come with me, my pretty Señorita," came a familiar voice from a masked man.

Ling-Ling screamed, bringing Sofia to her senses, but the man covered her mouth before a single word could be uttered.

Ling-Ling lunged as if to strike, but the man put his knife to her mistress's throat.

"You care for her do you," he licked his lips, "you little slant-eye. Well, if you love her you will not interfere. One move from you, and this knife might slip. You would not want her blood on your hands now would you?"

Ling-Ling blinked.

"Leave us or I will kill her!"

Ling-Ling could only watch as the man slipped into the alleyway.

The coach rolled into the drive of Darcy House and came to a stop in front of the portico. Ling-Ling flew from the carriage past two men coming to their aid.

"Mr. Darcy, Mr. Darcy, you come quick-quick. Bad man, he take mistress. He hurt her. Hurt Mr. Anslee. You must come," Ling-Ling cried as she pushed past the two gentlemen in search of her master.

"What the devil?!" cried the viscount.

"I think it would be ill advised not to investigate. It sounds as if Miss Molina is in trouble. Let us first see to the driver. He appears to be hurt," the general said.

Darcy had heard the commotion and had already appeared in the vestibule when Ling-Ling ran to him crying hysterically.

"He take her! He take her! You come. We find her. Bad man. He wear bandana."

Darcy grabbed Ling-Ling's frantic arms and looked directly into her frightened eyes. "Take a breath and calm yourself. Tell me exactly what has happened."

Ling-Ling nodded, her tears spilling down her cheeks. "Bad man, he hurt Mr. Anslee. He bleed much, but he get me home. He say get you. You come. Bad man take Mistress into alley. Me 'fraid he hurt her. Hurt her bad. He have *big* knife and cut Mr. Anslee. You come. Come now!"

Darcy dropped the maid's arms and ran out to the portico.

"Wex, what the devil is going on? Where is Sofia?"

"Your driver has been stabbed," said the general while helping the man from the driver's seat of the coach, "but he will live. He says a highwayman wearing a cloth tied around his head stopped the horses, frightening them badly. Your man tried to struggle against the robber who was attempting to take control of the carriage. But, when he saw it was futile, the masked man stabbed your driver. Even so your man would not let him have the coach. Apparently, the masked man has abducted Miss Molina."

Mr. Darcy grabbed hold of the driver and helped the general move him up the steps and into the house where they laid him on a divan in the front parlor.

"Fitzwilliam, dispatch a servant for the doctor. This wound is deep and needs attention. Then have my horse saddled. We have to find them before they leave the city."

"That I will!"

As the general left, Mr Darcy, turned to his coachman. "Mr. Anslee, can you tell me exactly where you were, and, if you can, where the man took Miss Molina?"

"Yes, sir." He nodded. "We were almost home. At the corner of Brook Street and Davies. I was weak and unable to respond, but I saw him take Miss Molina, though she was kicking and struggling. I had hoped passersby would stop and help, but there were none at that time on the road. The man has a limp, and he appeared to be wounded himself. Also, there was a large and ugly gash that I could see across his left eye. It is a recent wound from the looks of it."

Darcy glanced at the viscount. "The man from the ball."

"Indeed."

"Where did he take her?" Darcy asked, returning his attention to his coachman. "Mr. Anslee, if you please, were you able to get the direction of their escape?"

"Yes," the man answered. "He took her into the alley behind the large red brick house on Davies Street. Do you know the one, sir?"

"Yes, yes I do. It is the John Read Townhouse." Darcy looked up to his cousin who had just returned. "Is my horse ready?"

"I have your black stallion and two geldings. You are not going alone. The man is armed and dangerous. He could kill her or you, should you find them."

"Then let us be gone." He turned back to Mr. Anslee. "The doctor is coming. You are going to be well my good man. I will see you when I am back."

Darcy stood and turned to leave, but before he could, his servant called out.

"Mr. Darcy, sir."

"Yes?"

"I am sorry, sir."

"It is not your fault."

Darcy turned, and he and his cousins were off.

Sofia struggled against the man's iron grip on her mouth and waist, kicking and beating him with her fists, until finally she bit his hand as hard as she could, drawing blood.

He cried out in pain and slammed her body against the brick wall in the lane.

"You little wench! I will make you sorrier than you can imagine. It is because of you that I am scarred for life," he said as he removed his bandana and stuck his knife to her throat. "If you say one word, I will kill you right here and now, and I will surely kill Darcy for what he has done to me. Do you understand me, Lydia?"

Sofia nodded. He still did not know who she was, and for that, she felt some relief. But how much longer would it be until he discovered the truth, that she was not Lydia, and was, in fact, Elizabeth? Forcing herself to calm her fears, she took a deep breath and blinked.

"Señor, que espera de mi, what do you want of me?"

He slapped her. "I told you not to speak Spanish to me. Speak French if you must speak anything!"

Sofia swallowed back her fear and attempted her dead sister's voice as best she could. "La, Wickham! So it is you, my dearest love. What a good joke it is! Me! The youngest of them all has done something my sisters would not. La! They would never think of such a thing! But Wickham, you know very well I cannot speak a word of French. Papa taught us all Spanish. It is part of my disguise. Do you not think it rather clever, my love? You would not want people in society to know who I really am, would you?"

Mr. Wickham smiled and relaxed a little. "You little wench. I am duly impressed. Here I thought you had not one smattering of a brain in that pretty little head of yours, and you surprised me. Had we thought of this clever scheme years ago, I would not have had to leave you, my darling. But I have returned to you, and together we shall work all the nobility and gentlemen of distinction to our advantage. We shall make our fortune, and then we may retire to the life I so richly deserve—the one Mr. Darcy stole from me. You must give my compliments to your father for his good sense in instructing you so well." He laughed.

Sofia burned with righteous indignation. She wanted to slap him, spit in his face, knee him to the groin—anything to show her hatred. Compliments to her father indeed! But instead, she would play her part, hoping Mr. Darcy would come in search of her.

"You have always known I love you, and now that we are together, we will be a team. How much did Mr. Darcy settle on you? I have heard it was ten thousand."

Ignoring him, she responded, "My darling Wickham, if you loved me so, why did you abandon me to poverty? Surely you knew I could not return to Longbourn, that I would have to use whatever means I had to survive?"

"Debts, love, terrible debts. But now I am free of them. No one in London knows I am here, but you."

"La, Wickham I always knew you would make your fortune. How did you accomplish such a feat as to dispatch all those worrisome debtors? I worried so for your safety."

"How very kind of you, my love," he said, relaxing enough to ease his grip. "I managed to make my way north and find someone convenient to help me in my time of need. I eloped with Mary King, and made my fortune in that manner. Ten thousand pounds! Unfortunately, she was of a sickly nature and died soon after our wedding, but you are not to concern yourself with that small detail. I have always considered you to be my wife no matter what the circumstances. But, we must not talk of this here. How much money is Mr. Darcy giving you? Half of it is to be mine."

"Yours? Whatever for? It seems to me that it is I who must work for it."

"Because, my dear wife, if you do not give me my share, I will slit your slender little lily white throat or perhaps you will have an accident. You had best do as I say. We are to be partners, or we are to be nothing."

"Is that how Mary King died…an accident, pray tell?"

He laughed again. "She, in a weakened condition from her many ailments, took a tumble down the stairs and broke her delicate little neck. I was not home when it happened, therefore who is to say for sure what caused her to fall? Now, if you do not want to join Mary, you will make a bank withdrawal and pay me my share. Then, when you are through with Darcy, you are to come to me. I shall keep a very close watch to see that you do. I am going to release you at present. You are to say you fought off your attacker and freed yourself. On the morrow, you are to meet me in Hyde Park for further instructions, but first, you are to satisfy my longings. I, too, want to partake of your many charms—and mix my seed with Darcy's. He deserves no less for what he has done to me."

Cold fear gripped Sofia's heart as Mr. Wickham lifted her dress. She closed her eyes and bit her lower lip. Tears fell as his hands roamed her body at will.

"Wickham!" came a deep throated cry. "Unhand her at once, or I will run you through."

"Señor Darcy!"

"Sofia!"

Wickham turned with a sneer. "Do you care for her? If you do, then you had best leave us, or I will cut her throat," he said, pulling Sofia roughly in front of him and putting the blade to her neck once more. "That would avenge me for what you have done to me."

"What have I done to you, George? Loved you like a brother? Covered your gaming debts, looked after you whilst we were in school, and found homes for your many illegitimate children? I was your boyhood friend. We played and fished in the lake as brothers would."

Mr. Wickham clenched his teeth. "I loathe you. I have lived in your shadow since we were boys. While you had a silver spoon in your mouth, born the first son to the Master—heir to Pemberley, I had to take second best as the steward's son. Not only did you take my living, but you also stole Georgiana from me, and now you have scarred me for life. I believe you care for this little wench. It would be so easy to kill her. Just a little slip of the knife and it will be over. It is up to you, Darcy."

Darcy dropped back in fear, but the expression on his face was inscrutable.

"George, let her go. I will give you whatever you wish, but you must release her. This is between you and I. She has nothing to do with it."

"Oh, but she has everything to do with it," Wickham said with scorn. "If you want her to live, drop your foil, or I will take something from you as you have taken from me."

Darcy did as Wickham said, but his eyes were locked on Wickham's.

Wickham slowly released his hold on Sofia, and when she noticed he was distracted, she shoved him with all her strength and made haste; however, before she had gotten very far, he lunged at her, ripping her dress.

Darcy, taking advantage of the distraction, moved with lightning speed and leapt at him, knocking them both to the ground.

Sofia screamed as she saw them fighting over the knife, struggling for control, rolling over and over, the blade between them.

General Fitzwilliam stepped forward and placed a protective arm around her while the viscount stood by.

"Brother, what are we to do?" the viscount asked, holding the horses while he watched the struggle on the ground.

"There is nothing we can do." The general drew his pistol and had it poised to fire. "If we intervene, Wickham will kill him or quite possibly one of us, and if I fire, I may kill Darcy. We cannot take such a chance. However, should an opportunity avail itself to us, I will kill him myself."

"And if he kills Darcy?"

"Then I most assuredly *will* kill him."

Sofia held her fist to her mouth and cried. She privately whispered a prayer beseeching heaven to spare Mr. Darcy.

Rolling and tossing, the men struggled for the knife. Wickham had it poised at Darcy's heart with Darcy struggling for control of the handle grip, and then they collapsed on one another and both grew still. Sofia released a blood curdling scream. Finally Darcy rolled away to show a blood-soaked Wickham with a knife buried in his chest.

Viscount Wexford moved to help his cousin to his feet.

As Darcy stood over him, Wickham blinked and stared at the victor. "Darcy...you do not know."

"Know what, George?"

Mr. Wickham looked at Sofia. "The truth...I thought you preferred the other one..." An inaudible gurgle escaped his throat, fading into nothingness as the life force ebbed from his body.

Darcy moved to where Sofia and the general stood. "Come," he said, reaching for her.

She pulled out of the general's hold and flew into his arms, crying without restraint.

"Shh...'tis well. He will never hurt anyone again, and especially not you." Darcy glanced at the viscount. "Wickham sought to have his revenge on me once and for all by taking something I value and destroying it as he attempted to do with Georgiana."

"Take her home, Darce. I shall take the garbage out. The War Office at Whitehall wants him for desertion. I shall bring him in and tell the authorities he was killed in a street fight, which is the truth. The details need not be disclosed."

"I am in your debt. It is finally over between us." Darcy turned and soothed Sofia until she was calm enough to walk.

After several minutes of silence between them, Darcy finally spoke. "I am delaying my trip by one day. I want you removed to Richmond at once. I will hear no more opposition from you. Do I make myself clear?"

"No, Señor, please do not send me to Richmond," she pleaded in desperation. "I must remain in the city a few days more, and then I will go to Richmond and await your return. Please Señor, do not send me there!"

"Sofia!" Darcy replied in growing agitation. "You in your stubbornness have thwarted my every effort to see to your safety. First you refuse to have my man accompany you on your outings, and then you insist on remaining in town against my expressed wishes. I have been very patient with you—allowed you your way against my better judgment and instincts—that is, until now." He paused and glanced down at her. Her head was downcast. "Señorita," he said softly, "I fail to see why you must remain in town. You were supposed to return to Richmond weeks ago. But you refused. Sofia, had you done as I desired this calamity would not have occurred.

101

You would have been safe, my coachman unharmed, and George Wickham might still be alive, but as it stands, he is dead, Anslee is badly wounded, and you were nearly violated. You have taken a terrible risk, Señorita. He was going to rape you when I came upon you. Surely you know that!"

"Sí, Señor."

Darcy sighed heavily and glanced off into the distance.

"What you do not understand, Señorita is that George has been my enemy for many years. His motive for attacking you was to revenge himself on me. Had he succeeded in despoiling you, his revenge would have been complete indeed, and I would have been undone. Señorita, I cannot always be there to rescue you. ¡Had this happened on the morrow, you quite possibly could be dead, or worse! I will brook no opposition, Sofia. I want you to go to Richmond at once. ¿Do you understand me?"

"Sí Señor, I am well aware of what happened and what could have happened, but it did not come to be." She paused and looked up at him. "Señor, I beg of you give me but a few days, and then I shall go. You have my absolute word."

"Sofia," he said gently, but with firmness, as they turned into Darcy House proper, "if you wish to retain my good opinion, there can be no secrets between us. As it stands now, that is not the case. Therefore, you must tell me at once why it is that you must remain in town. I want to know where you go each day. I am a man who cares deeply for you. If I should lose you…well, I do not wish to think of it. Tell me once and for all, why must you go against my wishes and stay in town?"

She gritted her teeth and wiped her tears. She wanted to tell him. She wanted to tell him everything—who she was, why she must remain in town, what had become of her and her family, and most important of all, that she loved him, but something held her back, as if being Elizabeth Bennet was the only dignity she had remaining. He had not spoken words of love to her since the night of the ball, and she wondered if he regretted it. If only he would speak the words she longed to hear, she would break and tell him everything. But he did not.

"Señor," she said at last, "I must stay, and you must trust me on my reasons. If you cannot, then we have no future."

Her cool reply angered him and brought his temper to a boil, yet his demeanor remained calm. "Then I have no choice," he said in a clipped tone. "You may stay. I will not force you to Richmond against your will by dragging you kicking and screaming. However, let me make one thing clear to you, Señorita, so that there is no misunderstanding. When I return from Lancashire, I want a full accounting of where you go and why you feel the need to keep secrets from me. Our time of decision is coming upon us when you must reveal your identity. If you cannot tell me everything, then you *are* correct, we have no future, and we will part."

Pain shot through Sofia's heart at the sound of his cold words, and she began to cry anew. Could she remain as Mr. Darcy's mistress once he knew the truth? Would she still be able to hold her head up with dignity? Pride told her that she would not. This had been a bargain to save her family, and at the time, it seemed to be an acceptable bargain, but if it had been so *right* then why did it feel so wrong now? She sniffled as they came upon the portico.

Once they were in the house, he told her he would have his dinner alone, and that night, their last night together, Mr. Darcy refused her bed, preferring his own for the first time since they had become one on Christmas Eve. Alone in her room with nothing to comfort her but his masculine scent on the bed linens, Sofia ripped her veil and mask from her face and flung them at the closed door. She then threw herself down onto the bed, bursting into a violent flood of tears, sobbing bitterly into her pillow. Would she have to sacrifice everything, including her happiness, to save those she loved?

Darcy closed the door to his chamber and leaned against the dark oak frame. Anger still burned within his breast. What was she hiding, and why did she feel she could not confide in him? He did not want to believe it was another man, but doubts lingered. What exactly had Wickham attempted to tell him before he died? If it were either of the dukes, both of whom he knew wanted her, he was resolved to call them out. But in his heart, he knew it was not another man. Nonetheless, if she could not trust him, then did they really have a future? Just as that thought occurred, another replaced it.

She had not had her courses since they had been together. Could she be with child? He wondered. Of course, he knew nothing of these things, except that a woman ceased to bleed when she carried a child, and he had no knowledge of her bleeding. He had been told women could be quite difficult to live with in the early months of pregnancy. Perhaps she had fallen pregnant. With all of their amorous activity, it was certainly within the realm of possibilities. Should that be the case, he was willing to forgive her and try anew, provided that she bore the child and did not discard the pregnancy as so many courtesans were known to do.

He ran his fingers through his disheveled hair and shook his head. He would pen a letter and leave it with her before he left. He would give her one week in London, and then he wanted her removed to Richmond. He would write her there whilst in the North, and when he returned, he wanted the truth.

By the time his letter was complete, the hour was late, and yet his heart still yearned for Sofia. Stepping out into the corridor, he made his way to her room intending to enter and leave the missive on her dressing table. He would then discreetly leave to prepare for his trip, but when he came to her door, he heard her soft sobs, and his heart broke.

Darcy took a deep breath and released it slowly as he pressed his head to her door. This had been their first argument. He could not leave with this between them. He turned the latch and entered. It was dark and he could barely see, but he could make out her form as she lay in their bed. She was naked, and her mask was off. The black veil was there at his feet. He looked closer and in the dark she appeared to be asleep, but an occasional sob escaped her throat, as she was murmured, begging him not to leave her…pleading with him to love her.

Overcome with compassion, he laid the letter on her dressing table and stripped his dressing gown from his body. Slipping into bed beside her, he lifted her face in his hands and began to kiss her, tasting the dampness of the salty tears on her cheeks and lips. Tenderness and compassion overcame him. He kissed her eyes, her delicate upturned nose, her face, and her hair. He kissed her over and over again, and before he knew what he was doing, he whispered in her ear, "I love you, Sofia, more than you know. I am a man of few words who is not used to expressing himself, especially in matters of the heart. I say what I mean and mean what I say. I love you, my little Spanish siren, but do you love me? Can you love me for the man I am apart from my world of privilege and wealth, my connections and status?"

Her body reacted on instinct. She came alive in his arms and kissed him back with wanton abandonment. "Do not leave me," she whispered softly in English. "Stay with me...love me. I am not a faithless heart, and I love you, but can you love me once you know all?"

"I will love you until the earth melts away, until the stars fall from the sky. I will love you until the end of time. For an eternity, I will love you. Why can you not trust me?"

She whimpered and soon they came together as one, making love like two young lovers caught in the eye of a storm. They repeated it, and then she fell fast asleep in his arms, though he wondered if she had ever been awake.

As he held her to his chest, a tear slipped from his eye and trickled down his cheek. "Sofia, Sofia, I want to know who you are and why you cannot tell me what troubles you. You say you love me, but will you mean it in the light of day? That I am unsure of."

He slid her off his shoulder and gently tucked her into the soft comforter. He hesitated for a moment and contemplated lighting a candle so that he could gaze upon her naked face without the veil, but his conscience stopped him. They had a bargain, and he would honor it.

Darcy pressed a gentle kiss to her forehead, and then left for his room to ready himself for his trip. When he returned, it would be close to their time of reckoning, and then he would confront her for the truth, however painful it might be.

And so good reader, our heroine feels the weight of her troubles once again pressing down on her willowy shoulders. Pain wells up in her tender heart almost to the point of breaking it. As she weeps, so does another. Venus, Venus, where have you gone?

# Chapter 15

rue to his word, the right honorable General Richard Fitzwilliam and his reluctant noble brother, the Viscount of Wexford, have hired a man to follow our dear heroine and sleuth out her secrets. The former is convinced his man will find a faithless woman while the latter prays he does not. Meanwhile our courageous hero makes his way North with a heavy heart, and while he must conquer his demons, what of our heroine?

Now, my good and generous reader, let us have a look at how fares our dear heroine on the morning after her disastrous debacle.

Let us take a look, shall we?

Sofia awoke the next morning with a splitting headache and a queasy feeling in her stomach. Last evening had been the worst night she had spent since coming to Mr. Darcy as his mistress. She had cried herself to sleep, and truth be told, she felt like crying all over again, but the unsettling in her stomach threatened to overtake her if she made herself too distraught.

In an attempt to calm her emotions and abate the sickness that threatened to overcome her, Sofia lay back and began to breathe deeply. She would wait for her maid to come to her. She needed a hot bath and something to eat. Perhaps that would soothe her nausea and set things to right. Last night she had been too upset to eat anything and had gone to bed without her supper.

She glanced at his pillow and suppressed another sob. She had been so distressed that she had actually dreamed he had come to her in the night and had held her in his arms, telling her all the things she longed to hear, declaring his love and promising her the security she so badly needed. In her dream, she actually felt his warm breath on her skin as his lips caressed her face, the sensation of his gentle kiss upon her eyes and nose and mouth, and once again she broke down and sobbed.

*...Elizabeth you must control yourself. He did not come. It was only a dream. You are nothing more to him than his mistress, and that is all you shall ever be, a paid woman to satisfy his urges like the Duke of Ancaster said. That is all you can ever be...his paid companion.*

No sooner had the words coursed through her mind than her stomach lurched, and she had a sudden urge to retch. She leapt from her bed and made haste to the chamber pot just in time, dry heaving until she felt her stomach would come up through her throat.

"Oh Miss Sofie. You sick," Ling-Ling said, entering the room and coming to help her back to bed. "I get you tea for sickness. You need food and tea. Wait here."

Ling-Ling ran for a soft cloth and gently wiped her mistress's face with cool water, soothing her uneasy mind and calming her troubled spirits.

After Sofia had consumed as much breakfast as she could tolerate along with a cup of Ling-Ling's special tea, she felt much better and was ready to prepare for her day.

"Ling-Ling, pack our trunks. We are to stay at Newgate until my mother…until it is time for us to remove ourselves to Richmond."

"I pack, but Mistress be careful. She with child."

"What!" she gasped, folding her arms around her mid-section. "No, that cannot be…can it?"

"When you last bleed? Not since you come to Mr. Darcy. You no drink the tea, and he give you baby."

"Oh, no! Whatever am I going to do?"

"You tell master. He marry you, have baby, be happy. Ling-Ling see no problem."

"But there is a problem. Mr. Darcy is not in love with me. He will not marry me. He cannot marry me. Society forbids it."

"You blind. Mr. Darcy, he love you. I see his eyes. He love you. You very blind. You tell master you carry his baby." Ling-Ling poked her stomach almost sending her to her knees. "He marry you. No care 'bout society. Lord Berwick marry Miss Dubochet. She fashionable courtesan, too and very famous. He no care 'bout society. Mr. Darcy no care. Mr. Darcy marry you."

"Ling-Ling, we will see. I have no assurances I am with child, but if I am, that certainly changes things."

"Yes. Things change. Now have bath. I pack. We go to family and care for Mamma. She need us now. Think about baby later."

As soon as her bath was over and she was dressed, Sofia felt much better. She knew nothing about being with child, and there was no one to ask, except for possibly Ophelia. Elizabeth thought about speaking with her friend, but then thought the better of it. If she were with child, no one must know until she had clearly decided what her course of action would be.

Sofia turned to her maid busily packing their things for the extended stay at Newgate. "Ling-Ling, you are to say nothing to anyone about what you suspect. If I am indeed carrying a child, it is to be kept secret until I say otherwise. Do you understand?"

"Ling-Ling say no word. She understand."

"Good! Now while you finish packing, I will go to the library in search of something to read. Perhaps a book of poetry will soothe my mind and ease my troubles."

Just as Sofia was about to leave her room, she noticed a letter on her dressing table. In wonderment, she moved to the vanity and lifted it from the silver tray. A shiver traveled up her spine. She instantly recognized the elegant hand. She turned it over in her hand and examined the seal. It was from Mr. Darcy.

She looked up abruptly and wrinkled her brow. ....*So he* **was** *in my room sometime in the night.* "Was my dream a suppressed longing or did it actually happen?" she whispered to herself as she glanced at the bed clothes being stripped from her bed. There had been a stain, but she had paid it no mind. Now she wondered. She had not worn her veil, and for a moment she was concerned, but then she reasoned that if he had looked upon her face she would know by now. The Mr. Darcy as she knew him would not have left quietly if he knew her identity.

Breaking the seal, her heart leapt into her throat as she began to read.

*My Dearest Sofia,*

*Over the course of the last few months, I have come to know you, I believe, fairly well. You are a warm and generous woman with a kind heart, but, even after our very close and intimate connection, there is still much that I do not know about you. I do not know who you really are, nor do I know the face behind the veil. Sofia, why will you not allow me into that innermost chamber of your heart where your secrets are kept? Have I not been good to you? Have I not proudly taken you to the theatre, shown you about town and even brought you to my cousin's ball and his many dinner soirées? My dearest Señorita, I have given you more money per month than many wives are allotted for a year, generously showered you with anything that you could desire. I have allowed you the freedom to have whatever you wished, to come and go as you pleased. Yet you hold back. I do not understand. I know you care for me, Sofia. Your body does not lie, but do you care enough? For my part, I care deeply for you.*

*I do not know what more I can do. Perhaps you expect more from me in an intimate manner that I cannot comprehend, but understand this, I am not a man of eloquent words. I never have been one to quote poetry, write verse, or lavish compliments upon the fairer sex for the sake of meaningless flattery. These are things I have been told will win the heart of a woman. However, if it will turn your heart to me, let me express myself in the way I am best able. Miss Sofia Molina, I wish to tell you how much I admire you, esteem you, and how I have come to have a strong affection for you. It is my hope that some semblance of feelings and affection are returned. Maybe if we would have met under different circumstances and I could have courted you properly, as a gentleman courts a lady, things could have been different, but that is not our situation.*

She glanced up and released a hard breath. "No, that is not our situation, as I have daily proof. I am your mistress and you are my protector. We are not a gentleman and a lady." She returned her gaze to her letter and continued to read.

*We began our relationship as a business venture. I bought you and your services for, how shall I say it? For want of a better way, I will say we began our adventure together in a purely carnal sense. I paid for what is deemed solely sexual pleasures with the assumption that you would deliver on my demand, but our relationship has long since changed from that. I believe from our first night together it began to change, when I discovered you were not simply another courtesan, but an innocent maid caught in a web.*

*However, as we come upon the end of our trial duration, we have several very serious matters which we must address, and I must then decide our future. It is my desire to make our relationship permanent, but, mi querida, what I decide will depend entirely upon you and your honesty. If I cannot trust you, if you will not confide in me, then I see no future for us. The choice is left to you, my pretty Señorita. Do you want to continue, or do we part? For my part, I sincerely hope for the former and not the latter.*

*With great affection,*

*Fitzwilliam A. Darcy*

She placed her hand over the small of her flat stomach and shook her head with a laugh that was anything but humorous. *You never were a man of many words, Fitzwilliam, and these on this parchment...? ...They are no different than before. I am still unable to read your heart.* She bit her lower lip remembering the duke's painful words. *...all matters of exotic pleasures are what we expect. Mr. Darcy, especially, will not marry you. If that thought is in your pretty little head, you had best discard it now...*

"Elizabeth, you must judge carefully. Affection is not love. Henry VIII spoke of affection to the lady Anne Boleyn, and where did it get her? Without a head, that is where," she murmured to herself.

Glancing down at the letter in her hand once more, she nodded. "No, at this point, Fitzwilliam, if I carry your child, I will settle for nothing less than marriage. I will not continue to be your mistress and bear a child in open disgrace. Nor will I live with you in exposed shame for the entire world to see my humiliation. My son deserves better."

Rereading his letter more carefully than before, she searched for any semblance of meaning in his words that might address her concerns and desires. What did he mean by making their relationship permanent...*wife*...or mistress? She needed one clear word that she could cling to, but there was none. A small tear escaped her eye. She wiped it away and glanced up. "Sufficient for the day is the evil thereof. Let me not despair over that which I cannot control."

Neatly folding the letter, Sofia placed it in her trunk with another letter, which was always with her. He had written it to Elizabeth Bennet a long time ago, and now that letter was nearly in tatters from having been read so often.

She softly stroked the delicate letter with the tips of her fingers and then moved to close the trunk, but as she did, something else caught her eye.

Glancing over at her plans for their trip to Ireland, she lifted the papers from where they sat. The boarding passes were purchased, the contact information was established, and the bank draft sent. Satisfied that everything was in order, she slipped them safely inside her novel and placed it on her bedside table to be packed in her valise when she returned from the library.

Gently touching her hand to her stomach once more, she sighed. *...I will have to decide if this is really what I want...and I will decide—but not today.*

"Tomorrow," she said to herself, "Tomorrow is another day. You must be strong, Lizzy. So many depend upon you for their well being."

Faithful reader, I do believe it is now abundantly clear that our good friend Aphrodite, the goddess of love and fertility, has joined us in our quest for that much desired and ever coveted *happily ever after*. It could certainly be surmised that, at this point in time, our young heroine needs all the assistance she can procure, which brings us to another turn of events. I believe our dear heroine may expect a visit from a friend.

Let us listen in on their conversation and see how it transpires, and why should we not, for 'tis our story, is it not?

Lady Margaret's curricle sped through the streets of Mayfair as fast as her brace of ponies' little legs could carry it. She knew from the intelligence she had been given by her betrothed that Sofia would soon be leaving this morning for her outing, and after her conversation with Viscount Wexford the previous night, she was determined to see her before she left.

Over the years, Lady Margaret had become very close to the three gentlemen—Mr. Darcy, General Fitzwilliam, and Viscount Wexford—and to the best of her ability, she wanted to see them all happily situated in whatever way they chose. They had each offered her a respite in her own time of personal troubles, often sharing discussions of philosophy and the growing trends in society away from the old way of thinking to a new and freer style of living. And each in his own way had educated her in the ways of love. Therefore, if there was anything Lady Margaret could do to further Mr. Darcy's suit with the young Spanish courtesan, she was determined to see it through.

Handing the reigns to the footman, she hurried up the steps, lifted the heavy doorknocker, and gave it three hard raps. The butler opened the door, where she presented her card as he bade her enter.

Sofia was coming down the steps when she spied Lady Margaret and stopped cold. "Your Ladyship, to what do I owe the honor of such a visit so early in the day? If you seek Mr. Darcy, I must disappoint you. He has already departed for the North."

Lady Margaret curtsied and said, "It is not Mr. Darcy whom I seek. It is you I have come to see."

"Me?

"Yes."

"May I ask why you wish to see me, Your Ladyship?"

Lady Margaret removed her gloves and bonnet and placed them on the calling table. "My dear, Señorita, surely you are not so dense," replied the regal lady with an upturned brow. "I have come to see you concerning someone who is dear to use both: Mr. Darcy. The man is clearly in love with you, and if I know him, and I certainly do, he will soon ask you to marry him. For his sake, I beseech you to let Sofia Molina fade away—disappear to America or India. And then, from the ashes of her disappearance, let a Phoenix arise—a new identity, one who can marry such a distinguished gentleman as Mr. Darcy without the hint of scandal."

"Your Ladyship, you will have to excuse my disingenuousness, but I have to wonder at your telling me this. What could it possibly gain you?"

Lady Margaret sighed. "I tell you this because I once loved him, and I still care very deeply for his happiness. Also, I know what you face with the *ton* and those dragons who feel they must be the matriarchs of us all, that it is for them to decide whom they will allow entrance into the circle which many covet who are not born to it. It is a difficult undertaking to penetrate their sphere and can be an unpleasant experience to say the very least."

"Lady Margaret, you must excuse my manner of speaking, but I find this whole conversation very odd."

"I know it may seem rather strange to you now, but I come as a friend, for I fear you do not know what is at risk. You must understand how it is in our society. Love is something that is given little priority in matters of marriage and considered to be of little to no importance. Women are bought and sold for the advancement of their families. Our societal structure is not called 'the marriage mart' for nothing, but there are a few of us for which a cold and loveless marriage is not desired, and I can assure you Mr. Darcy is one of those who holds to the ideology of a love match. Many of us that believe men and women should marry because they love one another—not to better their families' standing within the ton. My cousin, Georgiana Cavendish, was an example to me. She became a duchess when she married one of the most powerful men in England in a marriage arranged by her parents to a man many considered a brute, and yet they wondered at why she was unhappy.

"As for myself, I came into that way of thinking when I was married off by my father to a much older man I could barely tolerate, much less love. Rodney was a baron and son of an earl. He desired me but not I him. However, I was a good daughter who never questioned my parents and did exactly as I was directed only to be miserable and lonely. Fortunately, our marriage was short lived.

"What happened?"

"He was killed in a carriage race brought on by strong drink and the members of the *Four Horse Club*."

"I am sorry to hear that."

"Do not be, for I am not. He was a drunkard, a miserly husband, and a cruel lover, especially when he was in his cups. And he smelled bad. It was Mr. Darcy who came to my rescue one day when Rodney was beating me in one of his drunken stupors. I fell in love with him then and have loved him ever since, and so, after Rodney's death, we had an affair, but he broke it off because he was not in love with me. Apparently he had met someone else, who captured his heart, a country miss from one of the southern counties, I do believe, but she, the simpleton that she was, spurned his generous offer and turned him down. I had hoped he would return to me, but it has been over five years now, and he has moved on as have I."

Sofia looked upon her visitor with astonishment. "Lady Margaret, I have to tell you I am not used to such forward conversation, and I am not sure what to make of it. You apparently harbor affection for Mr. Darcy and yet you wish for me to have him. Your Ladyship, you make no sense at all."

"My dear Sofia, I do still love him, but not in the way you might think. I love him now as a dear friend and much beloved cousin to my betrothed. We all want to see him happily situated. You, my dear, have made him happy for the first time in many years. I have his cousin, the Viscount of Wexford. I will give him an heir, but you must give Mr. Darcy one, for a man without sons is a man without a future. And I want Fitzwilliam Darcy to have a future. We have all worried about him excessively, and then you came into his life."

"If that be the case, then I have to ask, do you love Lord Wexford?"

"And I would have to answer, yes, I do. I have grown much since those early years. I am not the fool I once was, and I can say with all alacrity that Wex is a good man, worthy of a good woman. I will be that woman, but I shall also never forget Mr. Darcy and his kindness. He taught me that there could be pleasure in the union of two people and gave me hope. Therefore, it is my desire to see him in a happy situation as well with a woman who can offer him felicity in the married state—a woman with whom he can share a marriage of true minds. You, my dear Sofia, *are* that woman, but there is one thing you lack. Faith. Faith in the good man that he is. You must trust him, Sofia."

"Your Ladyship, I am sure I do not know what to say to your boldness. You are unlike any other woman with whom I have ever been acquainted."

"Then say nothing, but do regard my advice," the noble lady responded with a gentle smile and an upturned brow. "Miss Molina, I do not know from whence you came, but I am pleased you are here. Do not let your youthful foolishness cost you what it has cost so many. If you let him go, you will regret it for the rest of your life."

"I will consider your words carefully, but I have no assurance that Mr. Darcy feels as you seem to think. He has given no true indication that he loves me, much less that he wishes to marry me. It is foolish to desire things that are above one's reach. This is not one of the Brothers Grimm's fairytales. This is real life. Until I have such assurance, in my own opinion, I will not act on feelings that might constitute my utmost unhappiness."

Lady Margaret only shook her head. "That, my dear lady, will be your misfortune. I happen to know he loves you because he has confessed it to others, though maybe not to you. Allow me to impart a word of wisdom to you. If a woman conceals her affection with great skill from the object of it, she may lose the opportunity of fixing the love of the man she desires. A man needs encouragement. You must give Mr. Darcy reassurance that you reciprocate or at least are amenable to the idea of loving him. There is so much of gratitude and vanity in almost every attachment that it is not safe to leave anything to itself. You seek proof of Mr. Darcy's attachment to you. I give you Mr. Wickham. He would not have sought you out had you not been dear to Mr. Darcy, for it is a well-known and established fact within our close circle that Mr. Wickham has envied Mr. Darcy since they were boys, always taking and destroying that which was dear to him. If that man could have despoiled you, it would have been his ultimate revenge. That is what I know, Miss Molina. You do not trust me, and it is perfectly understandable. You do not know me and my forward ways. Someday you will, and then perhaps you will call me Maggie. Not all of us in the *ton* are narrow-minded bigots. Now, if you will excuse me, I have had my say."

Lady Margaret moved to the calling table and then glanced at Sofia once more. "On a final note, Miss Molina, I know you are not a woman of objectionable character. Nor are you an opportunist. I observed you at the ball and our many dinner parties. I think I know a woman in love when I see one. So, I shall say it once more. Think of what you are doing, Miss Molina! He loves you, and if you cannot see it, then perhaps you and the *Country Miss* share a common affliction, one I would call a lack of good sense. I shall see myself out."

Lady Margaret picked up her gloves and bonnet and was about to leave, but then paused at the door and turned back.

"Do you fence, Sofia? Every woman should know how to defend herself, especially when there are men such as Mr. Wickham about. Once you and Fitzwilliam are married, I shall take you to my master. I can handle a sword as well as James—maybe better by now. You must learn as well."

Sofia's jaw dropped, but Lady Margaret only smiled as she saw herself out, leaving Sofia to wonder after her.

While traveling from Darcy House to Covent Gardens, Sofia was in deep thought, reflecting back on her strange visitor and all she had said. Mr. Darcy was an enigma and just when she thought she knew him, she realized she knew nothing of the sort. Lady Margaret claimed he loved her, and if one judged on actions alone, one might come to that conclusion. But other than in the heat of passion, he had never expressed such sentiments to her, and in her position there was simply too much at stake to risk her heart on a mistaken assumption. She breathed deeply and emitted an unsteady sigh.

Suddenly she was jerked from her reverie by the sound of something crashing to the ground. The coach abruptly halted and she looked back. One of the trunks had come loose and slipped from its place tumbling into the street. A gentleman coming up behind dismounted his horse to stop and help.

"Miss, do not trouble yourself with this. I shall help your driver recover these items and set things to right. It's unusual for trunks to come unattached from a coach such as this. I will investigate and see what caused the mishap."

"Thank you very much, sir," she said, exiting the coach. "I appreciate your kindness to stop and help one such as myself."

Without a word, he smiled and tipped his beaver.

Once things were restored and the trunk safely refastened to the back, the man approached with a leather strap in his hand and bowed. "This tie was worn and snapped, ma'am. I replaced it with one from my own supply I keep handy for times such as this." He smiled and nodded.

"Again sir, let me thank your generosity. We are eternally grateful for your kindness."

The man helped her back into the carriage, and when Sofia turned back, she noticed him scribbling on a tablet. She mildly wondered about him but then shrugged it off. There were too many pressing concerns to worry over every stranger she met.

After having the trunks unloaded at Ophelia's house and then clandestinely reloaded to another carriage, Elizabeth settled herself into the drawing room with her friend to discuss all that had occurred the day before. Ophelia was more than a little distraught at the news of Mr. Wickham's attack and subsequent death, yet very relieved Elizabeth had been fortunate enough to have Mr. Darcy come to her rescue.

"Ophelia, it was the most harrowing experience I have ever undergone. I was frightened out of my wits."

"Yes, but now it is finally over," she said, "and you say Mr. Wickham never discovered your true identity."

"No, never, though I will admit, if I could have, I would have bent down and lifted my veil and mask so that the last thing he saw before he departed this life was my face."

"Lizzy, that is too cruel!" Ophelia laughed.

"'Tis not! It would have served him right, for I have no compassion for the man who was responsible for our undoing—my father's death and the dire poverty that resulted from it."

Ophelia sighed. "Yes, I certainly understand your sentiments."

Elizabeth smiled and poured another cup of tea. "There is one other thing, however, that I must request of you."

"And what is that?" Ophelia asked pouring her own tea.

"You are not to mention this to Jane or Kitty. I would not want them to worry anymore than they already do."

Ophelia nodded and reached for her teacup.

The ladies discussed Mr. Wickham and the events of the evening until that topic was exhausted, and Elizabeth changed the subject to her very strange and eccentric visitor, eager to know her friend's opinion of Lady Margaret and all that she had said and done.

"What do you make of her, Ophelia? I cannot make her out. I know what she says, but what does she mean?"

"Lizzy, I have heard of Lady Margaret for years. She is nearly thirty and unmarried. She was widowed when she was but twenty, and from what I recall, her husband was a notorious rake with a violent temper. She has also been a constant companion of Lord Wexford's for many years, and before him, I do believe she had a brief encounter with Mr. Darcy. Some say she was truly smitten with him, but now it is a thing of the past, and she is very much in love with his cousin."

"Yes, she told me as much. She also said she was very unhappy in her marriage. Apparently the baron had abused her."

"That, I believe is true. However, she is very fortunate to have had her own money from her late husband's estate, or I believe her life would fare no better than ours. From what I have heard, her family will barely speak to her. They consider her an embarrassment."

"I can certainly see why. She seems to have shunned everything society deems proper. She even drove her own curricle. Can you imagine that a woman would do such a thing? It would not surprise me if she drank whiskey with the gentlemen. She appears to do everything else."

Ophelia laughed. "I am sure I would know nothing of that. We move in very different circles, though I would say she is not that far removed from where we sit, for I hear she has had numerous affairs, but is now betrothed to Lord Wexford."

"Yes, they are to be married. I do believe the viscount truly loves her."

"Well, for her happiness, I hope it is the case, for she has certainly known very little of it in the married state, but Lizzy," Ophelia said pointing at the clock, "we must go before the hour becomes late."

Elizabeth sighed as she rose to her feet. "Yes, I suppose we must. I shall call for Ling-Ling."

When the last of the trunks were removed from the carriage and placed in the house on Newgate, Jane, Kitty, Ophelia, and Elizabeth gathered around the table to talk while the children played by the fire and Ling-Ling attended to Mrs. Bennet.

"Lizzy, I am so relieved you have come to stay. The doctor called round very early this morning. He says the end is near. Mamma's lungs are filling with fluid. It shan't be much longer. In addition, I have heard back from the vicar at Longbourn Parish. We have received permission from the Archbishop of Canterbury to have Mamma moved from our current parish to Longbourn Parish. The preparations are arranged for her to be buried next to Papa. It will be a simple funeral—not the elaborate mourning ritual the funeral director had insisted upon."

"Very good! I am relieved to hear it. Did the vicar speak of any interaction with Mr. Collins, by chance?" Elizabeth asked.

"No, none. I do not even know if Mr. Collins knows of our distress," Kitty answered.

"I am certain he knows," Elizabeth replied, "but as to whether or not he cares, that is another matter entirely. After all, he is partly to blame for our present predicament. However, for now, we will not concern ourselves with Mr. Collins and what he may or may not think or know." She turned to Jane. "Ophelia has volunteered to help us through our time of trouble. She has offered to take turns sitting with Mamma. Ling-Ling wants to remain the entire time, and so I suggest that she have the cot by the fireplace. We shall take the chair. I will go first, Jane you second, Kitty next, and then Ophelia." She then turned to their maid and housekeeper. "Daisy, watch the children. I do not want them exposed to what is transpiring. Let them remember her as she was, especially William, her only grandchild."

Daisy curtsied and went on her way with Flora, Edward, and little William.

After the children had cleared the room, Kitty turned to the others. "I agree," Kitty said. "It has been particularly difficult for William to understand. The others are taking things very well, I think, but Lizzy, they all want you to remain with us. Say it will not be much longer, Lizzy."

"I shall speak with William as soon as the opportunity presents itself. As for the other, I shall remain here for the week, and then I must go to Richmond where I must remain. I cannot delay it any longer." She glanced away, still uncertain as to what should be done about her situation with Mr. Darcy. If she was truly with child—no, she would not think of that now. She turned back to her sisters. "Let us act as if this were any other day. Continue on with what we do normally. Kitty, return to work. We will see you in the evening; you can sit with Mamma then."

"I know I should, but should anything happen, you must send for me at once."

"I will. Now go along. The three of us will manage."

Kitty took her cloak, bonnet, and gloves and set out for the modiste shop promising to return soon if the work was slow.

With Kitty gone, the ladies of Newgate settled into their routine. Elizabeth sat with her mother for her allotted time and then she began teaching the children while Jane picked up her workbasket and began mending clothes during her time, and Ophelia, when not sitting with Mrs. Bennet, helped the maid with the house work, as it was too much for Daisy alone with all the activity of caring for Mrs. Bennet and keeping the children entertained.

The morning passed into the afternoon, and the afternoon faded into the evening. All of the ladies took their turns sitting with Mrs. Bennet who was now only semi-conscious. Elizabeth took extra care to read and play with the children when it was not her turn to sit with her mother. This she did to distract them from her mother's room, but little William continued to ask questions. He had followed her to the garden when she had excused herself to once again purge her stomach as unfortunately she had done much of the morning.

"Mamma," William said, "Why is everyone here? A strange man comes everyday. Auntie Jane says he is the doctor, and now Auntie Ophelia has come. What is the matter with grandmamma? Miss Ling-Ling is always with her, and you will not allow me to see her. Why ever not?"

Elizabeth shook her head and looked down on the young child with sympathy. "It is time for Grandmamma to join your real mother in heaven, Wills. Very soon, she will depart for the beautiful city on the hill where I told you your true mother lives. Do you remember?"

He nodded, but then asked, "Are you not my mamma? I know only you."

With a gentle smile, she tousled his curls. She knew he was too young to understand any of what she was telling him. Finally, she replied, "I am your mother, but I am not the one who gave you life. Your real mother is Lydia. She was my sister."

"What happen to my mamma? Where is she?"

"She died bringing you into this world. She is with our Savior now. Remember how I have told you about Jesus and the little children and the other things we learned about in Church?"

"Yes." He nodded once more.

As they walked along Elizabeth contemplated how she might help the young lad understand things a littler better. Over by a large oak tree, she spied a fallen sparrow. She stopped and pointed to the bird on a mound of leaves.

"William, do you see that dead bird?"

"Yes." He nodded.

"It is a sparrow, and do you recall the story I read to you the other day about the sparrow?"

"Yes. You said my Heavenly Father knows when one falls from the sky, and He cares for them, but He cares for me even more than He does the sparrow."

"That is correct." She smiled. "If the Lord loves the sparrow, where do you suppose the sparrow is now? Do you think he might be in heaven with our Lord?"

William moved to where the bird lay and bent down studying it closely. He shook his head. "No, Mamma."

Elizabeth's eyes widen. "Why ever not?"

"Look," the small child pointed, "he is here on these leaves. He cannot be there if he is here."

She smiled and scooped her little gentleman up. "I see you do not understand my meaning. 'Tis just as well. Someday you shall know the meaning of life all too well, but for now, I think you should run and play with your cousins."

She tickled his ribs until he giggled and wriggled free. As she watched him go, her heart was once again pierced with sorrow. His mother and now his father were dead. He had never known either of them, but perhaps it was best he had never known his father. Elizabeth shook her head and wondered if George Wickham had known his son, whether or not it would have made a difference. "*Probably not,*" came the answer in her mind. Elizabeth then turned and walked towards the house.

The hour had grown late and the cook was preparing a simple supper. Ling-Ling was in and out of the kitchen. She did her part with soothing teas to help Mrs. Bennet to rest, and cool cloths to her head and face to give her comfort. Kitty had returned with a basket of sewing to complete so that she could have the next day off to tend to her mother.

Elizabeth sat to attempt a meager serving of mutton stew and hoped this bit of nourishment would remain with her throughout the long night she knew was ahead of them. Several times during the day she had found it necessary to excuse herself for a breath of fresh air lest she lose the contents of her stomach. It seemed that it came on suddenly; a certain smell or a flutter of emotion, and she was lost to her affliction.

Three long days and nights had come and gone. The ladies of Newgate had patiently sat and cared for Mrs. Bennet without much rest. It was the evening of the fourth day, and Jane and Elizabeth, exhausted from their tribulation, gathered round the small table in the drawing room for tea and conversation while Ophelia sat with Mrs. Bennet.

After seeing that the children were tucked in their beds for the night, Kitty slipped into the sitting room where her two older sisters were talking. Taking a seat by the fire, she picked up her workbasket and began to sew the items she had brought home.

With a sigh, she addressed her older sister. "Lizzy, since none of us will ever marry, do you mind if I ask you a question?"

Jane's cheeks flushed. "Kitty! You must not."

"But why not! I want to know, and Lizzy is the only one I dare ask." She glanced at her sister sitting across from her. "Well?"

"Well what?"

"What is it like to be loved—I mean in the physical way—by a man. Tell us. What is it like to lie with him as one would with a husband?"

"Oh!" Elizabeth blushed. But then seeing the pleading in her sister's eyes, Elizabeth's heart softened. "If you must know, Kitty, then I shall tell you," she said, setting her needlepoint aside as she glanced at Jane whom she could tell was just as anxious to know even though she would never ask. "It is the most wonderful experience imaginable. At first there is pain—a sharp burning pain, but then it is over and what follows is very pleasurable—at least it is for me. Mr. Darcy is kind, loving,

116

and gentle. No woman could ever ask for anything more. He fulfills all my expectations and then some I did not even know I had. "

"Is he healthy?" Jane asked.

Knowing her sister's meaning, Elizabeth smiled. "Oh yes—very," she said. "Mr. Darcy is rather virile I would have to say. He often keeps me awake throughout the night, and then when I am home he comes looking for me during the day. But now that he is working so much, I do have more time to myself."

"Lizzy, with that much…well, *you know*, do you not worry that there will be an unwanted consequence?" Jane asked.

"Who is to say it would be unwanted? Certainly not I."

"Lizzy!" Kitty gasped. "You would want a child? We would be further in disgrace than we already are. At least as Sofia Molina no one can connect what you do to any of us, but a child we can neither deny nor hide."

"I am not ashamed. In Ireland, I intend to be a modest widow. My sea captain was lost at sea. He died of fever on a Caribbean Island. That is what we will say."

"Do you love him, Lizzy?"

Elizabeth jolted at being asked such a question. She turned and wiped a tear. Then she turned back with a smile.

"Love who, Jane?"

"Do not be reserved with me, dear sister. You know exactly who I am referring to."

"Love is not an option for me, Jane. Besides, it was always you who held to such foolishness, not I."

"Foolishness! Yes, indeed, that does seem to be the way of it. First one wrote a set of verses on me, and very pretty they were. Then another flattered me with frivolous words that came to nothing." Jane smiled sweetly, but Elizabeth had not missed how she had wiped a tear herself as her needle moved in and out, darning a pair of socks for one of the children, and it made her all the more melancholy for her sisters.

The hour grew very late and soon it was the wee hours of the morning. Ophelia came to the drawing room with a worried look.

"Lizzy, Jane, Kitty, Ling-Ling says you had better come. Your mother is talking excessively. I think the hour is near."

Kitty gulped a sob and dropped her workbasket while Jane set her sewing aside and wiped her eyes, claiming the colors of the thread and the poor light strained her eyes, but Elizabeth knew better.

"Yes, we will come," Elizabeth said as she rose from her seat only to feel another bout of nausea strike, and she had to run for the basin.

"Lizzy, are you unwell?" Kitty asked coming to sooth her.

"I am well. It is only my nerves and my lack of appetite. When this is over I will return to my usual self."

After Elizabeth was able to control herself, all three sisters left and promptly went to their mother's side, each taking a seat by her bedside.

Mrs. Bennet tossed and turned. She was awake, and a smile graced her face. It was obvious to all in the room that she was experiencing a vision that only she could see. Elizabeth had one of her hands while Jane held the other. All three sisters and Ophelia sat and listened to her ramblings while Ling-Ling kept a cool compress to her face.

"Mr. Bennet, you have come at last. Why did you delay? Was there a storm? And Lydia! My dear, dear Lydia!" she cried. "This is delightful indeed! My dear girl, you have come home. You will be married! And to such a fine young man. Married at sixteen! Mrs. Wickham! Ohhh…How good that sounds! Oh! But you are not to give any directions about your clothes just yet. You must allow me to go with you, for you do not know which are the best warehouses. Oh dear girl, you need not worry. You shall have as much money as you choose to buy them with after you are married. Will she not, Mr. Bennet?"

Mrs. Bennet went on for the better part of a half hour calling the name of each and every relation who had preceded her in death until finally she collapsed into silence and breathed no more.

Her daughters broke down and cried. A chapter in their lives had ended with their mother's death.

# Chapter 16

My good and faithful reader, we have come through the thick of it, and yet there are still miles to go before we sleep. Let us go to Longbourn once more and take a turn in the garden—the garden of good and evil known as a churchyard, that is—and see what snake awaits our dear heroine there.

And what of our hero? How fares he in the frozen North? Well, my dear reader, we are about to find out.

Come along and let us be as gentle as doves in the trees above and watch as the plot unfolds, shall we?

Three days had passed since Mrs. Bennet's death, and the day to lay her to her final rest was at last upon the sisters as they set out from Cheapside to the little village of Longbourn in the southern county of Hertfordshire.

The trip to Longbourn Church proved to be long and arduous for Elizabeth. The weather was cold and the day dreary. A drizzling rain fell like a fine spray of mist from a waterfall pounding the rocks below on a mountain riverbed, enveloping them in its icy shroud as the funeral procession slowly and methodically made its way through the muddy streets of Meryton headed for its final destination.

By now, Elizabeth Bennet was very ill. She had been unable to keep more than bland soup on her stomach since her mother's death, and her strength was waning. She had, however, managed to see to it that she and her sisters all had new black matted dresses for the funeral, as was the custom. They, as well as little Flora, wore black bombazine and crepe with fashionable woolen felt bonnets and the appropriate black netted veils befitting the occasion of a funeral, though the pomp and circumstance was certainly missing. Additionally, each sister wore a handsome brooch with a lock of hair from both their mother and father. There were more mourning clothes to be purchased for Kitty and Jane, for they were to mourn for the customary six months, but Elizabeth, as Mr. Darcy's mistress, certainly could not.

She glanced to her left. Little William sat beside her in their rented carriage traveling behind the death coach. He looked solemn. He had not spoken a word since their departure from London. Flora and Edward were across from her with Kitty, and Jane sat on the other side of William as they all journeyed in silence.

Traveling down the lane to Longbourn proper, Elizabeth could not help but recollect the fond memories she had from spending her youth here—memories of running in the fields and collecting daisies. She, Charlotte, Jane, and Ophelia, who was then Harriette Goulding, would weave them into chains and pretend they were refined ladies of distinction being escorted to balls and assemblies by handsome gentlemen as they wore their daisy coronets like fine jewels. How they laughed and played back then, and how each of their mothers was vexed by the stains on their pretty frocks.

Then, she remembered Oakham Mount and how she would climb the steep incline for solitude to dream of a day when she would marry and have her own family, much as was the desire of every young girl of her acquaintance.

When she stood upon the highest summit, she could see for miles. She recalled with fondness a certain September day in 1811. That was when she had first spied Mr. Darcy on his black stallion galloping across the green fields of Netherfield with Mr. Bingley. She smiled to herself as she recalled her first impression of the elegant gentleman. He sat upon a horse like someone born to the saddle: tall, lean, and pleasing to the eye, moving as one with the black sleek animal beneath him.

She chuckled softly and glanced between her sisters. They too, she assumed, were consumed in memories of their childhood home, for Kitty could not contain her tears, and Elizabeth knew it was more than the loss of their mother that affected her.

The grave was terrible in its finality, and to lay one's parents to rest marked the end of their youth. Another page was turned in the book called life. Except for one another, the Bennet girls were alone in the world. They were the matriarchs of the family now, such as it was: three sisters, two cousins, and one nephew.

Out of the corner of her eye, she noticed a farmer with his cart stopped along the side of the road stuck in the mud, ranting and waving his arms because his donkey had stubbornly sat down and would not budge. She chuckled softly and shook her head, thinking of the time she and her father pulled a similar cart from the mud when she was a girl. She happily noticed a man on horseback had come along to assist him. She smiled. *...The Good Samaritan shall rescue you. I'm sure Cousin Collins would not trouble himself to muddy his boots ...*

Suddenly she was jolted from her reverie as the carriage turned into the drive of Longbourn Church proper.

Jane spoke softly, "We are here. I see the vicar coming to greet us."

"Yes," Kitty replied, "and that loathsome man is with him."

"Who?" Jane asked.

"Mr. Collins," Elizabeth replied.

As Mr. Collins approached, the footman opened the door, and the ladies of London, along with the children, exited the coach. The vicar greeted them cordially and then left to attend to the service arrangements. Mr. Collins subsequently stepped forward.

"My dear Cousins!" he exclaimed with a false smile. "I cannot tell you how relieved Mrs. Collins and I were to discover that you—well let me not speak of it, for 'tis not right on such a day. However, do let me say this much. It is with great feelings that I greet you on this mournful day. With great sorrowfulness, I feel myself called upon, by our relationship, and my situation in life, to condole with you on this grievous affliction you must now be suffering, of which we were informed on Sunday by Reverend Biltmore that your dear mother had passed from this life onto the next. Be assured, my dear Cousins, that Mrs. Collins and myself sincerely sympathize with you and all your respectable family, in your present distress, which must be of the bitterest kind, to lose your last remaining parent. No arguments shall be wanting on my part that can alleviate so severe a misfortune—or that may comfort you, under a circumstance that must be of all others most afflicting to your young hearts. Howsoever that may be, you are grievously to be pitied, in which opinion I am not only joined by Mrs. Collins, but likewise by the village of Longbourn and Meryton, and also, may I add, by the illustrious Lady Catherine and her ever so delicate daughter, the Right Honorable Miss. Anne de Bourgh, to whom I have related the whole affair in full. And let me further say how—"

"How very kind of you, Mr. Collins," Elizabeth finally cut him off with more coldness in her tone than she meant to convey. "You are most gracious in your declarations of sympathy. You may also give our compliments to the esteemed lady and her daughter, to whom we are in gratitude that she would remember us, insomuch as we owe our current situation in life mainly to her ladyship's most efficacious interference."

She and her sisters then turned with the children and moved towards the church leaving Mr. Collins with a look of astonishment upon his countenance.

"Well! I never. Ungrateful chits. They should be honored that such a woman of distinction as Lady Catherine would condescend to send her condolences at all, let alone to such impoverished sisters for whom their own father did not even care enough to provide for their future."

He squinted his eyes. The very poor, who often did not own more than one outfit, could not afford to follow the wardrobe rules of the established customs for mourning and yet…something was not right with the situation before him.

Mr. Collins stood rubbing his chin with his stubby little fingers as he watched the remnant of what was left of the former ladies of Longbourn enter the church. He narrowed his eyes even further. "I wonder," he mumbled to himself. "How can the poor afford such extravagance? The funeral…their clothes? They cannot! And yet they are dressed lavishly well in their bombazine and crepe. Mrs. Collins tells me bombazine is a costly cloth made of silk and woolen for mourning. Expensive attire for women of such impoverished circumstances. There appears to be no husband for any of them. How could they afford such finery? That boy, who is he? He bears a strong resemblance to Cousin Elizabeth. Could it be?"

The image of a painting in London in an establishment where he now frequented came to mind. "The jawline…it is similar, and did not Cousin Bennet take his two eldest daughters to Spain after Mrs. Bennet lost their son? Is Cousin Elizabeth the lady in the portrait? No." He shook his head. "Not even *she* would condescend so low as to disgrace her family even more than did the youngest."

He turned and followed the procession into the church where Mrs. Collins had joined the Bennet ladies near the front. As the only male in the family, he assumed himself duty bound to preside over the funeral ritual, since as women, the sisters were not allowed in the inner chamber where the body would lie in state.

After Mrs. Bennet had been laid to rest, the ladies of Cheapside ambled about, talking and socializing with the few friends they had left in Meryton. Most were

121

astonished that any of them had survived the terrible winter of 1813 when the grippe had claimed so many. One such lady who was extremely happy to see Elizabeth was Mrs. Collins, now fully rounded with her third child.

"Eliza," said she with tears in her eyes, "I *am* pleased to see you. You know not how often I have thought of you and longed for the conversations we formerly had over tea. I simply cannot believe my eyes. When Mr. Collins told me the news, I nearly fainted."

"Charlotte, as you see the rumors of my demise have been greatly exaggerated."

"So I do see, and I am joyous that they are not true," said she. "But Eliza, you do not look well. Your skin is pale, and I noticed you had to be excused during the sermon. Are you unwell?"

"I am well." Elizabeth nodded. "'Tis nothing fresh air and a walk in the country cannot cure."

"Then you shall come to tea, all of you," she said glancing around at the remaining sisters and the children. "We shall walk down the lane afterwards and talk as we once did."

"No, Charlotte, I think not. I must return to London before nightfall. I have a friend in the country where I will visit and take rest there, and," she glanced at Mr. Collins, "I would not feel comfortable at Longbourn. 'Tis best I do not come."

Her friend took her hand and gently squeezed it. "You must know, Eliza, Mr. Collins broke my heart the day he forced you and your family away. I had nothing to do with it."

"Yes, I am aware of that. You and I shall always be friends, but I can never return to Longbourn. It is your home now, not mine. Now, if you will excuse me, I must go."

Young William, who was standing with Elizabeth, tugged on her skirt. "Mamma, Mamma, may I go with Edward to the coach? I want to go home."

Elizabeth glanced around at the heads turning in her direction. She then returned to the child looking up at her and smiled. "Yes, you may go. I will be there soon."

Charlotte furrowed her brow. "Eliza?"

"It is not what you think, but neither do I wish to speak of it."

"Oh, dear Eliza. I do apologize."

"Please, Charlotte, let us remember things as they were," Elizabeth said with a sweet smile.

"Take care of yourself, Eliza. I shall never forget you or your family."

With a gentle smile, Elizabeth turned and moved towards the carriage. She did not wish to speak of Lydia here in front of the good people of Meryton. Let them think whatever they would. It mattered not, for she would never see them again.

Charlotte called to her husband as she watched her friend leave, "Mr. Collins! Mr. Collins!"

He nodded with a smile, and she continued, "I must return to the house before I catch cold from the damp."

"Do not worry yourself for me, my dear. I shall be but a minute more."

"Come when you are ready," she said, and then turned to walk up the lane to Longbourn leaving her husband standing under the large oaks in the churchyard.

Mr Collins leaned against a tree and licked his lips as he watched his wife disappear behind the hedgerow encircling the house. Returning his gaze to the carriage in which his cousins were preparing to leave, he tilted his head and muttered to himself. "Who is that child, or rather whose child is he? I wonder. Cousin Elizabeth does indeed bear a strong resemblance to the lady in town. The way her black veil falls over her face...it is very much like the one in the portrait. The jaw lines of both...hmm. Could my cousin be providing for her family as a...? Is the child hers, and why is she sickly this day?"

He removed his handkerchief from his pocket to wipe his sweaty brow.

Just before Elizabeth reached the coach, another bout of sickness seized her, and she ran for a wooded area where she might have privacy. When she felt well enough to return to the others, she moved out of the shrubbery to find Mr. Collins in her path.

"Cousin Elizabeth, are you unwell? You look very ill—very ill, indeed!"

"I am as well as can be expected for one who has just buried her remaining parent; please do not concern yourself for me."

Mr Collins reached with his sweaty palm and lightly brushed the jawline of Elizabeth's face with his fat stubby fingers.

"Perhaps you now regret your former decision, my sweet? Had you not been so hasty, you might—"

"I have many regrets, sir." *...but that is not one of them...*

"Ah..." He sighed. "Cousin Elizabeth, you must know that it gives me the greatest displeasure to hear that you have passed your time so disagreeably in utter poverty. My dear Charlotte and I certainly did our best to see to your needs, but alas, you did refuse my offer as maid and governess to our dear little William. However, my dear cousin, I want you to know that you are most fortunate in that I have it within my power to introduce you to a vastly superior society than that to which you now find yourself limited." He chuckled softly.

"I do flatter myself that my present overtures of goodwill are highly commendable, and that the condition of my being the current Master of Longbourn makes them all the more attractive, so much so that I believe you will find my generous offer to your liking. I wish with all my heart it may prove so, for you are destitute enough due to the circumstance of your late father and mother's unfortunate inability to produce the much desired heir. Things are settled very oddly by divine providence so to speak. Would you not agree?"

Her eyes widened, and she looked at him in astonishment.

"Surely Miss Elizabeth, you can hardly doubt the purport of my discourse, for you know that I am in a position to be of great service to you and your family if you will but allow me to do so."

Mr. Collins prattled on with his effusions of self-important accolades for the better part of five minutes. Finally, he came to his point.

"Therefore, my dear cousin, if you should be agreeable, I am of a mind to take a mistress in town, and since, given your present circumstances, placing you in a nebulous position, I thought you might—"

"Mr. Collins! Remember yourself!" Elizabeth blinked in shock. "You are a man of the cloth. Even if you do not preach the gospel at present, you are still a clergyman."

"Then you are not—"

"I am not!"

"Ah, my dear cousin, I should think that someone abiding in such abject poverty such as you and your dear sisters purportedly find yourselves dwelling at present would not find my offer of compassion so objectionable. Unless, of course, someone else buys your affections. My dear Miss Elizabeth, you do not appear to be so impoverished as one would think, given your proposed circumstances, for such is not to be believed as evidenced by the display of clothing and the cost of such a glorious funeral for your dearly departed mother. But then I might conjecture that there may be a reason for such fine display, considering as how you bear a striking resemblance to...let us say... a certain *Spanish* harlot."

"Mr. Collins, I am highly insulted by your claims. I know not of what you speak. I must beg you to take your leave." Elizabeth paled with anger. "If I give an appearance of anything except the state in which you plunged us, then it is because of hard work and frugal economy."

Mr. Collins gave a soft chuckle as he once more raised his hand to her face, brushing a stray strand from her face. "Such a colorless complexion for one so fair and delicate... Your pale lips...how they quiver in the damp chill. My dear sweet cousin, you *are* unwell."

She raised her hand and struck his face. "You sir, must control yourself. What do you care for my welfare? Before my father was even cold in his grave, you turned us out to starve. Do not ever speak to me again."

She turned and strode briskly to the hired carriage where her sisters awaited her.

Resentfully, he spat out, "You shall be sorry, my dear sweet cousin! I offered you two reasonable proposals, and twice you have refused me! You shall not get another!"

When Elizabeth reached the carriage, she was trembling with rage as she took her seat beside William. Kitty moved across the expanse and sat with her, trying to comfort her. She and Jane had seen the altercation near the churchyard but could not hear what had transpired between their sister and cousin.

"Lizzy," Kitty said, hugging her sister close. "What did that odious man say to you that has undone you and made you so distraught?"

Elizabeth glanced at the children with their wide-eyed stares fixed upon her.

"'Tis nothing. Let us not speak of such disagreeable things on this day. I shall tell you later when we have time to ourselves. We are going home. Daisy and Cook have a banquet prepared. Ophelia is waiting. We will talk then."

"As you wish, Lizzy," Jane replied, "but you must tell us as soon as may be. Anything that worries you is a concern for all of us."

Elizabeth gave a faint smile as Kitty returned to her seat. "If you only knew just what will affect you...affect us all. Insufferable man!" she said privately, gazing out the window as her hand instinctively went to her stomach in a proactive gesture.

"Lizzy," Jane said softly, "I'm sure it is just a misunderstanding between the two of you and shall all be forgot soon."

Turning to her sister, she bitterly replied, "You think that, do you, Jane? Well I think not. There are few people whom I really love, and still fewer of whom I think well of. The more I see of the world, the more am I dissatisfied with it, and every day confirms my belief of the inconsistency of all human characters. Just as the vicar said this very morning, the world is a wicked place."

"My dear Lizzy, do not give way to such feelings as these. They will ruin your happiness," Jane said in a comforting tone.

Kitty said as if an after thought, "This shall be the last time we see our home and the people of Meryton."

Elizabeth snapped at her sister's words. "I'm sure we shall bear the cruel depravation with equanimity."

Returning her gaze to the trees passing by her view, Elizabeth's mind began to ramble. *Could Mr. Darcy love me...Marry me?* She narrowed her eyes and took in a sharp breath as Lady Margaret's words came back to her. *...Miss Molina, I know you are not a woman of objectionable character. Nor are you an opportunist. I observed you at the ball and our many dinner parties. I think I know a woman in love when I see one. So, I shall say it once more. Think of what you are doing! He loves you, and if you cannot see it, then perhaps you and the* **Country Miss** *share a common affliction, one I would call a lack of good sense...*

She shuddered and looked away pensively. *If he loves me, then why does he not tell me? Love me indeed! What men say in the heat of passion is not necessarily what they mean in the light of day!*

Darcy sat at his desk pondering the events of the previous weeks as he poured himself a glass of Scotch. The morning had dawned cold and miserable in Wheaton Mills, much as it had every other morning since his coming to Lancashire. It was approaching the middle of March. Snow still covered the ground and Darcy had scarcely had time to think of much else during his days except the problems at hand.

The state of affairs upon his arrival had been much more acute than he had previously thought. A complete breakdown between his workers and management had seemed imminent, leaving him with the considerable task of settling the disputes before there were riots in the streets. He had set to work with all the determination he could muster, spending many long hours working through the tribulations before him, and at last, he could see the light at the end of the dark and weary tunnel.

After coming to the mill village, Darcy had spent the first week working through the numerous problems with his men at the mills, trying to obtain their good will and trust. He had offered them better wages than anywhere else they might choose to work, and he had set aside a fund for those disabled while working in any of his mills. One man had been unfortunate enough to lose an arm while trying to save a little girl whose hair had been caught in a weaving loom. She was saved with only a minor loss of hair, but Mr. Hammer's arm was lost to the grinding machinery. As compensation, Darcy had given him a sum of one hundred pounds and a pension for life consisting of half his regular wages.

That was another thing that bothered Darcy: children working in the mills. It would not do. The next week he had set about ensuring that instead of laboring for their families, children would be educated. Therefore, he had taken the initiative of forming a village school. All children would be allowed to attend until they were fourteen at no cost to their parents. Then, if they chose, a scholarship would be provided to go beyond the first stages of education to one of the available public schools in the nearby towns.

The third initiative he had undertaken was to set up an infirmary to provide the sick and injured with much needed medical care. He would see to it that a village doctor was found to the run the hospital and administer care to the patients. Then, among the other activities, he had chosen to work in the mills alongside his men, listening to their needs and complaints. The cost of corn for bread to feed their families was one of their utmost concerns. To assuage that worry, he would arrange subsidized grain from Pemberley to be shipped to the village and sold in the company store at an affordable price. By working in the mills with his workforce, not only did he earn their respect, but he also taught them to respect one another— Irish and Scots alike—so that they might labor together in harmony.

These were the things that had occupied his mind during the day, but at night when he was alone in the quiet of his quarters, Sofia commandeered his thoughts. Over the past few months, he had become accustomed to sleeping with her, and now, alone in the frozen, snow-covered North, he missed her acutely when the day was done. Without her, his bed was cold and dismal. He had written her two letters, and, as of yet, had received not one in return. Worry was ever present in his mind.

He reached for the bottle of Scotch and poured himself another full measure. Pushing back in his chair, he propped his feet up on his desk and thought of the many things they had shared in the evenings after his long days at work had come to an end: another night at the theatre to see *A Midsummer Night's Dream* which she had particularly enjoyed, and ice skating in the park—something else she enjoyed with enthusiasm.

He chuckled to himself. She had never owned a pair of skates, and it was a joy for him to share with her yet another first as he taught her how to skate with shoe skates—something she had never done before. The recollection of how he had held her close to his side as they glided over the ice warmed his heart. While skating with her, he was once again a young man with a young lady enjoying life as it was meant to be. He signed and took another drink. More than anything he wanted to make their arrangement permanent. And in his mind, he had devised a way in which he could achieve it. If only he could be sure that her heart truly belonged to him in the manner he desired.

He wrinkled his brow as another thought crossed his mind. Had she not said on their first night together that she had a family somewhere? He wondered if they could be in London. Why had he not thought of that before? Could that be where she went whilst he worked? Moreover, if it were, why would she not simply tell him and be done with it? Perhaps he could be of service to them. What was she keeping from him...and why? He groaned in frustration.

Darcy dragged his hand over his stubbly face and shook his head. He would write to her one last missive, and if she did not reply, then that would be the end of it until his return. There were too many pressing matters consuming his attention; why add yet another? When he was finished here, he would leave for Pemberley to settle the dispute there. He had received word just this morning that the unaddressed problems had escalated into more violence. Mr. McLarty had seriously injured the daughter of Mr. Rathbone leaving Darcy to decide the future of the former while compensating the latter.

With a sigh, he set his drink aside and removed his feet from the desk. Reaching for pen and letter-paper, he adjusted the nib, dipped it into his inkwell.

# Chapter 17

ur dear and most gentle reader, we have now come to a place of peaceful bliss for our young heroine where she can regain her strength and face her many fears. However, is it a respite from a storm or the eye thereof?

Let us join her in the gardens of tranquility.

Following a three days delay with her family in Cheapside, Sofia finally removed herself to Richmond House. She had chosen not to return to Mr. Darcy's house in town before departing, but rather to move directly to the country in hopes that she might find respite and solitude from all that had occurred over the last few weeks. More especially, she needed the time and space which the secluded paths and clean country air would afford her so that she might gather her thoughts and decide her future more clearly. Although the tickets were purchased, the plans made, and everything set for her to acquire the house in Ireland, she hesitated at the idea. Her heart was simply no longer engaged in the thought of moving.

She recalled with delight the event of but a few days ago when she had first arrive at the home she and Mr. Darcy shared. No sooner had she settled in with her trunks unpacked and her traveling clothes changed, than the butler presented her with three letters from the gentleman who was ever present in her thoughts. The jolt from seeing them was such that she immediately left for the garden and halted at the first stone bench she happened across, tearing into the first missive before she had even taken her seat. His close, elegant hand sent a flutter down her spine as she began to read.

But before she had gotten too far, her cat, Cocoa, appeared from the shrubbery to greet her with a field mouse, dropping the offering at Sofia's feet.

"Meow."

Sofia looked up from her letter and glanced at the mouse. "Cocoa! What on earth are you doing? Where is your bell?"

Sofia turned the small rodent over with her foot and then returned her gaze to the proud feline who appeared to smile.

"Miss Cocoa, it will not do to take Mr. Mouse from his family. Does Cook not spare you the fat from a pig or a bit of mutton from a leg of lamb? Really, Cocoa, I know cats are supposed to catch mice, but as long as they remain out of doors, let them live! You can have the remains of our meals from the kitchen."

Cocoa meowed again and hopped into Sofia's lap. Turning around twice, she dropped down and began to purr.

"I see what you are about. Well, just this once I shall forgive you, but you shan't do it again," she said with a smile, stroking the cat's soft fur.

Settling in once more with her cat softly purring, Sofia began to read anew. She read Mr. Darcy's account of the problems he had found upon his arrival in Lancashire and his proposed solutions to remedy them. She nodded at the various descriptions he had put to paper. Looking up, Sofia nodded once more.

Glancing down at her companion, she smiled. "He is a very thoughtful man, Cocoa—truly a good gentleman to care so much for those in his charge. He is just what a man ought to be: gentle and kind—the very sort I would want to align myself with in marriage. Do you not think so?"

"Meow."

Sofia laughed softly. "As if you understand anything. You are simply a cat."

"Meow."

Returning to her letter, she read on. There was not much in a personal way, but when she came to the final paragraph, her breath caught in her throat.

*Sofia, this time apart has given me the much-needed time to think about us. When I come to you in Richmond, we must talk and lay ourselves bare. There are decisions to be made and our future together to consider. I look forward to seeing you in three weeks' time.*

*With affection,*

*Fitzwilliam Alexander Darcy*

"You signed your full name! You have never done that before." She sighed. "Talk? Yes, Fitzwilliam Alexander Darcy, we shall indeed talk." She repeated his name once more with a soft sigh. "What a beautiful name. I certainly like the sound of it."

She folded that letter and placed it in her pocket and then ripped into the second. It was filled with the progress of the endeavors he had undertaken. From his discourse, it appeared that the desired results were coming to fruition. She smiled once more and nodded at the depth of his kindness towards others. Again, he had closed his letter with a desire to see her again and to discuss their future.

His third letter was not so much about business as it was about his feelings for her and his concern that he had yet to receive a response to his first two letters. Folding this letter and placing it with the others, she shooed the cat away and rose from her seat.

While she walked about the garden ambling through the paths leading to the small lake where they had first skated on ice, now a treasured memory, she spoke softly to herself. "Fitzwilliam Alexander, I will write, but I cannot explain why I have not written before now. It would not do to discuss such things of a personal nature in a letter. I will write directly once I have rested and my strength has returned. You cannot know what I have endured…or what I will yet endure if I indeed carry your child."

Turning, she walked back to the house.

The remaining days of Mr. Darcy's absence passed in quiet contentment for Sofia as she slowly regained her strength. Thanks to the ever careful attention of her faithful maid, the sickness she had experienced the month before had all but gone, leaving her feeling refreshed and able to spend many hours in the gardens of Richmond at her leisure. The cold grip of winter was slowly slipping into spring and was quickly giving way to the rebirth of the earth, leaving Sofia feeling the renewal of life, especially the one she now knew she carried in her womb. Every day she talked to the child and told him of his Papa and the great heritage he would have when he made his entrance into the world. Sofia laughed most days and enjoyed the warmth and beauty of a mild March. With a soft sigh, she pondered the splendor all around her.

Soon Persephone would rise from the underworld, marking the event by the flowering fields and sudden growth of new grain. Baby rabbits would be born and the birds would return. Sofia would have to be ever mindful of Cocoa, lest she feast upon the young rabbits in the fields and chicks falling from their nests.

Sofia once again laughed and played with her cat while running along the footpaths through groves and meadows, picking flowers and stringing them together in colorful chains much as she had done as a child at Longbourn.

She sighed with contentment as she spun around and hugged her bosom. She had long since given up the mask beneath her veil, and at night, she wore neither. Yet she would not go unveiled outside the safety of her apartment, for she had no desire to expose herself to the servants. The less they knew the better!

Walking along the lanes within the park, she approached the large stone fountain in the center of the gardens and took a seat on the wide ledge surrounding it. When she was comfortably situated, she pulled out his latest letter from her pocket and began to read.

Tomorrow was the twenty-fourth of March, and Fitzwilliam would return from the North. Over the course of time Sofia's feelings for him had deepened and her fears had somewhat abated. Each day she had received a letter, and every day she had sent one in return. They had not expressed their undying love for one another, but she knew he cared deeply for her as he had eloquently stated his feelings in this letter and the ones before it.

However, as to whether he intended to propose marriage when he spoke of a more permanent situation, Sofia was still uncertain. Therefore, she had decided that they would indeed talk, and when he knew the truth, she was hopeful that he would have compassion and not expose her to the ridicule and open shame she would most assuredly feel as Elizabeth Bennet in being his mistress. That would only make Mr. Collins' hateful words all the more painful for her to bear. Furthermore, what would Fitzwilliam's family think if they knew the truth…that the one to whom he had once proposed marriage was now in a much lower position? That, she could not bear to think of without severe mortification. She pensively folded his latest missive and placed it back in her pocket.

Pulling out another letter, she tore into it and read of all the news from home. It had been addressed by Ophelia, but it was from her sisters. Jane and Kitty were anxious for her to return. Jane was concerned lest Mr. Collins might yet prove to be their undoing even though she and Ophelia had assured her that he had as much to lose by such a disclosure as they, and quite possibly he would suffer more if it became common knowledge that he frequented a brothel. Sofia was confident Mr. Collins would not expose her without clear proof of the facts, and yet Jane and Kitty were clearly worried. They were ever diligent in their desire to carry through with the set plans without hesitation. Reading along, Sofia finally dropped her letter in her lap and glanced at Cocoa who rested on the ledge beside her, watching the goldfish shimmering in the cool water.

"What shall I tell them, Cocoa? They do not know of the babe. Only you and Ling-Ling know of him. Nor do they know I have all but changed my mind. Will they go without me? Can I bear to let them? They are the last of my family. I will not know what to tell Jane and Kitty until Fitzwilliam and I have talked." She lifted an eyebrow and shook her head. "It is not beyond the possibility that we shall all board the Northern Star Lines, but neither is it a certainty. I must look at our plans again and see what exactly it is I have agreed to. I never planned for this to happen," she said gently, placing her hand protectively over the child she carried.

Sighing heavily, she glanced toward the house. "Oh, Fitzwilliam, come home! I need you," she breathed out as she rose to her feet.

Walking back into the house and up to her room, she approached her maid after diligently searching with no results. "Ling-Ling, where are the plans for our move to Ireland? I do not recall packing them when we left Darcy House for Newgate Street. I had them in a novel. Did you, per chance, pack them away?"

"No. Ling-Ling no pack. She leave that to Mistress."

"Oh, no! I must have left them in town. Well, it is no matter. I will have time to retrieve them when we are next in town."

"Miss Sofia no go to Ireland. She stay here with Mr. Darcy. Ling-Ling insist. She have his baby. You tell him yet in letter?"

Sofia blushed scarlet. "No! That is not the sort of thing one says in a letter."

"You tell him soon! Ling-Ling not be put off. He should know! It his baby!"

"Yes...I suppose he should, but in my own good time, when I feel the moment is right—and not a second before!"

Ling-Ling cast her eyes downward. "Ling-Ling no understand you English. Very strange people. All these rules no make-a sense. You love man; man love you; he make baby. So what is problem?"

Sofia laughed softly and closed the distance between herself and her maid, pulling the little woman into an embrace. "What would I ever do without you to make me feel better? You are very much like my sister Jane and have been my rock and constant companion throughout this entire affair. Without you, I could never have persevered. Do you realize that?"

Ling-Ling nodded and looked up. "Ling-Ling know. She know many things. Tell Mr. Darcy, and he marry you."

Sofia took a deep breath. "I will tell him, but as to whether or not he will marry me, of that I am uncertain, as you well know. On our first night he told me we might have ten children together, and he never mentioned marriage."

"No understand English people," Ling-Ling replied, shaking her head.

Sofia laughed again. "We English are a difficult sort with our refined deportment and pageantry of elegant display, clinging in quiet desperation to our dignified manners," she said softly and then glanced down with a broad smile. "But we shall not think about that right now. Let us prepare for dinner. Mr. Darcy will be with us tomorrow. I want you to help me to look my very best. I shall wear my black veil, but no mask, and I want my most elegant, yet simplest, dress made ready—the one in soft cream-colored silk with lavender trimmings. It is his favorite. I shall bathe in lavender and rosemary with milk and sliced lemons, and my hair is to be rinsed in lavender and lemon verbena water."

"Ling-Ling make ready for Mr. Darcy."

Sofia smiled as she watched her maid flurry around grabbing first one thing and then another, straightening the room. How insightful in a pure, honest sort of way, Ling-Ling was. Sofia shook her head. If the truth be told, she could no longer repress the feelings that had long since taken root and grown in her heart almost to the point of controlling her rational thought. She was violently in love with Mr. Darcy, and for someone in her predicament that was a dangerous place to be.

Fitzwilliam Darcy sat in his carriage making his way to town on the thoroughfare between Derbyshire and London. Having completed his business at Pemberley earlier than expected, he had decided to return a day early and surprise Sofia this evening at Richmond. If all went as planned, he would reach London by nightfall where he planned to take his supper and have a hot bath. While there, he would retrieve his mother's ring from the safe in the library annex and head for their country abode. In the morning, they would talk, and if all went as he hoped, he would ask her to become his wife. If not, they would part in great sorrow. Even though he had not stressed the issue in his letters, he would have satisfaction to the many questions and concerns that still remained between them; for without answers, they could have no future together. Secrets—especially of the heart—were dangerous. It had always been in his character to despise deception in every form, and he would not compromise his principles now.

Mr. Darcy's carriage pulled into the drive of Darcy House just as the sun was setting over the housetops in London's Mayfair District. Having begun his trip just as the sun was rising with little to no time in between for rest, Mr. Darcy was tired and weary from the many hours spent on the road. Nevertheless, he was anxious to complete his business and be on his way, for there was only a short distance to Richmond *and* Sofia.

"Home again, sir?" the kindly butler asked as Darcy came through the door.

"Yes, but only long enough to bathe and have a small supper. I have something to retrieve from the library. Then I shall be off to Richmond should anyone ask."

"Very well, sir," the older gentleman said as he took Mr. Darcy's cane and then removed his cloak and gloves. "Your cousin, the general, called round today, sir. He said it was urgent that you see him the instant you were back in town. Shall I send word that you have arrived, sir?"

"No. I will see Richard when it is convenient for me to do so. The general can wait. I've more pressing matters to attend to at present."

"Very good, sir. I shall inform him of such should he call round on the morrow."

"Better yet, send word that I am back and will call shortly."

Darcy took his leave, wasting no time in his mission. First, he retrieved the key to the door behind the bookcase in the main library. Once inside, he lit several candles and then went to the safe hidden away behind another set of bookcases.

Retrieving the collection of black velvet boxes, he carried them to the reading table and set them out one by one, opening them all until he found the one he wanted. It was a blue sapphire surrounded by tiny diamonds set in gold. It had belonged to his mother, and before her, it had belonged to his father's mother. Tomorrow, if all went as he hoped and expected, at the hour of ten o'clock in the evening, three months to the day of the consummation of their contractual agreement, it would be Sofia's.

With a smile, he snapped the velvet case closed, placed it in his pocket, and returned all the others to the safe.

After his bath, a clean shave, and a bit of cold ham and cheese with bread and a flask of wine, he thought he might rest before setting out once more. Making his way down the hall to the room they had shared, he pushed the door open and entered. With a smile, he glanced around. They had spent much of their time together in this very chamber, and to him, it would always be special.

Stepping towards her dressing table, he picked up an ivory hairbrush and turned it over in his hand. Narrowing his eyes, he scrutinized the engraving. *Fanny, November 1789.* Who was Fanny? Was that perhaps her mother…or an aunt? It could not be her. She was too young to have received such a gift. As he replaced the brush, he accidently knocked the comb from the dressing table. Bending to retrieve it, he noticed out of the corner of his eye something carelessly dropped on the floor under the side table by her bed. The table skirt had concealed all but the edge of a book.

Moving to retrieve the novel, he saw a folded piece of paper carefully tucked in inside. He frowned as he opened the volume. It was a letter, and it was not from him. Instead, it was from an address in Ireland. Looking further under the table skirt, he noticed other papers scattered about. On closer inspection he reasoned they had all once been hidden in the book.

Picking up the first one, he saw that it was a sketch of a cottage by a grove of woods and a small lake. He gathered them all together and took them to the bed where he filtered through them one by one. His chest tightened in distress as he read them: a document describing an estate in Ireland, correspondences to Ophelia for an *anonymous friend* to be disclosed when she and her family reached Ireland, a proof of payment for seven boarding passes on his own passenger ship line, and a receipt from Sofia's banker for her request of a thousand pounds to be forwarded to a bank in Ulster in order to begin the process of purchasing Wilton Manor, the name of the estate in Ireland.

A low guttural moan escaped from deep within as the realization of her duplicity hit him squarely in the chest, bending him beneath the weight of it. Tears welled in his eyes, and his throat tightened. She was planning to leave him. He could scarcely draw breath for the restriction in his chest. There had not been any indication this was coming. In fact, it had been quite the opposite, if her letters were any indication of her feelings.

But…had she actually used him…betrayed him? At first he thought yes, but then on further inspection, no, not really. What exactly could he accuse her of? Being a seductress? No. She was being exactly what she was trained to be—a courtesan straight from *The Cyprian's Handbook* and instructed by him to perfection. He had received exactly what he had paid for and perhaps a little more. She had given him three short months of sheer happiness, something that was not in the handbook.

However, as he gazed at the papers strewed about their bed, his anger rose. Had her letters not led him to believe she held affection for him? Moreover, what of their many nights together when they had declared their deep feelings for one another as they made love? Had it meant nothing to her? He dragged his hand over his face as tears began to burn his eyes anew. He cried out mournfully. The most difficult part of loving her would be letting her go.

At long last, Darcy nodded in recognition of the truth. She, innocent as she was, had drawn him in with her charms that night at the Courtesans' Ball for his money—and, if it had not been him, it would have been another. Yet, he could not despise her. No, undeniably he did not. She had given him herself, and he had been happy. Now he would set her free; he would place her on the boat himself, if she indeed wished it.

However, he would not see her tonight and neither would he return to her bed. The thought of it was too painful. Tomorrow, he thought grimly, he would decide what he would say and what exactly was to be done about their situation. After all, he was her protector, and with that came responsibility. Unsure of what he would do, one thing he knew with absolute certainty: he did not want her to return to the life of a courtesan.

Gathering the sketch and papers, he grimaced as he left for his apartment. He would sleep in his own quarters tonight.

Hold onto your bonnets, my good reader. Conflicts have begun. Storm clouds gather, a tempest brews, but be assured, good and faithful reader, that the darkest hour is just before the dawn.

# Chapter 18

It is with a bit of anxiety, that I bring you this next installment of our tale, my dear reader, for instead of a passionate romance, I bring you the *Clash of the Titans*. Zeus and his brothers are once again involving themselves in the affairs of men with Zeus and Poseidon the champions of good and Hades once again lending his powers to the other side. I do wonder who invited them to our little tea party, for I assure you, good reader, 'twas not me. Perhaps it was one of the nine muses.

Yet man is born unto trouble, as the sparks fly upward. Job 5:7

Let us peek, if we dare, and see for ourselves how the gods have sported with our lovers, shall we?

The next morning, Darcy awoke still feeling the pain of loss in his heart. He could tell by the way his man moved around that Mr. Cunningham was concerned and was also wondering why their plans for the previous evening had been canceled. Darcy was not accustomed to discussing his personal matters with his servants, but for once, he did not care. Mr. Cunningham had been with him through thick and thin.

Darcy propped up on his elbows and glanced at his man as he polished his shoes.

"Winfred, have you ever been crossed in love, my good man?"

"Crossed in love, sir?"

"Yes…crossed in love. Has a woman ever broken your heart?"

"No, sir. I do not believe I have ever had that misfortune. I was once married, but she died in childbirth seventeen years ago last December—the third to be exact."

Darcy furrowed his brow. "I never knew."

"No, sir, I never told you."

"Children—do you have any children?"

"Three, sir: two girls and one son. Minnie, my eldest has recently married, and Sam is away at school. Barsheba, my youngest, lives with my mother in Hampshire."

"And you never remarried? With three children to bring up, you surely must have remarried?"

"No, sir. I have never seen the need to marry since my Molly. Once was enough. The thought of replacing my Molly was reprehensible. I could not even conceive of it. When you have loved and been loved, sir, you will understand."

"Loved…I have loved two women, and it is apparent I am to lose them both. However, I happen to think you are correct. Once…twice, is enough when you have loved—especially if you have been loved in return." *…By at least one of them… I know she loves me, so why is she leaving me…?*

"May I be so bold as to speak freely, sir?"

"Speak."

"When you talk of love, sir, do you speak of Miss Molina?"

"Yes, how very perceptive of you."

"Sir, if I am any judge of character, I do believe the woman does indeed love you. Therefore, if you love her, you must tell her so. Women are rather funny about that sort of thing. They have to have things laid out before them—in black and white—if you understand my meaning, sir.

"You see, sir, I had assumed my Molly knew that I loved her. It was quite evident to me that I showed it well enough, but I almost lost her to another because so confident was I in my suit that I never once felt the need to say the words. It was not until she began to receive the attentions of another that I realized the fault was mine. Women cannot hold on to a thin inclination, sir. They must have substance. Have you told Miss Molina that you love her in the full light of day, sir?"

"She knows I care—that I love her. I have told her…only recently in so many words, that is."

"Sir, if I may be so bold as to say: sir that will not do. You must tell her frequently, and you must waste no time in doing so."

"What if I told you she was planning to leave me? What would you think then?"

"I would think her a simpleton, sir, and I would further think it not consistent with her behavior. My eyes see and my ears hear, sir. If she is truly leaving you, something is most suspicious."

"Yes…it certainly is. Pack my things. I leave for Richmond in the afternoon. If I do not return, you are to follow suit on the morrow. For now, however, send below stairs for some hot water. I shall have a bath and a shave. Furthermore, see to it that my green coat is made ready."

"Very good, sir."

Darcy was about to board his carriage when he spied Viscount Wexford's coach coming through the gate. He released a frustrated breath as he paused to greet his cousin.

"Darcy, we have quite despaired of you. I was afraid you would stay in the North indefinitely, but when Richard told me he had received a letter that you had returned, I had to call round to invite you to cards and supper tomorrow night. It is only a small party, and Lady Margaret would love to see Sofia again."

Darcy shook his head, agitation building at being delayed. "No! Not now, Wex. You will forgive me, but I am in a bit of a hurry."

"Darcy, are you unwell?"

"I'm very well, thank you…very well, but I have a pressing matter of business. If you will forgive me, make my apologies to Lady Margaret, if you will. Tell Lady Margaret tomorrow is not convenient. Perhaps another time."

"What is wrong, Cousin? Have you and Sofia had a lovers' quarrel?"

"It is not something I wish to discuss—especially out of doors. If you will excuse me." Darcy abruptly cut him off and entered his carriage, signaling his coachman to drive on.

As the viscount watched his cousin's coach depart through the gate, he spoke to himself. "He's hiding something. I wonder if Richard knows of this."

It had been most unfortunate that the viscount had come upon him as he was about to leave. He knew if he and Sofia were to part, then he would have to tell Wex and Richard everything, for they would persist until they knew it all as they had done when Elizabeth had rejected him. However, this time things were different; he was older and more mature. He would not drown his sorrows in a bottle.

Wex and Richard were not only his cousins; they were his closest relations and dearest friends in the world. Darcy knew they loved him like a brother and cared for his welfare and best interests. That thought brought about another. He mildly wondered what it was that Richard had wanted, but then dismissed the thought as quickly as he began to consider other things of a more urgent concern. Shaking his head, he fell back against the soft cushions and closed his eyes to contemplate his present situation.

He had securely placed the sketch and letters from Ireland in his wallet along with his checkbook. He would lay them out before her, and they would talk. All the questions between them would be discussed and laid bare. If she was indeed planning to leave him, then he knew what he would do. Yes…he loved her enough that he would set her free, but not without careful consideration of her wellbeing. No matter what was the custom of his day, he simply could not abandon her to poverty. He would secure her future. She would have the full amount of ten thousand pounds, and she would have the proceeds from the sale of their home in Richmond as well. After all they had shared in that house, he knew he could never return there after she was gone. Then, if she would give him a written agreement that she would never return to the life of a courtesan, he would pay her the sum of one thousand pounds per annum over the course of her lifetime or until she married. As for himself, he would have to learn to content himself with the memories of the two women he had loved. Darcy paused at the thought and groaned. Longing and desire swept over him; the overwhelming urge to pull her into his arms and love her one last time tugged at his heart.

His eyes flew open. "Darcy, you are a fool if you allow that woman to twist you around her delicate little finger like a seductress twirls her hair when she wants something from a man. You are in control—*not* her. And you had best not forget it."

Sofia paced back and forth in the drawing room occasionally going to the window to pull back the heavy drapes and gaze out into the courtyard of Richmond House.

She glanced at her cat staring at her from the rug in front of the fireplace. "Cocoa, where is he? Why does he not come?! It is four o'clock in the afternoon."

"Meow," came the lazy reply from the cat as she jumped up and settled herself down on the hearth and began to lick her front paws.

"Of course you do not know. How silly of me to be talking to a cat!"

Sofia turned back to the window, her eyes searching the entrance for a sign.

She held his latest express in her hand. He was in town, and yet he had not come. She murmured privately, "Come to me, Fitzwilliam. I have missed you cruelly. Why have you not come?"

Once more, she unfolded the missive and read the few words he had written.

*I arrived in London last evening but was too tired to continue on to Richmond. I will see you later today.*

*Fitzwilliam A. Darcy*

"What is wrong, Fitzwilliam? Why do you delay?"

She looked up to the sound of a coach drawn by four large greys bearing the Darcy crest entering the gate. Excitement surged through her heart, and her body trembled in anticipation of seeing him.

"Finally, you have come!"

She threw back the curtains and ran her hands over her dress to remove any wrinkles. Moving to the large mirror in the drawing room, she smoothed her hair and pinched her cheeks. She took a deep breath as she heard the butler open the door.

"It is very good to see you, Mr. Darcy. I believe the lady awaits you in the drawing room, sir," he said taking Mr. Darcy's hat, overcoat, gloves, and cane.

"Thank you, Hobbs. I shall go directly."

When he came through the door, Sofia's heart burst for joy.

"¡Señor!"

He moved forward and poured himself a glass of brandy. Sofia's cat hopped down from the hearth and began to rub against his trouser leg.

Darcy smiled and bent down to stroke the cat's silky fur. "Run along, Cocoa. Your mistress and I have some things to discuss."

Sofia saw him look up at her, and suddenly her heart fell. Something was very wrong.

With a coolness of her own, she crossed the room and curtsied as he rose to his feet and bowed.

"Señor, I have been anticipating your arrival since you left. ¿Is something the matter?"

"No, not at all." He paused briefly and then responded, "¿Should there be something the matter?"

"No, Señor, there should not be, but I sense something is not right. You smile, but your eyes betray you."

Setting his glass aside, he smiled once more, and then reached for her and pulled her into his embrace as he gave a chaste kiss to the top of her head. "You know me well," he said. "I am exhausted from the trip and all of my negotiations. It has been grueling."

Breathing deeply, he caught her scent of lavender and lemon verbena and a low moan escaped his throat. It was his very favorite of all the scents she wore. Neither had he missed that she wore the string of pearls he had given her and his favorite morning dress—the one he had specifically chosen at the bazaar that wonderful day when they had first come to town. Her hair was down, long and flowing, just the way he liked it with tiny flowers woven in her tresses that curled prettily about her face. He knew she had prepared herself especially for him, but if her plans were to leave him, then why go to such trouble? Once again, a slow burn of anger began to take root and grow. Was she playing him for a fool, and furthermore, was he the fool for loving her?

He looked down and nodded.

She, to his utter shock, grabbed his face in her hands and drew him to her, taking his mouth in a wanton kiss filled with desire—raw and intense—pressing, demanding his attention. She kissed him again and again, running her fingers through his hair, until something finally broke deep inside of him, and he burst into flames, white hot.

He kissed her back with pure passion that surprised him even more than her forward manner. He loved her…he wanted her…and he would have her.

Lifting her up into his arms, he crossed the room and locked the door, and then took her to the mahogany table in the drawing room where he placed her on its sleek surface and lifted her skirt and petticoat. Unbuttoning his trousers, he parted her thighs with his hands and slid inside of her with ease. With a groan, he dipped his head into the curve of her delicate shoulder and proceeded to take her right there on the table as she wrapped her legs around him.

They made love as they had that night in January after the theatre—hot and passionate—taking and giving, consuming them both in a firestorm of emotion. It was not in his personality to completely lose control of himself like this, but when he was with her, all rational thought left him, and he was overwhelmed by the pure ferocity of the raw passion that flowed between them.

At the moment of his release, his jaw hardened and his teeth grazed her flesh, nipping her delicate skin. She shuddered from the sensation of his sheer force of power as she too reached her climax and cried out in pleasure, trembling in his arms.

Darcy, unable or unwilling to embrace her further, pulled back in unfathomable mortification of losing his resolve so easily. He withdrew and stepped away to adjust his trousers, and then turned back and returned her skirt to its respectable position. For a fleeting moment, all he could do was stare. Once more, she had taken him by complete surprise and reduced him to putty in her hands, so easily influenced as to lose control by her mere kisses.

Finally, he reached up in commiseration and caressed her soft face with his fingertips. That was when he noticed her mask was missing. He shook his head and once again stepped away.

"I am sorry, Senorita, I should not have been such a brute. Please accept my apology," he said with cool indifference as he turned to leave.

Fire flew from her mouth. "¡No! I will not! I have not seen you in over a month, and yet you do not want me when you return. ¡You apologize for making love to me and then turn away with such little consideration for my feelings! ¿What has come between us?"

"¿Consideration for *your* feelings, Senorita? ¿What of my feelings? ¿Are they to be neglected, or is it that I am a wealthy man and therefore must have no feelings? You are dismissed. I will send for you when I am ready!"

"Señor! You treat me like—"

"¿Like a courtesan? Señorita, that is what you are. Though innocent at first, you have employed your time much better than most and learned your skill well. You know how to seduce as well as the best of them: which look to give, which emotion to invoke, what to touch and where. No man admitted to the privilege of being with you for more than a little while can think anything wanting in your abilities."

"¡Señor Darcy! ¡Your assessment of my character is unfair! ¡Indeed it is! ¡It is insulting!"

"Señorita." He bowed and was about to leave when she pulled at his sleeve and addressed him further.

"¡And this is all the reply which I am to have the honor of expecting! ¿That I am a...a... courtesan, and you will send for me when I am needed?"

Her lower lip trembled.

"It is," he said, and then shook his head. "I will leave you now. We will have our much overdue talk in a half hour. Make yourself presentable and meet me in the study of this house when a half-hour has passed." He moved towards the window and pressed his hand against the sill as he gazed out into the lawn.

She ran after him and tugged at his coat. "Señor, I might, perhaps, wish to be informed why, with so little *endeavor* at civility, I am thusly rejected."

He glanced down at her and released his hold on the window as he turned to face her and replied, "If I have been uncivil, it might have to do with your deception. Disguise of every sort is my abhorrence."

"In that regard," she said with a small laugh, "you do not change, Señor. I will see you in half an hour at your discretion." She dropped a curtsy and then quit the room in a cool apathy all of her own.

He released a harsh breath and fell into a nearby chair as he watched her leave. Dropping his face into his hands, he wept. Why did he let his baser instincts drive away all conscious thoughts whenever he was in her presence? She had dressed and made herself up to please him—to pull him into her snare, and it had almost worked. He, in turn, had wounded her heart because she had wounded his.

Reining in his emotions, he moved to the table where his drink had been abandoned. Picking it up, he drained its contents and slammed it down. Darcy abruptly turned and removed himself to the small study in Richmond House where he poured himself another tumbler, this one of Scotch whiskey. He then took linen paper from the letterbox. He could express his thoughts and feelings much better on paper than in person, especially with one who drove him to distraction with a simple turn of her figure. The scent of her—the sight of her—the feel of her body pressed against his—drove all rational thought from his mind, and that would not do when negotiating a business transaction of this kind.

In great anguish, he put pen to paper. Repeatedly he tried to write, but it was of no use. His heart would not agree with the written words. Several sheets of linen paper lay wadded upon the floor. How could he dismiss her when all he wanted to do was fold her into his arms and keep her forever? He shook his head and tried once more. Finally, after breaking the last remaining nib, he fell back in his chair and threw up his hands in defeat.

He reached across the desk, took the half-empty glass of whiskey in his hand and downed it in one gulp before setting the empty tumbler aside. Returning his gaze to the half-written letter, he murmured to himself, "I cannot do this—not in this spirit of anger, for I fear the performance would reflect no credit on either of us."

At the sound of a sharp knock on his door, Darcy turned abruptly. Thinking it was she, he called out.

"Enter!"

"I beg your pardon, sir, but this express has just come from town. The courier says that it is of the utmost urgency and must have your direct attention."

"Thank you, Hobbs," he said, dismissing his butler.

Breaking the seal, he quickly scanned the contents.

*Darcy, you must return to London at once. Do not speak with Miss Molina until you have spoken with me. The matter is urgent. Come quickly.*

*General Richard A. Fitzwilliam*

Darcy folded the note and placed it in his pocket. He then took his latest attempt at a letter and placed it in the letter box. Retrieving the scattered letters about the room, he tossed them in the fire where he watched them burn, but in his haste, he forgot to lock the drawer where his last attempt lay.

Sofia watched the clock on the mantelpiece in her apartment as she paced the floor, crying as she moved back and forth. "What have I done? Surely he does not know it is I, Elizabeth? Surely not! No, if he knew he would have confronted me. What has happened? He says I have deceived him, but why would he think that…unless?"

"What wrong, Miss Sofie. Why you cry? You make baby cry. He feel when you upset."

"Ling-Ling! You have to remember! Where are those papers regarding the cottage in Ireland? They are not here. I meant to pack them before we left to care for Mamma. Where did I leave them?"

"Ling-Ling think….Umm…Last she see, they on—"

"—the table by the bed! Oh yes, I remember now!"

Sofia winced as realization dawned on her. "I placed them in a book so I would be sure to see them and not forget to pack them in my valise before we left for Newgate. Only I was distracted by Lady Margaret and forgot all about them." She turned to her maid, wringing her hands.

"I had hoped you had seen the book and packed it for me, but you did not." She stopped and shook her head and then nodded. "And he has been to London before coming here—before I had the chance to tell him or get the papers myself. Oh no! What shall I do?"

She glanced at her maid. "I know! I will tell him everything now and throw myself at his mercy. I have nothing to lose at this point...except my dignity, which truth be told, I lost a long time ago."

"Yes, you tell Mr. Darcy. He understand. He—"

"Yes, yes, I know. He loves me, and Ling-Ling, I do believe he does, or his reaction would not have been so violent. It was not indifference I saw in his eyes. It was pain! Yes, that is what I will do. I will remove my veil and tell him everything—all of it—now!"

Sofia heard a movement in the courtyard and moved to the window, pressing her small hand to the glass pane as she looked out with a worried look.

"Mr. Darcy!" Her hand flew to her mouth in shock. "Oh, no!"

He glanced up and saw her standing there, and then glanced back to his task at hand.

She quickly rushed down the stairs and hurried out to the portico.

"Mr. Darcy," she cried out in English, "where do you go in such haste? Shall we not talk?"

"When I return, we shall talk. I have an emergency in town. I will return when I can."

He mounted his black stallion and was gone in a full run, leaving through the gate as if the hounds of hell were quick on his heels.

Sofia choked back a sob and turned to reenter the house. Making her way to the kitchen, she had Cook fix some lemonade, which she took to the garden where she could find solace to think.

Cocoa joined her on the stone ledge.

"Meow."

"Cocoa! Oh, Cocoa, what am I to do? I wanted to tell him, but I was not given the opportunity."

"Meow."

"Silly cat! You cannot comprehend a word I say." Sofia tilted her head and narrowed her eyes. "Or can you? They say cats are stupid little creatures, but I do not think you are."

"Meow."

"Yes, yes, I know. Tell him, but how? After our last exchange, I am not sure where to begin. Will he even listen to me? And what if he sends me away? What about the babe? I well know that when he learns the truth, I shall surely disappoint him."

Cocoa answered once more, and then turned popped one of the large goldfish, who had ventured too close to the surface, out of the water. She then flew from her perch and snapped the flopping fish in midair and made her way to the shrubbery to feast.

"Well, I dare say I know where your sentiments are. Your belly overcomes your reason every time. Dear me, I will have to think about this all on my own with no Cocoa for solace."

Sofia sat and watched the animals playing in the lawn, squirrels running up and down the trees, jumping from limb to limb. For nearly a quarter hour, she sat thinking, pondering, and worrying, until at last she knew what she would do. She rose from her seat and made her way through the paths back to the house. She was aware of what needed to be said, and she knew there was only one way to say it. She would write him a letter. It was less mortifying than addressing the matter in person. Then, when the ice was broken, perhaps they could discuss the situation and come to a rational agreement concerning their future. There was one other thing she would tell him as well. She would tell him of their child. If Ling-Ling and Lady Margaret knew of what they spoke, it was her trump card.

Throwing open the study door, she took a seat and went to pull a piece of fine linen letter-paper from the letterbox. That was when she noticed the broken nibs scatter across the desk. She hesitated, but then opened the drawer and found his half-written letter to her.

Gently taking it in her hand, the tears began to fall as she read the words penned to her. When she reached the last word, she slumped in her chair and cried bitterly. But, she was not to cry for long as the sound of a familiar voice rumbled in the vestibule.

"Where is she? I demand to see her at once!"

# Chapter 19

h, my gentle reader, the storm in a teacup has been stirred. Hades is the culprit. Zeus has declared it from the heavens. Poseidon has announced it from the deep. *Excitabat enim fluctus in simpulo*—he was stirring up waves in a ladle, as Cicero would say. It is a frightful prospect, good and faithful reader, but let us not despair, for it is commonly known that even darkest cloud has a silver lining, or so the gods assure me.

Therefore, if we dare, let us once more take a look at our dear heroine and see how she fares as the wicked witch from the North blows in on the stormy seas.
Come along, shall we?

Sofia quickly left the study for the drawing room in dreaded expectation of the unwelcome guest. Before Mr. Hobbs could even make a complete announcement, the door was thrown open, and her visitor entered. It was Lady Catherine de Bourgh.

Sofia was, to say the very least, surprised, but her astonishment was beyond all expectations when Her Ladyship, entering the room with an air even more ungracious than was her habit, made no other reply to Sofia's salutation, other than a slight inclination of the head. She sat down without saying a word.

Sofia also took a seat.

"You have a very small park here," returned Lady Catherine, after a short silence. "Miss Molina, I assume you know who I am."

"Yes, Your Ladyship. Mr. Hobbs announced your entrance as much as he was allowed."

"Yes, I suppose he did." There was silence once more and Her Ladyship spoke again. "There seemed to be a prettyish kind of a little wilderness on one side of my nephew's lawn. I should be glad to take a turn in it, if you will favor me with your company."

Sofia obeyed, and, after running into her room for her parasol, attended her noble guest downstairs. As they passed through the hall, Lady Catherine opened the doors to the dining-parlor and drawing-room, and pronouncing them, after a short survey, to be decent looking rooms, walked on.

Her carriage remained at the door, and Sofia saw that her waiting-woman was in it. They proceeded in silence along the gravel walk that led to the copse. Sofia was determined to make no effort at conversation with a woman who was now more unpleasant than her usual insolent and disagreeable self that she had remembered from Kent all those years ago.

"How could I ever think her like her nephew?" she whispered to herself beneath her breath, as she looked in her face.

Once they entered the copse, Lady Catherine began in the following manner.

"You can be at no loss, Miss Molina, to understand the reason of my journey hither. Your own heart, your own conscience, must tell you why I have come."

Sofia looked at the older lady with unaffected astonishment.

"Indeed, you are mistaken, madam. I have not the slightest inclination of what might bring you to Richmond."

"Miss Molina," replied her ladyship, in an angry tone, "I am of such elevated status that you ought to know I am not to be trifled with. But however insincere you may choose to be, you shall not find me so. My character has ever been celebrated for its sincerity and frankness, and in such a moment as this, I shall certainly not depart from it. A report of a most alarming nature reached me two days ago. I was told that you, Miss Sofia Molina, are none other than Miss Elizabeth Bennet, and that you have for these three months been cohabitating with my nephew—my own nephew—Mr. Darcy, as his mistress!

"You wear a veil to conceal your true scurrilous character, but I know it all! I know who you are. How could this be possible—that you, Miss Elizabeth Bennet, would stoop to such a position as to form a sinful alliance of this shameful sort with my nephew and that he would agree to such an arrangement? Though I told myself it was impossible that such an outrageous falsehood could be so, by all appearances, it is true; you are his lover. How utterly shameful of you! It is disgraceful—reprehensible! I would not condescend to prevail upon him on such a scandalous affair! No! I could not! Therefore, I instantly resolved on setting off for this place, that I might make my sentiments known to *you*."

Sofia, coloring with astonishment and disdain, replied to the lady before her, "This entire supposition is absurd! I am not this *Elizabeth Bennet*. The accusation is as groundless as it is ridiculous. Your Ladyship, I have to wonder you took the trouble of coming here. What could you possibly hope to accomplish by such a display? To embarrass me with your abusive language or to impose your will upon Mr. Darcy by frightening me away?"

"There are reasons, and you know them, Miss Bennet. I will not sport with your intelligence, for that is not all I have heard. I have also heard there is a child, and that your designs are to trap my nephew into matrimony. If that is your *ambition*, Miss Bennet, you must be made to understand that it is a contemptible misconception. It shall never occur. That one, such as yourself, could even aspire to such a place as the wife of Mr. Darcy is incomprehensible; thus upon hearing such an outrageous declaration, I have come to insist on having such a report universally contradicted. It must be impossible. No! It cannot be! Tell me there is no child!"

Sofia's eyes widened beneath her veil and she thought she might faint, but from somewhere deep within the depths of her soul, she found the courage to face her foe.

"Lady Catherine, you insist upon knowing the truth of a great many things that you freely throw about. However, Your Ladyship, there are a few things I will insist upon myself, and one of those is to be called by my proper name, Miss Sofia Molina.

You will address me as such. If you cannot comply, all conversation between us is at an end this very instant!"

"Very well, then. Have it your way at present, but I insist on knowing the truth. Is the rumor true? Are you with child?"

"Your Ladyship ought to know that by your coming to Richmond, to see me," Sofia said coolly, "it will be seen, rather, as a confirmation of it, *if*, indeed, such a report exists, and therefore give credibility to the rumor Your Ladyship wishes to deny. But if it is your intent to spread gossip, you most assuredly will succeed."

"If! Do you then pretend to be *ignorant* of it?"

"I have never heard such a thing."

"And can you likewise declare that there is no foundation for it?"

"I do not pretend to possess equal frankness with Your Ladyship. You may ask questions which I shall choose not to answer."

"This is not to be borne! Miss Molina, I insist on being satisfied. Are you at this very moment carrying my nephew's child?"

"Your Ladyship has declared it to be impossible."

"It ought to be so; it *must* be so, while he retains the use of his reason. But you, Miss Molina, if that is truly who you are, have used your arts and allurements—your seductions, and in a moment of weakness have made him forget what he owes to himself and to all his family.

"I know what you are about—the likes of you and your kind. You may have drawn him into your bed, Miss Molina, but you will never draw him into matrimony—child or no child. He will never marry the likes of you! Now tell me at once. Are you carrying his child?!"

"If I am, I shall be the last person to confess it."

"Miss Molina, do you know who I am? I have not been accustomed to such language as this. I am almost the nearest relation he has in the world, and am entitled to know all his dearest concerns."

"But you are not entitled to know mine; nor is such behavior as this likely to induce me to be explicit."

"Let me be rightly understood. This match to which you have the presumption to aspire by trapping my nephew with the burden of an unwanted child, can never take place. No, never. Mr. Darcy is engaged to my daughter. Now, what have you to say for yourself?"

"Only this: that if it is so, then after all these years—he is, after all, two and thirty, and I have heard she is of a similar age, why has he not yet married her? He has free will to do as he chooses."

Lady Catherine hesitated for a moment, and then replied, "My daughter has been ill, but her recovery is certain. They will indeed marry before the year is out. Now, what have you to say?"

"If it is as you say, then you can have no reason to suppose he will make an offer to me—child or no child."

"Make no mistake. They will marry. The engagement between them is of a peculiar kind, intended and sanctioned by their parents. From their infancy they have been intended for each other. It was the favorite wish of his mother, as well as of hers. While in their cradles, we planned the union, and now, at the moment when the wishes of both sisters would be realized, they are to be prevented by a young woman of scurrilous reputation—a degradation to herself and a disgrace to all that is good and decent! Do you pay no regard to the wishes of his family and friends—to his tacit engagement with Miss De Bourgh? Are you lost to every feeling of propriety and delicacy? Have you not heard me just say that from his earliest hours he was destined for his cousin?"

"I have certainly heard your proclamations, but what is that to me? If Mr. Darcy is neither by honor nor inclination bound to his cousin, why is he not to make another choice? And if I were to be that choice, why may not I accept him?"

"Because honor, decorum, prudence—nay, common decency, forbid it! Yes, Miss Bennet because you are a—"

"Stop at once! Let us settle that subject here and now. For the last time, I am *not* Miss Bennet; though I know much of her, I am not she. Do not ever refer to me by that name again."

"And if you be not her, how would you know about her?"

"I know because Mr. Darcy once loved her. As his mistress, he has told me all. If his heart belongs to anyone, it would be she, though he believes her to be dead, and for all I know, she is dead. I am not she!"

"As you wish, Miss Molina, or whoever you may be. Miss Bennet is not dead, and even if he does love her as you say, it is of no consequence. A marriage with her would be as much of a degradation as one with yourself. Common decency forbids such an alliance with either of you, for should it occur, neither could expect to be noticed by his family or friends. Therefore, if you willfully act against the inclinations of all, you will be censured, slighted, and despised by everyone connected with him. Your alliance will be a disgrace; your name will never even be mentioned by any of us."

"These are heavy misfortunes, indeed," replied Sofia. "But the wife of Mr. Darcy must have such extraordinary sources of happiness necessarily attached to her situation that she could, upon the whole, have no cause to repine."

"Obstinate, headstrong girl! I am ashamed of you! Is this how you treat your betters? I am from among one of the highest ranks of society—the daughter of an earl, descended down the line from kings! Is nothing due to me on that score?

"Let us sit down. You are to understand, Miss Molina, that I came here with the determined resolution of carrying my purpose; nor will I be dissuaded from it. I have not been used to submitting to any person's whims. I am not in the habit of brooking disappointment."

"That will make Your Ladyship's situation at present more pitiable, but it will have no effect on me."

"I will not be interrupted! You will be silent and hear me out! My daughter and my nephew are formed for each other. They are descended, on the maternal side, from the same noble line, and on the father's, from respectable, honorable, and ancient, though untitled families. Their fortune on both sides is splendid. They are destined for each other by the voice of every member of their respective houses, and what is to divide them? A contemptible young woman who has descended into the realm of a harlot and now finds herself with child? Is this to be endured? No! It must not, shall not be! If you were sensible of your own good, you would remove yourself from this place and take that child to a land where no one knows who you are—what you are. This child you are carrying cannot—will not become the heir to Pemberley."

"I am a gentleman's daughter, born to a sphere equal to your nephew's. I came from a father with the same noble lines as Mr. Darcy's. Though my father was not titled, men in his line were."

"But you have long since quit that sphere. You are now a courtesan—a member of the demimonde with no connections other than that of mistress to the very rich—not considered respectable by—"

"Whatever I am," said Sofia, "if your nephew does not object, then it can be nothing to you."

"Tell me, once and for all, are you Miss Elizabeth Bennet as was reported to me, and are you carrying my nephew's child?"

"I have repeatedly told you I am not Miss Bennet."

"But what of the child? Are you or are you *not* carrying his child?!"

Though Sofia would not, for the mere purpose of obliging Lady Catherine, have answered this question, she was sensible enough to know that it could not be denied for much longer and thus, after a moment's deliberation, could not but say, "I am."

Lady Catherine was outraged.

"I knew it had to be true, but you must surely understand that no marriage can take place. Nor can a child born by the likes of you ever be associated with any of us. It shall not bear my nephew's name. No! Not ever! Decency forbids it. Therefore, will you promise me that the child will be disposed of—to an orphanage if you insist on birthing it?"

"I will make no promise of the kind. I intend to birth my son and keep him. You can depend upon it!"

"Miss Molina! I am shocked and astonished. You cannot keep my nephew's child, nor will he marry you! Despite your station, I expected to find a more reasonable young woman." She narrowed her eyes, her pinched mouth quivering. "Do not deceive yourself into a belief that I will ever recede. I shall not go away till you have given me the assurance I require."

"And I certainly never shall give it. I am not to be intimidated into anything so wholly unreasonable. Your Ladyship wants me to dispose of Mr. Darcy's child so that he may marry your daughter without guilt or consequence, but would my giving you the wished-for promise, make their marriage at all more probable? Supposing him to be attached to me and to desire this child I carry, would my refusing to accept his hand or birth his son make him wish to marry a cousin—especially one who is well on her way to being upon the shelf, as the saying goes, and, furthermore, is quite possibly unable to give him an heir? I can give him children—many of them."

Lady Catherine's face paled with anger, and Sofia rose to the challenge.

"Allow me to say this, Lady Catherine: you have widely mistaken my character, if you think I can be worked on by such persuasions as these. How far your nephew might approve of your interference in his affairs, I cannot tell, but you certainly have no right to concern yourself in mine. I carry his heir—something Miss De Bourgh quite possibly can never do. It is done, and that is it. On this subject, I have nothing more to say, no apology to offer. I must beg, therefore, to be importuned no further on the subject. I am keeping my child. Whether it is to your liking or not, I do not care."

"Not so hasty, if you please! I have by no means done. To all the objections I have already urged, I have still another to add. No matter what you may say, I believe you to be Miss Elizabeth Bennet. If that be so, I am not a stranger to the

M. K. Baxley

particulars of her background: your other child—William. I have it on good report that he too is illegitimate and the father unknown. Are the shades of Pemberley to be thus polluted by a wanton woman with one illegitimate child who is also carrying another ill begot?"

"Ill begot! Lady Catherine, your nephew has come to my bed these past months of his own choice. No one forced him to do as he has done. He sought me out and purchased me of his own volition. I will hear no more of this. You have said it all and can now have nothing further to say," she resentfully answered. "Furthermore, I have told you I am *not* Miss Elizabeth Bennet. You may choose to believe what you will. It will not alter the truth."

"If it is as you say, remove your veil this very instant and let me see who you are!"

"I shall do no such thing. Your Ladyship may ask, but I am not obliged to comply."

"Outrageous, headstrong girl of ill breeding! You are a disgrace to yourself and all that is good and decent! I know who you are and will not be dissuaded from my purpose."

"Lady Catherine, I have nothing further to say on the subject of Miss Bennet, marriage to your nephew, or the disposition of my child or any of hers! You have insulted me and the lady in every possible way you could conceive of. I must beg to return to the house."

She rose as she spoke. Lady Catherine also rose, and they turned back. Her Ladyship was highly incensed.

"You have no regard, then, for the honor and credit of my nephew! Unfeeling, selfish girl! Do you not consider that a connection with you must disgrace him in the eyes of everybody? Your children will bear the scandal of their mother for all their lives."

"Lady Catherine, I have nothing further to say. You know my sentiments."

"You are then resolved to have him brought down in scandal?"

"Lady Catherine, I am only resolved to act in that manner which will, in my own opinion, constitute my personal happiness, without reference to you, or to any other person so wholly unconnected with me."

"It is well. You refuse, then, to oblige me. You refuse to obey the claims of duty, honor, and decency. You are determined to ruin him in the opinion of all his friends, and make him the contempt of the world."

"Neither duty, nor honor, nor decency," replied Sofia, "has any possible claim on me in this present instance. No principle of duty, honor, or decency would be violated if I should enter into a marriage with Mr. Darcy. Many a lady has preempted her wedding vows and married with a child on the way. I am no different from any of them. Should we marry, my child would then be legitimate and therefore able to inherit all that is rightfully his. Lord Berwick married his mistress as did Mr. Thomas Coutts and the Duke of Devonshire theirs. It appears to be fashionable. Moreover, with regard to the resentment of his family or the indignation of the world, if his marrying me excited the former, it would not give me one moment's concern. As for the latter, I shall bear the deprivations with equanimity until it is forgotten in good time."

"And this is your real opinion, your final resolve! Very well, then, I shall now know how to act. Do not imagine, Miss Molina, that your ambition will ever be gratified. I came to try you. I hoped to find you reasonable, but depend upon it, I will carry my point. My nephew will not defy his family. Depend upon it."

In this manner, Lady Catherine talked on until they arrived at the door of the carriage, when, turning hastily around, she added, "I take no leave of you, Miss Molina, if that is indeed your name, nor do I give you any compliments. You deserve none. I am most seriously displeased."

Sofia made no answer, and, without attempting to persuade her ladyship to return into the house, walked quietly into it herself. She heard the carriage drive away as she proceeded upstairs.

"Ling-Ling, pack our trunks. We leave at once for Newgate, and do not forget Cocoa."

# Chapter 20

ow, my good reader, the truth will finally come to light, but not without consequence. A storm of cataclysmic proportions is brewing and uncertainties abound. The Wicked Witch of Kent blows in like a hurricane, settling herself upon our faithful hero as a vulture set to devour.

Let us once more gird up our loins so that we might make haste and retreat should scenes unpleasant necessitate a speedy exit from stage right. With trepidation, let us lift the shades of our peepers and once more take a look, shall we?

Darcy rode through the gate of Darcy House and quickly dismounted, throwing the reins to a footman. "See that Libertine is rubbed down and given a full measure of oats with some fresh hay. He's had a hard ride."

"Yes, sir. I will tell the stable boy to prepare his stall."

Darcy took the steps two at a time until he reached the top. Entering the house, he went straight to the library where he found the general waiting dispassionately, reading *The Times* while he sipped a brandy with his feet propped up on a table.

"Fitzwilliam, what the devil is the meaning of this! You had me come from Richmond to town in such a hurry that I nearly overturned a vegetable cart on the outskirts of London, frightening the poor farmer out of his wits. I might as well have thought the house was on fire from the vagueness of your express."

The general casually lowered his feet, one by one, as he folded his paper and set it side.

"Care to have a drink, Cousin?"

"What? You call me all this way to drink with you?!"

"No," he said, taking the decanter of brandy and pouring a full measure. "Not to drink with me, but you very well may need one when you see this report I have for you. Here, you are going to need it."

Darcy took the drink as he stood gazing at his cousin, contemplating his odd behavior.

"What report?"

"This one," the general said, reaching into his breast pocket and pulling out a portfolio wallet. He handed it to his cousin. "I took the liberty of hiring a man from the Bow Street Runners to investigate Miss Molina whilst you were in the North. I knew you trusted her implicitly, but I did not. Mr. Nickolas Fritchard and his men have followed her all these many weeks, careful always to observe from a distance and not look conspicuous. On occasion, I believe Mr. Fritchard said he was even of assistance to her, but he was always the professional he is paid to be. She has no idea that she was being followed or what is in this report."

Darcy stood staring at his cousin as a slow burn of resentment began to build. "Was Wex in agreement with this intrusion upon my privacy?"

"No, but he did know about it and was quite concerned himself."

Darcy took a sip of his drink and caught his cousin's gaze. "Fitzwilliam, what gives you the right to interfere in my affairs? I deeply resent this manner of meddling in things that are clearly none of your business."

"You may not feel so once you read the report."

"I will ask you once more, Cousin," Darcy said. "Tell me why you felt the need to take matters concerning *my* personal business into your own hands?"

"Darcy, when you read that report, you will once again be in my debt. Go on. What do you fear? The Truth?"

"I fear nothing!"

"Then read it and weep."

Setting his glass down, Darcy took a deep breath. With hesitation, he opened the leather wallet and carefully pulled out the account of his cousin's investigation and then laid the wallet aside. As he began to read, his face colored and then paled. He frowned. Then a look of astonishment spread across his face.

The general spoke, but Darcy made no answer. He seemed scarcely able to hear him. Walking up and down the room in earnest meditation, his brow contracted; his air was distressed. He stopped and glanced up. Everything she had ever said or done flashed before his eyes. ...*Elizabeth*...? He shook his head. ...*no, this could not be...?*

He turned to the general. "Are you saying Sofia Molina is...?"

"It is as you see."

"No, that cannot be. I tell you she is *dead!*" Darcy shouted, his countenance reflecting an expression of mingled astonishment and mortification.

He began to move once again, pacing in great agitation, realization slowly gripping him even as his mind struggled against it. George Wickham's last words came to mind ...*I thought you preferred the other one*... Darcy's chest tightened as he shook his head. ...*I wonder what he meant.*

The general leaned against the chimneypiece with one leg crossed over the other, watching every expression his cousin displayed: shock, disbelief, even—it would appear—pain.

"She is dead!" Darcy repeated.

The general pushed himself away from the stone mantel and spoke with a tone meant to make his point. "You think that," he said. "What proof do you have? Were you there for the interment? Have you even seen her grave? Did you mourn over her stone?"

Abruptly, Darcy came to a stop and looked at his cousin with piercing eyes. "No...I have not. I took the word of her uncle's business partner. Why would he lie to me?"

"*That,* I do not know, but I can imagine why he might. Can you not?"

"Yes," Darcy said as the truth of the situation began to take form in his mind. "If it is as you say, I certainly can."

The general nodded in response. "He wanted the entire commerce for himself, Darcy. Therefore, he must have sought a clause in the contract that would allow him to legally steal it from the remaining children—a disreputable business practice by one with no scruples. Moreover, quite common where there are no male relatives to offer protection for the defenseless. Read on."

Darcy held the few sheets of paper, trying to still his shaking hand. He fell into the nearest chair and reached for his brandy; then he returned his gaze to the details, pausing every now and then to sip his drink. He continued through the second page onto the third.

Looking up yet again, he said, "This is where she would go whilst I was involved with Mr. Mann and Mr. Steadman…to this address on Newgate?"

"The residents at No. 12 Newgate Street are Miss Jane Bennet, Miss Catherine Bennet, Edward Gardiner, Miss Flora Gardiner, and a small child, William Bennet, believed to be the son of…*Miss Elizabeth Bennet.*"

Darcy's jaw hardened. "No! That cannot be. I tell you, Fitzwilliam, she was untouched by any man when she came to me! The child is *not* her son!"

The general replied with little emotion expressed. "I believe you, Cousin. A man knows whether a woman is chaste or not when he beds her for the first time."

"Of course I knew! There was evidence on the bed clothes—plenty of it. I know what she was!"

"I never said you did not. The child could be the offspring of any of the Bennet sisters. It just so happens that he refers to Miss Elizabeth as his 'mamma.' But you must read the entire report before much more discourse."

Darcy raised his hand and rubbed his chin, staring off into the room in deep thought. *...Not just any Bennet sister, but Lydia…and Wickham. That is why Wickham attacked Elizabeth. He must have believed her to be Lydia. That must have been what he meant when he was dying.*

Darcy turned to his cousin and started as if he would speak, but the general held up his drink and nodded.

"Read on."

Darcy returned his eyes to the printed page, his drink abandoned until he had finally read the complete report.

"She came from Beggars Street in Whitecastle—the poorest part of London where people live in deplorable conditions: rats, fleas, squalor, filth. My dogs live better than the people on London's East End." He paused and looked to his cousin. "And this is how my money has been spent."

"Yes, I took the liberty of having Mr. Mann audit her accounts. The money was spent for clothing, food, decent lodging, and medical care for her mother as well as her mother's funeral whilst you were in Lancashire. Hardly a penny went for Miss Elizabeth's personal use. That is why she sold herself to you, Darcy—so that she could provide for them, one life given for another."

"Newgate Street is barely a step up from Beggars Street," he whispered beneath his breath.

"Yes, but it is the best she could afford. She gave her all for them and their comfort. Very much like you, I would say. Sofia Molina, or rather Elizabeth Bennet, is a remarkable woman. Not many could persevere as she has done, and what it must have cost her! But there is more."

"More? What possibly more could there be? If it is as I've read so far, I am not at all certain I can manage it!"

The general took the wallet and retrieved seven boarding passes for North Star Lines. "You will manage it, Darce; you have to. It looks as if she plans a trip—or move is more like it, I would say. They are to leave on the first of April."

Darcy's head fell as he slumped in his seat.

"Yes…that I know." He closed his eyes and took a deep breath. "I found a sketch of a cottage in Ulster and the correspondence between her friend and the person in charge of settling the affair, as well as the bank draft where money was sent to a bank in County Down. Had I not gotten your express, I was going to give her a letter of dismissal along with a check for ten thousand pounds—the full amount of our contract."

"Exactly why I had to see you before you could. From what Wex relayed to me, I knew something was very wrong."

As the general spoke, the memory of their last exchange flashed before his eyes.

"¿Like a courtesan? Señorita that is what you are… You know how to seduce as well as the best of them: which look to give, which emotion to invoke, what to touch and where. No man admitted to the privilege of being with you for more than a little while can think anything wanting in your abilities."

Darcy winced and swallowed against the restriction in his throat as he groaned from deep within. "What have I done to her—to my Elizabeth—the woman I have loved all these years? I have taken her—ravished her—despoiled her much as any rake would have done, and I was about to cast her off."

"That is where you are wrong, Darcy. You have loved her as any husband would love a wife. And as for casting her off, the man I know would not have been able to do that. You know you could never have let her go completely. Wex and I have both been witnesses to how much you love her, and Maggie is in agreement. In fact, she is truly taken with Sofia, though she does not know who Sofia really is at present. We are all in agreement. Go to the woman you love and ask for her hand, but you might want to let her tell you the information I have given you rather than have her find out you know by other means. Allow her to keep that much dignity, as I am sure this will be a humiliation too much to comprehend when she has to face you as Elizabeth Bennet.

"As for the family, you know they will not approve, but take heart in knowing that Wex, Lady Margaret, and I fully support you. If father raises any objections, let us remind him of one salient point. You are your own master, Darce. You can do as you please.

"And do not berate yourself a minute more. Far better for you to have purchased her than either of the Dukes. You know Prinny's set. Miss Elizabeth Bennet is a gentleman's daughter of high caliber—a diamond of the first waters. Even as Sofia, she was always a lady. They would have degraded her and then discarded her like the morning newspaper when they were done—and quite possibly, with one or more mouths to feed that they would neither have cared for nor supported. Of all the gentlemen there that night, you are the one she chose—and Darcy, you may not have known *her*, but she certainly knew *you*."

Darcy breathed deeply and let out a noisy breath as he stared into the expanse of the room. "No, Fitzwilliam, that is were you are wrong. I knew. The truth was right there in front of me, all around me. Everywhere I turned, Elizabeth was there. Though she tried her best to hide it, somehow I knew, and yet I did not." He paused and shook his head, sipping his drink before continuing.

"The manner of her addresses, her laughter, her intelligence, the turn of her countenance and her implacable self confidence when she would challenge me. She bantered and sported as she had done at Netherfield and Rosings, and I could never forget her lavender scent—of all she wore, it is my cherished favorite. Those things were etched in my mind.

"Incredible it is that I should see how remarkably similar Sofia was to Elizabeth, and yet, still I was blind. It was all there, but I did not see it because I was not looking for it." Darcy glanced at his cousin. "Fitzwilliam, there have been two women I have loved, and they are one and the same."

His cousin gave him a look of sympathy as Darcy stated with conviction. "I believe she did love me—and that she loves me still. I have not the slightest notion as to why she is going to Ireland, but I *know* she loves me." *Or at least she did if I haven't destroyed it.*

"If that be the case then, what are you going to do about it?"

"I don't know. I will have to think about it—*and* about her."

"Do not think for too long, Darce. You would be a fool to let her slip through your fingers after all you have been through together. The Fates… or God, whichever way you may choose to look at it, are giving you a second chance, and that is rare. Take it without delay, Cousin."

Just then there was a disturbance at the front door. Both gentlemen turned at the sound of it.

"I will see my nephew this instant. Take me to him at once." The grand lady pushed by the older gentleman nearly knocking him to the floor.

"Madam, if you will allow me, I shall announce you to the master of the house."

"No! Get out of my way," she exclaimed, whacking him with her cane. "He is my nephew. He will see me at once!"

Bursting through the library doors, she entered like a whirlwind.

"Darcy, I have the most alarming news. Miss Elizabeth Bennet is alive, and she is posing as your mistress. Though she denies it, I know it all. You must throw her off before she brings shame down on us all!"

Lady Catherine hobbled into the room, her cane clicking on the polished floor as her feet shuffled along. "The way you searched for that young woman when you discovered her father had died, I was afraid you would do something foolish then. I will not have you do it now."

Darcy was on his feet in a matter of seconds. "Lady Catherine, may I ask of what are you speaking?"

"Miss Molina!" The Grand Dame said as she took the seat her nephew had just vacated. "I have been to Richmond and seen her. Though she will not confess it, my former parson, Mr. Collins, tells me it is true."

"Excuse me Darce, but this is my cue to leave." The general bowed to his aunt and discreetly found somewhere else to be.

Darcy's eyes widened. Glancing between his aunt and his departing cousin, he pulled himself up straight and moved to where Lady Catherine sat. He gave a slight bow.

"Excuse me, Lady Catherine, but did I just hear you correctly? Did you say that you have been to Richmond and have seen Miss Molina?" He looked at her in stunned disbelief. "And pray tell, exactly what did you hope to achieve by interjecting yourself into my personal affairs? Even if she were Miss Bennet, which I assure you she is not, I am a grown man with a full set of teeth—well past the age of consent. I owe no consideration to you or anyone else as to whom I choose to share my house or, dear aunt, need I say, *my bed*. Therefore, please enlighten me. What was your purpose in accosting Miss Molina? I have a contractual agreement with her. Did you mean to frighten her off? She is a courtesan, there at my request, and need I dare add, she is well paid for her services."

"Darcy! How could you?! Such disgraceful behavior."

"I can do it very well, madam. The same as other rich men in my position—the same as your brother, the Earl—the same as my grandfather, the Earl before your brother, and the same, I might add, as Uncle Lewis, *your* late husband. Need I continue?"

"Outrageous! I am not used to such vulgar language as this."

"No, I am sure you are not," he said with a shrug of his shoulders.

"Fitzwilliam Alexander Darcy! You are not to take that tone with me. She means to trap you into a marriage that will disgrace us all. Mr. Collins—"

"Mr. Collins! Is he not the very clergyman who put an old woman with four unprotected daughters into the hedgerows—and I might say, at your direction? What could he possibly have to do with any of this? Has he not done enough?"

Lady Catherine straightened in her chair and narrowed her beady eyes. "Nothing was done at my direction. I merely made a suggestion. The rest was up to him! However, once it was done, it was done for the good. But this…this Miss Elizabeth Bennet, a young woman brought up in the wildest manner of circumstances with no governess to speak of—unfit to be mentioned by any of us, has had the forwardness to return to Longbourn to bury her mother, and while she was there, she would make a spectacle of herself parading about a child who carries the name Bennet. Who would know the identity of his father? He calls her 'Mamma.' Then if that were not enough, she could not even be sociable because she was unwell. There is more in her belly than ever passed through her throat. Are you to forsake your heritage and disgrace us all with such a woman? No! It shall not be borne!"

"What! What are you telling me, Aunt?"

"I am telling you that woman is carrying a child."

"What woman?"

"Miss Molina—the woman you are carrying on with. I have seen her!"

He looked at her in shock and astonishment and repeated what he had asked previously, "You have been to *my* house in Richmond without *my* knowledge or consent and have accosted *my* mistress with such accusations as you have expressed to me?" He rolled his eyes in revulsion. "I can only imagine what you must have said." *...and how she must have felt...!*

"Fitzwilliam Darcy! Somebody must look after your affairs. Yes, I have been to that house of iniquity!"

Darcy turned and walked to the window, gazing out and slowly shaking his head. Breathing out in disgust, he pivoted on his heel and addressed his aunt directly. "And did she tell you she is Miss Elizabeth Bennet—a woman I have believed to be dead these five years?"

"Well, no—not exactly. Mr. Collins—"

"Mr. Collins! And what proof did *he* offer?"

"He saw a portrait of her in, well a place where he does missionary work for the church, and he recognized Miss Bennet from the portrait—something about her jawline and the fact that her father toured Spain with his children when they were young."

"Now, let me see if I have this straight," Darcy said. "He recognized Miss Bennet as Miss Molina at Madam Papillia's establishment where he does...*missionary work*...for the *church*? Very interesting." Darcy rolled his eyes once more and shrugged as the missionary *position* came to his mind.

Clearing his throat, he continued, "Lady Catherine, there is one thing I would wish to ask of you, if I may."

She nodded.

"Why is it that I have been with Miss Molina in, shall we say, *very close* and confined quarters for some months now, and yet I did not see the connection? I would say that I know both women fairly well, though one better than the other, obviously. Hence, I can assure you from my most *intimate* and very pleasurable contact with Miss Molina that she is *not* Miss Elizabeth Bennet. I should think I would know with whom it is that I have slept all these many months. Do you not think, Lady Catherine that I would not recognize her—especially if she is *indeed*, as you have said, carrying my child, which I might add I know nothing of? I mean, how could I sleep with a woman and not know who she is?"

Lady Catherine colored deep shades of red and purple. "But if she is *not* Miss Bennet, then *who is* she, and what of the child this woman claims to carry? What will you do there? It is a disgrace! What have you to say to that, Darcy?"

"Lady Catherine, I am not sure I know who you mean—Miss Molina or Miss Bennet. You have spoken of each and claimed them both to be with child because one says she is and the other is merely unwell. Which is it, Lady Catherine, Miss Molina, or Miss Bennet?"

"I—I—"

"If it is Miss Molina which you mean, then that is my concern, but if Miss Bennet is with child, I am sure I would know nothing of it. I have not had the privilege of seeing her in years. And, if it is Miss Bennet you meant—on sheer speculation, I might, because she is merely in poor health, then maybe it would be that she is simply unwell from the stress of caring for her only remaining parent who has, according to you, just died. If caring for a dying parent were not reason enough to make one ill, then I am afraid I do not know what might be. A case of nervous vexations is enough to set anyone's stomach to fits, would you not think, Lady Catherine? But it is not enough to claim one has fallen with child."

"Yes-yes, but if Miss Molina is *not* Miss Bennet, then what do you say of *her* condition? She has admitted to being with child—your child! Now what do you say to that?"

"Only this: If it is, in fact, true...that my mistress has fallen pregnant, then this might be considered a heavy misfortune for some, but—"

"Stop at once!" She held up her hand, her mouth twisted in anger. "I am not used to such patronizing treatment; nor will I abide by the crude vulgarity as you have thus far displayed. No! I will not hear any of it any longer. I will have my share in this conversation, and *you*, nephew, will listen. Hear me in silence. I will not be interrupted again!"

He turned and privately said, "I feel like little Jack Horner, sitting in a corner eating his Christmas pie. I stuck in my thumb and pulled out a plumb. Oh, my, what a good boy am I! Two women have fallen pregnant, and I am supposed to have sired both their babes." He sighed heavily in disgust and turned back to his aunt's dour face. Yes…he would hear her out, and then he would shut her up.

Cool and calm with his hands linked behind his back, twisting his signet ring, Darcy paced the floor, glancing at his aunt every now and then, while she continued on her discourse, disparaging first Miss Bennet and then Miss Molina, ranting and raving about disgrace and family honor. On and on she went for the better part of a quarter hour.

"The little trollop told me she would not dispose of the child she carries. Obstinate, headstrong girl! Give me your word, Darcy that you will not do anything foolish, that you will take care of that…that insolent, willful woman who seduces with her arts and allurements. I was astonished at the boldness of her declaration. She even has the notion that you might marry her, ill-conceived that it is. Promise me, nephew that you will never enter into a union with such a scurrilous woman, that you will have her and her child sent away. I want no scandal to touch this family."

Darcy's eyes flashed in warning, but Lady Catherine would have her say. "If you do not listen to the voice of reason, my brother the Earl will call on you next. He will—even more than I—be most seriously displeased."

Finally, he nodded and spoke. "There is no need to involve the Earl. I give you my solemn word that I will indeed take care of the matter and no scandal will touch me or *this* family." *…or her… as I consider **her** to be part of my family as well.*

"Good! I knew you would listen to reason even if she will not. Unfeeling, selfish girl! You will send her away then."

"I will put her on a boat bound for America for the entire world to see if it pleases you. In fact, I have been considering it and have the ticket in hand. Will that do?" he raised up a ticket so that his aunt could clearly see the boarding pass.

"Excellent! The little strumpet. Make sure she never returns. And what of the child? What is to be done there?"

"Sofia Molina will never return, I assure you. As for the child, if there is one, he or she, which ever it may be, will be provided for in America, and you, Aunt Catherine, are to speak nothing of this ever again lest you bring scandal down on us all with the spread of gossip."

"You can be assured of my silence." She smiled, releasing a breath of relief. "I shall take my leave. I want a public display of her boarding that ship."

"As you wish."

"Then I am going to announce your engagement to my daughter. The time has long passed since it ought to be done."

"You will announce no such engagement until I give you leave to do so."

Lady Catherine smiled once more. "I knew you would come to your senses. You are correct in your thinking. A goodly amount of time must pass to remove the stench of that woman from you. I do not want Anne to suffer from the talk of wagging tongues."

"Allow me to see you safely to your carriage."

When Darcy reentered the library, General Fitzwilliam came from the alcove where he had taken refuge. He gave a low whistle.

"Well, Darcy, that certainly presents a whole different set of problems. What are you going to do now?"

"I am going back to Richmond as quickly as I can. I have a lady to whom I wish to propose."

"But Darcy! You heard Aunt Catherine. Elizabeth is with child."

"All the more reason to marry—and marry without delay."

"But what about the scandal? True, no one knows Sofia Molina's true identity, but how will you hide Elizabeth's pregnancy—especially if you marry so soon after the affair with Miss Molina is ended? The world will know, or at least have suspicions."

Darcy gave a lopsided grin. "I have a plan. No one will know anything, and as for those who suspect, I have a way of closing their mouths. I may not have spent as much time at the gaming tables as have you and Wex, but I know how to play the game just the same. I have a card or two up my sleeve. You can count on it!"

The general broke into a wide grin. "I believe you do at that, Darcy. Yes...I certainly do. Remember, Wex and I are with you."

"And I am grateful for your support, but I must make haste, for I've not a moment to lose. Tell your brother that he and Lady Margaret are invited to a wedding, and I expect you to stand up with me," he said, retrieving the report and tickets from the side table and stuffing them securely inside his coat.

"We wouldn't miss it for the world, Darcy...not for the world. Good luck, Cousin!"

Darcy laughed as he made his way up the stairs to fetch the ring and then to the stables for a fresh horse. There was not a second to spare. He had to get to Sofia— no, *Elizabeth* before she had time to disappear from his life again as she had done before.

# $\mathscr{C}$hapter 21

$\mathscr{G}$ ood and gentle reader, we have now come to that moment which has long been anticipated. The spring rains have fallen, and now the flowers shall bloom. As the Bard would say, "Let not the marriage of true minds admit impediments." I think our hero will endure.

Let us take this one and final look and see, shall we?

Galloping through the crowded streets of London, Darcy had but one thing on his mind: to reach Richmond House before Sofia—nay, *Elizabeth*—did something they would both regret. How desperate she must have been to choose as she had done to save the others! Darcy knew very well the appalling conditions of London's East End. He was currently working with other liberal minded men to offer relief to the families trapped in that particular purgatory.

But that was not what pierced his heart as he finally made it to the outskirts of town. Elizabeth was ever present in his thoughts as he galloped on the thoroughfare from London to Richmond. All this time she had been right in front of him, and he had not seen it. Everything was there: the turn of her countenance, her glib jovial banter, her keen wit and thirst for knowledge—especially carnal knowledge. He smiled at the images his last thought brought to mind. Elizabeth had a passion for life, and she was everything he had ever dreamed she would be—that and more. She suited him splendidly in every regard, and he could only imagine that theirs would be a remarkable marriage for two souls that were created to be as one.

Had he not thought Elizabeth dead, he would have insisted on knowing the truth of Sofia's identity well before now. There had been times when he had wondered, but then his lust had pushed those thoughts away as quickly as they had appeared.

Coming into the gate of Richmond House, he quickly dismounted and threw the reins to the footman. "Take care of him, Jennings," Darcy snapped.

Taking the steps two at a time, he burst through the door and quickly searched the house, but she was nowhere to be found—no singing, no jovial chatter. Only silence greeted him. Finally, he found the butler polishing the salver.

"Mr. Hobbs, where is Miss Molina? The house is quiet."

"They have left, sir," he said rather casually.

"Did she happen to say where she was going?"

"No sir, she did not. However, she left this letter."

The elderly man took a missive from the table and presented it to Mr. Darcy.

"Thank you, Hobbs."

Darcy took the letter and moved quickly to the library. Glancing around, he noticed what he had not noticed earlier today. The shelves were stocked full of books: classics in literature and poetry, histories and philosophies in Greek and Latin—everything he would have chosen; she had selected and filled the room to perfection. Even the selection of paintings reflected her style—and his.

Turning the letter over in his hand, he noticed the seal: 𝕭 for Bennet encased in a coat of arms. His eyes welled as he broke the seal and unfolded the elegant, lavender scented stationary only a woman would choose.

*My dearest Mr. Darcy,*

*If you are reading this letter then by now, you must know who Sofia Molina truly is, in reality. Be assured that I have not betrayed you, nor did I use you as you might think. I gave to you all that I had to give: my innocence…and my heart.*

*Nevertheless, I can no longer remain in England with the grievous threats that have been made to the security and safety of my family; nay, the injuries that have already been realized upon us have been of such severity that I cannot and will not allow another injury to be inflicted. Please forgive me. I never meant to wound you as I surely must have done.*

*You have been the only man I have ever loved and my only lover. There will never be another for me.*

*God Bless,*

*Elizabeth R. Bennet*

Darcy looked up, his countenance set in determination. "No! I will not accept it. Elizabeth, you cannot escape me—not this time. I will find you, and we will talk face to face. You will hear me out. Then, if you still think you must leave, I will give you the money to secure your future, and I will put you on the boat myself. But our child? No, I cannot give him up. You cannot take my child from me. That, somehow we shall share. I am intertwined in your life until he is a man, and there is nothing you can do to reject me—not this time, my lady."

He folded the letter, placed it in his coat pocket, and then pulled out the report with her address.

"No. 12 Newgate. That is where you are, and that is where I will go."

With a fresh horse, back to London he flew.

Elizabeth stared dejectedly out the carriage window with her cat in her lap, the scenery passing in a blur. She felt as if her heart would burst from the pain that the hateful woman had inflicted upon her. And furthermore, she was fearful of the reaction Mr. Darcy would have once he knew the truth—especially the truth coming from his aunt who would have no sympathy for her plight. "What will you do, Fitzwilliam Alexander...what will you think?" she whispered to herself as she reached to wipe a tear. "Fitzwilliam Alexander...that will be the name of our son, and should this babe be a girl, she shall be called Alexandra Jane Darcie after you and my sister."

Jolted out of her thoughts by a hole in the road, she turned her head and caught her maid staring at her.

"Big mistake. You no let bad woman chase you away. Mr. Darcy—"

"Please, Ling-Ling, not now. You do not understand us or our ways. That woman can destroy not only me, but my family as well, and I will not allow that. I have come too far, sacrificed too much to see it all undone."

"Ling-Ling no understand the English. Strange people," she said shaking her head.

They traveled the remainder of the trip in silence until they were finally on Newgate Street. The house sat up on a rise surrounded by a flowering hedge and was not entirely in view from the street. The only thing identifying it was a hitching post with the street marker No. 12 at the entrance of the drive.

When the carriage turned into the drive, Miss Ling-Ling shook her head and once more glanced at her mistress. "We here," she said. "Miss Jane, she sweep porch. I take Cocoa. You go to her."

Elizabeth nodded and handed the cat to her maid before the footman opened the coach and helped her out.

"Lizzy!" Jane called in astonishment as she dropped her broom and ran to her sister. "I did not expect you so soon. I..." she stopped in mid sentence and stepped back. "Lizzy, you look pale and sickly. Are you unwell?"

"No—yes!" Tears began to flow anew.

Jane turned to Ling-Ling. "What is the matter with my sister?" she asked. "I have not seen her distressed in such a manner since Papa died and we were forced to leave Longbourn."

"Bad, wicked woman come. She make Miss Sofie cry. She hurt baby."

"Baby! What baby?" she turned to her sister. "Lizzy, of what does she speak? Are you with child, and who is the bad, wicked lady?"

"Where are the children?" Elizabeth asked, wiping her tears. "They mustn't see me like this, and I do not want them exposed to any of this sordid business."

"They are in the garden with Daisy taking their morning exercise. We have just completed our geography lesson. Come with me and sit. I was just about to have my tea. I will pour you a cup, and you must tell me everything." Jane turned to the footman unloading the trunks. "Leave those there on the drive. I will have someone take them in. When you are done, you may return to your master's house."

Jane placed her arm around her sister's shoulder gently directing her into the house where she guided her to the divan and then ordered the maid to bring another a pot of tea.

Elizabeth sat and removed her veil and over two pots of tea, told Jane all that had happened. When she had finished, she felt much better for the wear, but her heart could not be comforted from the dull ache that had now become her constant companion.

"Mr. Darcy's aunt came to see you, did she? Well, we both know who it was that sent that most alarming letter. I suspected this would occur, and now that it has, we

162

will have to leave England immediately. Let us go outside. I will have John bring your things in. He has been so handy with the firewood and coal. I am glad you hired him. Once all is settled, we will pack and leave within the week. Kitty will be here this evening, and we will discuss the particulars then."

Elizabeth sighed despondently and nodded.

Jane and Elizabeth talked between themselves while they watched the trunks being brought into the house. Jane was concerned that there might not be enough money for them to do as they had planned since Elizabeth had not collected her five thousand pounds from Mr. Darcy.

"Jane, I cannot face him to ask for the money. We will have to make do with what we already have. With diligent care, we can manage."

"Lizzy."

"Kitty will have to find employment, and I shall have to do much of the work, plowing the fields myself, if need be. This is going to be a grand adventure, and we can—"

"Lizzy."

"Jane, have you by chance collected the tickets for Ireland?"

"Lizzy!"

"What is it, Jane? Can you not see that I am trying to discuss our futures?"

Jane gave a nod indicating that her sister should look behind her.

"Are you looking for these?" came a man's deep voice, holding up several boarding passes.

"Mr. Darcy!" Elizabeth's jaw dropped, and her eyes widened in shock.

"Miss Elizabeth Bennet."

"Oh!" she exclaimed on a sharp intake of breath. Her eyes rolled back, and she promptly fainted, but before she could fall to the ground, Darcy caught her in his arms.

He turned to Jane. "Miss Bennet, where might I take your sister?"

Stunned, Jane reacted. "Oh yes! Lizzy needs to come inside. She has not been well for some time now. Oh Mr. Darcy, you must please forgive her, for I know what you must think of us."

"I would imagine not. Now where must I take your sister? She needs immediate attention."

"Follow me," Jane said.

She quickly moved up the front steps and opened the door for Mr. Darcy to enter. The maid, who had just entered the room to remove the tea service, looked up in utter astonishment.

"Oh Miss! What has happened?"

"My sister has fainted; that is all," Jane answered. "Please Daisy, get some fresh tea and fetch Ling-Ling. Right this way, Mr. Darcy," she said, leading him up the steps and to the first room on the left. "This is Lizzy's room when she is here with us. Shall I bring you anything? A glass of water or perhaps some wine?"

Darcy glanced up after placing Elizabeth on the turned down bed. "A pitcher of water for your sister and a decanter of wine for me."

"Yes," she said as she curtsied. "I will be back shortly. Come with me Daisy."

Jane returned with a basin and clean cloth for her sister. Daisy came behind her with the water and wine and set them on the side table.

Darcy looked up. "Thank you, Miss Bennet, but if you will, might I have some private time with your sister?"

Jane stared at him as if unsure, and he replied once more, "Please, Miss Bennet. I care very deeply for Miss Elizabeth. I would never hurt her."

Jane glanced between the door and Mr. Darcy. With her compassionate heart, she caught his pleading gaze and smiled. "I see that you are sincere, Mr. Darcy. Therefore, I shall leave you to yourselves for a little while. After what you and my sister have shared, I suppose it is rather pointless to think of proprieties now."

"Yes, I believe that is so."

"I will return within the hour to see after my sister. She has suffered in her own way, Mr. Darcy. Please be gentle with her. Forgive her if it is within your power to do so." Jane curtsied, and then quit the room.

Darcy turned back to Elizabeth. He took the cloth and dipped it into the cool water. Wringing it out, he washed her face with great tenderness, cleaning the dust from her skin and placing tender kisses on her cheeks and delicate mouth. Forgiving her was not what he had in mind, but rather to seek her forgiveness instead.

"Elizabeth. Elizabeth!" Darcy called out, gently turning her face from side to side. "Elizabeth, can you hear me? I am not angry, love. Please come back to me."

"Fitzwilliam…Fitzwilliam," she moaned softly.

"I am here, Elizabeth. I am here. Wake up, my love. Come back to me."

Elizabeth tossed back and forth, tears escaping her closed lids. Finally her eyes fluttered open, and she looked into his worried gaze with the expression of a small frightened animal caught in a hunter's snare.

Darcy reached over to gently caress her face, pushing back her hair which still held the small pale blue buds clinging to her curls. He shook his head and momentarily glanced away to pour her a glass of water. He then lifted her head with his hand.

"Drink."

When she had drunk her fill, she looked at him with a contrite spirit. "Can you forgive me, Fitzwilliam?" she asked as a fresh round of tears began to spill down her cheeks. "I never meant to hurt anyone. What I have done was done for them…Jane and Kitty, and the children." She paused and glanced away, staring out the window by her bed. At last, she turned back. "I…I…know I should not have, but I found your letter in the letterbox. I was going to write you a letter and…" She shook her head violently. Darcy waited patiently. Finally she turned her eyes to him and swallowed back her tears. "Mr. Darcy, I am a very selfish creature, and for the sake of giving relief to my own suffering and that of my family, I have caused you pain. I set aside my feelings of all that I knew was good and right. I am dreadfully sorry for I know how you must feel…what you must think of me."

Darcy sorrowfully looked away. Returning his gaze to her tear streaked face, he said, "No, I think not, for I could never be angry for what has transpired between us. I am not ashamed of the love—the feelings we have shared. They were beautiful in their simplicity and goodness—perfectly right and natural for a man and woman falling in love. Elizabeth, do you not know…can you not know?" He paused and swallowed to suppress his own tears threatening to fall, his throat constricting. "Perhaps you do not; therefore let me tell you. A good friend has told me that women need certain assurances to be secure in a man's feelings and devotions, so let me try to express myself clearly so that you might know the depths of my attachment to you. Elizabeth Bennet...I am a man who *loves* you—loves you deeply...and passionately," he said as he cleared his throat. "You have been with me these three months more as my wife than my mistress. You know how I feel for you...for *Elizabeth Bennet*, and what I think, so there is no use in pretending otherwise.

"When I wrote that letter," Darcy replied, "I believed myself to be doing what I perceived was your desire—to be free of me. I had found your plans in our room in London. They cut me to the quick, and I came to Richmond with the intent of leaving you. But first I was going to ask you for an explanation. I believed myself to be in complete control of my emotions and rational in my thoughts. Then, when I saw you dressed in a manner that I knew was to please me, bitterness, and yes, anger, did spring up in me. Then when you kissed me, I lost control and did the very thing I had told myself I would not do. For that, I blamed myself as much as I did you. It was then that I decided irrevocably that we would part, but...when I tried, I could not bring myself to do it." He swallowed past the lump in his throat once more and continued. "I believed myself to be entirely calm and cool when I sat and began my letter. However, I am since convinced that what little I composed was written in a dreadful bitterness of spirit. I tried to order a perfectly logical letter with sense and reasoning, but I could not complete it. My heart was at war with my mind, and...what can I say? I am sorry you saw what I wrote then, for it is not how I feel now, nor was it what I honestly felt at the time if I am to be truthful."

He reached and took her frail hand in his and gently stroked her fingers. Tears sprang into his eyes, and his voice almost faltered.

"My dearest Elizabeth," Darcy said with a slight nod, "it has been many years that I have cherished and loved you. My feelings, though I do not easily show them, have, from the beginning of our acquaintance, been a struggle. First I struggled to overcome all that I knew was expected of me by my family, society, and yes, even my friends, to ask for your hand. And you rejected me, leaving my pride wounded." He momentarily glanced away. "Your reproof, so well applied, I shall never forget: 'Had you behaved in a more gentlemanlike manner.' Those were your words. You know not, you can scarcely conceive, how they tortured me; though it was some time, I confess, before I was reasonable enough to allow their justice. Nevertheless, in time I recovered and resolved to be a better man, though I never supposed I would see you again.

"Elizabeth, it tore at me—ate away at my conscience. I could not go on living in the world believing you thought ill of me, and so, when I heard of your father's death, I came for you to offer what assistance I could, but you were gone—lost to me for what I believed to be forever. And again I struggled thinking the only woman I had ever loved was dead. I grieved your loss as one who loved you dearly surely would. And then, when I was not expecting it, Sofia Molina came into my life, and I had to struggle anew when I thought you to be her—a woman I admired from our first night together, and yes, came to love. I struggled against the feelings of my heart and my desire to ask a courtesan to become my wife, and yet I overcame that as well, but, as you must surely know by now, when it comes to affairs of the heart, I cannot make speeches." Darcy paused and shook his head, and then replied in a tone of sincere tenderness.

"If I loved you less, I might be able to talk about it more. But you know what I am beneath *my* mask and veil. You hear nothing but honesty from me, even in its severest reproof, and to that I might add I am heartily ashamed of my behavior earlier today. I said things that should not have been said, and you endured them as no other woman in England would have endured them. Bear with the truths I tell you now, dearest Elizabeth. God knows, I have been a very indifferent and difficult lover at times—treated you with less than the respect you deserved, held my tongue when I should have spoken. I assumed you knew my intentions and feelings, and you did not. My reserved manners and temperament, resentful at times, are in much need of improvement still. However, in spite of it all, I believe you understand me as no other can. My veil is removed; my mask gone. You now see me as I am and understand my feelings—and I pray will return them if you can."

She turned aside and fixed her eyes on the wall, crying softly. He gently cupped her face in his hand and turned her back to him. "I must ask two things of you, Elizabeth, and I want you, as a woman of honor and integrity, to answer them truthfully." He paused and looked deeply into her doe-like eyes. "I must know, and you must tell me. Do not keep any more secrets. Open your heart as I have opened mine."

She nodded. "Speak and I will answer."

"Are you, Miss Elizabeth Bennet, carrying my child?"

She nodded once more and wiped a fresh round of tears from her cheeks. "Yes…It is true. I am with child." She gave a small smile, but he burst forth in a wide grin causing her to laugh.

"Now the second question. You know my feelings. I have expressed them freely. In truth, they are unchanged from Hunsford all those years ago. And, if anything, they go much deeper now than they did then. I love you enough, Elizabeth, that I will not hold you against your will. Therefore, if you wish to go to Ireland, I will not stop you, *but* if there be a chance that you can love me in the same deep and abiding way in which I care for you, then…I want you to legally become my wife…to share my bed, my life, my home, my fortune, and all that I have for as long as we both shall live."

He paused and awaited her response, his eyes ever searching hers for what he hoped to see.

Once again, she nodded, slowly at first and then vigorously as her face erupted into a tearful smile. "Yes! Oh yes, I will marry you, and I do not care what people shall say. I have loved you these many months—esteemed you for years, and I want to love you for the rest of my life in every way a woman is supposed to love her husband. You know me well enough to understand that I do not care for fortune and all the trappings that come with it. All I ask is for a simple life—to be loved and cared for—cherished and respected as someone worthy to be respected, to be your companion in all things."

"And I do…cherish you, respect you…and ardently love you. My one regret is that I did not find you sooner. I could have saved you from all that has happened to you and your family over the years. However, I am grateful that I have found you now. You will never again have to worry about the tribulations of life or the trials there of. You will have no cause to repine. I will never leave you."

He lifted her up, and her arms instinctively circled his neck. Darcy sprinkled tender kisses in her hair before she turned and took his lips in a deep passionate kiss. Breaking the kiss, they held one another and cried for joy.

"My Elizabeth, *dearest, dearest, Elizabeth*," he said releasing her gently to her bed and kissed her face as he laid her down. "You have seen me at my worst, and yet you love me for the man I am."

"And I have seen you at your finest," she said with upturned lips. "And I do love you. You are the best of men."

He chuckled and gave a roguish grin. "Will you sometimes wear the black veil in the privacy of our bed chamber, only without the mask? And I might add with your hair down, long and flowing, as your only covering. Will you always be my fantasy, my reality?"

"If you wish it," she replied with a salacious smile.

"Indeed, I wish it and so much more. Your heart and mine are forever one. You will always and forever be my temptress. I am undone when you cast your eyes upon me, and when we kiss, it does indeed cause my torch to burn."

She laughed, and he laughed in return. But then he grew silent and once more took her hand, pressing it between his larger ones.

Darcy sighed and briefly closed his eyes. Opening them, he stared into her curious ones. "They say that women like pretty words—poetry. I am not very good at reciting verse for the sake of turning a woman's head, but let me recite something from my youth that has always been meaningful to me. And though the text reads *charity*, I prefer the word love." He paused and then began. "Though I speak with the tongues of men and of angels, and have not love, I am become as sounding brass, or a tinkling cymbal; for love bears all things, believes all things, hopes all things, and endures all things. Love never ends."

"Char—" She paused and then smiled. "I will follow your lead as I think it expresses my feelings as well." She took up the lines and continued. "Love suffereth long, and is kind; love envieth not; love vaunteth not itself, is not puffed up; doth not behave itself unseemly, seeketh not her own, is not easily provoked, thinketh no evil; rejoiceth not in iniquity, but rejoiceth in the truth. Beareth all things, believeth all things, hopeth all things, endureth all things. Love never faileth.

"Yes, Fitzwilliam, it is a favorite of mine as well. I learnt it in catechism when I was a girl."

"As did I. The catechism of enduring love, 1 Corinthians13:1 and 4 through 7 and part of 8, as taught to us by St. Paul. Elizabeth, I believe those verses capture our spirits and minds completely."

"Yes, I believe they do. Two melded into one—a marriage of true minds and hearts."

Darcy reached into his pocket and pulled out a velvet box and gave it to her.

"It was my mother's and before her, my grandmother's. Now it is yours. Open it."

She glanced from him to the black case.

"Go ahead, open it."

When she did, her heart nearly burst for joy. "It is so very beautiful! I have never seen anything so lovely."

He took it from the case and slipped it on her finger. "I was afraid it would not fit, but it looks as if three Mrs. Darcys have had similar hands. It looks so beautiful on your finger."

"Indeed it does." She giggled.

Before either could say another word, there was a knock at the door, and Jane and Ling-Ling entered. Jane beamed from ear to ear.

"Jane! Were you listening?"

"Yes, Miss Jane she listen. I tell her no-no, but she no listen to Ling-Ling. Not let Ling-Ling bring tea to make Miss Sofie better."

Darcy laughed. "That was very clever of Miss Bennet, but Ling-Ling, this is no longer Sofia Molina. You must call her Miss Elizabeth or Miss Lizzy if you will; however, soon enough, you will address her as my wife, Mrs. Darcy."

Jane's hand flew to her mouth, and Ling-Ling nearly dropped her tray.

"Lizzy! I knew this is how it would be."

Ling-Ling said matter-of-factly, "Ling-Ling tell Miss Lizzy, but she no listen. Now she see Ling-Ling know what she say is right."

"Indeed I do, Ling-Ling, but Mr. Darcy and I have much to discuss. Our old life, brief as it was, is now gone, and I am Elizabeth Bennet once more."

"Lizzy, drink the tea, and then you should rest. Ling-Ling and I will leave you two to talk. Much has to be decided."

"Yes, Miss Lizzy you drink tea. Chamomile and anise make you and baby rest. We must take care of baby. No more upset. Make baby upset! Ling-Ling no a like it for baby to be upset!"

Darcy laughed and replied, "Ling-Ling, I will see to it that she finishes her tea. I want a strong healthy son with a full set of lungs to announce his arrival."

"But what if it is a daughter?" Jane asked.

"Then we will have a beautiful little girl for her proud papa to bounce on his knee and cradle to his chest and... a strapping son next time," Darcy answered with a smile.

Jane smiled at them both, shook her head, and turned and left with Ling-Ling, pulling the door shut behind them.

Once they were alone, Darcy bent down and kissed Elizabeth's soft lips. "I am sorry, exceedingly sorry, Elizabeth," Darcy replied, in a tone of remorse, "that my aunt could make such a vulgar exhibition of herself as I am certain she must have displayed when she called on you at Richmond. I hope that the wounds inflicted will be of short duration. Had I known she would come, I would have stopped her, but as it is, there is a silver lining to the cloud she hung over us both."

Elizabeth glanced up at Darcy with a contrite look while she sipped her tea. "You are not to worry. It is all forgot. Though, I am curious. I assume she did visit you as she implied she would. What did she say?"

He chuckled. "Yes," he nodded, "indeed she did. She called on me on her return through London, and there she related her journey to Richmond, its motive, and the substance of her conversation with you. Her Ladyship dwelt emphatically on every expression you displayed which, in her apprehension, curiously denoted her perverseness and assurance, in the belief that such a disclosure must assist her endeavors to obtain that promise from me which you had refused to give. But, unluckily for Lady Catherine, its effect has been exactly contrariwise."

Elizabeth laughed. "I am sure you were quite surprised by her declarations. Though I would admit to something I could not hide, I would not give her the satisfaction of knowing Sofia's true identity."

"Yes, her revelations were quite eye-opening, to say the least, and are how I first knew you loved me for certain and that we were to expect a child. Though I must say

I was not surprised, given our frequent amorous activities. You are, after all, an exceedingly healthy woman and I a healthy man; therefore the natural course of things must allow us to expect a child, but I had desired to wed before the happy and much desired event would occur. Nevertheless, that is not the case. So, we will marry as soon as I can arrange it, and then, when my business affairs here are set in order, we will leave for the continent. You will give birth abroad, and we will return with our child giving him or her a date of birth that will be within a respectable time from our wedding date. We will, of course, celebrate the true date privately."

"And thus you will have saved my reputation as a respectable gentlewoman and spared our son the shame some would attempt to bestow on him."

"A son can bear it better than a daughter, but either way, son or daughter, no scandal will touch us or our children. Dukes and lords are able to provide respectable situations for their children born out of wedlock. I can do no less for one whose conception preempted his parents vows should it ever be an issue—which I am certain it will not."

"But how are you going to explain Sofia's sudden disappearance and why you are no longer with her? And Ling-Ling, I do not want to give her up. She is as dear to me now as family."

"You are not to worry. I told Lady Catherine I would place Sofia Molina on a boat bound for America in front of all who care to see, and so I shall. As for Ling-Ling, I paid for her contract. She belongs to me for one year. There was no duration clause attached to her. She is mine, and I will keep what belongs to me."

"What about Lady Catherine and Mr. Collins? They could cause great harm to me and to you, through me."

"You are not to worry there either. I am in the process of purchasing your portrait at the *House of Pleasure*. It will remain in the attic of Pemberley until a time such as one from our issue can display it without concern. All things relating to the truth will be recorded in my journal for the annals of Pemberley to preserve the truth of our family's history for the following generations, but it will never be exposed in our lifetimes. As for Mr. Collins and my aunt," he glanced around the room, "are there any writing instruments and paper in this room?"

"Yes, over there on my writing table. The ink is on the table, and the letter-paper, blotter, sealing wax, and quills are beneath in my writing table on the shelf. The letterbox is unlocked."

Darcy removed himself and sat to jot a few lines. Blotting the paper and making sure it was dry, he returned to Elizabeth's bedside."

"Now, allow me to read what Lady Catherine will shortly receive once Miss Molina is securely aboard a ship bound for America."

*Aunt Catherine,*

*This letter is to inform you that Sofia was indeed dear to me, so much so that I have, out of gratitude, secured her future within the former colony of South Carolina. She will be well received and treated kindly by my family in Charleston to which you are not to relate one word about her, me, or our connection to one another.*

*She, as well, recounted to me the details of your conversation at Richmond, that you believe her to be none other than Miss Elizabeth Bennet, which as we have previously discussed, is utter nonsense. She also related to me what you believe* about her being with child. Let me assure you, the matter is taken care of, and you need not be concerned. Nevertheless, if you have any further design about interfering in my life, let me advise you not to carry through on those notions.

If you should even think of disclosing what you suspect concerning either of the two women connected to me, take heed, Madam. Uncle Lewis kept a detailed record, which I found in the rubbish you discarded to be burned after his death, of his accounts concerning your marriage to him and your condition upon entering such marriage. Should you even think of slandering either of the two women who have shared my life, I will not hesitate to make Uncle Lewis's journal public.

As for that simpleton, Mr. Collins, should he interfere in my life or the life of anyone connected to me, he may find that his name is mentioned among the patrons of Madame Papillia's establishment, the **House of Pleasure**. I am sure a man of his distinction in good standing with the Church of England would not wish for that knowledge to be widely known.

Lastly, I am forever in your debt for relaying to me the information that Miss Elizabeth Bennet was not only alive, but was, in fact, quite well. We have renewed our friendship and have recently become betrothed. We will marry within the fortnight.

In closing, let me say that I hope all past differences between us will be forgot and that you will wish me joy upon entering the married state. My wife and I will take an extended tour of the continent as soon as we are wed. If it is agreeable, you may call upon us at Pemberley when we return.

Your devoted nephew,

Fitzwilliam Alexander Darcy, Esq.

Returning to the table, he dripped hot wax on the folded sheet and sealed it with his signet ring.

Elizabeth smiled. "You have thought of everything."

"Not quite. I need a double willing to board a ship. That I have not found as of yet."

Elizabeth was quiet for several minutes then finally she asked how Darcy had found her address and how he had acquired her boarding passes, and Darcy told her all. He told her how his cousins had been concerned and had hired a Bow Street Runner to ferret out the truth.

She nodded. "The man with the carriage strap."

Darcy quizzed his brow, and she explained how a trunk had come loose and fallen into the street and someone just happened to be passing by and stopped to help. Then she told him of the man on horseback who had stopped to help the farmer in Longbourn village near the church.

"Yes," Darcy sighed, "that is how they work. They appear as ordinary people doing ordinary things. And you never know the difference. The farmer was most likely a Bow Street Runner, as well."

William peered through the half-closed door to his mother's room with a pensive look on his face. He had heard his mother was home and that she was ill. Would she die as his grandmother had and leave him all alone? He had begged to go to her, but Aunt Jane had refused, so, when his aunt was not looking, he crept up the stairs silently, ever so careful so as not to be noticed. Edging his way to the door left ajar, he pushed it gently and stuck his face just in the crack to listen. He gazed at the tall man sitting by his mother's side. He looked brave and strong. Was this his papa? For he looked as William had always supposed his father would. Furthermore, he seemed to care about his mother, and that made William think well of him.

Elizabeth noticed him and smiled.

"William, what are you doing standing there like that?"

"Mamma, are you going to die, too?" he asked with a trembling voice.

"No, Wills. Mamma is only a little sick. Mr. Darcy is seeing to me. I shall be fine in a little while."

William glanced at the man beside his mother's bed. "Sir, are you my papa? You look like the drawing we have of him."

"No, son, I am not. But I would like to be."

The child's eyes widened as he nodded his reply.

Then he came running to Elizabeth's bed and threw his arms around her. "I love you, Mamma."

"And I love you, too, Wills. Now, I have someone I want you to meet. Wills, this is Mr. Darcy, a very good friend of your mamma's, and he will be a good friend to you, too."

Young William straightened himself and bowed. "How do you do, sir?"

Fitzwilliam rose to his feet and bowed in return. "I do very well, Master William. You are a fine looking boy with exceptional manners for one so young. How old are you?"

"Five, sir. I just had my birthday. Mamma gave me a book of fairytales, and Aunt Kitty made me a new set of clothes. Aunt Jane helped, but it was mostly Aunt Kitty."

"Five years of age…that is very young, but still, it makes you the man of the house and therefore, if I may be so bold, I would like to ask for the hand of your mother in marriage."

"Oh, sir, if my mamma loves you, then yes, you may marry her, but you must promise to make her happy. Poor Mamma has had to work hard and could not be home with us. We missed her terribly. You must promise to work and let her stay home with us."

Darcy laughed. "*That* I think I can manage. I shall take care of you all. And you, young William, shall go with us to the continent. How would you like that?"

"Oh, I should like it very well, sir. To the continent! Aunt Jane showed me pictures in Edward's schoolbook." He danced from foot to foot. "I will go with Mamma! I love Mamma, and now I have a Papa, too. I have wished every night on the wishing star for my own dear Papa, and now I will have one. Next I will wish for a little brother."

"Ha! Keep wishing, son. Papa wishes for one, too."

Elizabeth laughed contentedly. "Come, give me a hug, Wills, and then you run along and play. Mr. Darcy and I must talk."

"Yes, Mamma!" He reached and hugged her tightly and then hugged Darcy before he skipped through the door.

Darcy turned to Elizabeth. "Whose child is he? He is a delightful lad and looks very much like you, but I know he is not your natural child."

"He is my sister Lydia's son. She died when he was born. It was a difficult birth, and her body was too weak to sustain the exertion. She passed two days later. As to his father, I think you can guess who he was."

"Yes. George Wickham. Elizabeth, I must ask, did George know who you were before he died? I recall he was trying to tell me something, but I could not make it out as to what he meant to convey at the time."

"No, he did not. He believed to his death that I was Lydia. He recognized me, or I should say Lydia, by the mark on my shoulder—the one you think lovely. Lydia had one, too. Our grandmother Gardiner used to tell us it was the mark of the devil." She laughed. "It threw my mother's nerves into fits and vexed my father greatly. But, as circumstances would have it, it was not too far from the mark.

"Mr. Wickham was a patron of Madame Papillia's *House of Pleasure*, and that is where he saw my portrait and recognized the mark. He naturally assumed I was Lydia. He then stalked me with the intent of selling me for services and taking half the money. When you came upon us that is what he had demanded—that I give him half of what you were to pay me. I agreed, of course, lest he do me harm, and when you entered the alleyway, he was about to violate me. He said something about mixing his seed with yours."

Darcy's countenance darkened. "Yes, he would have liked nothing more than to despoil that which was mine. All of our lives that was what he had done. First with my sister, and then you. Did he think I was in love with Lydia, then?"

"No, not exactly. He knew you did not know who I—or rather, she was. He thought that I was your property, and that is what he wished to insult. My being a person with feelings was not a consideration. What he said to you as he was dying was, 'I thought you preferred the older to the younger.' I think, if he could have, he would have called my sister's name."

"I see." Darcy nodded. *...so it was as I thought...*

After some time of silence, Darcy broke the ambiance. "Where was the child christened?"

"At my Aunt and Uncle Gardiner's church in Cheapside."

"And how was the record put in?"

"My sister Lydia is listed as the mother, I the godmother, and George Wickham as the father. I assumed my responsibilities as his mother when my sister died. That is why he calls me Mamma."

"Umm...well, it is over, and we shall raise his son as our own. If he so chooses, I will allow, of course, that he have my name when he comes of age."

"You know people will whisper about him. He does favor you in many ways."

"Yes, there will be talk at first, but it will be hushed up soon enough. His birth record stands as a witness to his unfortunate birth, and you are, after all, his godmother thus making me his godfather by proxy. It is not the first time something of this nature has occurred, and I dare say it will not be the last. He cannot inherit my estate. The son you carry will have that, but I will provide for him and give him an education and a good living."

"For that, I am grateful, for I do love and cherish him as any mother could a son." Elizabeth paused with a bemused smile and laughed. "So you think I carry your son, do you?" she asked putting her hand to her stomach.

He laughed in return and placed his atop hers. "It matters not, but if I have anything to say about it, one day you will carry my son, for I know your disposition and your desires. You could not stay away from our bed even if you wanted to."

"Mr. Darcy! That is not a thing a gentleman says to a lady."

"Miss Bennet, behind closed doors you are not a lady, and I am no gentleman."

They both laughed.

"Mr. Darcy—"

"Fitzwilliam. You are to call me by my Christian name when we are in private."

"Very well, Fitzwilliam." She took a deep breath. "If you do not mind, I have one thing I would like to know—for the sake of my family and all that you aspire to do."

"Ask. I do not mind."

She lowered her lashes and bit her lower lip. Slowly raising her gaze to his, she asked. "Fitzwilliam, exactly how much money do you have?"

He laughed out loud. "You mean do *we* have. Let us say we have enough. I have recently acquired a railroad and invested in a locomotive venture. If things progress to half my and Mr. Steadman's expectations, we will be amongst the richest families in England—twice that of the Duke of Devonshire."

She smiled. "If we were at home, I would ask you to love me."

He chuckled softly. "As much as I would like to, that will not happen again until we are wed. I will give you the proper respect due as my betrothed. You are no longer a paid companion."

She sighed and pouted adorably. "Very well, then, if it must be, but I wish you would change your mind."

"No, Elizabeth, on that subject my mind is fixed. There will be time enough for conjugal pleasures once we are wed."

"As you wish, though I think it unnecessary after all we have already experienced, but I will abide by your wishes. Now, you were telling me of your plans. How are we to marry and make ourselves respectable? What do you propose?" She yawned sleepily and stretched out.

"Not now, my love. You look very tired. We will discuss this at another time. For now, you need to rest and let my son rest as well."

"Yes, I am tired. Ling-Ling's tea is having its desired affect." She yawned once more and nodded as he pulled the counterpane up over her shoulders. "Sleep well, Elizabeth," he said, brushing a few silky strands from her forehead as he leaned in and kissed her soft lips one last time. She was already fast asleep.

Darcy came down the stairs and found Jane, Kitty, and Ophelia all sitting on the settee in the small parlor. The children were playing by the fire with the toys he recognized from the bazaar, and Cocoa was curled contentedly in Ling-Ling's lap.

"Mr. Darcy, will you join us for dinner tonight? Now that you are engaged to my sister, I think you should get to know the family a little better."

"Miss Bennet, I would be honored to dine with you this evening. Truth be told, I am loath to be parted from your sister as we are, after all, fairly well acquainted."

Jane blushed scarlet, and Kitty giggled.

Darcy, realizing he had committed a *faux pas*, quickly recovered and cleared his throat. "What I mean is that we are betrothed, and I hate to be away from her presence—especially when she is unwell."

"You shall manage, Mr. Darcy, I am sure," Ophelia said with a smile. "Turning to Kitty and the children, she said, "I think we are needed elsewhere.""

Kitty, quickly understanding, hurried the children out of the room, and Ling-Ling left with them.

Jane rose from her seat and closed the door. Wrapping her shawl tightly over her shoulders, she resumed her seat and beckoned Darcy to do the same.

"I gather you wish to speak with me," he said taking the seat opposite her.

"Yes, Mr. Darcy I do. I am quite concerned for my sister. I am sure you know this was very much out of her character to have taken the measures she felt she needed to take, but she is still a lady and I am exceedingly anxious for her reputation. She will be maligned, but you are an extremely wealthy gentleman. Nothing will be attached to you though it will quite possibly affect your children. How do you propose to protect my sister and your children, Mr. Darcy?"

Darcy crossed his legs as he fiddled with his signet ring. "I love your sister and would have married her six years ago if she would have had me. Nay, I would have married her had I found you in London on Beggar's Street. That is how much I love her. You have my assurance and promise nothing will happen to her."

"But what if scandal should erupt amongst your peers in the ton? Then what will you do?"

"I am telling you it will not be a question. I care little for society and what they think. But should it become one, it shall soon be forgot when a new scandal comes along to take its place. That is how things are within the ton. However, I do not think that will be a problem."

"Will you not be introducing my sister into your society, then?"

"In time, yes, but that is not what is on my mind at present. First and foremost, I must marry your sister and secure our future and that of our children, and for that I have a plan that will spare us all. I am only in want of another woman."

"For what?" Ophelia asked, returning to the parlor.

Darcy turned and furrowed his brow. "I need someone to board a ship bound for America, someone to take the place of Miss Molina who will allow me to escort her aboard so that my aunt and whoever may care to will know that we have separated."

"You need someone to act as your mistress and dress in her disguise, so that you can marry Elizabeth without any hint of scandal attached to her from her past as a courtesan."

"Yes, precisely. Would you, perchance, be interested, Mrs. Dior?"

"If you make an offer worth my while, I believe I would. How much would you spend and where would you send me?"

Darcy bid her to take a seat.

"I will pay you the amount owed to Miss Molina—a sum of ten thousand pounds. If you are agreeable, I will send you to South Carolina where I have a cousin who is a banker and factor to the local planters there. He will, on my promissory note, deposit the money, and when all is cleared, give you the total sum to spend as you like. With that sum, you should be able to afford a small townhouse and live comfortably well if the remains are invested properly, which I, on your behalf, will ask my cousin to do for you."

Ophelia tilted her head quizzically. "Exactly where in South Carolina is this cousin?"

"The port city of Charleston. I have been there. It is a gay city with many attractions and many wealthy gentlemen, whom I might add desire anything English. You are a beautiful woman, Mrs. Dior. If you set your mind to it, you could have any of them. What say you?"

She smiled. "When do we board?"

Darcy gave a wide grin. "In one week. You will dress like Sofia. And since Elizabeth cannot be seen in anything that belonged to Sofia Molina, you may take what I bought for her as well as the jewelry I purchased, and you will be set for a new adventure."

Ophelia stood up and wrapped her shawl a little tighter about her shoulders. "We eat at exactly eight o'clock. I will see you then," she said with a smile.

Once she had left, Darcy turned to Jane. "Miss Bennet, I have something that I must confess to you as well. Nearly six years ago, I interfered in your life and that of my dear friend, Mr. Bingley. He now knows the truth of it, and I must say, he did not take it very well. He too believed you to be…well…not among the living. If I may, I would like to send an express and tell him the good news that you are, in fact, alive and well. May I have your permission to do so?"

"Do you need my permission, Mr. Darcy?"

"Well, no, but I would like it just the same."

She smiled sweetly as she rose to her feet. "Then go to it," she said. "If you will excuse me, I will see to dinner. You may visit my sister above stairs or come to the kitchen with me, whichever you prefer. The choice is yours."

Darcy gave a wide grin and glanced at the staircase. It was highly improper for him to be above stairs alone with Elizabeth, but what did it matter after all they had come through?

My good reader, in the words of our most admired friend, let us present a verse that so aptly sums up our dear couple. For who could say it better than the master of the written word himself, Mr. William Shakespeare?

*Let me not to the marriage of true minds*

*Admit impediments. Love is not love*

*Which alters when it alteration finds,*

*Or bends with the remover to remove:*

*O no! It is an ever-fixed mark*

*That looks on tempests and is never shaken;*

*It is the star to every wandering bark,*

*Whose worth's unknown, although his height be taken.*

*Love's not Time's fool, though rosy lips and cheeks*

*Within his bending sickle's compass come:*

*Love alters not with his brief hours and weeks,*

*But bears it out even to the edge of doom.*

*If this be error and upon me proved,*

*I never writ, nor no man ever loved.*

William Shakespeare

(1564 - 1616)

# Epilogue

N ow, my good and gentle reader, the day has finally come. Our dear hero, Fitzwilliam Alexander Darcy, without show of emotions, escorted his mistress, Miss Sofia Molina, to the boarding plank of the *Claremont de Bonté* set to sail for America at high noon from the port at Dover. Close by stood a chubby little parson turned country squire and his newly delivered wife who held their baby girl bundled in blankets. I must say that Mrs. Collins looked rather cross. Perhaps it was the cool wind blowing in from the Channel that affected her so, or perhaps it was the stench of the ocean, or more like it is the disagreeable circumstance of her present situation in marriage, for who can really tell for certain?

Not far from them stood the Right Honorable Lady Catherine de Bourgh, her face dour and wrinkled as was customary. She bore the smug look of someone who had won a great victory or perhaps had eaten too many prunes. I could neither tell nor care. Then there was present his uncle, the Earl of Matlock and the earl's two sons, standing to the left of Her Ladyship. The Dukes of Ancaster and Castlebaum, and many more from the nobility were also present, claiming it was a damn shame that such magnificent beauty should depart these shores and with none except Darcy to have tasted her pleasures. In fact, Ancaster did beg for one tryst, but to no avail. I might say, my dear reader, that from my position above the fray, I did observe many things that day. The ladies were glad to see her go, I do believe, and the gentlemen did most assuredly appear to be despondent with dejected and forlorn looks upon their countenances. I nearly felt half sorry for them—almost, but not quite. But, nevertheless, let us not dwell on that bit of unpleasantness.

After much pomp and circumstance, at last the *Claremont* did finally set sail. Darcy waved goodbye and some said there was a tear in his eye, but I must tell you that I never noticed such a thing. Perhaps it was merely the sun blinding their eyes, or that some wished it to be so.

When the ship had passed over the horizon and people moved to leave, our hero, ever diligent to his word, turned to his aunt and handed her a letter which she, with all alacrity, broke the seal and began to read. At first Lady Catherine appeared to be in a bit of confusion, but soon her countenance grew dark. She looked in utter shock at the written words she held in her hand.

She had been rendered so exceedingly angry by her nephew's letter, announcing his pending marriage that her face contorted with great emotion, and she gave way to all the genuine frankness of her character in her very vocal reply to him. Denouncing its arrangement, she let her sentiments be known to each and all who cared to hear with one insult heaped upon another, disparaging poor Miss Elizabeth Bennet and berating her nephew for breaking her dear daughter's heart. The language she spewed forth was so very abusive, especially of Elizabeth, that all intercourse between nephew and aunt was irrevocably put at an end.

Once made aware of what had distressed his sister so, the earl was also extremely indignant over the engagement and declared it to be an abominable display of willful arrogance. He ranted for several minutes, making a spectacle of himself, while his sons secretly smiled as they glanced between one another and Mr. Darcy, who also sported a smile threatening to lift the corners of his mouth into an out-and-out laugh. But at last, good manners prevailed, and with a shrug of his wide shoulders, he merely turned and walked to his carriage where his soon-to-be wife awaited.

Upon observing her saucy grin as he climbed into their carriage and took his seat beside her, he did break into a hardy laugh, for they had accomplished the grand farce of the century and were now free to marry at will.

The special license was obtained, the announcement was placed in the London papers, and within a few days they were joined as man and wife.

Alas, my dear reader, one week has now passed, and our hero and heroine are finally joined in the blissful state of matrimony. As they stroll along in the park, let us, as we have done from the beginning, drop in and see how love fares, shall we?

Mr. Darcy helped his new bride of but a few hours from their carriage. They had been wed this very morning in the parish church of St. Paul's. It was not a formal wedding, and there were no guests to speak of, other than close family and a few friends. When Darcy asked his bride what she would desire for the afternoon, Mrs. Darcy requested a stroll in Vauxhall Gardens—one of her most favorite places in London.

Spring had arrived with warmer weather, and the gardens had burst forth in brilliant color with a mass of early spring flowers. Daffodils, bluebells, lords and ladies, and English primroses were throughout the park in neatly kept beds. Hawthorn and blackthorn hedges had come into leaf. The thick, white blossomed blackthorns contrasted beautifully against their dark, bristling twigs. From a distance, Elizabeth thought it looked as though snow had fallen, so densely covered were they. Swans, geese, and ducks now played in the calm waters of the lake where just a few short months ago it had been frozen in ice, and Darcy and Elizabeth had skated there in the moonlight as their love had nurtured and grown, bursting into full bloom much as the flowers around them had sprung to life.

Strolling through the garden paths arm in arm, Elizabeth thought about all her husband had told her of her new home in Derbyshire where they were to go on

Saturday to spend a few days before traveling to Liverpool to board a ship bound for France. She recalled with great delight all his tales of the wild and untamed north, of the natural beauty of the peaks and lakes and of their estate with its sunken gardens and thick copse of woods where she could walk to her heart's delight. She had admired the portraits of the house and estate when she had first seen them in the halls of Darcy House, but he had assured her there was much more to be seen in Pemberley's gallery than the relatively few paintings hanging in the smaller gallery in town.

He had also informed her that when they returned from their wedding tour of the Continent, Pemberley would be their home. His children, he had said, must learn to love that which would one day be theirs, and she knew that family honor and heritage were very much a part of the man who was her husband. Of course, he had said that business would necessitate they be in London from time to time, but with so many matters settled and ventures made, it would not consume him as it had when there was no other reason to care of little else.

She breathed in the cool clear air of this glorious afternoon and glanced up at him. Her felicity upon entering the married state was so much more than she had ever dreamt was possible. There could be no doubt of its reality, for it was settled between them from the beginning of their understanding that they were to be the happiest couple in the world.

"Fitzwilliam, you have not said two words since we left our wedding breakfast at Lord Wexford's. I feel we must have some conversation."

He glanced down with a mischievous smile. "Do you talk by rule, then, while you are walking?" he asked.

"Yes! One must speak a little, you know. It is odd to be entirely silent while walking together among such beauty as we see before us."

"Are you consulting your own feelings in the present case, or do you imagine that you are gratifying mine?"

"Both," Elizabeth replied archly, "for I have always seen a great similarity in the turn of our minds. We are each of an unsocial, taciturn disposition, unwilling to speak, unless we expect to say something significant. But on such a glorious day as this, I think we should have some conversation. The weather is uncommonly warm for this time of year, and makes for a very pleasant afternoon. Do you not think so, Mr. Darcy?"

He glanced at her once more and shook his head with a smile, but said nothing.

"It is your turn to say something now, Mr. Darcy—I have talked about the weather, and you ought to make some kind of remark on how the gardens are particularly beautiful this time of year, and I might agree and remark how the pond seems so different from a few months ago when we were last here. Skating in the moonlight was beautiful, but ducks, geese, and swans, especially those black swans, gliding across the water are equally lovely."

He laughed. "I do believe, Mrs. Darcy that we have had this conversation before."

She gave a coy smile and replied, "And so we have, but really, Fitzwilliam, we should talk just a little. I cannot abide silence when so much beauty is before us."

He looked down upon her upturned face once more with amusement. "Then we shall talk. There are many things I have wanted to discuss with you, but for want of time and opportunity, I have let them be. But now that your sisters and cousins are happily situated at Richmond, and you are officially in my house as my wife, I think it is time to address the future for your family which I now consider to be my family as well."

"Proceed."

"It is time for young Edward Gardiner to enter his formal education. Before we depart for Pemberley, I wish to enroll him at Eton. I want our nephew to have a gentleman's education, and when his public school studies are complete, he will attend Cambridge where I was educated."

"I like that very well, though I did not expect it."

"And why not? Your family is as much a part of me as are you. We are, after all, man and wife," he said, "but there is more."

She gave him a quizzical look. "More?"

"Yes. I have begun the investigation into the business dealings of the late Mr. Gardiner's partner, Mr. Bateman. He has a dubious reputation, I have discovered, and is known for dishonest practices. I intend to recover the losses for young Mr. Gardiner with interest and restore that which is rightfully his and his sister's.

"What's more, I have provided a dowry for Miss Flora Gardiner. She will receive an education suited to that of a genteel young lady, and when she is of age, she will have her come out in the same manner that we would present a daughter of our own. Additionally, the arrangements for William's future have been secured. In fact, Mr. Mann spoke to me in the church this very morning before you arrived. William is to be my ward. I have assumed full responsibility for his welfare and have made provisions for him in my will. He will carry my name for informal use, but, of course, not legally." Darcy hesitated and glanced at his wife. "Elizabeth, now that William is five, he should have a proper governess. There is no need for Jane to work so hard, especially if Mr. Bingley should return, which I believe that he will. She will need to attend to a courtship if things proceed as we both desire. Then, hopefully, nature will take its course, and we will have a letter telling us of their happy nuptials."

"If Jane will be happy with Mr. Bingley, then so shall I. She deserves all the happiness in the world."

"Yes, I agree, and that is why I have also set aside a sum of twenty thousand pounds for each of your sisters. I want them to have the luxury that should have been theirs had your father lived. It is not right, but in order to make a good match, they must have something to offer so that they can secure a good future."

She nodded. "Thank you for everything—especially for the children and my sisters. And I agree that Wills should have a governess."

They continued on in silence for several minutes further until finally he caressed her gloved hand on his arm and broke the silence yet again.

"There are two things about which I am curious, Mrs. Darcy."

"Yes?"

"The ivory hairbrush on your dresser; to whom did it belong?"

"Oh that," she said. "It was a complete set, a wedding present to my mother from my father. The mirror has long since been broken. Lydia threw it at Kitty when they were children, but the brush and comb were given to me, and I have kept them ever since. What is the other thing you wish to know?"

"Your birthmark. You say Lydia had one as well. Did hers become red and irritated as yours did the night of the Twelfth Night Ball?"

"Yes, it often did. Hers was identical to mine, only perhaps a little larger. Our mother had one, too. My grandmother Gardiner thought it a mark of the devil. My father would become angry whenever she said such a thing, but she insisted it was a sign that we would be a bane to our family. And, I suppose if one were to look at it as such, then in a regrettable sort of way, that has been true—Lydia with her seduction, and me with my choice."

"That is now forgot. However, I did look into some of my mythological tomes from school and came upon one strange passage. It appears that the mark is considered a strawberry placed on a young girl at birth by Aphrodite. It is a mark of fertility. When it becomes inflamed bright red, you are fertile."

Elizabeth's hand flew to her mouth. "George Wickham!"

"Wickham? What about him?"

She glanced up at him and tilted her head. "He mentioned to me on the night of the ball that he remembered Lydia's mark had been red, and that...well...I'm embarrassed to repeat what he said."

"He enjoyed her charms...and now you think that was the night William was conceived?"

"If what you say is true, then, yes."

"It is also believed that a son will be conceived when the mark is red. We shall see. Come, Elizabeth," he said, tapping his cane along the graveled walkway, "'tis time to return home. William will be anxious to see us, and I can tell him the good news. Now that we are married I am, in fact, his Papa in every sense of the word."

Strolling down the lane they soon came to their carriage and entered, driving off towards Darcy House.

In conclusion of our road well traveled, dear reader, I shall take in upon myself to tell you what became of all who have been a part of this tale, since I know it is your wont to have curious, enquiring minds and all. So, without further delay, this is what became of our cast.

Mr. and Mrs. Fitzwilliam Darcy did, in fact, tour the Continent for one year. First, they visited France, then Spain, and finally Italy. On the return voyage, they stopped briefly in a small village in the South of Spain where Elizabeth had previously spent a summer with her father and sister, Jane, when she was but ten. Whilst there, Mrs. Darcy gave birth to a fine strapping boy—Alexander Bennet Darcy, who was the delight of his father and older brother, Master William.

In the ensuing years, Elizabeth Darcy would give her husband three more sons. In addition to four sons, they would also have six daughters, all rambunctious girls as their mother had been when she was a child. Fitzwilliam, much to his delight, always knew when his sons were conceived, because, true to what he had read, his wife's birthmark would indeed glow red when she was to conceive a male child.

As for Mr. Bingley and Miss Jane Bennet, they did eventually wed, but not before a stormy courtship. It seemed Mr. Bingley was to find an unexpected surprise when he returned from York. Believing that an angel awaited him, he instead found a fully mature woman whose heart was not so effortlessly touched as it had been before, and thus, Mr. Bingley had to win the heart of a woman whose affections were not so easily impressed with rapt attention and handsome smiles. But, our dear Mr. Bingley did win her heart, for in spite of her own resistance, Miss Jane had not forgotten her first love and so eventually gave him his desire and consented to be his wife, much to the displeasure of his spinster sister, Miss Caroline Bingley. In the course of their long life together, she bore him two sons and three daughters, all of which were such good natured children that their poor parents worried excessively about them, albeit needlessly, as they proved to be quite able to carry their own in the changing age of Queen Victoria's sovereignty.

After her older sister had given up the name Bennet, Miss Catherine was soon to renounce her own surname to a charming red coat. For it seems the general was passionately smitten upon first acquaintance with the strikingly beautiful and quite spirited Miss Bennet. He admired her forthright ways, strong will, and strength of mind. But there was more to it than merely that. He knew she was a diamond in the rough, a gem to be treasured, and let us not forget, a woman of uncommonly physical beauty. In truth, she had matured and developed into one of the handsomest women the general had ever had the pleasure of meeting. Her sky blue eyes, dark hair, and alabaster skin held him captive when he was in her company. She, of course, gave all the credit to an Oriental maid who had taught her the secrets known only to Asian beauties.

And so Miss Catherine Adeline Bennet did take the name of General Richard Arthur Fitzwilliam on the twenty-third day of September in the year of our Lord 1819. They were married for nearly fifty years, and she bore him six sons and no daughters. They did also keep the Gardiner children when they were home from school up until they married.

Master William Bennet grew into a fine young man under the diligent instruction of his godparents to whom he always referred to affectionately as Mamma and Papa. Thus accordingly, because of his great love for them, he did indeed take the name of Darcy when he came of age, and consequently overcame his affliction of being born a bastard. With the connections of his step-father and the Darcy money, no one dared to show him anything less than the respect which his adopted name commanded.

Young William was educated in the best schools in England and went on to join his brothers in their father's business. Together they laid the foundation for what would become one of the most powerful and influential families in the United Kingdom. He married his third cousin by marriage, Celina Angeline Darcy of South Carolina, and made an empire in his own right apart from the family dynasty.

Furthermore, it was said of William Bennet Darcy that he grew in stature and moral fortitude to become one of the best men the Old City had even seen, resembling his step-father in every way a son could. He was generous of heart and spirit and always mindful of those less fortunate than himself, and therefore overcame the stigma of his natural father and the folly of his silly and unfortunate mother.

Now, what became of our young courtesan on a ship bound for South Carolina, you may ask? Well, Mrs. Ophelia Dior, nay Harriette Goulding Dior, arrived at the port city of Charleston approximately two months after the *Claremont de Bonté* set sail. There she was greeted by a Mr. Francis Benedict Darcy, second cousin to Mr.

Fitzwilliam Darcy, who, it just so happened, was not only a wealthy banker and cotton and rice factor to many of the Lowcountry planters, but also a young widower with a small daughter and very much in want of a wife—especially one as beautiful as Mrs. Harriette Dior with her refined English comportment proved to be, which, I must relay to you, charmed everyone she met.

Mr. Darcy was lost to her dark eyes and teasing manners the day Mrs. Dior stepped foot on American soil. And, as such, after a whirlwind romance of less than a month, he would have her for his wife, and she would accept him. His two-year-old daughter, Celina Darcy, who was destined to become the bride of young William Darcy of London, England, loved Harriette dearly, especially when her five boisterous brothers and three charming sisters joined the happy family, one by one, of course. Celina was the ideal older sibling, ever diligent and ever attentive, and with great devotion she always kept her siblings, especially her brothers, from things they ought not to do, and encouraged them in things they should. And let it never be said that the American Mrs. Darcy was ever amiss in her eloquent ability to entertain and forward her husband's business interests, especially in the Season when the finest of the Lowcountry came to town. Mrs. Darcy was a favorite at the St. Cecilia Balls and the many musical performances given every year at St. Andrew's after the harvest; she was pronounced the most admired hostess to ever set a table in that fair city.

However, she never forgot to whom she belonged and whose bed she would share when the last candle was extinguished. Mr. Francis Darcy was never wanting in connubial bliss—as was evidenced by his unruly brood.

Now you might ask whatever became of the viscount and his eccentric lady? Well, in the autumn of 1818, tragedy befell the house of Matlock. The third Earl of Matlock succumbed to heart failure, and breathing his last was thus no more. The Viscount of Wexford gave up his title and became the fourth Earl of Matlock. Later that year, in the heart of the Harvest Season, he and Lady Margaret married as planned in Pemberley Chapel with all their friends present save two, as Mr. and Mrs. Fitzwilliam Darcy were yet to arrive back on English soil.

The fourth earl and his countess lived a long and happy life. Lady Matlock gave the earl two sons and one daughter. She was not as prolific as the others, but then she was a good deal older.

Much distinction marked the tenure of the fourth earl in the House of Lords. In his lifetime, Lord Matlock would become responsible for several pieces of legislation to give relief to the poor and underprivileged. He would see to it that legislation to abolish the Corn Laws and unfair trade practices were set in place. The hideous practice of entailment was also to come to an end under his influence, for like his younger cousin, he too had a heart of gold.

And Lady Matlock? She and Mrs. Darcy became as close as any sisters could be. The countess's influence on her friend was considerable. Maggie, true to her word, did teach her dear friend to fence and enjoy all sorts of things otherwise unavailable to the fairer sex.

Now I suppose you wish to know what became of Miss Ling-Ling. Well if you insist, then I will tell you. Mr. Darcy hired a Chinese gardener to create an elaborate oriental pavilion for his wife's twenty-eighth birthday. When the young man from Shanghai met the young woman from Singapore, sparks flew. Though he would have her, she would not have him. However, after a long and arduous courtship, the lady did relent and became the wife of a most successful gardener and herbalist. Together, they did much good for those they served.

Yes, yes, I know. You wish to learn the fate of poor Charlotte and Mr. Collins. Well, on that subject there is both good news and bad. First, the bad or the good, whichever way you choose to think of it. Mr. Collins, it seems suffered a seizure and fell over dead in Madame Papillia's *House of Pleasure*. It appears he was once again in service for the Church. Unfortunately, his service was in the boudoir of Miss Pandora, who claimed he was instructing her in some great doctrinal thesis. What I never could understand was why he would attempt to impart such wisdom while wearing no clothes. 'Tis no joke, for I tell you it is so. He was as naked as the day he was born I say. Curious...umm...curious indeed.

Charlotte Collins was then free to do as she chose without the embarrassment of her late husband's foolish prattle continuously extolling the many virtues of his betters with many eloquent compliments. For many years, Mrs. Collins was content with her children, her grandchildren, her poultry, and her gardens, but eventually she would meet an honorable older gentleman who would persuade her to marry. She lived out the remainder of her life in relative peace and happiness, loved and adored by a husband who endeavored to deserve her.

And what of Lady Catherine de Bourgh, you say? Well, I am here to inform you that she never forgave her nephew and died alone with her money and elevated status as her only company. Anne had long since preceded her in death, having caught a trifling cold while daring to venture outside the range of her mother's overly protective eye for a walk in the gardens. Caught in a rainstorm, she was soaked to the bone and succumbed to a fever one week later for which Mrs. Darcy was to blame, according to Her Ladyship; for if she had not interfered, the Grand Dame believed Mr. Darcy would have married her daughter and thus Miss Anne would not have ventured out on her own on such a stormy day in late October. Though she would never voice it publicly, Lady Catherine believed to her dying day that Elizabeth was, in fact, Mr. Darcy's mistress behind the black veil.

Umm...now I suppose you wish to know what befell the randy dukes of lust—Ancaster and Castlebaum. Well, since you asked nicely and I just happen to know, I think I will tell you. Unfortunately, like so many others who practiced their lascivious habits, they contracted the pox and succumbed to the effect of the cure. They died of mercury poisoning.

Now last, but I hope certainly not least, I am sure you have wondered about Mrs. Darcy's cat, Cocoa. Well, she did live out her life to a ripe old age of one and twenty at Pemberley. She, all the days of her life, a most excellent mouser, preferred mice to mutton. Mr. Darcy did acquire a male cat of her kind, and together, they did produce many generations of kittens, thus introducing the Siamese cat to Derbyshire.

And that, my dear reader, is what became of our dear hero and his most excellent lady. Elizabeth Rose Bennet Darcy was the love of his life, as was Fitzwilliam Alexander Darcy to her. Their love was said to have been a deep, strong, and abiding one—the kind that only comes once in a blue moon, or when heaven intervenes to see it through.

inis

184

9446192R0

Made in the USA
Lexington, KY
27 April 2011